HERE WE GO ROUND THE MULBERRY BUSH

AN ANTHOLOGY OF POEMS & CONVERSATIONS [FROM OUTSIDE]

"UTTER"

PRESS.

"UTTER" & PRESS.

Published by "Utter" & Press
Unit 1, Viaduct Works, Ponsanooth,
TR3 7JW, England

www.utterandpress.co.uk

First Edition, 2021
Second Printing, 2022

Set in Edita.
Paper: Arena Ivory Bulk, 90 gsm.
Cover: Keaykolour Pumpkin 300 gsm.
Printers: Calverts, London

ISBN 978-1-9162226-6-3

To us.

CONTENTS.

(Poems denoted by ¶)

C O N T E N T S.

(Poems denoted by ¶)

CONTENTS.

(Poems denoted by ¶)

CONTENTS.

(Poems denoted by ¶)

DRAMATIS PERSONÆ.

A list of Key's channels. His fellow yardbirds; shackled, restless, pinned back by the circumstances. All of them keeping lines of communication open for Key. Taps; ready to be turned on.

‖‖

In order of appearance.

THE COLONEL:	Not made for this. Designed to pour ale into himself near a fire. Not this. Vexed. Defiant.
EMILY JUNIPER:	A swirl of typewriter ribbons and printing blocks. Breathes only sea air. Thirties. Cornwall.
CHIGGY:	Agent to people of talent. Snouting out opportunities for Key. Keeping him upright.
DANIEL:	Born to lock down. Inch-thick spectacles. Fogey cords. Checks in regularly. Owns a kiln.
CAROL KEY:	Mother figure. Welsh. Cheesed off. But will not break.
BILL KEY:	6' 4". Thighs like Sir Chris Hoy's. Equine tendencies. Homebrew whisperer.
BUDDY:	Vast, brown eyes. The heartbeat of this or any lockdown. Big sunglasses. Marshals Rick.
RICK:	The guy lucked out, married Buddy. Human Scooby-Doo. Good energy, mind. Local. Big old jaw.
YOUNGUZI:	Headmaster. Wearer of Scandinavian running vests. Father and NW5 stalwart. Impressive.
STEVEN:	Barely appears.
MAGGIE:	Young. Resilient. A lot like a goldfinch. A ray of hope in the middle of it all.
COFFEE GIRL:	Effervescent. Smooth. With subtle hints of citrus and enticing caramel notes. Possibly impossible.
LORD:	Zero interest in eating things like meat or eggs. Reaps the rewards. Slim. Athletic. Marshals Bobby.
BOBBY:	Four now. Cheeks like furnaces. Why must this young man endure a lockdown?

PC GOURD:	Squidged into his square-o uniform. Constantly getting bollocked at home. Chipped truncheon.
SWEETIE PIE:	Reformed proof-reader. A latter-day Bertie Wooster-figure, with appealing fellow-well-met disposition. Stretchy dog.
FRANK:	Black Country favourite. Veins pulsating with vax. Spry as hell.
CATH:	Coasting it. Long, comforting cuppas with her sister. Marshals Frank.
GAZ CORN:	Journalist. Can move his pen smoothly between his knuckles like a conjuring trick.
LIZ AND KENNY:	Forties. Ten years in the force. Bullet-proof vests. Guns. In love. Have eaten doughnuts in Number Ten.
LAUREN:	A voice. Like warm syrup. A beacon. A comfort. A bright lamp in the abyss.
TRISH:	Specialist in swabs. Lots of refrigerated boxes in her Daihatsu. Leather skirt. Men's watch.
JUMBO:	From another era. Needs a moment to reflect on how he goes about things. Hard work.
SAM AND SAOIRSE:	World-class actors. Heavily garlanded. Sprinkled generously with stardust. Patient with Key.
MOUSE:	Despicable. Scandalous. Thick whiskers like uncooked spaghetti. The worst.
QUINT:	Scratch that. This guy's the worst. Quint.
BINKY WILLIAMS:	Works for the NHS. A hero. Pierced nose. New Balance trainers.

And primarily.

KEY:	In the middle of all of it. Wincing at the chains. Trying to keep moving.

Week I.

In which a book spills into the world,
Christmas languishes on the streets,
and the keys tremble in their
locks once more.

THE BEST LAID PLANS.[†]

My diary arrived.

2021!

All new and wrapped in Cellophane!

I grabbed my scalpel and touched the blade to the diary's spine.

The radio was on and news charged into my ear.

I frowned as it whizzed around my skull.

I slowly pulled back my scalpel, resheathed it.

I tapped the Cellophane with my palm.

I shoved the diary in my drawer; its gleaming skin still intact.

I slammed the drawer shut with my hip, fixed myself a gin and a flapjack.

[†] **JUNIPER:** I want to read them all.
KEY: What's stopping you?
JUNIPER: Gah.
KEY: We have nowhere we need to be.

THE TREE MUST GO.

Two figures on the street. Key and The Colonel. Key stuffed inside a dark-blue Mountain Warehouse anorak; The Colonel trussed up in sheepskin. They're either end of a Christmas tree; behind them a trail of sweat and needles. Yule evaporating. A chill in the air. Midday. No one out. Everyone in. A moment in history. Stretching.

COLONEL: I don't understand why we're doing this on New Year's Day.

KEY: Get rid. That's all. A new start.

COLONEL: What's wrong with Twelfth Night?

KEY: Fuck that, Colonel. I swear. I'm not hanging about this year. Get the tree out. Drag it, kicking and screaming. Get it on the street.

COLONEL: *(Looking over his shoulder)* Where am I going here?

KEY: Keep going, bro, there's a whole bunch of 'em up the hill. Let's leave it with them. Whole gang of 'em. Give the old fella some company.

COLONEL: Why am I at the sharp end? It keeps – agh!

The Colonel walks backwards up the hill, the tip of the tree keeps slamming into his bollocks. Key's in the engine room, shoving the base forward as the tree shakes its way past the Thai Café – closed; the dry cleaner's – closed; Costcutter – open, empty.

COLONEL: Be careful, can't ya?! Keeps jamming into my boy!

KEY: 2021, Colonel. Out with the old. Let's be having yer!

COLONEL: New Year's Day and he asks me to dispose of a Christmas tree.

KEY: How was New Year?

COLONEL: How's anything these days?

KEY: Yeah well.

COLONEL: Same as Christmas, same as bloody fireworks night! Always the same! Can't do shit. Gab's down in the dumps, she loves a bloody festival.

KEY: We're through the worst of it, Colonel.

COLONEL: Agh! Stop pushing it, can't ya!

KEY: These are the hard yards, Colonel. He'll open it up soon, I swear.

COLONEL: Well, I bloody well hope so.

KEY: It's a time for optimism.

COLONEL: Plague's gone, man!

Key nods. He blinks. The air is full of bugs. Millions of them. Their wings clacking, their eyes dead, sullen. He blinks again. They are gone.

COLONEL: Well, he's bollocksed up Christmas so I hope there's some method to his madness. Careful!

KEY: He's got it mapped out, this guy.

COLONEL: Jeesh.

KEY: The Maestro. He knows what he's doing.

COLONEL: Yeah, well.

KEY: In more positive news, I'm on Richard Osman's House of Games all this week.

The Colonel doesn't register any enjoyment at this. Key nods.

KEY: Colonel, bro! You think The Maestro's plunging a dagger into Christmas if he ain't got something up his sleeve?

A huge surge forward by Key, and The Colonel is lifted up by the seat. Like an angel he swings momentarily in the frozen air, then comes back down, skids on a manhole cover.

KEY: This time next week. I'll knock on your door.

COLONEL: Well. That'll be something.

KEY: "Room for a little one?"

COLONEL: "Come on in! Come on in!"

KEY: It's imminent, bro, I'm telling ya. Watch it!

The Colonel smashes his hip into a traffic light and pitches backwards. His arse hits the deck but he bobs back up like a Weeble. Across the road, two girls carry their tree up the hill. Laughing, red-cheeked. Two bright blobs, dabbed by the winter sunlight on the barren, urban stage. Key gestures to them with his jaw.

KEY: Two metres, look.

COLONEL: Yeah.

KEY: Should bring it in as a policy.

COLONEL: Carrying Christmas trees?

KEY: Yeah, you wanna meet up; you gotta carry a Christmas tree. Two metres. I'd buy into it. Anything that gets the pubs back open, I swear to God.

COLONEL: Yeah, no dafter than the rest of their policies.

KEY: Well.

COLONEL: Look at this shit! They gotta unlock, man!

The Colonel puts down his end of the tree and yells into the arctic air.

COLONEL: Unlock us, man! Come on, let's go!

The girls turn round, their cheeks ablaze. Then they move off again. And that's it, no one else. Emptiness. Like last year. Everything like last year.

KEY: You wait, next briefing. I swear, we're a briefing away.

COLONEL: Always a briefing away.

KEY: He'll have some good old stuff up his sleeve.

COLONEL: I'm gonna get a keg in, you know.

KEY: You always say you'll get a keg in.

COLONEL: I'm getting a keg in, I swear. He unlocks: you're coming over.

KEY: You got that right.

They round a corner, there's a heap of trees and an adult supervising them. Key lets his trunk hit the deck, the tip flies up The Colonel's nose.

KEY: This week, Colonel, I'm telling you. He'll stand behind that bloody lectern and do his "let there be booze" speech.

COLONEL: Yeah?

KEY: Like Martin Luther King himself. The Maestro, in full flow. "Sorry about December! Faulty gasket! Couldn't be helped! But I bring good tidings from the front. Pubs: open! Cinemas: snip the locks! You wanna guzzle from kegs? Be my guest! Now hop it, you horrible lot, before I change me mind!"

COLONEL: Now that's a speech I could get behind.

KEY: Then he'll fill his pint pot with some absolute muck and neck it, right there and then.

COLONEL: Cheers!

KEY: Straight down camera one. "Get out there my pretties! As of precisely now, you are officially UNLOCKED!"

COLONEL: I'd love that. When was the last time you went in someone's house?

KEY: This is my point, Colonel. Let's not live in the past. What did 2020 ever do for us?

COLONEL: Yeah.

KEY: We're days away from a pint, Colonel, mark my words.

COLONEL: I hope so, thirsty work this.

A final effort, laying the tree at the adult's feet.

KEY: I'm coming over, Saturday night.

COLONEL: We can pencil it in, I guess.

They move away, still two metres. The tree now gone, the distance still there. The world still broken. The locks barely trembling. The streets dead. Flat. They reach the corner.

KEY: *(Out of sight now)* Pencil? Ink it, bro. Thick, gloopy ink. Gallons of it. Rip open your diary, brother, pour it in! Saturday night. Me, you and your bleedin' keg!

We stay with the adult. He takes the lower branches off with an axe, slings what's left onto the heap. The tree looks funny without those lower branches. Like she's showing a little ankle. The adult pulls a rollie from behind his ear and lights it. Clouds of ice-cold breath change indistinguishably into smoke.

HERE WE GO ROUND THE MULBERRY BUSH.

LOCKING.†

A KEY.

Cold, heavy, shoved in a lock.
Its teeth smooth now, ineffective; hunting for grip.
A fist jiggling it.
Panicked voices.
The key licking its teeth with its tongue.
Willing its canines to sharpen.
Willing them to find some purchase.
Yearning for the mechanism to clunk open.
Desperate for a release.
Its shaft: ice cold.

† **JUNIPER:** Christ.
KEY: It's from January.
JUNIPER: Eugh. "Desperate for a release." I love it!
KEY: Ha!
JUNIPER: Toothless keys, scratching about!
KEY: I'll get two more Bulmers.
JUNIPER: Yes! Come on let's get lashed and go through them.
KEY: Might get some loaded fries.
JUNIPER: Ha! Yes! The poetry pigs!
KEY: It's so good to see you, Em.

OUR BOOK.

Key is walking through the wintry streets of NW London. A man in his forties in size-eleven Adidas Gazelles, swinging a Ryman's bag. He holds his iPhone in front of him, following himself on a map. A blue dot, millimetering itself across a screen, Key powering the dot. The dot powering Key. The iPhone lurches round a corner, Key quicksteps after it. Like he's being dragged by a bloody daft dog. The map disappears and a name replaces it. Emily Juniper. Key's heart melts and he swishes the screen; connects the call. To Emily Juniper.

KEY: Emily Juniper. Designer Dispatcher. Genius.

JUNIPER: Tim!

KEY: Tim Key!

JUNIPER: Yes!

KEY: Poet. Voiceover artist. Renaissance man.

JUNIPER: Huh?

KEY: How are you, Em?

JUNIPER: I'm out and about.

KEY: Oh, you are?

JUNIPER: The Sun's on my back.

KEY: Best place for it.

JUNIPER: Tim, people are buying the book. They're buying it, Tim!

Key looks down at his Ryman's bag. His eyes fogging over with pride. His Gazelles skipping along the pavement.

JUNIPER: They're buying it. I sent out ninety this morning. Oh, Tim!

KEY: Mine came this morning, Em. Ten of 'em.

JUNIPER: I'm hand delivering one now! I'm walking to the bakery.

KEY: Oh, you are?

JUNIPER: I'm on the beach. Scenic route. We made a book!

Key stuffs his brand new AirPods deep into his lugholes and they connect. Click. He can hear the sea. He can hear miniscule shells being delivered onto the beach. He can hear fat guys in wetsuits, surfing on the horizon. He can hear a designer smiling by the ocean.

JUNIPER: I have boxes of them. I cut the first box this morning. The stink!

KEY: The stench of new books, Em. It cuts through.

JUNIPER: I reached in, pulled out a book.

KEY: Our first book together.

JUNIPER: Our first... yes...

Emily Juniper stops speaking. Emotions. The sound of the sea. A blue sky. A chill in the air.

KEY: I'm delivering one now, Em. To Rick and Buddy.

JUNIPER: We made a book, Tim! We made a book!

Key sits his fat arse down on a wall. He unfurls the Ryman's bag, pulls the book out. "He Used Thought as a Wife". The Sun cuts through the trees, throws a dappled sunlight onto the faded blue cover. It is beautifully designed, to within an inch of its life.

JUNIPER: I love our book, Tim. I hope I wasn't a pain in the neck.

KEY: How were you a pain in the neck?

JUNIPER: It just goes to show. When we put our minds to something –

KEY: I wasn't easy to work with at times, that's a fact.

JUNIPER: Oh, Tim. You were a nightmare but look at it –

KEY: Huh?

JUNIPER: Just look at it.

Key listens as Emily Juniper turns the pages; he discerns her sobs of joy. Tears run from the handset, flow down Key's wrist, drip onto Key's copy. Deep breaths in Cornwall, Emily Juniper composing herself.

JUNIPER: I saw you on House of Games last night.

KEY: Oh, yeah?

JUNIPER: Fuck me, you're clever.

Key's chest puffs up.

KEY: Oh, you know. It's the luck of the draw on that show. You know 'em or you don't.

JUNIPER: Says you! You won a bath-robe last night.

KEY: I'm not the first, I'm sure I won't be the –

JUNIPER: Didn't know what had hit 'em, them other three!

KEY: Well, four more days, you know. It's stripped across the week.

JUNIPER: Bet you grind their beaks into the dust. Ha ha!

KEY: How was Christmas, Em?

JUNIPER: Buggered. Couldn't move a single inch.

KEY: No.

JUNIPER: Trapped.

The sound of the waves. The sound of the pages. Key looking down the street. Silence. The nip in the air.

JUNIPER: Why'd he do it, Tim?

KEY: The Maestro? I dunno. I... I dunno.

JUNIPER: The rat that stole Christmas. We had our bags packed. My mum –

KEY: Lynne Juniper –

JUNIPER: She'd killed the turkey. Peeled the spuds.

Key peers across the street. A man in a Christmas jumper hurls a sackful of meat into a wheelie bin.

KEY: It'll unlock now, that's the thing. That's what you have to remember, Em. He's nicked one Christ-mas, that's all. Now it's easy street. Gradual unlocking. You watch.

JUNIPER: Didn't have anything in, me. Defrosted some rice, had it with a weird meatball thing.

KEY: Oh.

JUNIPER: Me and Stu went to bed about ten. Crapola.

KEY: You're freezing rice these days?

JUNIPER: Watched Dibley.

KEY: Oh, yeah?

JUNIPER: Surprised he didn't ban telly, if I'm honest. What's going to happen, Tim?

KEY: Nothing. Normal year.

JUNIPER: They won't press the button again will they, Tim?

KEY: No.

JUNIPER: The man who sews the fish-ing nets said –

KEY: No one's pressing any buttons, Em.

JUNIPER: I don't want another lock-down, Tim.

KEY: Stop saying lockdown, Em. Stop even saying it. Let's talk about the book. People are buying the book.

JUNIPER: Clomp, clomp, clomp. Onto people's doormats. I can't get my head round it. Oh, Tim!

The tears are sucked back into the iPhone and away. Emily Juniper's smile is back.

JUNIPER: What are you doing tonight?

KEY: I might... I sometimes go to the pub.

JUNIPER: They're not open.

KEY: It's a pilgrimage, Em. I go there some nights. Pay my respects.

JUNIPER: Oh.

KEY: Stand there looking at it, like a chump.

JUNIPER: I want everything to be fine this year.

KEY: On the outside, looking in.

Key pushes off from the wall, picks up speed, heads towards Rick and Buddy's. The gate. The coffee. The friendship.

KEY: Happy New Year, Em.

JUNIPER: Oh, I hope so, Tim. I do hope so.

KEY: It will be.

JUNIPER: I don't want another bollocks one, that's for sure.

KEY: They'll put their keys in the locks, Em. They'll turn them clockwise, I swear.

JUNIPER: I love our book, Tim.

KEY: Speak soon, Em.

Swipe. Back to the map. The blue dot twitching, pulling, yanking Key down the road. The air: ice-cold, gnawing into his ears. Pinching his testicles.

†**JUNIPER:** From before.
KEY: Christmas.
JUNIPER: Behind the scenes.
KEY: Gawd knows, Em. Gawd knows what they were up to.
JUNIPER: You been?
KEY: Fabric?
JUNIPER: Yeah.
KEY: Yeah.
JUNIPER: Ha ha.
KEY: What?
JUNIPER: No, no. So you've been to Fabric.
KEY: Yeah, you're still smiling.
JUNIPER: I'm sorry. Was it fun?
KEY: I was out of my depth.
JUNIPER: Ha ha.
KEY: You keep laughing at the idea I went to Fabric.
JUNIPER: I know, I do, I do! I'm sorry.
KEY: Try and stop laughing though, Em.
JUNIPER: I can't imagine you in a nightclub, I'm sorry, I'm so sorry,
KEY: I was in my thirties.
JUNIPER: Ha ha ha. Oh my God!
KEY: You've spat your cider out, Em.

WHATEVER HAPPENED TO CHRISTMAS?[†]

THERE was a big old Christmas meeting in *Numero Ten*.

All the MPs in Christmas jumpers and shit-tons of plum duff and mulled wine and M&S treats on the table.

Bohnson was wearing his Rudolf onesie.

"I fucking love Christmas, me! Just putting it out there."

He'd brought his Bluetooth speaker down and Jingle Bells filled the air.

Matt Boytwitch was changing the words!

He was singing "Mingle Bells" and guffawing and eating mince pies and farting.

It was a great atmos, apart from a couple of sad-as-hell nerds pointing to their dismal little graphs and eating their Prets.

One of the junior MPs floated the idea of all the youngsters going to Fabric on Twelfth Night.

"Never mind the youngsters!"

Bohnson was on the table now, swinging his vast hips to Frosty The Snowman, pouring piping-hot mulled wine down his flabby old gullet.

He smashed his thumbs into his chest and smacked his lips.

"Yours truly'll be there, off his tits, on a podium."

And now everyone was on the table and dancing, and a chap in a suit was typing it all up and chewing pensively on a fig.

WHERE'S BEADLE?

Key's quads are roaring inside his Uniqlo jeans as he clambers over fallen Christmas trees, jinks round stockings, slides through gravy. His brand new AirPods in. Switching station when the music stops and people start to talk about the world. "The government have –" and out, new station, goodbye. Into some Eliza Doolittle. Into some Debussy. Into anything. His thighs bulging, tearing up Parliament Hill, the locked city drifting out of focus behind him. Click. The music cuts out, and the ringtone cuts in. Chiggy. The agent. The ray of hope.

KEY: Season's greetings, Chig. I hope you managed to salvage some festive cheer amongst the gash!

CHIGGY: *(Heavy, flat)* Darling boy.

KEY: No. Not that tone, Chig. I can't, I just can't.

CHIGGY: Darling boy, how are you –?

KEY: Tell me they're unlocking. Tell me something decent, Chig. Tell me about the rabbits. Tell me about the rabbits, Chig!

Key continues to walk. His eyes are pink with the stress of it all. 2021. Unlock it, man! 2021 must be unlocked! Onwards, up the hill.

KEY: What's happening, Chig?

CHIGGY: Yeeeeers.

KEY: No!!! Find a different tone, Chig. We can do better than this, Chig.

CHIGGY: Oh, Gawd. You'll have seen the news.

KEY: Chig, I'm avoiding the lot. Duvet cover over the telly, pillowcase over the head. I don't wanna know.

CHIGGY: Well, let's look at the positives.

KEY: We're locked up for the foreseeable, aren't we, Chig?

CHIGGY: Nothing confirmed.

KEY: I'm a big boy, Chig!

CHIGGY: I've heard Easter.

KEY: Ha! Ha ha ha! Easter! Ha ha!!!

Key roars with laughter. Other poets – dotted around the heath – turn sadly and face him. He continues to laugh for some minutes.

KEY: Ha ha! Where's Beadle?

CHIGGY: Highgate Cemetery.

KEY: No, as in: this has to be some kind of wind-up, Chig!

CHIGGY: I know. I know. Now, obviously this means comedy clubs are kaput until late spring, earliest.

KEY: Bleugh. Bleeeeeeugh!!!

CHIGGY: You were great on House of Games last night!

KEY: Bleugh. Yuk. Bleeeeeeugh!!!

CHIGGY: Briefing incoming. Maybe they'll have flattened the curve. Might surprise us all. Tell us to snip off our masks, tell us it's done.

KEY: Don't patronise me, Chig.

CHIGGY: It looks grim.

KEY: Don't use words like "grim", Chig.

Key moves backwards and a black, cast iron bench appears behind his knees. He collapses onto it.

KEY: 2021. Chig! I pinned my hopes on it.

CHIGGY: You get a girlfriend?

KEY: Did I...?

CHIGGY: In the window?

Key looks down at his hand. It's not holding anyone, that's for sure. He balls it into a fist, strikes his jaw hard, spits out teeth.

KEY: Chig?

CHIGGY: Yes, darling boy.

KEY: Are there people who just say, "I don't want to be locked down!"?

CHIGGY: I think we're all saying that, Tim.

KEY: I know, I know but aren't there people who are saying it and then actually not locking themselves down? Are there people who just... carry on?

CHIGGY: Well, yes –

KEY: Then I'll be one of them, Chig. Honestly. I'm not doing another three months in there, honestly.

Key points his arm, rifle-straight in the direction of his street. The direction of his flat. The direction of his lounge. The direction of his slow cooker, his Post-it notes, his bath, his Perrier Award, his frozen soup, his mousetraps, his record player. The direction of his first lockdown.

CHIGGY: Now, I've spoken to someone in SAGE.

KEY: Chig, man, what's SAGE? You're talking in riddles.

CHIGGY: Robert's brother works for SAGE.

KEY: I don't even know who Robert is, Chig.

CHIGGY: We were doing an online quiz on Saturday –

KEY: No! Noooooo! I'm not doing it, Chig. No quizzes! No banana bread! I'm not doing it!!!

Key picks up a good-sized stick and hurls it into the ether. It spins and spins and lands a mile away. Key watches it land. Thunk. Straight in the ground. Bolt upright. Key stares at it. 'Well, how d'ya like that?'

KEY: Okay. It's okay. I'm good, Chig. It's all good.

CHIGGY: Now the important thing is not to write another book.

KEY: Huh?

CHIGGY: It's a time for cool heads.

KEY: The first book's selling, Chig. Did you get your copy?

CHIGGY: It came through safe and sound. Emily Juniper's done a great job.

KEY: We both did.

CHIGGY: That cover!

KEY: D'ya open it at all?

CHIGGY: Did she choose the paper?

KEY: She chose the paper, I chose the words, Chig. 'Twas a team effort.

CHIGGY: I read it. It's a real snapshot of life in Lockdown One.

KEY: Ha. We're on Lockdown Three now! Whipping through 'em.

CHIGGY: Did you lose it, in Lockdown One?

KEY: Nah, Chig. Gained it, if anything.

CHIGGY: You talk to a mouse in it.

KEY: Yup.

CHIGGY: It was an eye-opener, that book, that's for sure. But that's done now.

Key is fixated on the stick. Stuck in the ground there. Why did it plant like that?

KEY: Chig, I couldn't write a single 'nother word about my flat.

CHIGGY: I know.

KEY: I've read it through. It's the diary of a madman.

CHIGGY: Be a sight easier to read if you'd gone outside once in a while. Described the trees.

KEY: Get my DH Lawrence on. Yeah, yeah I know.

Key looks down beyond the stick. A tree, old, professorial almost, appears to be taking stock of developments.

CHIGGY: I think flush the orange pen down the bog –

KEY: I binned the orange pen, Chig. On the heath –

Key squints down the hill. Squints at the streetbin by the heath's entrance. The end of Lockdown One.

CHIGGY: You gotta do something constructive.

KEY: I know, but what's that?

CHIGGY: Well, pray for the bloody clubs to open back up!

KEY: Yeah. Yeah, I know that's what I should be doing. I know that.

Key rises. He moves down, off the path, back onto the wet grass of the hill. Moves towards the stick.

CHIGGY: Now, will you keep me posted? Let me know how you're getting on.

KEY: Yes.

CHIGGY: You must talk to people, otherwise you bottle it all up and then that becomes a book again, that's all.

Key stands by his stick. It is stuck deep in the turf. A special stick. His stick.

KEY: Is he really in Highgate Cemetery, Chig?

CHIGGY: Who?

KEY: Beadle. Is Beadle buried in Highgate Cemetery?

CHIGGY: Yuh. They're all in there. Marx –

KEY: I'm not so interested in whether they're all in there, Chig.

CHIGGY: Then yeah, Beadle's in there.

KEY: Ha!

CHIGGY: Bye, darling boy.

KEY: Bye, Chig.

Key pulls the stick out the ground, like King Arthur himself. He surveys the city. He looks to his left. Towards Highgate. Towards the cemetery. Towards the stones and the skeletons. Towards Beadle. Ha ha. Jeremy Beadle. What would Beadle have made of all this? With his new stick, Key points across at the sleeping jester.

TOP POCKET.

An old swindler came into my orbit on the heath.

He was 1.65 m away from me and I shot him a look.

Such was the velocity with which I snapped my neck in his direction that a bead of sweat flew from my eyelash and landed on the swindler's monocle.

He touched it with his mitten and took a step back.

We stared at one another, quite afraid.

He seemed to have something under his tracksuit top.

What was that?

Cigs in his top pocket?

A tin?

KILL MY DELL.

I TOOK my laptop in.

I got the guy to amend the settings.

He ripped out Zoom and also Facebook and smashed the camera apart with a small ice pick.

It was a relief to be honest.

He poured gasoline on the machine and then he ignited it and we danced around it.

I would walk this lockdown.

Fill my legs with kilometres, take the air, pull my shoulders back, have a good old think.

DO NOT SLEEPWALK.

Key is sweating in the heart of N22, trudging up through the woods towards Alexandra Palace. He's wearing a bright red bobble hat that says 'Norway' on the front, and he's clutching his new stick. Christmas lights are still slung in the boughs of birches. Some flash intermittently. Some are cracked. Occasionally, Key catches a glimpse of The Palace through the trees. In his brand new AirPods: The PDC World Darts Final. Talksport 2. 1053/1089MW. A double sixteen, and another set clinched by Price. Relentless. Then: click. Comms replaced by ringing. Daniel. FaceTime. Key peels off a Thinsulate glove, connects the call.

DANIEL: You need to join a bubble.

KEY: Happy New Year, Daniel.

DANIEL: You need to join a bubble!

Daniel. In all his glory. As bald as Michael van Gerwen himself. Gawping out of the screen, his nose no less bulbous this year than last.

DANIEL: I've got your back, mate, and I'm telling you: you need to join a bubble.

KEY: What the hell's a bubble? What the hell are you talking about?

DANIEL: I'm joining a bubble.

KEY: What bubble? Happy New Year, Daniel.

DANIEL: They're double-locking.

Key stops. Daniel's looking about as serious and square as always. Silence.

KEY: Nothing's been confirmed, there's a briefing –

DANIEL: They'll add more locks.

KEY: They'll set us free. There's a briefing tomorrow. Teatime. They'll set us free, chill yer knackers.

The Christmas lights flickering. There never was a Christmas, and now it is over. Extinguished. Embers.

DANIEL: You're not made for lockdowns.

KEY: Hog's bollocks!

DANIEL: You went la la in the first one.

KEY: Thick wet hog's bollocks.

DANIEL: You need people around you. Decent people, people who can steer you in the right direction. That's what you need.

KEY: La la, how? What are you talking

about? I kept it together. I thrived. I don't need you, believe me.

DANIEL: Did you get the AirPods?

KEY: Yes, cheers, they came on Monday.

DANIEL: You gotta look after yourself, that's all.

KEY: I nail lockdowns, Dan. That's what I do.

DANIEL: Where are you?

KEY: Stiff walk.

DANIEL: Yeah well. Get home, do the admin. Find yourself a bubble. You gotta be on it with this stuff.

KEY: La la, how?! How d'ya know I went la la?

DANIEL: I'm holding it.

KEY: Huh?

DANIEL: *(Significantly)* I'm holding it.

Key hears a book being whacked against a thigh. Then the book rises slowly into shot. Key nods. It's his book. The blue one. A poetical response to the first lockdown.

KEY: I wanted you to have it.

DANIEL: I'm half way through.

KEY: It's the first time I've seen it in someone else's hands.

Key peers in. At his book. Held. By another. Key nods, holds back whatever tears might be available.

KEY: Well?

Daniel softens. Runs his hands through where his hair should be. He sighs.

DANIEL: It's a great book, obviously.

KEY: Thanks, Daniel.

DANIEL: I hate how I come over.

KEY: I know.

DANIEL: But I can't deny it's a great book.

KEY: No.

DANIEL: Clearly it was something you needed to write.

KEY: It's mad that it's published, eh.

DANIEL: I come across poorly.

KEY: I think I've nailed you.

DANIEL: You've got it out of your system.

KEY: I've lanced the boil.

DANIEL: Smeared it onto the pages.

Key leans against an elm, glares up at The Palace. He imagines it pulsating. The great events of yore. The Kaiser Chiefs, Jamiroquai. In simpler times. Björk and The Betfred Masters Snooker Championship. The snooker: gone. No crowds permitted. In ruins. Key pushes off.

DANIEL: You're in denial, that's all. The sword's about to fall and you're waddling around like Little Boy Blue.

KEY: Stiff walk, Daniel.

DANIEL: They're locking –

KEY: Out on my stiffy. That's all –

DANIEL: With nothing in place. Make plans! That's what!

KEY: And what plans have you made?

DANIEL: Out with the old.

KEY: Oh, yeah?

DANIEL: Paring it down. Getting rid of the crap. Clearing the decks.

KEY: Why've you got a sledgehammer?

A dull metal drop-forged hammerhead keeps honing into view. Daniel's on the move.

DANIEL: I dunno. Thinking about giving it a swing. Having me a knock-through.

KEY: We haven't even locked down yet, man! Give the rest of us time to work things out. We're trying to get our heads round things, you're putting walls through?

Daniel switches his camera round. Walls. Chalk on the walls. Potential. The sledgehammer kissing the chalk. The camera switches back onto Daniel. The nose.

DANIEL: How's your mental health?

KEY: Up the spout! The Maestro's pulling my plonker.

DANIEL: You've got your teddy bear?

KEY: Bear!

DANIEL: Bear then.

KEY: "Teddy bear." Makes me sound like a baby.

DANIEL: So you won't be alone, that's what I'm saying. You have your bear.

KEY: No, no. Gave the bear away.

DANIEL: Oh.

KEY: End of the first lockdown. Which was supposed to be the only lockdown. Which they were calling The Lockdown.

DANIEL: Who'd ya give the bear to?

KEY: A four year old. A young adventurer.

Nah. The bear is gone. Bobby has the bear. Lord's lad. The bear will look after Bobby this lockdown. Key scrapes his teeth along his lip.

DANIEL: Walking's good.

KEY: Yeah. I know walking's good, Dan. I'm not thick, cheers.

DANIEL: I'll send you a Fitbit.

KEY: Yeah. Yeah, Fitbit. Yeah.

Daniel looks concerned for Key. Key nods. He appreciates the concern.

DANIEL: A bubble is where –

KEY: I don't wanna know, Dan.

Daniel nods.

KEY: I just wanna walk.

DANIEL: Where are you walking?

KEY: I'm on a pilgrimage, that's what.

Key spins his iPhone onto The Palace. Apparitions seem to emerge from the vast windows. Tom Jones emitting into the night like a vapour. Back on Key's face. Dismal bulbs, flickering, exploding behind him.

DANIEL: Let's speak soon, huh. You bubble up, eh.

KEY: Happy New Year, Daniel.

DANIEL: Great book, bro.

The call concludes. Key stands, arms outstretched, in front of The Palace. And inside it: Price and Anderson. In The PDC World Darts Final. Playing without an audience. Key takes his AirPods out, pops them in their little tin, like travel sweets. He cranes his skull towards the vast windows. Thunk. He hears a dart go in. And around him silence. Thunk. Thunk. And then Russ Bray's distinctive, powerful roar, spewing from the chimneys. "One Hundred And Eighty!!!! "

HERE WE GO ROUND THE MULBERRY BUSH.

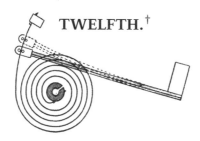

TWELFTH.[†]

Twelfth Night and I hacked up my tree and wazzed the branches out into the street.

Old biddies scurried into the road and collected the needles for soup.

Tinsel blew through the air.

Children gathered to devour toffee apples and stamp on their toys.

Rain fell in vast sheets.

And the streamers and paper hats disintegrated.

And Christmas was swept away in a torrent.

[†]**JUNIPER:** Deary me, that one's bleak.
KEY: It was a bleak time.
JUNIPER: I know.
KEY: My old man ate five Yule logs on Boxing Day.
JUNIPER: Slices? Or whole logs?
KEY: I'm not bringing it up if it's just slices, am I?
JUNIPER: So what, a whole one for breakfast –
KEY: I don't know his schedule, Em. I just know he got 'em down him.
JUNIPER: The last one in front of MOTD, I imagine.
KEY: I imagine so, Em. I imagine so.

WELCOME TO THE HOUSE OF FUN.

Key vaults the stiff black gate, stomps down his path and is away. He crosses the road, muttering about the briefing, spitting highlights of it into the January air. His knees are loose and his movements lack clarity. He spins. Looks back up, up to his lounge window. His flat is still thick with the cruelty of the briefing. His windows are crying. Key blinks, turns and staggers up the hill.

KEY: *(Snorting)* Lockdown.

The occasional knock-kneed ghost sways past him and Key does his best to salute. Key's lockdown clothes are fully up and running now. He has a dark snood, warming his neck. Then the red Norway bobble hat, the blue Uniqlo jeans, the dark-blue Mountain Warehouse anorak, the Puma rucksack clinging onto his back for dear life. The yellow Adidas Gazelles complete the picture. He stumbles past the shops, rapping his new stick on their ice-cold windows. Past the dry cleaner's – closed. Past the Thai Café – closed. He staggers past the vast tower of spent Christmas trees. He salutes the desolation. His iPhone begins to ring. Mother. He clamps her to his lughole.

CAROL: We've just watched –

KEY: The briefing. I know. I know, Ma.

CAROL: Your dad's spitting feathers.

KEY: It's Groundhog Day, Ma. They've gone cuckoo. I dunno what to say. I promised this would finish.

CAROL: No, not the briefing!

KEY: Huh?

CAROL: House of Games! We've just watched House of Games!

KEY: Oh. Oh okay.

CAROL: With Richard Osman! Be still, my beating heart!

Key hangs a left and moves further into the night. The Moon beats down, splashing into puddles, bouncing down the street, lighting Key's way.

CAROL: You're so clever!

KEY: Well, there's been a briefing, Ma. That's what's happened.

CAROL: She'd met her match with you, I'll say that!

KEY: Huh?

CAROL: Gaby Roslin.

KEY: Logan.

CAROL: My son! Giving Gaby Roslin a hiding –

KEY: It's Gabby Logan –

CAROL: On House of Games!

KEY: So you haven't seen the briefing?

CAROL: Of course we haven't seen the briefing, Son! We're watching you! Pressing your little buzzer! Showing 'em all what's what!

BILL: *(Off)* They give 'em the answers, Carol.

CAROL: Your father thinks you get given the answers in advance. He's furious.

BILL: *(Off)* Well, how else is he doing it? Aaaagh.

CAROL: Your father's hacking up the Christmas tree.

KEY: Hacking?

BILL: *(Off)* Getting rid of Christmas, Son. Good riddance to bad rubbish!

Key's plodding past Christmas trees on the pavement. Left to their fate. Sad, wilting, these once-proud beasts wait to be collected and buried by the brave workhorses of the local borough council.

CAROL: Why'd he gotta go and ban Christmas?

KEY: Yeah, well.

CAROL: He should keep his bloody beak out, if you ask me.

KEY: You had an okay time, I thought –

BILL: *(Off)* Ha! The guy's yanking my chain!

Key squints as he glances at a skip full of tinsel, the Moon making it sing.

CAROL: No grandchildren. All our bloody presents in the wrong city. Eating curry on our laps in front of Lewis –

KEY: Curry? Eh?

BILL: *(Off)* Tinned chicken korma, Son!

KEY: Christ. Didn't know it had come to that, Pa.

BILL: *(Off)* No Key's ever had coconut on Christmas Day.

KEY: You at least had some homebrew, I hope.

CAROL: He was plastered.

KEY: Good man.

CAROL: Off his tits, started doing DIY during the Queen's Speech.

Key nods. Blinks and nods. And plods.

CAROL: Waving the drill at Her Majesty.

BILL: *(Off)* I wasn't in my right mind, Son.

KEY: No.

BILL: *(Off)* Not on Christmas Day, I wasn't.

KEY: I'm gonna send your prezzies this week. Now the post's calming down a bit.

CAROL: Four perfectly good grandchildren and we can't cuddle a single one of them, and no bloody prezzies to open. It's inhuman, is what it is.

Key's eyes are moist. The ice-cold wind teases tears from them, pulls them down his cheeks. He thinks of the four grandchildren. His parents. The sixty-mile gap between them. His tongue reaches onto his cheek, steals back some tears. The circle of life.

KEY: Well, they're doing it again, Ma. The top dogs. They're jiggling the locks.

CAROL: Where do you get your brains from?! Like lightning!

BILL: *(Off)* They get given the bloody answers. Fake news.

KEY: We don't, Pops, I swear.

CAROL: We've got a clever son, that's all.

BILL: *(Off)* He ain't cleverer than Gaby bloody Roslin.

KEY: Logan. She was good, Pa, I had to work for it.

BILL: *(Off)* Fake news! Stop the Steal.

CAROL: Who was the nice man on the right?

KEY: Jeff Stelling.

BILL: *(Off)* Didn't know what had hit him, that guy.

KEY: You need to watch the briefing.

CAROL: Can you get a hold of one of Richard Osman's books, then?

BILL: *(Off)* Champagne, Carol!

CAROL: Oh, yes, you won a bottle of Richard Osman champagne!

BILL: *(Off)* When are we getting smashed?

CAROL: He wants to know if we can all have it together, to celebrate your win!

KEY: But the briefing, Ma!

CAROL: We didn't watch the briefing! We're not watching the briefings! We're fed up with the briefings!

The Moon is shining hard on Key's tears. Drying them.

BILL: *(Off)* If you want us to watch that pillock's updates, don't be going on a game show at the same time.

KEY: Record the show then, Pa.

BILL: *(Off)* If my son's locking horns with Gaby bloody Roslin –

KEY: Logan –

BILL: *(Off)* I'm afraid I'm tuning in live. And that noodle-haired buffoon will have to get to us another way.

KEY: Do you even know what he's said?

CAROL: What's he said?

BILL: *(Off)* Yeah. Come on, Son. What's he said? What is it now?

CAROL: Short of another lockdown, I'm sure nothing would surprise me.

Key climbs the stile to the heath and stops. January is making his jeans cool and harden. A hundred yards away there is a bench, drawn in black ink, on the top of Parliament Hill. An old swindler has one foot on the bench. He has a saxophone and leans into it, rasping a melancholy tune into the night. Key swallows and moves slowly out onto the heath, catching his parents up on the briefing as he walks.

BACK INSIDE.

I LOOKED out of the window, and vomited out of it, too.

I hoicked it back down, locked it, welded the lock, pissed on the lock, dried the lock, welded the lock again and wandered back into the bathroom.

I did myself a couple of buzzcuts and dived into my bath.

My jaw smashed into the taps and my tangerine toppled off the side of the bath and rolled away.

I reached out, but my arm wasn't long enough or the distance was too great.

My fingertips tapped the puddled tiles and the second hand on my Casio watch ticked steadily on.

Week II.

In which bubbles emerge,
marshmallows sink
slowly into mocha,
and a ritual is put to bed.

HERE WE GO ROUND THE MULBERRY BUSH.

ICING.

I FLICKED through the latest regs, seeing if there was anything there I could get on board with.

Unlimited exercise seemed good.

I gave it a big fat tick with my Sharpie.

No one coming over for cake: less so.

I poured out my Tipp-Ex; troweled it over the shit I wasn't down with.

Absolutely caked it on.

I blew on the Tipp-Ex.

Waited for the white puddles to dry over the meanness.

I pulled on my little tracksuit bottoms and headband.

My frown dribbled down my singlet as I stretched out my calves and sliced myself a couple of inches of Jamaican Ginger Cake.

BUBBLING UP.

Key and Buddy are walking on the heath. Up past the water fountain, forking right, towards the ponds. They've picked up coffee, and have springs in their steps. Key has a mocha in his mitts and a warm glow around his cheeks. Buddy's hat is cosy as hell. It portrays a fun-looking seal, with friendly eyes and flippers that dangle down, taking care of the ears. Key listens to Buddy. Key is interested in what she has to say.

KEY: And that's a bubble, huh?

BUDDY: That's a bubble.

KEY: They're calling that a bubble.

BUDDY: They are.

KEY: The old Michael Bublé.

BUDDY: And me and Rick... Well, we're asking you into ours.

KEY: Ha.

Key's welling up.

BUDDY: Just makes the whole thing... well, I mean d'ya wanna do another one on your own?

KEY: Yer know... um...

BUDDY: Lockdowns aren't a walk in the park, that's all. On your own.

They continue to walk. Key can't talk yet. Something in his eye. A bubble with Rick and Buddy, huh? That'd be something. Go to Rick and Buddy's place. Pancakes with Rick and Buddy. Buzzcut party at Rick and Buddy's. Movie night at Rick and Buddy's. Popping over to Rick and Buddy's. A doughnut. Maybe two. At Rick and Buddy's.

KEY: I mean... Is there no one else you want? In your bubble, I mean?

BUDDY: We want you, Kiddo.

KEY: Ha.

BUDDY: You're into it, aren't you, Boo!

She yells back at Rick. He's walking fifteen feet back, espadrilles splooshing in the puddles. He's straining to keep up with the conversation. He's not in their group. Three would be a conviction.

RICK: *(Yelling)* The more the merrier!

BUDDY: Well, you think about it, anyway, Kiddo. The offer's there.

RICK: Pizza party.

BUDDY: Huh?

RICK: Pizza party!

BUDDY: You see, we could have pizza. It'd be like 2019.

Key's eyes glaze over. He remembers that year. 2019. He remembers the foil tins of Indian takeaway, everyone cleaving into them with ladles. He remembers hips clipping against hips. Champions League nights. Nine people in a room, no regulations broken. No spirit of the rules breached. Laughter. Fun.

BUDDY: Everyone's bubbling. CJ's bubbled up with Claire and Pete, you know.

KEY: Oh, nice.

BUDDY: He's round there half the time, doing weird cheese-tasting afternoons and the like.

KEY: *(Smiling)* It would be nice to do that sort of stuff.

BUDDY: They're having a great time with CJ, by all accounts.

RICK: CJ would have been good!

KEY: Huh?

Rick's found a tree and is climbing it. Twenty feet now the gap. Rick bawling from the branches.

RICK: Nah, you'd be good, too, bro!

KEY: You tried getting CJ, huh?

RICK: CJ was snapped up before the key was turned, believe me!

KEY: So you went for me?!

BUDDY: *(To Rick)* Shut up, you big loafhead. *(To Key)* You're first choice, Kiddo. Always have been.

Rick's upside down. His mouth, swinging backwards and forwards over the frosted tips of the grass below.

KEY: I mean, I can't do another like last time, Bud. Not all on my own.

BUDDY: I know, right? Just you and the bear.

KEY: Not even. Gave the bear to Bobby.

BUDDY: Oh, Christ, yeah, you're buggered.

KEY: What would I do?

RICK: Write another book!

KEY: Who's talking to you, Tarzan!

RICK: Get your Dickens on!

KEY: Ink's not dry on the first one, he asks me to write another.

RICK: I was being saucy!

KEY: So was I, pal! Don't worry about that!

BUDDY: We're reading it at the mo, Kiddo. Thanks for dropping it round.

KEY: Yeah? You like?

BUDDY: It's a beaut. But...

KEY: What, Bud? What?

BUDDY: Your lockdown sounded intenze!

Key nods. His eyes catapult back to Lock-down One. The disintegration, the struggle. The orange pen. The ray of light. The book. The blue cover. The beautiful design. The salvation.

RICK: I come across as a pillock in your book!

BUDDY: Ha ha. He hates it!

RICK: There should be a government department where you can complain about this kind of shit!

KEY: What? What department?

RICK: Make me out like I'm a dingo in there.

BUDDY: Ignore him.

RICK: I'm serious!

Rick falls from the boughs and starts to catch up. Key and Bud speed up. Keep the gap. Separate groups. Twelve feet. Fifteen. Twenty feet. The further the safer. Buddy's iPhone goes. It's Rick, from behind. She picks up, puts it on speakerphone.

RICK: Should have used the unlocked bit to get a girlfriend.

Key and Buddy stare at the iPhone. Keep walking. Key doesn't speak.

BUDDY: He didn't know it was gonna lock down again, did he?

RICK: This was always on the cards, Doll. Absolute cert.

KEY: Hardly, Dumbass. Had The Maestro in my ear, didn't I? Boasting about how ideal it was all gonna be.

RICK: Facing a lockdown without a girlfriend, come on, man. Like fighting a war without a rifle, that's my honest opinion.

BUDDY: Well, he doesn't need to now, does he? Because he's joining our bubble.

RICK: Hey, can we swap around, I walk up front, one of you drops back?

Buddy hangs up, slings him in her handbag. Rummages around. She's after something in there. What's she after?

BUDDY: I'm sure you have other offers on the table.

KEY: I dunno.

BUDDY: There'll be interest. Believe me. You're a commodity.

KEY: I am?

BUDDY: If you bubble up with some nice young lady, we'll not stand in your way.

KEY: Young lady, yuh.

RICK: Missed the boat! He had his gap, Doll!

Buddy removes herself from her handbag. She's holding a small plastic bottle of Peppa Pig bubbles. Key smiles. Buddy shakes, untwists the lid. Key smiles.

BUDDY: Well, there's no hurry, seriously. Let us know next week.

RICK: Or the week after!

KEY: Lockdown will have ended by then lol.

BUDDY: It really won't.

Buddy blows a stream of bubbles in the air and Key has tears in his eyes. As they continue to walk, so they hear Rick thudding towards the bubbles like a red setter, leaping up at them, bursting them with his palms, his tongue swinging out of his mouth, his involuntary yelps filling the air with joy.

HERE WE GO ROUND THE MULBERRY BUSH.

THE TEAM.

A LITTLE boy, rosy cheeks, blond hair, sleeps in lockdown.

A vast bear fills the spaces around him in his bed.

The bear is sleeping, too.

Occasionally the bear mutters: "Fucking lockdown, pointless faeces."

But he is barely audible, and his words are slurred, and he is speaking in bear.

And the little boy is asleep anyway, so nay bother.

And the whole thing is insanely cuddly.

Two adventurers, resting.

Before the next day's excellent quests behind the locks.

TO CLAP OR NOT TO CLAP?

Key is on the street. House of Games bathrobe, slippers. An amber glow dribbles out from his flat, fifteen feet above him. It's Thursday night. He's bought a cymbal off of eBay and he's whacking it with a truncheon his old man gave him when he turned eighteen. Again and again he whacks the cymbal. 8:02 PM. His iPhone vibrating in his pocket. His breath freezing in the air, falling, clinking onto the cymbal. He whacks and he whacks and the sound echoes up and down the empty street. 8:04 PM. A window opens opposite, men howl at him. Howl into the night, slam their shutters closed. And now there is silence apart from the iPhone. Ring ring. Click.

JUNIPER: Tim!

KEY: Thought we didn't phone on Thursday nights in lockdowns, Em.

JUNIPER: Huh?

KEY: 8 PM, Em. Think about it. It's the clapping, Dumb-Dumb.

JUNIPER: They're doing the clapping in London?

KEY: Huh?

Key looks up and down the street. No open doors. The windows shut fast. No palms, no wrists. No love. Key blinks.

JUNIPER: Think it got kind of cancelled most places. People kind of over it this time –

Key slings the cymbal to the floor.

KEY: But the nurses!

JUNIPER: The nurses need money, Tim. Not applause. You can't put food on your table with –

Key slings down his truncheon and it dents the cymbal and rolls into the street. Key marches off. Up the street, outta town.

KEY: I can't do lockdowns! It's pointless, Em! I can't do lockdowns! I can't do them!

JUNIPER: Oh, fie, of course you can! Just takes a few days to get your rhythm, that's all.

KEY: I get myself ready for the clapping, the clapping ain't on. Aaggh! They still saying no cuddling? No footy? Masks still happening?

JUNIPER: Of course!

KEY: What of course? Clapping's gone! They're all over the place, man!

JUNIPER: *(Sad)* Nurses need a pay rise, that's all.

KEY: The Maestro's not made of stone, Em.

JUNIPER: They're taken for granted.

KEY: He'll open his chequebook, you watch.

Key's walking fast now, away from civilisation, into the night. Deeper into the darkness. Deeper into Lockdown Three.

KEY: It's not fair, Em.

JUNIPER: Hey, look, it'll be over before you know it.

KEY: It's okay for you. You've got the ocean. You've got a weird cottage with a fire and a man in it.

Key's path is unlit. He is rudderless. Stomping onto the heath now. A hunched beast.

KEY: I mean, what's the point of even writing a book about the lockdown, of putting it all to bed, so to speak, if they're gonna keep having lockdowns.

JUNIPER: Write another book!

KEY: No ma'am! That thing killed me, Em. I emptied the tank. Fuck.

JUNIPER: What?

Key is flailing under the moonlight. Flailing in his slippers.

KEY: Need to go back, in case the trucks –

JUNIPER: You're allowed to walk.

KEY: Oh, you are? But the trucks.

JUNIPER: What trucks?

KEY: We're allowed to walk? We can walk this time?

JUNIPER: I'm walking now.

KEY: Okay. Okay, I'll walk.

The ground is wet. Key's slippers want to sink into the mud, so Key moves quickly. He is spry, like a mouse. He has to be.

JUNIPER: He locked down too late, that's the problem.

KEY: What?! No, Em. He's locked down too early.

JUNIPER: The tolls, the science says –

KEY: Look at us, Em! They're playing us for fools!

JUNIPER: Flatten the curve though.

KEY: He's flattened my boy here, Em! That's what! No Christmas! No Boxing Day! And now no bloody January. If there's no Pancake Day I swear I'm taking the pills!

Key's slipper comes off in the puddle. It is sucked down into the planet. Lost in the mud. One slipper left.

JUNIPER: It's just for one year; you can have a quiet Pancake Day.

KEY: I'm not asking for a loud Pancake Day, Em! I'm not asking for parades down the streets! No one's demanding a carnival for Pancake Day! But the way this is going he'll be outlawing any kind of Pancake Day.

JUNIPER: It's a ways off, anyway.

KEY: *(To the Moon)* I will have my pancakes, so help me God!!!

The Moon becomes golden momentarily. Jif Lemon flows across its face.

JUNIPER: You got yourself a bubble?

KEY: Ha!

JUNIPER: What?

KEY: Everyone wants me in their bubble, Em.

JUNIPER: I bet! You should come join our bubble!

KEY: *(Stopping, blinking)* Yeah?

JUNIPER: Be a hoot!

KEY: *(Voice shaking, words catching)* Join your bubble?

Key pulls his final slipper off, spins on his naked heel, moves back towards civilisation. Moves quickly. Talks excitedly.

KEY: I mean I can pack a bag, the trains are still running.

JUNIPER: Ha ha! Don't tease! You wouldn't leave the bear!

KEY: I don't have the bear, Em. I'm on

my tod, Em!

JUNIPER: Ha ha! Like a little evacuee. Popped on a train in London, picked up the other end by his designer –

KEY: And friend!

JUNIPER: Ha ha, of course friend!

Key running. Key breathless. Key clomping barefoot over a cattle grid. Key's House of Games bathrobe billowing like a sail.

KEY: Ha ha! Imagine! Me pitching up in Falmouth! Like Paddington Bear himself!

JUNIPER: "Please look after this Poet. Thank you!"

KEY: Please!

Key running. Key laughing. Key available. Key mentally in Cornwall already.

JUNIPER: Ha ha! We've got this poor sod from the fish market wants to join our bubble.

Key's tank empty. Key swaying. Key upright in a puddle, like a fork rammed vertically into a thick-as-pigshit chilli. Key slowly sinking.

JUNIPER: Quint.

KEY: *(Key's lights going out)* Goes by Quint, huh?

JUNIPER: He's all alone.

KEY: *(Key's heart slowing)* Quint's alone. Yeah.

JUNIPER: Give the old sod somewhere to have a glass o' red.

KEY: *(Key submerged)* Quint in your bubble.

JUNIPER: Well, we'll see. He's strong favourite, let's put it that way. Oh, hey, I've emailed you all the fun stats about the book. How many we've sold, which shops I've emailed, all that...

But Key isn't listening. Key is focusing on remaining vertical. Key can't disappear into the mud. Not in the first week. Other people remain upright in lockdowns. They keep it together in lockdowns. They keep moving. And so must Key.

BIG DOPY MARE.[†]

BOHNSON was horse riding in Lowestoft now!

The streets were rammoed.

Everyone wanted a glimpse of The Maestro.

"Tough month, fans, huh?!" Bohnson was waggling his fists and his cheeks were scarlet as the wind tore in off the ocean.

He was raising a smile amongst his people as per, though.

"Never mind Dry January, anyone else here doing Bollocks January?"

The hordes were wetting themselves at his humour.

Downing Street Spokesmen and police officers shovelled people up and slopped them back into their homes.

Bohnson's crop top rode up as Mulberry pranced over the cobbles.

---

†**JUNIPER:** One rule for one, then a bunch of all different ones for the rest of us.
KEY: That's the idea.
JUNIPER: Did he do this? Did he ride to Lowestoft?
KEY: How the hell should I know, Em? You think I'm across his diary?
JUNIPER: Lol.
KEY: Put it this way, I wouldn't exactly put it past him.
JUNIPER: Prancing around the streets of Lowestoft. The rest of us stuffed in our houses, ploughing through our box sets.
KEY: Ripping open craft beers like they're going out of fashion.
JUNIPER: Munching Butterkist and scrolling through Twitter.
KEY: Doesn't sound so bad when you put it like that.

QUICKIE.

T HEY started and ended The
Clapping on the same evening.
No pissing about this time.
Just get the thing done.

NOT ALL HEROES WEAR CAPES.

Key's Adidas Gazelles, stepping through the frozen dew, destroying patterns, crushing cobwebs, stomping onto the heath. Past the pétanque piste – empty, past the bowling green – closed, past the public toilets – shackled, taped off, dead. He arrives at the water fountain and laments it. It is a relic now, frozen in time, its refreshing jet suspended in mid-flow: icy, stiff, glistening. He taps the jet with his stick, moves in to lick it.

YOUNGUZI: Keyzee!

It is Younguzi! Jogging down the hill in his Copenhagen Half Marathon running vest and white headband. Younguzi!

KEY: Younguzi! The man, the myth!

Key opens his arms wide and Younguzi pulls up two metres short.

YOUNGUZI: Ha ha. How are you, brüter?!

KEY: Don't know!

Younguzi nods. No one knows. That's the beauty of Lockdown Three. It's a head scratcher.

KEY: No chance of a hug?

YOUNGUZI: I can't, bro.

KEY: Nah, I know.

YOUNGUZI: Sorry, bro.

KEY: Can't buy a hug, me.

YOUNGUZI: Gotta think of my students.

Key nods. Keeps his arms open wide, on the off-chance.

YOUNGUZI: Going back to school, you know.

KEY: Oh, yeah. Fastening the tie, huh?

YOUNGUZI: Tomorrow. Fifty children.

KEY: Wow.

YOUNGUZI: I know.

KEY: *(Liverpudlian accent)* A lorra lorra kids.

YOUNGUZI: It's usually nine hundred. We've just got the children of key workers, for now.

KEY: Yeah. Yeah. Gotcha. So if they've got a nurse as a mum or... I dunno... their dad's a baker, they're in.

YOUNGUZI: Not baker, but –

KEY: Superhero then.

YOUNGUZI: Ha ha. Yeah yeah! Kids of superheroes. I like that.

KEY: You're telling me a superhero's not a key worker now?

YOUNGUZI: Well, I'll say this: all key workers are superheroes.

KEY: Come on; give us a hug, man. You can have a bath after. Hug me, bro!

Key's arms curl towards Younguzi like daisies craving the Sun. He's hugged this man over four hundred times. He takes another step forward and Younguzi takes another one back. They move up the hill in this manner for some time. They stop. Their breath is forming a dense cloud between them, slowly descending under its own weight.

KEY: You know who *is* a hero?

YOUNGUZI: They're everywhere, bro. I swear. The pando finds heroes, that's what –

KEY: This guy!

Key unzips his dark-blue Mountain Warehouse anorak, unzips his red Adidas tracksuit top; reveals a grey t-shirt. On it, in silhouette, Captain Tom. Edging along on his Zimmer frame.

YOUNGUZI: They're putting him on t-shirts now, huh?

KEY: I have no idea what "they" are doing, Youngsten. I know Snappy Snaps are still slapping photos on anything that moves.

YOUNGUZI: You had it made?

KEY: I'm not walking around without the captain on my chest, I swear.

YOUNGUZI: That guy got huge; I'll give him that.

KEY: Yeah I know he did. Round and round the garden.

Key zips up. Stretches his arms out again. Hug me, Younguzi. Lift me up.

YOUNGUZI: Where's your teddy bear?

KEY: I don't need a bear. I'm doing this lockdown without.

YOUNGUZI: Locked down alone. You got a bubble? Rick says he and Bud have put in a bid.

KEY: They've come knocking, yeah.

YOUNGUZI: You taking 'em up on it?

KEY: They're in the frame, yuh.

YOUNGUZI: Looking for something better?

KEY: I don't know.

YOUNGUZI: You don't know much.

KEY: The tyranny of choice.

YOUNGUZI: Nice to have options.

KEY: I know what'll happen. End up getting myself in a pickle, slamming my fists against any old door, demanding to be let me in!

YOUNGUZI: "Let me in your fucking bubble!"

KEY: Yeah. Yeah.

They are by a streetbin now and Key leans his fat arse against it. Its feet sink further into the ground. The muscles inside Younguzi's running tights are beginning to calcify.

KEY: You do a great job, Younguzi, I'll say that.

YOUNGUZI: It's stressing me out.

KEY: 'Course! You got a lot of people relying on you.

YOUNGUZI: We're in a pandemic, what can you do?

KEY: I couldn't do it, I'll say that.

YOUNGUZI: *(Gravely)* No.

KEY: What do you mean "no"?

YOUNGUZI: I mean, as in –

KEY: You think you could have written a book, then?

Key stamps his foot down. A chunk of mud, chilled by the elements, flies up like a hardened piece of chocolate ice cream. The dull orange lid of an ancient pen is revealed by the foot of the streetbin. What Sun there is catches it, yet it does not glint.

YOUNGUZI: I'm saying everyone has to keep going.

KEY: We swap places, huh? Let's see. Let's go. I don the tie; stride out in front of thirty ten-year-olds –

YOUNGUZI: My school's secondary, eh.

KEY: Run rings around 'em, that's what.

YOUNGUZI: I think you'd keep them engaged.

KEY: Jaws on the floor, that's what!

Younguzi nods. Smiles.

KEY: You think you're penning a book

for the ages? Good luck, mate. You'd've hit the bottle more than I did, I swear.

YOUNGUZI: Turned to the drink, eh?

The book has appeared in Key's hand and he is slapping the cover hard.

KEY: We both have our roles to play, that's all.

YOUNGUZI: And I'm saying the same.

KEY: Hug me, man! Hug me!

YOUNGUZI: I can't!

Key slings his book down, picks it up, puts it in his Puma rucksack, stamps his foot, misses the orange pen by a millimetre. And now here they are. Two men stood by a streetbin. Children of the pandemic, both with their assigned roles. Heroic. Like waxworks. Figures from an emerging history. Eyes watering, frosting up, cheeks like glaciers.

KEY: Well, I'm gonna deliver this 'ere book to my accountant. See what that does. You?

YOUNGUZI: Fine-tuning our hybrid teaching strategy; distribution of free school meal vouchers.

KEY: Rashford, huh?

YOUNGUZI: Guy's something else.

KEY: Running rings around The Maestro.

YOUNGUZI: I can't talk about him, I'll cry.

KEY: Everyone doing their bit.

Key's book is out again, the Sun bouncing off it. He sighs.

KEY: Well, can I at least hug you goodbye?

YOUNGUZI: Not really.

KEY: Because...

YOUNGUZI: You know why, man.

KEY: Flattening the curve, keeping the bugs on the down low.

YOUNGUZI: Good to see you, bro.

Key nods. His arms are outstretched again. Younguzi adjusts his headband, pings it, and is away. A thoroughbred, his long strides take him quickly down the hill and he hurdles a fence, a hedge, another fence and the public toilets. Key puts his arms down, collects his thoughts and moves slowly away, up towards the ponds.

†**JUNIPER:** They should be ashamed of themselves, that lot.
KEY: It's about the school dinners sitch, you know.
JUNIPER: Rashford put them to shame.
KEY: He did, Em. He really did.
JUNIPER: Cooking all those lovely dinners, while the hogs –
KEY: Don't think he cooked them himself, Em –
JUNIPER: No, I know. Probably his teammates helped.
KEY: Ha ha. Yeah.
JUNIPER: McTominay grating the carrots.
KEY: How do you know McTominay?
JUNIPER: There's a lot of things I know.
KEY: And why's he grating carrots?
JUNIPER: Helping Marcus.

PORK PASTE.[†]

"**T**OTALLY get it, that's a gash dinner that."

Bohnson was sucking his tummy in behind his podium thingy, wiping crap off his gob.

Another slide came up, a little girl gnawing on a pea.

"Yarrrrs, *mea culpa*, she should have more than that. Will sort!"

Bob Piston ITV narrowed his eyes in his screen and asked his follow-up question.

"And is there any truth that you treated yourself to a Double Deliveroo today?"

Bohnson clearly had detritus from two different continents on his bib.

"Get this little girl some pie, can we! Poor little angel!"

Bohnson thumped his fist on his notes and belched out a pungent burp.

The room was filled with an intoxicating stink of Bengali spices mixed with the unmistakable pong of oregano and 'nduja sausage.

HERE WE GO ROUND THE MULBERRY BUSH.

228*.

Key is on his loop. Past the pétanque piste, left at the table tennis table, right at the water fountain. Stretching out past the ponds. And on. Listening to the cricket. Listening to Joe Root flaying the Sri Lankan medium-pacers. On into the spinney Key goes; right through the bogs, left up the slippery hill and a moment at the gate, gazing back down, across London, across the past, the future. Hands on hips. Root slapping Fernando into the stands. Key purring. The commentary cutting out. The ringing cutting in. Steve this time. Thanking Key for the book, most probably.

KEY: Steven! Get the book?

STEVEN: Got the book.

KEY: Yuh. I sent you one, just 'cos you're in it.

STEVEN: One line.

KEY: I'm sending it to people who were in the book, you know.

STEVEN: One fucking line!

KEY: Oh, right, ha ha!

STEVEN: Never mind your fucking laughing, why am I saying one line in your book, Steinbeck?!

Key glances down at his iPhone. Imagines Steve inside it, smashing stuff in his vest, kicking chairs about. He squeezes the iPhone.

KEY: Hang on, what the fuck is this? You're in it, so I send you a book. I don't understand –

STEVEN: It's a fucking pisstake. The kids are in it loads.

KEY: Steve, man! It's nothing personal, bro. How's lockdown? How are the kids?

STEVEN: Jo's in it.

KEY: That's why I sent the book, Steve; you're not listening to me!

STEVEN: Shit book!

KEY: What is this, man? What's this about? I've immortalised you!

STEVEN: Yeah, as a fucking gel who says one line and pisses off back under his rock, never to be seen again.

Key slings down his Puma rucksack. Looks for somewhere to sit, rest his damn legs.

STEVEN: You write another book –

KEY: I'm not writing another book.

STEVEN: You write another book, I want the full treatment.

KEY: What the fuck is that? "The full treatment"?

STEVEN: You got Lord in there properly; you got Rick in there. I'm just in the background of one dialogue. You write another book –

KEY: I'm not writing another book, Steve. Not this lockdown. I'm flogging the first one and walking.

STEVEN: It's fucking embarrassing is what it is.

KEY: No one knows it's you, man.

STEVEN: Getting texts from Rick. Photos of the book. Yanking my chain about my one fucking line.

KEY: I can't do this, Steve.

Key's found a log. Some fallen tree bullshit from years ago. He brushes the frost off it, slaps his fat arse, plonks it on the log.

STEVEN: You've got two pages of you talking to a mouse.

KEY: It doesn't matter, Steve. It's just stuff from my mind. I was working through stuff.

STEVEN: Yeah well, work through me next time, hey!

The line goes dead. Key's feet are cold. His trainers rest on the icy lid of a puddle. The blueness of his toes is turning the yellow of his Gazelles into a putrid green. Frost builds on spiders' webs.

KEY: Cheers then, Steve.

The ice cracks and Key's feet fall through into the depths of the puddle. Crystal clear water moves slowly through his Gazelles and reaches for the hems of his jeans. Key leaves his feet in the drink. What's the difference? He looks to his left. A whisker, covered in moisture, then frozen solid sits, gleaming in the sunshine. Key frowns.

WARBOYS.

WHAT a load of old bollocks.

Now you had to choose three people and spend the next six months in a car with them with the windows up.

I bought sweets and texted a few people.

Same old story, everyone all fixed up already.

I entered the Leftover Scheme.

Filled out about a million bloody forms.

Got hooked up with an old biddy called Sylvia and a couple of hulking great twins.

We got in a Volvo and locked the doors.

I glanced at the clock.

Ten minutes in and we were already winding each other up like anything.

The gruesome twosome sat in their singlets with their music up on full.

Sylvia stuffing her face with Doritos and droning on about the government.

THE NATIONAL EFFORT.

I SPENT the morning making huge sacrifices as part of the national effort.

I was whistling hard, veering this way and that to keep a patriotic distance between myself and other organisms.

At approximately half past eleven I saw a small minority who apparently didn't want to follow the rules.

I frowned hard, crumbling some of my teeth.

Why was this small minority not following the rules, for heaven's sake?

I found a five-litre pot of paint and waded over to them.

"Why can't you make a huge sacrifice as part of the national effort, like me?" I said, teasing off the lid with a teaspoon.

They started following the rules even less and I splooshed them with paint.

About four litres went on the small minority who didn't follow the rules and the rest went down my jeans and splattered my Gazelles.

WALRUS.

Key's laces are pulled tight, his Gazelles clomp forward, he moves through the mud like a duck. On he goes. Up towards the ponds, his stick plugging and unplugging in the muck. The light is going. His AirPods are wedged in his lugholes; there's another briefing in his ears. Key imperceptibly shaking his head as the political gunk sloshes in. Key is a zombie, no more, no less. The briefing cuts out, the ringing begins. The Colonel. He connects the call.

KEY: What we gonna do, Colonel?

COLONEL: These guys are mad.

KEY: Yeah, yeah I know they're mad.

COLONEL: Broken promises.

KEY: I'd rather not dwell on what they're breaking, Colonel.

COLONEL: Broken hearts.

KEY: These people don't understand the needs of their fellow man.

COLONEL: You're supposed to be round my gaff tonight.

KEY: You think I don't know that?

COLONEL: *(With gravity now)* You can still come.

Key has reached the ponds. There's moonlight there, a light wash of it skims over the water. Trees cast ominous shadows. Key's shadow, too, impresses itself on the water.

KEY: But I can't, Colonel.

COLONEL: But don't you see? You can!

KEY: But the regs, bro!

COLONEL: See, I've talked with Gab.

KEY: Okay. You've talked with Gab.

COLONEL: I have. I've talked with Gab.

On the opposite side of the ponds, Key spies a lady: thickset. She has a tracksuit on and a swimming cap. Key looks around, sits himself down on a fallen willow.

COLONEL: We'd like to throw our hat in the ring.

KEY: Huh?

COLONEL: We'll have you in our bubble.

KEY: You will?

COLONEL: We've talked it through. We had a meeting.

KEY: Meeting? What?

COLONEL: You're fucked on your own there.

KEY: Fucked? Huh?

COLONEL: Gab's worried about you.

KEY: Worried? What?

COLONEL: She read your book, she asked her University friends. She read around it a bit. She's worried about you.

KEY: You'd have me in your bubble?

COLONEL: We'd take you like that.

The Colonel clicks and it's like a gunshot. Key nods. He leans on his stick; continues to watch the lady. She's stripped to her black swimming costume and is moving down towards the shore. She is impressive, bringing to mind a walrus or possibly a decent-sized tyre. A toe lowers itself into the water, breaching the surface, sending moonlight up her legs.

COLONEL: You know about bubbles, right?

Key nods.

COLONEL: I'm getting the keg.

KEY: The keg, again.

COLONEL: From the boozer. It's a done deal.

KEY: Me join your bubble?

COLONEL: Yeah. A gallon o' beer. I've signed on the dotted line.

KEY: Keg of beer in your flat.

COLONEL: The three of us watching Newsnight. Whenever you're out of beer, simples, into the kitchen, flick the switch. Blow the foam off, wander back in. The three of us, lashed off our tits, hanging off Maitlis's every word.

KEY: Join your bubble, huh?

COLONEL: We'd love you to.

KEY: The offer's there.

COLONEL: It is.

KEY: A gallon o' beer.

COLONEL: And when that's done I'll buy another.

The walrus is finally submerged. The water rises a millimetre across the board and the cap disappears. The lagoon becomes peaceful, serene once more.

KEY: You've got my back, Colonel. And I love you for it.

COLONEL: Why wouldn't you join with us?

KEY: It's definitely food for thought.

COLONEL: I'll keep buying those kegs. We can have a keg a day, I really don't mind. You can still get a takeaway. We're gold members on Deliveroo. We get the best cyclists.

KEY: Okay, okay.

COLONEL: We've had it where the doorbell's rung before the card's gone through.

KEY: Really?

COLONEL: Gab pays extra. We're gold members, I'm telling you. We've had it where we've been discussing getting fish and chips and the doorbell's rung and there's a guy with a big brown bag full of the stuff.

KEY: That can't be true.

COLONEL: It's the gold membership. What d'ya say?

Key nods. The pond is placid and he leans forward. The silence of lockdown is tightening. He peers at the water's surface. He looks at his watch. January.

KEY: I'm gonna go home, work this out.

COLONEL: Don't go home, come straight here.

KEY: I've gotta go home. I've gotta...

COLONEL: Gotta what? What's happening in there? What'ya gotta do?

Key closes his eyes.

COLONEL: Who else is in the frame?

KEY: It's not about the frame. I... I've never been in a bubble, Colonel.

COLONEL: Well, I don't know what to say.

KEY: It's a great offer, John.

COLONEL: What if I get a car?

KEY: What car?

COLONEL: Like Rick and Buddy. You think I can't get a car?

KEY: This ain't about cars, Colonel!

Key pulls a Penelope Pitstop flask from his Puma rucksack. He slops 250 ml of Camden Pale into the lid, which also serves as a cup.

COLONEL: Go on then: a keg each! Me, you and Gab. I'll label 'em up; Gab's got a label-maker. "Colonel", "Gab", "Keyzee". Our own tankards. Show the powers that be what's what.

KEY: I love you and Gab.

COLONEL: Then let's do it. I'll nip out, grab some cashews. You head on over.

KEY: I'll think it over. I need to... you know. Think it over. If that's okay.

Bubbles rise up in the pond and the two vast nostrils emerge from the depths. This beast is free. She is not locked down. She pulls herself through the waters, back to her beach, reaches for the thick roots, plugged into the bank, hauls herself out. Moves with an enormous, leathery dignity, back to her tracksuit.

COLONEL: Let's meet at least. You'll do me that honour.

KEY: Pubs are buggered.

COLONEL: I'm not asking to go into a pub, man. That ship's sailed. I'm saying let's get our tramp on, thrash it out, eh.

KEY: A bench?

COLONEL: Pick a bench, any bench.

KEY: A bench in winter.

COLONEL: Get our laughing gear round some decent IPA.

KEY: Hazy Janes.

COLONEL: I can put the keg in my bicycle basket.

KEY: Let's stick to cans, Colonel. At least for the negotiations.

COLONEL: Fair play, we'll go cans. Just want to be on a bench, with your fat arse next to mine, gulping down something. Anything.

KEY: Are we allowed to sit on a bench together?

COLONEL: If we stop sitting on benches what's left?

KEY: Of course I'll meet with you, Colonel.

COLONEL: We can wrap up warm.

KEY: And you can make your case.

COLONEL: We've got central heating, bro. We can learn chess.

KEY: I already said I'm meeting you, didn't I?

Key ends the call and his brain is immediately flooded with a governmental update. He gets to his feet and the vast walrus opposite turns. They stand momentarily, looking at one another. The pond, the moonlight, the situation: it all hangs heavily between them.

†**JUNIPER:** One star jump, lol.
KEY: Ha ha, I know.
JUNIPER: I thought you had a personal trainer.
KEY: Naw, got rid.
JUNIPER: Oh, you dumped your PT!
KEY: Kept seeing him on the street.
JUNIPER: Awkward!
KEY: Whole lockdown, kept having to squat behind bins.
JUNIPER: Ha ha!
KEY: Legging it when I saw him. Jumping over fences to avoid this guy.
JUNIPER: Kept you fit, eh!
KEY: Pulling up manhole covers, jumping into the sewers, swimming through faeces.
JUNIPER: Proper workout, ha ha!
KEY: Four, sometimes five times a week.
JUNIPER: Gotta stay active, eh.

SLOTS.[†]

A ROTA arrived.

Government sanctioned, it outlined when people from my block could exercise so we didn't fill the local air up too much.

I got 2:25 PM–2:35 PM.

Ten measly minutes!

I pulled on my tracksuit and warmed up in my kitchen.

At the appointed hour my door unlocked and I burst onto the street.

I charged up to the tennis courts, did a star jump and raced back down the hill.

I squeaked back home at 2:35 PM and heard my locks whirr shut.

The nick of time.

I was breathing out of my ass and restored my fats with a cream bun and a handful of pâté.

I heard the chap opposite leaving his flat in a hurry.

He was swearing and apparently wearing roller skates.

BUBBLING DOWN.

A fingerless glove. Tips protruding. Pink, cold, but glowing. Blackcurrant fingernails. They clasp a disposable cup, piping hot. A poet's hand comes in, takes the paper cup. Marshmallows erupt from its summit. An empty counter now. A blank canvas. The Poet's hand comes back in with coins. The fingerless glove re-enters, too. The coins are poured into the naked fingertips. They clink and jingle and it is like a fairytale. Momentarily, The Poet's hand hovers above the naked tips. An iPhone, ringing. Click. A connection.

KEY: Niece?

MAGGIE: Uncle! Are you joining our bubble?! It's boring here! Well, are you?!

Key is walking away now. Behind him the coffee concession, the fingerless glove, a girl's eyes. In softer and softer focus. Key's face sharp, we're right with him.

KEY: Watcha doin', Niece?

MAGGIE: Not much lol. Bored out of my skull. Drinking cherryade.

KEY: Old-school.

MAGGIE: I've drunk around about a gallon of it, ha ha!

KEY: Ha ha! I drunk six 440 ml cans of Staropramen last night, Mag. The phrase "cut from the same cloth" barely covers it.

MAGGIE: I'm full of the fizz, Unc. Keep thinking I'm gonna float away!

KEY: Stiff email to Panda Pops if my niece floats away, I'll say that.

MAGGIE: Ha ha.

KEY: Lockdown Three then, Mags. You prepped? You pumped?

MAGGIE: School's cancelled!

KEY: Yes! That's what I'm talking about!

Key fist pumps and his marshmallows tremble.

MAGGIE: Nooooo! It's bad!

KEY: Huh? When I was a kid, school was faeces. You're telling me it's fun going to school all of a sudden?

MAGGIE: Of course! And the big children's exams are maybe being cancelled!

KEY: Let me tell you this, when I was a big child I'd have given my left bollock to have my exams cancelled. No joke.

MAGGIE: I can't play football and we have to do home schooling. Oh – hey, if you join our bubble you can do home schooling! We –

KEY: I'm gonna stop you there, Niece, I ain't home-schooling shit.

MAGGIE: Oh.

Key can hear a straw. He can hear a niece blowing into it. He can hear red, vibrant bubbles flying round a kitchen.

MAGGIE: It's alright for you!

KEY: What is? What's alright for me?

MAGGIE: You've finished school and you don't really do much. What's the difference?

KEY: Don't do much? Pah!

Key is at the top of Parliament Hill now. He sits his fat arse down on the black, cast iron bench – his bench – and surveys his city. His mocha is hot in his hands and he smiles into it. He looks down the hill. Looks for the coffee girl. She is masked by a vast bald chap now. A latte eclipse.

KEY: *(Dreaming)* Mocha.

MAGGIE: You can just waddle round, wait for it to finish.

KEY: It's worse for adults, Mag. Believe me. Comedy, sport, love: all on their knees, I swear.

MAGGIE: Mm. Maybe it's bad for everyone then.

KEY: Nope. Worse for us. You know nothing about lockdowns.

MAGGIE: I've done a lockdown, haven't I?

KEY: Yeah, I'm talking about doing one as an adult. Kids are clueless, it's like rolling down a hill for you lot. Lockdowns are tough for adults, believe me.

MAGGIE: Well, I don't know because I'm not an adult.

KEY: Yet.

MAGGIE: Yet.

KEY: Read my book, doll. Educate yourself.

MAGGIE: We're not allowed to read your book.

KEY: Too sophisticated, that's why.

MAGGIE: If you home schooled us –

KEY: Not happening –

MAGGIE: You could teach us the book.

That could be our English Literature.

KEY: Aye. Bang it on the curriculum, see who salutes, type of thing.

MAGGIE: We've got plenty of other boring stuff on there already, what's the difference?

Key peers into his mocha. Fingertips rise up from it, blackcurrant fingernails, they beckon. Key smiles. They submerge themselves back into the corps de chocolat.

MAGGIE: So what do you do then? Just waddling and boozing and turning your calendar then, is it?

KEY: Stop saying waddle, can ya? Long strides, me. Like a young John Cleese. Gotta stay active when you're an adult, darling.

MAGGIE: When Dad goes for a run he fills his rucksack with bricks.

KEY: To each his own, Magbury.

MAGGIE: He can't fit his legs in his jeans!

KEY: 'Cos of his new muscles, right.

MAGGIE: He says it's what soldiers do.

KEY: You think I'm rampaging about without a rucksack on my back?

MAGGIE: Your Puma one? Ha ha! You'd be chucked out of the army with that one! You could carry about one hand grenade in that thing.

KEY: Slating your own uncle's rucksack, who's bringing you up, Mags?

MAGGIE: Fill it with bricks, that's what you need to do.

KEY: Bagful of bricks, lol. She's finally lost it. Open the schools! We've got a generation of numpties on our hands!

MAGGIE: Something heavy anyway.

KEY: "Something heavy," she says.

The Sun peeps between the clouds; it hits the vast windows of The Shard and a thin spear of light glances towards NW London. It strikes the coffee girl's awning and is dispersed around the heath. Sunshine.

MAGGIE: Uncle?

KEY: *(Dreaming)* Mocha.

MAGGIE: What? What's wrong with you today? You're not at the races!

Key sips from his mocha. A fingertip touches his lip, scratches lightly against his gnashers, settles momentarily on his tongue. Key kisses it away, swallows.

KEY: If you must know, a beautiful

girl's just flogged me a mocha.

MAGGIE: Oh, are you in love with the coffee girl, now?

KEY: No! You're twisting my words.

MAGGIE: Ha ha! Uncle Tim and the coffee girl!

KEY: She smiled. I don't expect you to understand –

MAGGIE: She's not going to come into your bubble, you know!

KEY: And you know that, do you? You know that for a fact?

MAGGIE: Come and stay with us, Unc!

KEY: Adults don't smile at one another for the benefit of their own health, you know.

MAGGIE: Probably smiling at your divvy clothes!

KEY: This smile had nothing to do with my gloves, Magioshi.

MAGGIE: Please don't pick the coffee girl instead of your number one niece. I'll be furious, Unc.

KEY: I gotta go, Mag.

MAGGIE: Are you getting the vaccination?

KEY: *(Beat)* What?

MAGGIE: Daddy says you might be.

KEY: Do you think I'm seventy? What are you talking about?

MAGGIE: Daddy says you're vulnerable...

Key glances down at his bicep. His eyes bore into his veins, travel round his body. Vulnerable? Who's vulnerable?

KEY: I'm gonna go daydream, if you really wanna know.

MAGGIE: Oh, okay. Maybe I'll do that.

KEY: There's worse things to do, Mags.

MAGGIE: I'm gonna daydream about hockey.

KEY: Scoring all the goals?

MAGGIE: Ha ha! Yeah. Running rings around the boys.

KEY: Your stick'll be rattling into their shins before we know it.

MAGGIE: Hubble bubble, uncle in the bubble!

KEY: Goodbye, Niece.

Key gazes down the hill, sips his mocha. As he does so the marshmallows seem to form themselves into a duvet-soft smile and mouth the word "dream".

HERE WE GO ROUND THE MULBERRY BUSH.

VACANCY.†

I SET up formal interviews.

Households sat before me, balloting for my services.

They wanted me, these folk.

They wanted me in their bubbles.

Some had put together PowerPoint presentations.

Others bought me gifts.

Leather jackets, exotic perfumes, taxidermy.

There was often desperation coming from the other side of the trestle table.

Desperation for my signature.

---

†**KEY:** You have to know your value, Em.
JUNIPER: You were in demand, yeah.
KEY: Understatement of the year. Think about it.
JUNIPER: You're a laugh.
KEY: Erm. Yes. I am, Em.
JUNIPER: You could have charged people.
KEY: Perrier Award Winner. So, yes, I think I'm probably a laugh.
JUNIPER: 2009.
KEY: Pedigree, Em. That's what. You think that's all dissolved into nothing over the past twelve years.
JUNIPER: Can't have.
KEY: 'Course, it hasn't, Em.

Week III.

In which an old friend returns,
a poet reaches into his reserves,
and desperate fists
slap against the
gossamer-thin walls
of a bubble.

HERE WE GO ROUND THE MULBERRY BUSH.

A REFLECTIVE GLOW.

I DELVED into the reserves, found the courage to ask her out.

All the pubs were closed and the cinemas were welded shut so we sat on a wall in the bitter cold drinking some port from the neck 'cos I forgot the plastic glasses.

The atmosphere was bitter and at one point the police pulled up and talked to us and checked our papers and she flirted with them.

As our date came to an end, she did some pretty bleak stuff about not wanting to hug, elbow-touch, say she'd had a nice time, or commit to meeting up again.

She pinned the lot on the bug.

My nose was bright red because of the cold.

I could read its glow in her cheeks.

A MOCHA FROM HEAVEN.

Key is marching along by the playground – empty – dragging his stick across the railings. His Puma rucksack is heavier than before and his legs bow slightly under the weight of it. In the distance, the coffee concession. He squints. It's a beautiful little stall, kind of like a little wagon almost, hand-drawn and coloured-in with crayon. Key strides towards it, his skin glowing brighter the closer he gets. Will she be there? Emily Juniper – designer, human being, voice – is in his ears.

JUNIPER: It's only week three.

KEY: I can't do another one, Em. Not a long one, honest I can't.

JUNIPER: Everyone's in the same boat.

KEY: I know, Em. It's a faeces boat. That's the problem.

JUNIPER: Just do as much as you can.

KEY: We need to rise up, that's what.

JUNIPER: I think the trick is, plenty of exercise. You can't be a blob.

KEY: We need to make placards. I swear, show these people what's what.

JUNIPER: Are you getting out and about, walking still?

KEY: Walking right now, Em. Inspired by Captain Tom himself. Gonna walk and walk.

JUNIPER: That guy makes me cry.

KEY: I've ordered walking trousers, Em.

JUNIPER: Oh.

KEY: Calves like resin, Em. Filled my rucksack up, extra weight, you know. Like Rambo.

JUNIPER: Did Rambo have a knapsack?

KEY: Beck's Viers in there, Perrier Award, Champagne.

JUNIPER: Got your Perrier Award on your back?

KEY: Calves like resin, Em, I swear.

JUNIPER: You got yourself a bubble yet?

Key is getting closer to the coffee wagon. He squints. A figure, hunched over the nozzles, her back to him. Is it her? Key stands motionless. He can see his breath as it honks out of his nostrils. It is thick. Grey. Key is a dragon.

KEY: I dunno, Em. I dunno about the bubble. The bubble stresses me out.

JUNIPER: You gotta join a bub, Tim! The lady who sells the cockles has bubbled up with her brother. They eat chowder together every evening. It's what keeps them going.

KEY: *(Optimistic)* And... have you, um... filled your... vacancy?

JUNIPER: You know what, we have. We went with Quint. Poor sod. All on his own like that.

KEY: You've gone with Quint.

Key negotiates a fence. His face is stretched to its limits with disappointment. He sighs. He can hear the spoon in the milk jug. Clink clink.

KEY: Em, I can come up with content for these placards, I swear. Then you design them, Bob's your uncle. March on Parliament –

JUNIPER: I'm not marching on Parliament.

KEY: What's the difference? It's one afternoon. Wiggle the placards, fuzz some rocks. Pop you back on the train.

JUNIPER: I'm not supposed to leave Cornwall.

KEY: We gotta get unlocked, Em!

Key can smell the coffee. It's her. The same girl from before. Must be! The blonde ponytail snaking down the back of her thin, black anorak. He loses control of his knees. He is now being swept towards her, his heart pumping, his arteries desperately trying to disperse the blood. Being pulled into her orbit.

JUNIPER: The book's selling, Tim. I mean, it's selling. We're gonna have to print more at this rate.

KEY: Control-P, Em. Control-P.

JUNIPER: We're gonna run out, I swear.

KEY: People are reading it, Em, that's all.

JUNIPER: Well, I mean... should we?

KEY: Control-P.

JUNIPER: Fuck. How many?

Key is like a zombie, drifting towards the wagon, his feet six inches above the stiff, frosty grass.

KEY: Too many.

JUNIPER: Too many?

KEY: Yes. The only way. Be bold. Overprint. Pulp if necessary.

JUNIPER: You're gonna have to do press, Tim. To shift the units.

KEY: *(Transfixed by the girl)* Press. Yes. Quite right. Press.

And now: boom. She spins round. It's her. The coffee girl. Smiling.

JUNIPER: Do you think you can get on 6 Music? Chat to Lauren Laverne, oh my God! Can you chat to Lauren? Is that a thing?

KEY: One second, Em, I'm just getting my mocha, you know.

JUNIPER: Oh.

KEY: *(To the coffee girl)* Hi.

Emily Juniper falls silent. The girl is looking at him. Her eyes are alive. Lockdown has not extinguished them. These are 2019 eyes. Mischievous. Undefeated by governmental constraint. Two azure puddles of optimism.

KEY: Hi.

COFFEE GIRL: Hello. Mocha, is it?

KEY: Huh?

COFFEE GIRL: You got a mocha yesterday.

KEY: Oh.

COFFEE GIRL: And the day before.

Key blushes. Covers his cheeks with his mittens to hide their rays. The coffee girl's fur hat is white as snow. Beneath her eyes: a mask, horses running free all over it, beneath that a black jumper, disappearing underneath the black anorak, the fingerless gloves, denying Key her hands, allowing him tips and nails, then the obligatory dark-blue jeans and then nothing. Her body evaporating under the weird wooden front of her 18th-century stall. The most beautiful coffee girl he ever did see, with just the eyes and the very tops of her cheeks exposed. They emit only warmth, making Key's cheeks burn ever harder.

KEY: Yes. Mocha please.

COFFEE GIRL: Coming right up.

KEY: Good-o.

COFFEE GIRL: Good-o?

KEY: That is to say, thank you.

COFFEE GIRL: Ha ha.

Key salutes, retreats to a wooden stump.

JUNIPER: *(Back in his ear)* Oh, he likes the coffee girl, does he?

KEY: No he doesn't. He doesn't like the coffee girl.

JUNIPER: He does.

KEY: He doesn't! He bloody hates her.

JUNIPER: I've not seen you like this for a while, I must say.

Key watches the coffee girl as she hammers her metal jug on the counter. Clouds of frothy milk leap from the jug, sail into a paper cup.

JUNIPER: Bubble up with her, Tim!

KEY: What you going on about, Em! Stop it, man! Come on!

Key is done for. He keeps himself upright on his stump using his stick.

COFFEE GIRL: *(Off)* Tim!

KEY: Oh, hang on.

JUNIPER: How did she know your name?

KEY: Huh?

JUNIPER: You never told her your name.

KEY: Shush, Em. Please!

Key nods. He stands. He supports himself with his stick. Like Willy Wonka himself. He moves to the counter. To his destiny.

KEY: Hi.

COFFEE GIRL: That's your mocha.

KEY: Uh-huh.

COFFEE GIRL: I put marshmallows on it.

KEY: Oh, you did?

COFFEE GIRL: I took the liberty.

KEY: All different colours. Ha.

COFFEE GIRL: I'll see you tomorrow.

KEY: Tomorrow.

COFFEE GIRL: Well? Won't I?

KEY: Um...

Key is dazed. He gazes at his mocha. The coloured marshmallows spin around like a kaleidoscope. He gazes back up at the girl. Her cheeks are bright purple. Key moves away; sips his mocha. It is from heaven.

JUNIPER: You need to be bubbling with that girl, Tim.

KEY: Um. Uh-huh. What?

JUNIPER: I've never been as certain of anything in my entire life.

KEY: Certain. Yeah. But.

Key smells his mocha. It is strong with the scent of perfume, and high-class stuff at that. He spreads a nostril out around the whole thing, shuts his eyes and is transported into the coffee girl's bubble, her lounge, her bedroom, her walk-in wardrobe, her mind, her embrace.

KEY: She's just the coffee girl, Em.

LISTEN TO TIM. [†]

"**W**EAR a mask, eh! You know you want to!"

It was Jermaine bloody Jenas!

They'd got celebs telling us the drill.

They were marching them out, one at a time.

"And keep your distance, for heaven's sake, this thing's fucked!"

They'd only roped in Ian flipping Hislop.

We were on tenterhooks, chowing down on pizzas and continental lagers around Bugsy's, the place buzzing, standing room only.

Who the hell were they gonna wheel out next??

The doorbell went and Steve and his lot piled in, too.

It was like a carnival here!

"The new variant's the issue."

How the hell had they got Henman?

[†]**JUNIPER:** Why didn't they do more of this?
KEY: Money, Em.
JUNIPER: Get someone like Schofield –
KEY: Right, £20k probably, Schofield.
JUNIPER: Madeley then.
KEY: You're still talking £5–10k, I bet.
JUNIPER: Can't they do the one where they *make* them do it?
KEY: Conscription?
JUNIPER: Drug them and bung them in front of a camera.
KEY: I don't think the Great British public are gonna take orders from a woozy Graham Norton, Em.
JUNIPER: Let the drugs wear off a bit before they roll camera?
KEY: Possibly. Lot of logistics with your way of doing it, Em.
JUNIPER: I know.
KEY: Pain in the nutsack, if you're trying to get the drugs the right balance between docile and inspirational.
JUNIPER: Yeah! I know, I know.
KEY: End up with a dopy Tarrant, slurring his words.

RULE OF NONE.

Now you could only see no people *including* yourself.

I reread the rules again and again on my smartphone.

"No people, including yourself."

Splatboy phoned.

"Seen the new regs?!"

Splatboy hated the govt.

"Yeah I seen 'em."

I edged away from myself, hissing.

I could hear Splatboy breathing through his nose.

I could imagine him shaking his head and stretching his fingers in disdain.

♥

† **JUNIPER:** Bonn always makes me laugh.
KEY: Yeah.
JUNIPER: Why call somewhere Bonn?
KEY: Yeah.
JUNIPER: Just *why*?
KEY: Why call somewhere Oslo then?
JUNIPER: Yes! Exactly! That's another one.
KEY: I'm sure there was method to their madness.
JUNIPER: Even ones like Caracas. What's that all about?
KEY: Yeah, Caracas is a fun one.
JUNIPER: I think they're on mushrooms half the time, these people.
KEY: Who though, Em? Who are you talking about?
JUNIPER: Ha ha.

A CONTINENTAL ADVENTURE.[†]

"**Y**OU can't go Interrailing, Bohnson. Not at the mo, it won't play well."

Bohnson was wearing a blue crop top with yellow stars on it, and a beret.

"But it's not Interrailing! Moggeth, you swine! It's not, man!"

Bohnson was pointing at his little diagram thing.

"Look! I actually get a weird coach thing between Barcelona and Prague, how's that Interrailing?"

Moggeth screwed his eyes up like fleas as he scrutinised the route.

Bohnson had written down what snacks he was going to have on what train.

Prague – Vienna: boiled eggs.

Interlaken – Bonn: cocktail sausages and Percy Pigs.

Lisbon – Bucharest: chives and buns.

DOWN-AND-OUT IN NW5.

Key and The Colonel at night. Stomping from one pub to the next. Like old times. But these aren't old times. These are new times. And they cannot go in the pubs. They plod with cans. Jet black carrier bags in their left hands, Tropical Deluxe 3.8%abv, ripped open and bubbling, in their right. The pavement crackling with the cold, their noses damp, red. And on, on they go.

COLONEL: You gone la la yet?

KEY: Why the hell am I going la la?

COLONEL: Ha ha. Stuffed up in your flat there. Shuffling about.

KEY: What shuffling? Make out like I'm some kind of weird mammal, up there.

COLONEL: Ha ha! Yeah, a dopy old tapir!

KEY: I'm out and about, don't you worry about me.

COLONEL: Oh, yeah?

KEY: Not rotting in my flat, believe me.

COLONEL: House arrest, lol.

KEY: Yeah, weird house arrest when you can bang a snood on and crank out ten miles.

COLONEL: Getting your Wainwright on, huh?

KEY: I read some pamphlets this time, believe me. I'm across it this time. Walking. You know? Maestro says I can walk. Okay, I'll walk.

COLONEL: Bite his hand off.

KEY: Thank you Maestro. You got yourself a walker.

COLONEL: Yeah, they've given us walking. Fair play to 'em.

A text. Key checks it. Key can't look at The Colonel. Pockets his iPhone. The Colonel's eyebrows knit hard.

COLONEL: *(Tormented)* People want you in their bubble.

KEY: *(Yes, it's true)* No, John.

Key winces like he's just been smacked in the face by two hockey balls. And on they go. Four trainers. Walking. Four feet inside. Cold. Eating up the pavement. Moving down the street. The empty street. The Colonel shivering. The Colonel sighing. The Colonel building up to it.

COLONEL: Let's stop, huh?

KEY: Thought we were walking.

COLONEL: Let's sit down. Like we're in a pub, eh.

KEY: But... the regs...

There is a bench. Key holds his beer under his chin like an old-school telephone, pulls the regs out of his inside pocket. Some lime-green Post-its, heavy with scrawled directives. Key thumbs through them.

COLONEL: Bugger me, man. They can't ban stopping. Let's rest our legs.

KEY: I swear to God, Colonel. This is how it's spreading, man!

COLONEL: Huh? We walk, it don't spread? We sit down, bugs fly out? It don't make sense, man!

KEY: Have I said it makes sense?!

COLONEL: I've brought foil for us to sit on.

KEY: What the fuck? What foil?

COLONEL: Bacofoil. Gab gave it me as I left the house. Said we could sit down on the foil. Sink a few cold ones.

KEY: They'll all be cold, bro. Believe me.

COLONEL: Yeah. Knackers like ice cubes over here.

The bench is cold, damp, bad. Its wood has taken a soaking and is hardening up a treat. A thin layer of lumpen ice, lacquered over the top.

COLONEL: Say what you like about Lockdown One –

KEY: Lockdown One was jizz, John –

COLONEL: Say what you like about it, it was at least warm.

KEY: Yeah. Yeah, you got that right.

COLONEL: Hard to stay angry with Lockdown One.

KEY: It was warm, I'll say that.

COLONEL: Gonna be a cold-ass lockdown this one, I swear.

KEY: *(Looking up)* At least snow, can't you!

COLONEL: *(Looking up)* Yeah, give us a giggle at least!

KEY: How are we going sledging if the big guy doesn't chuck down a few flakes?

The Colonel sits. Key sits. A rule breached. He slides to one end. Descends into thought. Opposite: The Duke's Head. Its doors: shackled. The amber glow in the window: absent. Key in thought. He drinks.

COLONEL: Me and Gab even in the frame?

KEY: Yeah.

COLONEL: Ha. Who else?

KEY: I'm working it out, man!

The Colonel's hands are maroon and he is shaking with the cold.

COLONEL: Work it out now! Sign on the line! Come back to ours!

KEY: I said I'm working it out, man!

COLONEL: Fifteen minutes and we're home! The keg, bro. I'm serious. Radiators. Music. Come back, bro!

KEY: Colonel, man! Don't do this.

COLONEL: I've said to Gab! I've said I'll get ya. I've said to Gab, man!

His lungs empty themselves of love and the lockdown air freezes into a cloud, drifts up into the night. The Colonel slides back across the ice, to his end of the bench.

COLONEL: This is bananas, being this far away from one another on a bloody bench.

KEY: It's the way things are, Colonel. I'm not having you on my lap, I'm afraid.

COLONEL: If we were in a bubble...

His words trail off, freeze, ascend. Across the street, a burbling old drunkie walks past the pub. A sleeping bag, knotted round his neck, falls down his back. He has a fag in his trap and carries beer. He raises his can.

COLONEL: We are him and he is us.

KEY: We get to go home, John.

The man moves slowly along. He is pushing a shopping trolley and one of his shoes is a box-thing. Key closes his eyes. The rain starts.

KEY: We need to walk.

COLONEL: We should be in that boozer.

KEY: We need to walk.

COLONEL: We should be through that window. In that boozer. We should be sharing Twiglets. We should be taking it in turns to get rounds –

KEY: I know how the pub works, John.

COLONEL: We need to say it out loud, so we don't forget.

Key nods.

COLONEL: We should be slamming down two more pints. Foam should be sploshing on the table. We should be going for a wee. We should be hitting the quiz machine.

KEY: Mark Philippoussis!

COLONEL: Join our bubble, man! Has to be!

Key begins to howl lightly. His eyeballs are cold. Why must he choose? Why must the government make him choose?

COLONEL: You're going to Rick and Buddy's, ain't ya?

Key looks up. The Colonel is opening a Hazy Jane. He blows the foam out of the tongue-hole. Offers up a smile.

KEY: I'm not gonna lie, Colonel.

COLONEL: It's alright.

KEY: It's not signed and sealed.

COLONEL: Percentage. For Gab. She'll want a percentage.

Key stands, he's too cold. His iPhone goes. Another text. Another overture. A cough. The tramp leaning over them.

DRUNKIE: Excuse me.

COLONEL: Huh?

DRUNKIE: I couldn't help overhearing... that is to say...

He is faltering, but his voice is clipped, Dickensian almost.

DRUNKIE: There's a bubble going?

Close-up his sleeping bag doesn't half look warm. Key steps back, gives him his space.

DRUNKIE: I could do with a bubble. That was all really.

COLONEL: Erm.

DRUNKIE: If you're not going in with him.

The Colonel is open-mouthed. Frosted breath pouring down his fleece.

COLONEL: He *is* coming in with me.

KEY: We don't know that, Colonel. I don't know what I'm doing, Sir. It's up in the air.

There is a stand-off. Three men, holding three cans. Deep into January. Trying to get themselves organised.

HERE WE GO ROUND THE MULBERRY BUSH.

RPE CONVENIENCE STORE.

I CONTRAVENED lockdown in order to meet a chap I didn't know that well for a couple of cans on a bench opposite an off-licence that also sold leeks.

He was called something like Stelfort (Mike Stelfort?) and was from work and I think we'd once had to carry something through when they reconfigured the office.

His hair was the colour of ginger and he had skiing gloves and he didn't laugh at much I said.

Anyway, we advanced the bug, him passing it to me and me giving it to the chap in the offy.

Then we went our separate ways.

THE RETURN OF A FRIEND.

Key cuts past the public toilets and strikes out towards the children's playground. What rain there is hangs in the air in the form of a thin mist. Key ploughs stoically through it, his face becoming damp, his features softening. As the mist clears, so the playground emerges. Small, vaguely drawn figures climb frames and rocket down slides. Larger versions watch on. As Key gets closer, two in particular come into sharp focus. Key pulls a handful of rain from his eyes. He squints. Lord and Bobby! He smiles.

KEY: *(Yelling)* Lordoss!

LORD: Keyzee! Thanks for swinging by.

Key vaults the fence, rips his jeans, twists his ankle and hobbles over to the seesaw. On one end we have Bobby. Four years old and handsome as hell, he's trussed up in a green anorak, as warm as a button. Lord stands, loyally by his flank. Bopping him up and down like a mole. On the opposite end of the seesaw... a third figure. Key blinks. No, surely not.

KEY: *(Astonished)* Fatberg?

LORD: The same!

BOBBY: Um-um-um-um we brought him for you!

Sure enough, right there on the B-side, is Key's erstwhile bear, Fatberg. Five foot tall, he's dressed in his red tracksuit and his amber fur is sparkling with precipitation.

KEY: Fatberg! Why've you brung Fatberg down?

LORD: Ha! His idea.

KEY: Bobby!!!

BOBBY: Um-um-um-um I'm on the seesaw!

KEY: You certainly are, Bobby. Why's he brung Fatberg, Lord?

Key wanders round to his old bear and pushes him down as a counterweight. Lord pushes Bobby down and Key lets Fatberg rise back up. Then he pushes him down again, and so it goes on.

KEY: The old seesaw. You can't whack it.

LORD: How are you doing, bro? Going stir-crazy?

KEY: Getting out. Walking.

LORD: They can't stop us walking, huh.

KEY: Like to see 'em try.

LORD: There'd be a revolution.

KEY: Gonna strike out to the peak, run my peepers over the city. Say a prayer.

LORD: You in a bubble? What's happening?

Key looks at Lord, looks at Bobby, looks at the bear, shuts his eyes, imagines Megan, imagines the lot of them chowing down on an Indian takeaway, seeing away a number of 500 ml bottles of Bishops Finger, Lord getting the guitar out, Key being forced to help wash up after.

KEY: Not yet. I'm on the lookout.

LORD: You can bubble up with us. You know that.

BOBBY: Um-um-um-um what's a bubble?

KEY: You know what a bubble is, you little scamp.

Key mimes blowing a bubble, climbing inside it and floating up into the sky. Then he mimes a pelican, soaring through the clouds, spearing the bubble with its majestic bill and the bubble smashing into a million droplets and descending to the ground, Key mimes tumbling through the sky. Landing with a bang in the middle of the lot. He stands up, dusts himself down, pulls some feathers from his collar. Bobby is wide-eyed in his little anorak.

KEY: Someone's dressed up nice and warm. Did you knit your own hat?

LORD: He's three. 'Course he ain't knitting.

KEY: I don't know what the guy's capable of doing, do I?

BOBBY: Um-um-um-um nana knitted me my hat!

KEY: Well, there you go. And what is that, a frog coat?

BOBBY: Um-um-um-um it's my frog coat.

KEY: And why'd ya bring Fatberg, Bobs?

BOBBY: Um-um-um-um.

Bobby is too excited and he goes purple for a moment. He takes some deep breaths. Lord hands him some Hubba Bubba.

LORD: He wants you to have it.

KEY: Huh?

BOBBY: Um-um-um-um he's for you.

KEY: No, no. He's yours now.

The seesaw stops. Everything is still. Bobby unwraps his Hubba Bubba, flicks it into his gob, smiles. Key puts an arm around Fatberg. He feels good.

KEY: Why's he giving me my bear back?

BOBBY: Um-um-um-um because it's lockdown.

KEY: Hey? You don't want him then, Bobs?

Key glances down at his bear. He's coming back? The bear seems to wink. Is he behind all this? What stroke of luck is this?

BOBBY: Um-um-um-um you can have him for one week.

KEY: One week, what?

BOBBY: Um-um-um-um for lockdown.

KEY: Hey?

LORD: I've told him the lockdown's gonna be a week.

KEY: Huh?

LORD: Shhh.

KEY: A week. That's a joke right there. What do you mean a week?

LORD: He hates lockdowns.

KEY: And I don't? You think I'm rubbing my hands together over here? We all hate lockdowns.

LORD: Well, no. But he doesn't need to know it's gonna go on a bit.

KEY: A bit? This one's gonna run and run.

LORD: Shhh.

KEY: I've heard Easter.

LORD: Well, we're telling him it's a week then we'll kind of add a bit on each time a week runs out.

BOBBY: Um-um-um-um you can have him for one week.

Key pings the bear's headband. The rain is getting thicker, each blob now the size of a pine nut, or maybe not that big even.

KEY: You're playing him for a fool. Don't listen to them, Bobs.

LORD: Well, what else can we do?

KEY: That's what the government does, Lord! Don't you see! Making a mug of all of us. Same as last year. Lockdown always ending next week. Tore me apart. It ain't right! This runs till April, Bob! I'm telling you this! Minimum.

BOBBY: Um-um-um-um –

LORD: Don't listen to him, Bob. We're out of this next week.

BOBBY: Um-um-um-um...

Bobby runs out of steam and looks forlorn. His eyes are damp from the mist.

KEY: I'll take him for a week, Bob.

BOBBY: Um-um-um-um it's so you're not lonely.

KEY: Exactly, Bob, so I'm not lonely. *(To Lord)* Humour the chap.

Key hoicks Fatberg into his arms. Christ he feels good. Key stands holding him for a minimum of ninety seconds.

LORD: Cheers, mate.

KEY: No worries. Thanks, Bob.

LORD: Sorry, bro. Now you've gotta lug that bloody bear around the heath. You'll get some looks!

KEY: I don't mind walking my bear. What do you reckon, Bob? Nice to have someone to walk with. Ha ha!

BOBBY: Ha ha.

LORD: Ha ha.

BOBBY: Um-um-um-um goodbye, Fatberg.

KEY: Huh?

Key pulls his tummy in. Gets the bear comfortable on his hip. Elbow-bumps Lord. Bobby blows a bubble and Lord frowns.

LORD: Appreciate that, Keyzee. Let us know if you wanna bub.

KEY: Yeah. Yeah I will. Salut.

Key moves out of the playground. He turns to see Lord lowering his son onto a horse thing. Bobby's waving hard. Key waves back, and makes the bear wave back, too.

KEY: *(To the bear)* Humour the kid, hey.

†**JUNIPER:** I don't like this one so much.
KEY: Have you got cigarettes?
JUNIPER: I gave up in the lockdown.
KEY: Oh.
JUNIPER: Did you really think the government were in your head?
KEY: No. No, don't think so. Lot going on in there though.
JUNIPER: But it's usually your voice.
KEY: Yeah. Yeah, as a rule. Fortunately.
JUNIPER: I'd love to have your voice in my head.
KEY: Ha ha. Yeah.
JUNIPER: Voice of Burger King.
KEY: 24/7 it gets a bit much.
JUNIPER: They've got cigs, look.
KEY: Oh, yeah, see if you can cadge a couple, eh.
JUNIPER: Hang on, why am I cadging them?
KEY: Dunno.
JUNIPER: Do your own dirty work.

WHO TO LISTEN TO.[†]

I TOOK off my mask and a voice in my head told me to put it back on again.

I couldn't work out if it was just me thinking or if the government had injected me with some weird serum that was now speaking to me.

I decided to just ask it a straight question.

"Says who??!"

"Says me, you dozy cunt!!"

Okay, it was my own voice so it was obviously me just thinking.

I hated the idea of a tiny government mouth sloshing about in my skull.

I put my mask back on all the same.

Mask on, earphones in, podcast on, eyelids closed, wait for my stop.

IF YOU DON'T ASK.

A rain has fallen; the heath is looking particularly green. Key is coming down off Parliament Hill, walking in the wilds, no interest in paths, just getting it done. As the crow flies stuff. Straight down, through the lush, sopping grass and the mud. Sliding down the hill now, to his destiny. Emily Juniper is in his ears. The pep talk. And Key sliding down. In control, but only just.

KEY: I'm doing it, Em!

JUNIPER: Because you must, Tim. You only live once. It's a love story. I sense it.

KEY: I can smell the coffee.

JUNIPER: Wake up! Jolt yourself out of your slumber. You can't sleep-walk through another lockdown, Tim. I'm certain of that.

KEY: I'm doing it, I said. I'm sliding down now.

JUNIPER: Sliding?

Key disconnects the call as he slips down the final fifty metres of thick mud. He accelerates; he is now out of control, falling. Falling towards the coffee stall, the coffee wagon, the coffee fairy tale. He pitches into the temporary steel fencing, flies over the rim, lands on the asphalt, gathers his thoughts. The thick stench of Arabica and the tinny radio in his ears. He slices the mud off his back with his stick and pulls himself up to his full height. He fiddles in his pocket, straps on his mask.

COFFEE GIRL: Hello. Need I ask?

The coffee girl. She is behind Key. Her voice, itself warm and addictive. Key turns slowly, imperceptibly, as if standing on a plum-coloured record player. In time he is delivered to her, and steps from the turntable. She has shades on this time, and also earmuffs. With the mask and her other comprehensive trappings in place he can only see the tops of her cheeks. Again they are radiant, and knock Key backwards twelve inches.

KEY: Yeah, yeah it is. It's a mocha.

COFFEE GIRL: With the marshmallows?

Her facemask ripples as she speaks. Her eyes sparkle.

KEY: Yeah. Yeah it is. Marshmallows.

COFFEE GIRL: Here.

She hands over the mocha. It is beautifully devised, as always, the marshmallows rising out of it like volcanic candy.

KEY: You already made it.

COFFEE GIRL: Only that you always seem to come around twelve.

KEY: Set your watch by me.

She mimes resetting her watch. It's a Swatch watch, green. Key laughs. Buoyed by this, she clambers onto a crate and grabs the clock that's hanging on a pipe at the top of the stall, mimes fiddling about with the hands.

KEY: Ha ha. It's good stuff.

There's a pause. Charged. Key can't bear it. Takes out his Barclays Premier bankcard.

COFFEE GIRL: Oh, God no.

KEY: No?

COFFEE GIRL: No, fuck that, this one's on me.

KEY: Fuck that?

He can't see more than ten square millimetres of this girl. What is happening to him?

KEY: Ha. I'll get you one back.

COFFEE GIRL: Ha ha. Yeah, why not? Once this jizz is all over with. Make mine a whiskey sour.

KEY: *(Almost inaudibly)* Classy.

COFFEE GIRL: Anything else?

KEY: No. Um –

Key looks at her cheeks. Examines her squamous cells, wonders at the soft blonde down that shrouds her pores like a duvet. His knees buckle and he grabs the counter. What is happening to him?

KEY: That is to say, yes.

COFFEE GIRL: Yes?

KEY: Yes, I'll have a...

Key is floundering. He looks up at the blackboard. Too much choice. Too much, all in chalk. Coloured chalk. "Sparkling water" in purple. "Homemade". Yes. Sparkling water. Stay in her orbit. Sparkling water. Sparkling water.

KEY: Sparkling water.

COFFEE GIRL: Sparkling water?

KEY: Please.

COFFEE GIRL: Coming right up.

She spins round. Grabs a large glass bottle, fills it from the tap. As it fills he observes her ponytail, becomes lost in it, blindly wanders through its silken fronds. She turns round, moves to her right. Shoves the bottle into the SodaStream. Smiles at Key.

COFFEE GIRL: So what's your story?

KEY: Pardon me?

COFFEE GIRL: You live around here?

KEY: Oh, okay.

COFFEE GIRL: Or you come down from, I dunno, Dundee each day.

KEY: Dundee?

COFFEE GIRL: Joke.

KEY: Oh, I see, Dundee! Lol. Nah I live down that way. Stone's throw.

COFFEE GIRL: Oh, I live that way. Stone's throw, too.

They're pointing in different directions. They're smiling. She pulls the arm down, troubles the canister; bubbles flood the placid waters of the bottle. Millions of bubbles.

COFFEE GIRL: So who you cooped up with anyway?

In his mind Key strips her of her mask, of her scarf, of her shades, of her white fur hat. She is beautiful, open, warm.

KEY: Just me.

COFFEE GIRL: Aw.

KEY: And a bear.

COFFEE GIRL: Ha, me too! But no bear.

KEY: You live alone!

COFFEE GIRL: I know! Bollocksed it up! No bear even!

KEY: You gotta have a bear!

Key's eyes flicker between her cheeks and the bubbles. She pulls the arm down again. Again: an explosion. Key is drawn into the bubbles. Spinning in the bottle with them. The bubbles. The bubbles.

KEY: Well, there ya go.

COFFEE GIRL: There ya go.

Bubbles everywhere. Bubbles in the air. The two of them floating in the bubbles. Spinning around amongst the bubbles. The energy, the excitement.

KEY: Do you want to bubble up?

COFFEE GIRL: Huh?

KEY: With me?

COFFEE GIRL: Oh.

Every single bubble in the world bursts at once.

COFFEE GIRL: Ha ha. Amazing.

The coffee girl laughs. She pulls the bottle from its dock, grabs a paper cup that has an illustration of a penguin on the side. Pours in the homemade sparkling water. Places the cup on the side.

COFFEE GIRL: Will you come past again?

Key's Barclays Premier bankcard is wiggling about again and her cheeks politely decline it. And now Key has his mocha in one hand and his homemade sparkling water in the other.

COFFEE GIRL: Because you must.

Key places his mocha down, fetches up his stick under his arm, picks up his mocha again. He is unsteady on his feet.

COFFEE GIRL: It's boring here. I like it when you come by.

KEY: I'll come by again, I said.

COFFEE GIRL: I hope so.

Key smiles. The coffee girl hooks her little finger over the top of her mask and pulls it down. She is smiling too. Smiling as Key turns; smiling as he walks along the steel railings; smiling as he increases his pace towards the water fountain and breaks into a run; smiling as she fills the next glass water bottle from the tap; smiling as she rams it up into the SodaStream and hoicks the arm down.

HERE WE GO ROUND THE MULBERRY BUSH.

LEANING.

THE government banned leaning.

"What the – ?!"

I could barely believe what I was reading on www.bbc.co.uk/news/uk

I leant against the betting shop, jaw wide open and swinging, poring over my iPhone.

Twitter was going mad, hating the leaning ban.

"Well, fuck 'em!" I said under my breath.

"Get your flank off the wall, Son."

A rozzer.

He prised me off the wall and pushed me upright with his truncheon.

I threw a couple more masks on and bowed deeply.

I moved away, back towards my flat.

I'd have a proper lean when I got home.

A lean and a Peroni.

There was fuck all anyone could do about that.

THROUGH KENTISH TOWN.

Key is running now, his stick in one hand, his mocha in another. His sparkling water is in a third and in his fourth: his iPhone; chirruping, twittering, clacking and clucking. He wraps a fist around it to quell it and he runs and he runs. He sweeps by the bogs, bursts past the pétanque piste, clambers over the stile and is on the road. The iPhone getting louder, vibrating, burning up his wrists. Offers of bubbles, gifs of bubbles, his whole iPhone carbonated. He presses hard into its interface; his thumb sinks right in, right into his iPhone.

And now this poet is charging down the street. More texts coming in. More bubbles, more choices, too much. He hurtles past a streetbin, slings the hand with the sparkling water in it into the streetbin. Mocha is jumping up and down in his cup as he accelerates past Costcutter – empty, and down past the strip of broken businesses. The dry cleaner's – closed, the GP surgery – new systems, the Italian restaurant – closed. Past his own flat – empty, a silhouette of a bear in the window. He waves his stick in the air; the bear appears to waggle the TV remote. Is he smoking?

On Key goes. Down the hill. His dark-blue Mountain Warehouse anorak lacquered now in the velvet slosh of the mocha. Mocha down his jeans. Mocha on his Gazelles. The coffee girl's mocha. Marshmallows pinging off his laces, skipping into the kerb. He clatters down the street, skidding sometimes on the icy asphalt. Dead centre of the road now, following the white lines; his mocha splooshing onto them. His iPhone still buzzing and cooing, bubbles forcing their way from the speaker and out into the ether. Bubbles in the air and Key pounding down the street. Plunging his iPhone into his mocha, fuzzing another hand into another streetbin, accelerating. A man without a bubble, but surrounded by them. They are like a fog. Like Winnie-The-Pooh himself, surrounded by his cloud of bees, on Key goes. Popping what bubbles he can.

Past a policeman. A blur. Compassion in his eyes. Everyone with their role to play – the policeman's role now: to watch a panicked poet charging towards sanctuary.

And now Key is on Rutherford, and onto Gaisford, and onto Burghley, and onto Osprey. And he hurdles a Christmas tree, a dismal Christmas tree, and why is there still a Christmas tree? And he slows down and now he is a rubber man, broken and moving only by dint of the hill. Pulled towards asylum. He flows past houses. This is the street. Nice houses! Fifteen, seventeen, nineteen and now he jams his stick into a fence, holds on tight and swings himself in front of a gatepost. And now he is stood before a big front door. A front door that glows, that is warm. The icy footpath defrosts as Key gets closer to the door and now here he stands. Like a ten-year-old. Eight. Six. A deep breath. He bungs his mocha into the garden next-door, fetches his stick up.

And now Key hammers his stick against the door. Hammers it again and again. The thick stained glass begins to creak and dent. Key spins the stick round, he'll use the foot of it, get some proper purchase. Whack! Then... click. The door opening. A doormat revealed. "Welcome". And on the mat two slippers, and in those slippers: feet. And suds, falling onto the feet. And Key's gaze moves up the tights. Past the Snoopy jumper. Past the Marigolds. Past the plate, dressed in silken foam, generated by Fairy at the sink. And there is her face. It is Buddy, sweet Buddy. And behind her, gormless as ever, Rick.

Key clutches his red Norway bobble hat against his chest. Stands before his friends.

KEY: "I'm in."

And Key smiles, and hope surges out between his teeth and rises in the crisp air.

*And Buddy's
face lights up. And
she drops her plate and
claps her hands together and
bubbles fly into the air. These
sweet bubbles; they dance beyond
the threshold and one lands on Key's
eyelash. The brittle acid of a tear
slides into the bubble and it sizzles.
Key blinks. He hears an ice-cold can
of Beck's Vier being opened and then
another. He looks beyond Buddy's
kiln-like cheeks. Rick is smiling.
His perfect gnashers gleam as
he opens a third beer and
slopes off towards the
Twiglets.*

Week IV.

I n which the syringes start plunging
into valiant limbs,
a hero falls,
and a bubble starts to sparkle.

LIPPY.[†]

THERE was a briefing.

Nine addresses were pinpointed.

If you lived in one of those addresses you could no longer go into the lounge and you had to install Perspex barriers down the middle of beds and sofas and wear a Perspex cap and have different meals from your wife.

"Fuck it!"

Wuggles slung his Pepsi at the wall.

"That's our bloody address, right there!"

His Missus poked her head into the lounge.

When she saw her address on the graphic she clamped her lips so tightly shut that her bottom lip rode up above her nose and she resembled one of those gurning guys who do it professionally in Cumbria.

[†]**JUNIPER:** Ha ha, I know these people.
KEY: The gurners. Fantastic guys. Really.
JUNIPER: Up and over the nose.
KEY: See who salutes.
JUNIPER: Bet they had their league cancelled.
KEY: League? What?
JUNIPER: 'Cos of the pandemic – if they're binning Wimbledon I'm sure these chaps will have had to pack their faces down for a year.
KEY: You think they've got a league?
JUNIPER: Gawd knows what a gurner does when their fixtures disappear.
KEY: I think it's fire up Zoom, isn't it? Gurn remotely.
JUNIPER: It's not the same, Tim.
KEY: Have I said it's the same?

THE COLONEL'S WHEELS.

Key is walking down Chetwynd Rd. He has his new walking trousers on. Hard, unforgiving material, baking his shins. In his head, his AirPods. And in his AirPods: The Beatles, of all things. The Fab Four: making hay – quelle surprise. His dark-blue Mountain Warehouse anorak is zipped-up tight and his pale-blue lips would be curling into a smile if they weren't so bleedin' cold. His legs are stiff like icicles. A well-aimed thwack with a cricket bat and they'd shatter. There's no bend in the knee and he walks stiffly, like a duke. Occasionally his breath dissipates in front of him and he can see the way. Suddenly a honk. Key continues to shuffle along, like a wooden boy. Another honk. And another. And now Key swings round. There is a Volvo. Grey as the very lockdown itself. Key squints to see through the window; what beast is driving this?

KEY: Colonel?

The Colonel winks and pulls up alongside Key. He slows his wheels to walking pace. And the two men move down the hill. The Colonel: exultant.

COLONEL: Keyzee!!!

The Colonel presses some kind of mad button and his window recedes. Key pulls his AirPods out of his ears, puts 'em back in the tub. The Beatles continue to play momentarily, then relax.

COLONEL: I got wheels!

The Colonel hammers his hooter and frost is shaken from the hedges. His face is red with joy and Key basks in its terrific glow.

COLONEL: I got wheels, man!

KEY: I can see 'em. Love it!

COLONEL: They dropped it off today! *(In sinister voice)* It's miiiiine! Allll miiiiine!

KEY: Finally got yourself a car, huh! This is fantastic.

The Colonel whacks his horn and slaps his windscreen. He unclips his seatbelt and waggles it around, pretends to smoke it like a cigar, then clunks it back in to its dock.

COLONEL: Drove straight here.

KEY: Volvo.

COLONEL: Not pissing about.

KEY: I'm real pleased for ya, John. Real pleased for ya.

COLONEL: Swedish.

KEY: What's the damage?

COLONEL: Seven grand, baby! Well, come on! Get the fuck in!

KEY: But...

A beat. Then a wink from The Colonel. Then another wink. Then The Colonel speeds off. He spins her round and burns past Key, whacking his horn like a mad man. Key watches bewildered. The Colonel hoicks the handbrake and the car spins one hundred and eighty degrees and then roars back by Key's side, like a faithful dog. His tongue is out and they move down the hill for a minute. After some time The Colonel's tongue licks his lips and returns to its cave. Then he speaks. His tone is serious. Practised.

COLONEL: You gotta join our bubble, man.

KEY: No. John...

They continue down past the Osteopath's – closed, the fish and chip shop – dark. A child's scooter, abandoned, leans against a Christmas tree. When will someone collect these trees?

KEY: I'm fixed up now, John.

The Colonel winces. Grinds his gears.

COLONEL: What more can I do? I'm serious here! I've bought a car.

KEY: To get me in your bubble? Colonel, this is madness!

COLONEL: A Swedish car!

KEY: Why have you bought a car, John?

COLONEL: Me, you and Gab! What d'ya say?

Key's open-mouthed. The pallid-blue outline of his lips gawps at his friend. The truth emerges from his lungs.

KEY: I've signed with Rick and Buddy.

The smell of burning rubber. He's gone again. Key stops, leans against a wall. Watches the car, spinning in the road like a whirligig. And now it's by his side once more. The two men move off again. The window still open. The Colonel's eyes fixed on the road. A Waitrose bag, sat on the passenger seat. A sticky toffee pudding peering out.

COLONEL: The Happy Throuple then, is it?!

KEY: Huh?

COLONEL: Throuple. Three people in a couple.

KEY: Oh, I see. Ha ha.

COLONEL: This ain't a joke, man!

KEY: Naw, just, that's a funny word, that.

The Colonel presses something or other and now his windscreen is covered in tears, his wipers blinking them away.

COLONEL: It's not you who has to break it to Gab.

KEY: Look for another bubble, Boo.

COLONEL: It's you or nothing.

KEY: Dean Wren's after a bubble –

COLONEL: Come on, man!

KEY: He's hawking himself on Facebook. Saying he'll bring his tagine –

COLONEL: We're not having Dean fucking Wren.

KEY: We can still meet to exercise, John.

COLONEL: Cosmic, two twerps in leotards doing sit-ups in a bloody car park. Perfect. Not.

KEY: The athletics track. We vault the fence. Get our Farah on.

The Colonel has tuned out. He's gone. He ain't there.

KEY: When the snow comes –

COLONEL: What snow?

KEY: We'll go sledging. That's exercise, too. Lots of these things are exercise. It may not seem it but –

COLONEL: We just wanted you, man. That's all. Wanted to see it out with ya.

Key nods.

COLONEL: That's all it was. I know you've gone with them. I get it. But we wanted you, too. That was all.

Key's breath is shallow. His tongue keeps momentarily sticking to his icy lips.

KEY: You think it was easy?

COLONEL: I dunno, do I?

KEY: Picking them over you? You think I liked making that pick?

COLONEL: I said I dunno, didn't I?!

KEY: I had to disappoint someone.

COLONEL: Yeah… yeah you did.

KEY: Colonel, man.

COLONEL: Goddamn Lockdown Three.

The Colonel shields his eyes with his caramel-coloured driving glove. Key keeps walking.

KEY: You wouldn't want me under your feet, Colonel. Lucky escape, bro. I'm telling you. Lucky escape.

The glove comes down to operate the window. Key can see The Colonel's eyes once more. They're red now. The guy's devastated. With what's left of his eyes The Colonel seems to say, "Maybe we have some fun on the heath some time?" Key nods in affirmation. The window is up now, and Key observes The Colonel's form shaking as the breakdown continues. They move side by side for another fifty-or-so metres. And now The Colonel has composed himself and is ready to drive. The honk and the deep cough of the engine readying itself. And then the power. The Colonel puts the hammer down and he's gone. Key spins round and shields his eyes as he looks down the road. Scorched asphalt and flames dance and die in the street. And beyond – flying into the skies – the Volvo, silhouetted against the setting Sun. Key nods and blinks as the honking becomes indistinct. He finds The Beatles in his tub, shoves them back in his lugholes. "He got feet down below his knee… Hold you in his armchair, you can feel his disease."

HERE WE GO ROUND THE MULBERRY BUSH.

THE STREETS.[†]

A TIGHTENING.

The government banned "inside".

People had to vacate their houses now, since that's where the bug was getting spread about.

We moved into the streets with our packs.

I could actually see my building from the chalked out square in the road in which I sat.

I was a good ten feet from the next citizen.

We were masked up and the breeze blew what bugs there were into the sky.

I leant against my pack, looking up at the amber glow emanating from the living room window of my flat.

I went on Twitter, see if anyone else was pissed off with this new policy.

†**JUNIPER:** This one I don't like.
KEY: You don't.
JUNIPER: Too scary. Dystopian, you know.
KEY: Go on then.
JUNIPER: What?
KEY: Put me out of me misery, Em. What does dystopian mean?
JUNIPER: Well, you know. This.
KEY: Chalked-out squares, etc.
JUNIPER: Basically yes. And other futuristic bits and bobs, you know.
KEY: It's the world we live in, Em.
JUNIPER: They've not chalked out squares.
KEY: Yet, Em. Yet.

CHAMBERLAIN.

Key – poetical, stout – ripples down the hill. Past the fire station – open; past the Co-op – open; past the weird community centre thing – God knows. He stops outside the curved window of an estate agents – closed. 11 AM and there is Key, reflected in the glass. The curve of the window makes the mirrored Key seem even fatter than the real-life one. Key IRL scrutinises himself. He blows his cheeks out. They are worn. Four weeks into Lockdown Three, and they are already thinning in places, threadbare. Key squints. Can he see his teeth through his cheeks? In his hand, his book. For comfort, for safety, for identity. It is his gun, his shield, his diplomatic bag. In his other hand, his iPhone; ringing now. He raises it; tips his parents into his ears.

BILL: *(Off)* I have in my hand a piece of paper!

KEY: Hi, Dad.

BILL: *(Off)* I have in my hand a piece of paper!

CAROL: Don't be daft, Bill, this is serious.

KEY: What's happening, Ma? What's he talking about?

Key stares at his reflection. He blinks and – doink! – his parents appear on either side of him. Three Keys now, crystal clear in the glass. His father is shaking his documents above his head like Chamberlain himself. His mother is clutching earthenware to her bosom, moving some dough round with some weird spoon from Key's childhood.

KEY: What's going on, Ma?

CAROL: We've just got the letter through, Tim. We're getting vaccinated.

Key nods. Gunk booked into his parents' veins. He smiles.

CAROL: Feb 19th.

KEY: Ha!

CAROL: Have you got yours?

KEY: Huh?

CAROL: Your papers. You gotta get jabbed, Son. You're vulnerable.

Key nods. He's vulnerable. Anyone can see that.

BILL: *(Slapping his bicep hard)* Bang it in, see who salutes!

CAROL: He's excited. He's buying a horse.

KEY: Pardon me?

CAROL: He's got too much money because we can't go on holiday.

KEY: Buying a horse though?

BILL: *(American accent)* Ya gotta have a project, Son!

KEY: What horse? You can't buy a horse!

BILL: *(Slapping his bicep, stamping his foot)* Yeeeee-haaaaa!

CAROL: I'm doing sewing and weight-lifting. How about you?

KEY: Huh?

CAROL: Writing another one of your books, is it?

KEY: No, Ma. That ain't happening.

BILL: *(That American accent again)* Buy a horse! Saddle up!

KEY: Buying a horse isn't the answer, Pa!

BILL: Not for you maybe!

CAROL: *(Suddenly crestfallen)* Oh, Tim, we're at our wit's end down here, I swear.

Key gazes at his parents. They smile back. It's not fair. None of this is fair. Two stalwarts. Fine wines, incarcerated in the cellar.

CAROL: How many will there be, Tim?

KEY: Gawd knows, Ma. They lock. It's what they do. They can't help themselves. They're lockers.

CAROL: Wretched things. Two last year, one already this year.

KEY: I know, I know. Gives 'em a boner, Ma, that's what. They love it.

CAROL: This isn't why we retired, you know.

KEY: I know, Ma.

CAROL: And that's not just me saying that, Christine from the village thinks exactly the same.

KEY: Christine boyed off with it too, huh?

CAROL: And Joan. She had Egypt up her sleeve. Good luck getting to Egypt with this bloody lot in charge.

KEY: Joan's plans up in smoke, huh?

CAROL: She was in floods earlier.

KEY: It'll pass, Ma.

CAROL: Sobbing into her Motorola. Thinks she's never going to hold a scarab.

KEY: Nonsense, Ma! Of course Joan will hold a scarab!

CAROL: You've got your whole life ahead of you. It's difficult for our mob, you know.

KEY: Joan will hold a scarab, Ma. This year. She'll hold dozens, I swear!

BILL: We didn't retire to look like dickheads, Son.

Key nods. His father is wearing a cowboy hat, his mother's apron depicts a naked muscleman.

CAROL: Now, Tim. Joyce from the village happened to mention that Steven's moved back in for lockdown.

KEY: Oh, he has?

CAROL: Well, 'cos otherwise he'd have been on his own, you know? So they've taken him back in, you see.

BILL: Like a rescue dog, Son.

CAROL: It's nice for them, you know.

Key, staring at the tableau. His mother moving the dough. His father, unscrewing the lid on a thick, glass Schweppes lemonade bottle, full of homemade beer.

KEY: I...

CAROL: Are you in a bubble, Son?

KEY: There was a bidding war, Ma.

CAROL: Of course there was! People –

BILL: Feel sorry for you –

CAROL: Bill! No, they know you'd be a laugh, Son, isn't it?

BILL: She wanted you here, your mother.

KEY: Well, it hasn't come to that.

The three of them, stood there, in 2D. Key shivering.

CAROL: Well, you must know that, should it burst, you've got a bed here. That's all.

KEY: It won't burst, Ma.

BILL: Bubbles burst, Son. Famous for it.

CAROL: We'll get the old Mr Men wallpaper back up, dig out your posters. Peter Beardsley –

BILL: Cindy Crawford!

KEY: I've bubbled up with Rick and Buddy.

BILL: They got homebrew, Son?

Key nods. He can see his eyes glazing over in the window, intoxicated by the prospect of homebrew flowing through a lockdown. His father hitching up his beige shorts, creaking up the stairs. The distant sound of lemonade bottles, the clinking becoming louder as his father plods back down and into the lounge. Buddy Holly squawking on the turntable. Endless Mini Cheddars. Safety.

CAROL: I don't like imagining you on your own, that's all. I know you've got your bear, but it's not the same.

KEY: I'm in with Rick and Buddy, Ma. All signed up.

CAROL: Sitting with your bear, walking the bear.

KEY: I'm not walking the bear, Ma.

CAROL: Round and round the garden, like a teddy bear. One step, two step, tickly under there!

KEY: I guess.

BILL: He's not walking his bear, Carol.

CAROL: Well, if it goes pop...

KEY: My bubble ain't going pop.

BILL: No shame in bubbling up with the dinosaurs, Son.

Bill Key raises his tankard. It clinks against the window and the two of them disappear. It is just the curved mirror now. And Key observes himself. Rivulets of water track down the window and Key realises it is raining.

KEY: Bye, then. Love you.

Key is motionless as the drizzle intensifies. He holds his book above his head. Rain passes through its pages and the conversations of Lockdown One soak through his pate, run through his frame. Standing in one lockdown; clutching another. The azure cover leaks into him and his skin takes on a pale-blue hue. He moves down the hill. Becoming bluer and bluer as he approaches the fishmongers.

†**JUNIPER:** Test and trace. Test and *waste of time*, more like.

KEY: You get into it in Cornwall?

JUNIPER: What a bloody palaver, honestly.

KEY: Didn't do it right, that's all.

JUNIPER: Phone pinging every time I go to the gym. Stressful enough in there as it is.

KEY: If they'd put half the time and resources into that jizz as they put into things like locks and making stuff like Tiger King and The Serpent we'd have been out in a matter of weeks.

JUNIPER: I don't like the idea of the Health Secretary having my email, that's all.

KEY: What's he gonna do with your email?

JUNIPER: I dunno. Forward me gifs, invite me to shows.

KEY: What shows?

JUNIPER: I'd just rather he didn't have my email, that's all.

KEY: I don't think he's putting on shows, Em.

JUNIPER: Keep it professional, that's all. Don't try and sneak into my life through the back door.

TOM, DICK AND HARRY.[†]

THE government built a series of *walking tunnels* under the city.

If you tested negative you could take a stroll.

Bung on your walking boots, flash your lanyard, in you go.

They had food concessions down there, too.

Negative guys sold doughnuts and hotdogs and a negative steel band played tunes on their pans.

It was fucking busy down there and the lighting was very poor and people kept banging into each other and falling into the thick silt and a lot of the radio stations laid into the project and said the government should be focusing on having a robust test-and-trace system.

ASK MY FRIENDS.

Key is walking around Highgate Cemetery, his hands clasped tightly behind his back. One Thinsulate glove locked into another. A slow, respectful pace. Moving between the skeletons. Sometimes he reads about a corpse; nods his appreciation of a life well-lived. He sips his can of gin and tonic; flicks frustratedly at his brand new Fitbit. He stands in front of a French guy's tomb. His iPhone squawks. Even amongst the dead he can be found.

DANIEL: You gotta get vaccinated, bro.

KEY: Good morning, Daniel.

DANIEL: A splurt in the arm.

KEY: Why you telling me this?

DANIEL: Everyone has to!

KEY: Yeah I know that, Daniel. I've got a telly and half a brain, I know what the next bit of the bloody pando is. Stuff my arms full of jizz and whirl 'em about.

DANIEL: My parents are getting done.

KEY: Do you want a medal? Everyone's bloody parents are getting done. My parents are getting done.

DANIEL: Oh, they are, huh?

KEY: They're working down a list, Dan, that's what. Queen at the top, babies at the bottom. One by one, slam in the lamb. See who salutes.

DANIEL: They're doing seventy-five plusses next week.

KEY: Why are you trying to school me on vax, bro? I know the drill.

DANIEL: We're in June, they reckon.

KEY: Hmm.

DANIEL: What "hmm"? We're in June, me and thee, maybe July.

KEY: Yeah well. Maybe I'm before that.

DANIEL: Huh?

A chill wind blows through. Key pulls his red Norway bobble hat right down over his jowls. He waddles towards some dead thinkers. His eyebrows are knitted, his fist is on his chin.

DANIEL: What do you mean you're before June? They doing poets first? What's going on here?

KEY: Maybe they are. Get us back out there, could do with us. Smashing out odes, lifting the mood.

DANIEL: Chap next door goes down looking for returns.

KEY: Heh?

DANIEL: If someone doesn't turn up, he

"volunteers his bicep".

KEY: Never heard anything so stupid in all my life.

DANIEL: Window cleaner. Wants to get juiced-up so he can get back on his ladder.

KEY: Hangs out the back, wait for scraps type of thing?

Key warms his cockles with a slurp of G&T, moves deliberately between the graves.

DANIEL: Where are you?

KEY: Up the cemetery.

DANIEL: Pervert.

KEY: Hardly. Keeping it in my trousers.

DANIEL: Who you after? Marx?

KEY: Pah.

DANIEL: What "pah"?

KEY: I don't need Marx in my bloody life, believe me.

DANIEL: Who then?

Key moves easily amongst the relics. He peers between them. Squints. Where is the one he really wants then? Where does he recline? Let's be having you.

DANIEL: *(Casually)* Removed a joist this morning.

KEY: Jesus wept.

DANIEL: Making some changes, me.

KEY: You shouldn't phone people up and bother them with the word "joist", you know.

DANIEL: Getting rid of my bed, too.

KEY: You've gone mad, bro.

DANIEL: Why do I need a bed?

KEY: To sleep on! Come on, man!

DANIEL: Nah, I've dismantled it.

KEY: Remantle it, bro. What's it with you and lockdowns?

DANIEL: Out with the old.

KEY: Not beds, though.

DANIEL: Pointless bourgeois gash, slowing me down. Bunged my awards 'n' all.

KEY: What?

DANIEL: Can't be fucked. Don't mean shit.

KEY: No? Threw 'em out, huh?

DANIEL: Taken half down the tip, doing another run this afternoon.

KEY: Lot of awards.

DANIEL: Lot of acclaim. Where's yours?

KEY: Huh?

DANIEL: Your Perrier.

KEY: Oh, that old thing.

DANIEL: Bet it's in your flat, no? Pride of place.

KEY: No. No it isn't in my flat, cheers.

DANIEL: Exactly. You can't cling on to these things. Get rid!

The award is heavy on Key's back. His ligaments cling to his knees. He staggers past a clonking great stone, sat at the tip of the originator of the postal service.

DANIEL: I've unplumbed my pipes, I've bought a nice box for my Lego –

KEY: Be still, man, can't you? Take stock, that's what lockdowns are for. They're a sign.

DANIEL: Naw. Make the best of 'em. Bring out the big tools.

Key cuts between an electrical engineer and the inventor of cinematography. Dead as ice-cold catfish.

DANIEL: Well, what are you doing?

KEY: Gonna ask the coffee girl out.

DANIEL: You can't live in your head, man.

KEY: It's not in my head though. I'm asking her.

DANIEL: You're living in a dreamland, pal.

KEY: I most certainly am not. Why shouldn't I invite the coffee girl out?

DANIEL: Because you haven't got the stones, that's why.

KEY: I've got more stones than you'll ever have, pal.

DANIEL: Still enjoying your walking?

KEY: Quads like concrete.

DANIEL: You get the Fitbit?

KEY: Pah!

DANIEL: What "Pah!" I sent you a Fitbit.

KEY: Fitbit's a load of steaming gash by the way, that's what.

DANIEL: How about we try, "Thank you for the Fitbit"?

KEY: How about we try, "Send old Key something that actually works". Shitbit, this!

Key is whacking his wrist. Slapping his palm against the face of the Fitbit.

DANIEL: How many steps you done?

KEY: Huh? What steps?

DANIEL: How's your mental health?

KEY: Up the spout! This thing's bust! Shitbit!

DANIEL: Bust how? You're walking now, right?

Key stalks across towards a two-hundred-year-old novelist.

KEY: Of course I'm walking. No thanks to this thing.

DANIEL: What are you talking about?

KEY: Still have to do the legs, like before.

DANIEL: The Fitbit tells you how many steps you've taken.

KEY: Huh?

Key is smashing the Fitbit against a gravestone now.

DANIEL: It doesn't power your legs.

KEY: Well, apparently not!

DANIEL: It registers how many steps you've taken, I'm saying.

KEY: Huh?

Key shuts up and marches. Marches round the gravestones. Marches down at his Fitbit. Squints through the shards of smashed up glass. Peers into the flickering LED. The numbers are going up. He marches like Botham and the numbers rise.

KEY: Oh, yeah. I see. Very good. Ah.

DANIEL: What?

KEY: I gotta go.

DANIEL: Why?

KEY: I'm here.

DANIEL: Marx?

KEY: Stop saying Marx, you wombat. Tatty bye.

Key slides his iPhone down his drawers and flicks his G&T into a streetbin. He is stood before Beadle. Writer, Presenter and Curator of Oddities. He nods at the trickster. Smiles. Beadle perished twelve years before all this gash. Key crouches down and strokes the great man's stone books. For a moment he thinks he can hear Beadle chuckling at his best pranks. Yes, Beadle had a good vibe. He'd've coasted through this. Key shuts his eyes, locks his Thinsulate gloves behind his back once more.

HOUSE DOLLS.

SOME local councils provided Lockdown Dolls.

If you lived alone you could rent one for a lockdown.

The price came down if you committed to the next three lockdowns.

They came with a ripcord.

Pull the cord and the doll spoke.

"Tut. These bloody lockdowns."

"I'm getting cheesed off here."

"Shall we hit the hay?"

If you placed the Lockdown Doll under the covers it became warm and raunchy.

It would say things like, "I don't want this lockdown to end, Bubs."

Even if you didn't pull the ripcord.

JARDIN DES SPORTS.

I ARRIVED back at Heathrow and was told I had to quarantine for ten days at Center Parcs at my own expense.

We were bunged into minibuses and given cans of JD and Coke and were tight as hell by the time we got to Sherwood Forest.

Fuck me we racked up some activities that week.

I had about five archery lessons and got my arse handed to me on the badminton court, and in the evenings we did bowling and drank pitchers of lager and hot-wired golf buggies.

My chalet was me, a young family from Lewes, three Spanish businessmen and an old man called Leonard who we had to look after a bit.

On our final day we had one last frolic in the rapids, then ice creams and hugs and then back in the minibuses.

We returned to Heathrow to have our temperature tested and fill out forms.

Then home.

Stinking of chlorine, reinvigorated, clean as whistles.

A HERO FALLS.

Key has propped his Puma rucksack against a streetbin on the pavement opposite his local surgery. He's sat on his arse, his back against his pack. His book is on his lap, but he ain't reading it. He's squinting across the road. A queue seeps from the clinic's doors. Socially distanced biddies and swindlers, stood in line for their vaccines; sleeves rolled up, biceps glinting in the afternoon haze. Key, unblinking, watches them like a lizard. His iPhone goes. The clouds separate. He flicks the ball, connects the call.

KEY: Emily Juniper!

JUNIPER: The Captain's fallen.

Key is stopped in his tracks. He is agog. Doesn't speak, just nods. Moisture creeps from the roots to the tips of his eyelashes. He opens his mouth and closes it once more, blinks instead.

JUNIPER: Tim?

KEY: Captain Tom? Gone?

JUNIPER: This morning.

KEY: Jizz.

Key leans back. A third of his head goes into the streetbin and he scrutinises the sky. The clouds seem to form themselves into discernible shapes. A Zimmer frame. A medal. A smile. Key smiles back. The cloud winks. It's okay.

JUNIPER: A good innings, anyway.

KEY: Barely covers it.

JUNIPER: An amazing innings actually, to be fair to the dopy old sod.

KEY: Like Viv Richards in his pomp.

JUNIPER: The government's making everyone clap later.

KEY: Classy. The Maestro wants a piece of it, does he?

JUNIPER: Well, I'm clapping.

KEY: Yeah, I'll give the old hen a clap.

JUNIPER: I'm making a weird needlework thing in his honour.

KEY: 'Course you are.

JUNIPER: You drive me to it, nothing to design. Whilst you're not writing.

KEY: Turn the old dear into a ragdoll, is it?

JUNIPER: It's not a doll, this is needlework, Tim. A montage of some of his highlights.

KEY: Like at the end of Match of the Day.

JUNIPER: Except mine's needlework.

KEY: The Captain, gone.

Key is shaken. His pale-blue hand reaches behind him into his sack. A Beck's Vier, ice-cold. He coughs as he rips the pull off and sinks his teeth into the German pop.

JUNIPER: Can you bear to do admin?

KEY: *(Pulling himself together as best he can)* Speak to me, Em.

JUNIPER: We need to talk stock, Tim. What am I ordering here? You gotta engage.

KEY: I'm reading it now, Em.

JUNIPER: Ha! Reading his own book.

KEY: Makes me yearn for the first lockdown.

JUNIPER: Fie. You hated that thing.

KEY: Least it was new, Em. This one's all gash, without any of the novelty. Well, that's my opinion, anyway.

A car piles through. Its registration is G77 435H but who cares about that stuff?

JUNIPER: Where are you?

KEY: Oh, right. Leaning against a bin, yer know.

JUNIPER: I do like our little chats, lol.

KEY: I'm just up at the GP's, yer know.

JUNIPER: How so?

KEY: Sniffing about. That's all.

JUNIPER: Sniffing about for what?

Another slurp of Vier. He wipes an eye with a Thinsulate glove. His nostrils flare.

KEY: Vax, baby. Vax.

JUNIPER: You're getting vaccinated?

A swindler marches out from the clinic, bins his sticks, skips up the hill.

JUNIPER: You're not on the list are you? I thought it was seventy-year-olds this week.

KEY: You thought right, Em. You thought right.

JUNIPER: Fuck – I thought you were my age.

KEY: I'm waiting for, you know. What's-the-word. Offcuts.

JUNIPER: Is it?

KEY: Someone doesn't turn up, I'm in.

JUNIPER: Really?

KEY: They've got a fridge full of this shit, needs to go into an arm, Em.

JUNIPER: Oh, right. Like returns.

KEY: Putting myself in the shop window, Em. My sleeve's rolled up, it's ready for the gunk.

JUNIPER: Yeah.

KEY: Flow it in.

JUNIPER: Ha! Waiting for returns!

Key's tongue reaches down into his Beck's Vier, squeezes through the thumbnail entrance, swims in the golden juices, is winched back into The Poet's mouth.

JUNIPER: We used to do that at Wimbledon. Returns.

KEY: Higher stakes of course, this.

JUNIPER: Stayed overnight, me and Dane Woods.

KEY: Who the fuck is Dane Woods?

JUNIPER: Drank five cans of Pimm's and Lemonade, used our fleeces as pillows. Next day we're shuffling forwards, nearer and nearer the front.

KEY: SW19.

JUNIPER: 4 PM, two big ones for Centre Court.

KEY: The Chocolate Factory.

JUNIPER: Michael Chang, Todd Martin, a young Kournikova –

KEY: Is there any other kind?

JUNIPER: Jenny Capriati in the doubles.

KEY: Late nineties, I'm saying.

JUNIPER: 2001.

KEY: Give myself that, I think.

Key slaps his bicep, looks across at the queue. Looks for weaknesses. Wills a relic to give up on the whole exercise, waddle back up the hill unpierced.

KEY: Need this shit in my arm, Em.

JUNIPER: I know. The old seadog who maintains the buoys had his first shot yesterday.

KEY: What the fuck?

JUNIPER: They're rolling it out all right, you have to hand it to them.

KEY: How do you "maintain a buoy"?

JUNIPER: The Health whatdyacallit guy was on the news yesterday. Did you hear him?

KEY: Man's a clown.

JUNIPER: He said he'd watched Contagion, got it in his head he needed to get huge with a vaccination programme.

KEY: And he's welcome to it, Em. I'm gonna drink my drink, keep my eye out for spare vax, that's all.

JUNIPER: Ah ha!

KEY: What?

JUNIPER: Mocha, huh? Another visit to the coffee girl, was it?

Key slings his Beck's Vier over his shoulder. Reaches behind him, gropes into his pack, pulls another out. Like an archer drawing his next arrow. He coughs loudly to cover the pssscht.

KEY: I auditioned for Contagion, Em.

JUNIPER: Avoiding the question!

KEY: 2010. "Park it back bitch!"

JUNIPER: Pardon me?

KEY: That was my line. Had to do it about a million times. What's the bloody point?

JUNIPER: Did you see the movie?

KEY: No, Em. Pointless jizz, could never happen, not wasting my time, cheers.

JUNIPER: You did read the script though.

KEY: I read my line, let's put it that way.

JUNIPER: Shouldn't you read the whole thing?

KEY: People do.

JUNIPER: Well, listen. I'm going to get my embroidery on. Depict The Captain getting knighted using bullion knot stitch.

KEY: (*Loud; intense*) "We all have little ones and money, park it back, bitch!"

Emily Juniper hangs up. There is some action amongst the biddies and the swindlers. Clearly one has a grandson's Samsung or a transistor radio. Either way, the news of the fallen captain has hit the queue and it dampens with the sadness of it all. Key heaves a sigh; sips his wallop. The queue stays together, fortified.

STRONG TO THE FINICH.[†]

THEY opened the vaccine shack up 24/7.

I got lashed off my tits and took my bicep down there.

"Fill this cunt up!" I slurred.

I was the least drunk guy in there, including a couple of old people.

My sleeve was peeled right back like salami, exposing my Popeye tattoo.

"Maybe I should be injecting him with spinach, hey?"

The nurse was the most pissed of the lot.

I tried to remember Popeye's catchphrase.

[†]**JUNIPER:** His laugh.
KEY: Huh?
JUNIPER: His laugh's his catchphrase, isn't it?
KEY: I don't think your laugh can be your catchphrase, Em.
JUNIPER: *"Ag ag ag ag ag ag ag!"*
KEY: Yes, but it's not his catchphrase.
JUNIPER: Well, is Jimmy Carr's laugh a catchphrase?
KEY: But it's not like... I mean it's not a phrase.
JUNIPER: Oh, well, I think it's a catchphrase.
KEY: It's like saying Jimmy's suit's his catchphrase or doing all those shows is a catchphrase.
JUNIPER: Yeah I'd go along with that, I think.
KEY: You think Jimmy Carr's suit's his catchphrase?
JUNIPER: Well...
KEY: By that rationale let's just say Popeye's pipe's his catchphrase and be done with it.
JUNIPER: Yes! His pipe!
KEY: Bugger me.
JUNIPER: His pipe and his laugh.
KEY: Ha ha.
JUNIPER: *"Ag ag ag ag ag ag ag!!!"*

HONOURING A HERO.

"**M**ORNING folks!"

Bohnson was looking fantastic, eyes less sunken than usual, proper definition in his tennis shorts.

"Just some more stuff we've done about Captain Tom – thanks for clapping last night, eh."

The captain was splooshed across Bohnson's crop top and he was leaning on sticks.

"We're gonna bung the poor sod on a plinth. There'll obviously be a stamp made, he'll be added to the flag and we're changing the name of the vaccine to "The Captain" out of respect for the man, the myth, the legend."

He banged his fists together, blew a kiss off his knuckles into the camera and lowered his eyes, bashfully.

"And someone – mention no names – is off to your friend and mine, Deed Poll, right after this 'ere briefing. News as it comes in as to what I'm changing my name to!"

He winked so hard his right eyeball shot across and appeared in his left socket so he fleetingly had two eyes in there.

Then it pinged back into its rightful socket, and he stared down the barrel once more.

His eyes were blue, hopeful, full of empathy for the fallen hero.

A FRAGILE ORB.

The Sun is low; on the verge of dipping behind the leafless trees on the hill. The bright sky is fading. It is, give or take, the colour of the cover of "He Used Thought as a Wife", Key's book about the first lockdown. Three figures approach in silhouette. They laugh, they stamp, the big one splashes through puddles. They sing as they move effervescently down the muddy track. Rick's deep baritone making the oaks shake. Three old friends. Three. Like blind mice. Three. Like The Scarecrow, The Tin Man and The Cowardly Lion himself. Splashing, laughing, singing.

"Three best friends, singing this song.
Pissing about, in the setting Sun.

Three best friends, is it so wrong?
Don't see what's wrong, we're just singing our song."

They spill off the heath and move down the hill. They are three abreast as they come past Costcutter. And Key can't speak. Buddy leaps for joy.

BUDDY: Oh, hey, we can go for a car wash tomorrow!

Key's eyes, all brown, all lost. He cannot speak.

RICK: Oh, now we're talking! Now we are talking! Give Old Faithful a bloody good wash.

KEY: *(With his eyes)* Me? In a car wash? Me? In Old Faithful?

BUDDY: You're in our bubble, aren't you?

Key is in dreamland. They walk past the estate agents – closed. They walk past the Thai Café – closed. Three abreast. Some old swindlers cast eyes at them. Fire judgment across the street. But the three will not be shamed. They stand up straight. They are legit, these three. In a bubble.

BUDDY: We put "Car Wash" on when we're in the car wash.

RICK: Yes!

KEY: You do?

BUDDY: Rose Royce. Have a boogie.

RICK: Boogie-woogie.

BUDDY: Have a good old singsong, let the brushes do their worst.

RICK: Bubbles on the outside. Bubbles on the inside.

BUDDY: I think we'll close the windows, Rick.

RICK: I mean this bubble.

BUDDY: Oh, right. Bubbles on the outside, support bubble on the inside, then.

KEY: Yeah, get it right, bro.

Rick envelops his arms around the lot of them. Swindlers bare their teeth as this gigantic clown disrupts the matrix with his embrace. Where they were a two and a one, they are now a three. They press on, Rick moonwalking, Key and Buddy laughing at this soppy old sod's interminable vibe. They come to Key's flat.

RICK: Why you stopping?

Key is a child. He is five. He has nothing left. He is in a bubble.

KEY: Pointless Celebs, no?

BUDDY: What are you going on about?

KEY: Ravioli on toast and bawling at the telly, no?

BUDDY: Saturday nights are with us now, Kiddo.

KEY: Huh?

Rick stretches out a vast arm. It is like a bough. He lifts Key, like a crane would lift a girder; swings him round, deposits him twenty metres down the road. Buddy catches up and the three continue to walk.

BUDDY: Now, what are we gonna eat do we think?

KEY: Huh?

BUDDY: What "huh"?

KEY: You mean...

BUDDY: You're coming to ours, Kiddo.

KEY: Really?

RICK: Do we definitely want him on Saturdays?

BUDDY: Of course!

RICK: Well, there you go!

BUDDY: I'm bored shitless of this one.

RICK: Exsqueeze me?

KEY: You are?

RICK: Be our guest!

BUDDY: Our houseguest.

Rick spots a skateboard outside the William Hill's – closed. He jumps onto it, pushes off, loops around the bus stop, leaps into the air on it, lands it. He does it again, gets proper air.

KEY: "Houseguest".

RICK & BUDDY: Yes!

KEY: Like when Pooh and Piglet visited Rabbit.

Rick props the skateboard back up against the bookies and bows.

RICK: Just don't eat too much honey and get stuck inside.

KEY: Huh?

BUDDY: Of course he's not going to eat that amount of honey, Dolfus.

KEY: What honey?

RICK: That's what happened to Pooh. Read up on your Milne, Broseph.

KEY: Well, more fool you if you're feeding me that much honey.

BUDDY: Think we might err on the side of a Tiffin Tin.

KEY: Indian?

Key stops right there on the pavement, he is motionless. Thunderstruck.

BUDDY: What's up, Kiddo?

RICK: This is what happens in a bubble, Broseph.

BUDDY: Lamb Bhunas all round, one of Rick's woeful cycling docs on the flatscreen.

Rick gets to work miming that he's a pro-cy-clist. Spinning imaginary pedals, ringing his imaginary bicycle bell, plunging drugs into his arms with imaginary syringes.

RICK: Yes please, Louise!

Key is mouthing some of the things he wants to say. Trying to express that he fears he is dreaming, trying to ask if they are serious, serious about sofas and saag.

KEY: Will there be beer?

BUDDY: If the Bubble Boy wants beer then there most certainly will be beer.

KEY: You got a keg in?

RICK: What keg? We got Cobras, bro! Hisssssss!

KEY: Frigid Cobras slithering down my throat, heh.

BUDDY: You'll come over then?

Key angles away. His eyes are moist, his cheeks beginning to puff. He doesn't want them seeing him like this. Rick is on the blower already.

RICK: *(Off)* Fine sir! I should like to order an Indian feast for my newly formed and very attractive bubble.

He marches ahead, his whole body curving into his iPhone as he barks his suggestions down the pipes. Key watches transfixed, he imagines the orders landing, the dishes being yelled into the kitchen, the cumin seeds exploding in the pan.

BUDDY: Tim?

KEY: Huh?

BUDDY: Come on, Kiddo, before the government shovel us into a death van, drive us to the camps.

KEY: Well, you know. If you're sure.

BUDDY: We picked you in our bubble, you soft-shell crab. Hardly any point in doing that if we're not gonna get shit-faced and watch some investigative journalism about Lance Armstrong.

Key nods. They catch up with Rick, who is doing star jumps.

RICK: Done.

BUDDY: Fabbo.

RICK: Nine papadums. Oh, whoops.

KEY: Three each.

RICK: Yeah, I think I know it's three each.

BUDDY: A medieval feast!

KEY: With Indian lager.

RICK: Three times 660 ml.

KEY: 1980 ml. Classy.

RICK: I know it's classy, and four meat dishes between three. Don't mind if I do per se.

KEY: Well, we're not sharing.

BUDDY: Oh, we share at ours.

KEY: Fuck no, really?

RICK: House rules, Bublé!

BUDDY: He hogs the chicken Madras, this one, watch out for him.

Rick's doing a chicken impression.

BUDDY: Uses his arm like a massive wing.

KEY: Not if I can help it he won't.

We watch them go. A row is brewing but the steps have a spring in them. Buddy grabs both of their scarves at one point and begins to run. They spin after her, unravelling, laughter filling the air in arctic clumps.

HERE WE GO ROUND THE MULBERRY BUSH.

A NEW WORLD.

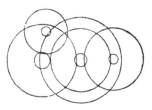

I DECIDED to spend some time in the hall bit, in between the bathroom and the bedroom.

It was a not bad area.

I got some crisps and sat on a cushion.

I plugged my phone into the socket.

This area had everything!

The paint around the socket was neatly done.

A tradesman had clearly taken a pride in his or her work.

Fucking wonderful.

I checked my phone.

Instagram, Twitter, the date.

Battery: 63% and rising!

I snaffled a Frazzle.

What a time to be alive!

♥

Week V.

In which ink is splattered onto paper, Key does some old-school promo, and the man of the moment plumps for a Pret Swedish Meatball Wrap.

†**JUNIPER:** Why didn't just one company make all the muck, do we know?
KEY: Same as anything, that's like saying let's have just one kind of beer. Go into the pub and say, "Yeah, beer please."
JUNIPER: People *do* do that, don't they?
KEY: But there's lots of different types of beer, Em, you know.
JUNIPER: Ha ha. Really? Ha ha. For any occasion.
KEY: You must know there's more than one type of beer, Em.
JUNIPER: I've got my nose in a gin and peppermint usually.
KEY: Kronenbourg, Hofmeister, you know. I could go on.
JUNIPER: What about tomatoes then. We wouldn't have lots of different companies all chopping tomatoes and bunging them in tins.
KEY: We do, Em. The free market, all different labels, thats all.
JUNIPER: Funny buggers, aren't we?
KEY: Honestly, yeah. Yeah, we are a bit.
JUNIPER: All different companies all devising the same gunk, popping it in our arms.

TIPPLE.[†]

SCIENTISTS did some experiments and typed them up *et cetera*.

Now your best bet was to have the Baxter jab first, then wait four days, then have the Baxter jab again, then a week later have the Gaulem-Roddick jab, let that take and then have a jab of Perrier, then one more Baxter, give your arm a good old shake, wait a month then half a dose of piping-hot Bisto, a final Baxter and that should be you.

Letters would go out to people who had rickets or earache or were particularly middle-aged and most of the injections would be in gyms and would be administered by sportspeople and you could also take pills or shove stuff up your arse if that was more your vibe.

A POLICE OFFICER IN UNIFORM.

Key's big fat arnuzzi is splodged onto a bench next to a streetbin near the entrance to the heath. A biting cold carves a grey road through Key's spine and slows his blood. Key is trying to open a Mars Bar Duo with his Thinsulate gloves on. He fumbles with it like a heroin addict might grapple with the syringe. A policeman's coming. Key drops the skag, scrabbles around amongst the frosty leaves next to the streetbin, trying to retrieve it. Momentarily an orange pen reveals itself, then disappears under black leaves. Key grabs his nougat bar. His needle. The bobby is closing in. The wrapper finally acquiesces and Key plunges the first of the twins into his trap.

POLICEMAN: *(Approaching)* Good morning.

The bar is ice-cold and hard, and Key's teeth explode around it as he bites down. He spits out the ivory, replaces his Mars Bar in its sheath, nods at the policeman.

KEY: I ain't doing anything wrong, Officer.

POLICEMAN: You shouldn't be sitting on a bench, Son.

Key rocks his head back. Stares into the skies. Where once there were aeroplanes, hot-air balloons, parachutists, flamingos, now there are only weird bits of blue and atmosphere. Key rocks forward. The policeman's eyes are covered by his divvy helmet. His chinstrap squeezes all his features together. His bottom lip is tucked up against his hooter, which is bright red like the great Sir Alex Ferguson's situation.

POLICEMAN: You even know the rules?

KEY: Got a fair idea, yuh.

Key pulls out an unsightly purple notebook. The lime-green Post-its are glued into it and it pulsates; pulsates with the muck he's heard in briefings and on the grapevine. It's as thick as a Kit Kat, this notebook, bound together with staples; some that have taken, others that are crumpled like squished fireflies. On the cover, in Tipp-Ex: "Fuck The Pando".

POLICEMAN: Fuck the pando, huh?

KEY: *(Squeezing his lips into a type of smile)* Oh, you like the pando, do you?

POLICEMAN: Don't have an opinion on it.

KEY: No opinion on the pando? Ha!

POLICEMAN: We've gotta be impartial, that's all.

KEY: Well, I think the pando's a disgrace and I bet you do, too.

POLICEMAN: You shouldn't be on the bench, that's all.

The policeman's weird walkie-talkie thing crackles to life. He presses some device thing in his floppy old ear and the crackling stops. He is listening. He peels his lower lip off his nose and speaks into his chest.

POLICEMAN: Yes, Sarge. Right away, Sarge. Aggressive? Very well, Sarge. Of course I will, Sarge.

The policeman shoves his walkie-talkie back down his drawers.

KEY: Who was that?

POLICEMAN: There's a group of three down by the canal there.

KEY: Yikes! In a bubble?

POLICEMAN: Pisstakers, sounds like.

KEY: And what, you're gonna read them the riot act, type of thing?

POLICEMAN: And them laughing at my chinstrap and calling me every name under the Sun, yah.

The bobby sighs and his brass buttons catch what rays of Sun there are. Key observes this daft old bobby's truncheon. He bends his knees a bit.

POLICEMAN: What do you do then?

KEY: Me? Diarist.

POLICEMAN: What does that mean?

KEY: Got my Pepys on in Lockdown One, flogging it in Lockdown Three.

POLICEMAN: Right. Monetising the pandemic, is it?

KEY: And you're not? Shifting people off of benches, dispersing groups of three like your life depends on it. Bet you're coining it in, pal. Flying up the ranks.

POLICEMAN: Just following orders.

KEY: Come on, matey, anyone can see, you're getting a right old hard-on about this pando. Waggling your truncheon at anything that moves.

POLICEMAN: You wanna be dispersed?

KEY: Can you disperse a group of one?

The policeman's thumbs rifle through Key's notes. He is muttering about dispersing people, muttering about common sense, making additional noises.

KEY: But it doesn't make sense. Nothing makes sense. You can't disperse a person, honestly you can't.

POLICEMAN: You live local?

KEY: I ain't breaking any rules here, mate.

The policeman hands Key back his purple book. He sits down on the bench. He adjusts his bollocks in his thick trousers, stares grimly into the distance. They sit like this for a spell. Then the policeman speaks.

POLICEMAN: I'll level with you, mate. I just want a chat.

KEY: Oh, well. I mean... I'll chat to anyone, me.

A healthy pause. Let's say a minute. The policeman and The Poet. Acquainting themselves. Key sometimes nodding. The policeman occasionally making little noises.

KEY: So... well, I mean... d'ya like the lash?

POLICEMAN: Me?

KEY: Glass of wine after a long shift?

POLICEMAN: I'm fond of a drink, yeah.

KEY: The nose.

POLICEMAN: Huh?

KEY: I worked out how much beer I had in the last lockdown.

POLICEMAN: Not pretty?

KEY: You think a hundred and ten pints a month's pretty?

POLICEMAN: Pretty mad.

KEY: 'Twas a mad three months.

POLICEMAN: Try being a policeman.

KEY: Try writing a blend of poetry and dialogues in a vacuum.

POLICEMAN: I got spat at yesterday.

KEY: Yuk!

They stare across the expanse. The coldness is visible in the air. Silver shards of the stuff. More little noises from the policeman.

POLICEMAN: I'm a bit of a right old dumpling, I'm afraid.

KEY: Oh, you are, huh?

POLICEMAN: Live with my boss, never a good idea.

KEY: You live with Cressida Dick?

POLICEMAN: Ha ha I wish! Naw, not Dick, live with my Sergeant.

KEY: I live on my own.

POLICEMAN: Get in each night, wanna veg out, look at The Serpent, drink some cans. Got him pissing about in just a towel, asking how many people I've dispersed.

KEY: Jeesh, put some clothes on.

POLICEMAN: I know, right.

KEY: We should open a couple of bottles of ale in the not-too-distant future.

POLICEMAN: He eats his breakfast in just his helmet.

KEY: Oh, he does, huh?

POLICEMAN: Kippers on toast, wedding tackle dripping off his stool.

KEY: I live on my own.

POLICEMAN: The dream.

KEY: Mm.

POLICEMAN: No?

KEY: Read my book. Seriously.

Key has taken his Thinsulate glove off and is signing "He Used Thought as a Wife". "To..."

KEY: What's your name, mate?

POLICEMAN: Gourd. PC Gourd.

KEY: As in... ?

POLICEMAN: Well, a marrow's a gourd, put it that way.

KEY: I get the idea.

Key hands the policeman the tome and they stand. The policeman's still making little noises.

POLICEMAN: Know where I can get a coffee round here?

Key picks up his stick; waggles it towards the distant coffee wagon.

POLICEMAN: Well, look. Thanks for the chat.

KEY: I'll talk to anyone.

POLICEMAN: Meant more than you think.

KEY: Ha!

Key nods. The policeman makes a little noise. Then he wobbles away. Key shakes his Mars Bar Duo back out of its sheath, bungs it in his mouth. He lets it sit in there, waiting for it to thaw. Like how an emperor penguin keeps its eggs warm by placing them on their red-hot feet. The policeman moves towards the wagon.

CRIME AND PUNISHMENT.[†]

MY facemask slipped down whilst I was talking to Mrs Gardener.

A policeman arrested me and I got given life.

Mrs Gardener got sixteen years for being an accomplice and was in the next cell.

Her grandson smuggled in weed in hollowed-out walnuts and we'd smoke that after our prison meals until she was released.

†**KEY:** My mum made us all masks.
JUNIPER: Ha ha.
KEY: No experience in masks and now she's making them for every Tom, Dick and Harry.
JUNIPER: Good masks?
KEY: Masks for the grandchildren, masks for the camping lot, anyone with a face, basically.
JUNIPER: I wouldn't know where to start, making a mask. I'll stick to my blue ones from Superdrug.
KEY: She was making them out of a colander and bungee cord.
JUNIPER: Oh.
KEY: Madness. Size of the holes, yer know. Bugs are gonna fly in, anyway.
JUNIPER: A colander.
KEY: You know how tiny covids are?
JUNIPER: Yeah masks have to be cloth. You can't give those critters gaps.
KEY: No.
JUNIPER: That's playing into their hands, that.

INTERLAKEN.

"**G**UTEN *Tag, mein ducklings! Ich habe einen neuen policy,* M'dears."

Bohnson had been drinking and, judging by the mud on his tennis shorts and his grazed thighs, he'd come off his bicycle.

He turned to a slaphead.

"Slide me up, Macduff."

A slide came up: a man stood in a clear plastic tube.

"May I present to you... The Swiss Doll policy."

Journalists blinked on screens.

Bohnson unscrewed another bottle of Dooley's and explained that everyone would have a see-through cylinder lowered over them in the next few days.

He put his Dooley's to his lips, kissed the rim and drank.

"These will stay for the foreseeable," he winked.

Toffee liqueur ran in rivulets down his neck, tarnishing his crop top.

"It'll be a bit of a pain in the plus fours for a month or three -"

His ear was bleeding hard.

"But boy, are we gonna have a good summer! Yessirree, I should bloody cocoa! Slide, Macduff! Slide! Slide!"

A video played.

Tubes falling through the air in Letchworth, separating people into individual tubes, palms slapped against the Perspex, faces stretched in terror.

HERE WE GO ROUND THE MULBERRY BUSH.

THWARTED.

Key tramps the barren streets of N10. The February Sun occasionally elbows its way through the clouds; splats on rooftops. Key whacks his stick against streetbins; whistles along to his chill playlist. Suddenly: a voice. Friendly, familiar. The merest hint of Nottinghamshire colouring it.

SWEETIE: Keyzee!

Key's AirPods explode out of his ears and he spins round. It's Sweetie Pie! Of all the people. And his one-metre-long sausage dog, Vermouth, on his pink leash.

KEY: Aha! Now then! Sweetie Pie!

SWEETIE: You're in Muswell Hill!

KEY: I'm everywhere, Pie, I really am!

SWEETIE: I'd heard you were walking.

KEY: Oh, I'm walking, alright!

Key snaps his shattered Fitbit in front of Sweetie Pie's face. The front bit of Pie's sausage dog wanders off towards a sports shop – closed – and sniffs at the shutters.

KEY: So, what's new, Pie? You're smiling like a larrikin there.

SWEETIE: Ah, well. Not to put *too* fine a point on it, me and Joan are… "embracing lockdown", as it were. As in, well… yer know. We're expecting. A baby.

KEY: Ha! Well, how d'ya like that?

SWEETIE: Gotta have a project!

KEY: Indeed, I've got my walking!

SWEETIE: Nailing it.

KEY: Ha! A lockdown bairn!

Whoompf. Key's sack is on the deck and he's hauled out his champagne. He holds it aloft like Bobby Moore himself.

SWEETIE: *(Uncertain)* Champagne.

KEY: For getting Joan pregnant!

SWEETIE: It's 10 AM.

KEY: Five past, to be fair.

SWEETIE: Ha ha. Erm. I mean, it'd ruin me.

KEY: Bro, it's champers! We gotta celebrate! This is perfect.

SWEETIE: Burning a hole in your rucksack, is it?

KEY: I won it, look. "House. Of. Games."

SWEETIE: You were sharp on that, huh. We watched it. Sharp on the buzzer there.

KEY: Had to be, Pie.

SWEETIE: And now you carry it around, waiting for good news to fall into your lap.

Key is scratching at the foil. Vermouth is transfixed. His front portion has rejoined the back portion. His middle is now stretched around a bollard outside the sports shop – closed.

SWEETIE: Truth is, I don't drink in lockdowns, not really.

KEY: Ah. Uh-huh. I hear that.

Key is fiddling with the foil. He wants it to go pop. He wants the cork to ricochet around Muswell Hill. He fingers the cork.

KEY: Yer know, you really shouldn't be telling people good news if you're not prepared to sit on the kerb and get lashed on champers.

SWEETIE: I know, I know.

KEY: You can't be spilling your tidings and then not accept the consequences, Pie. Really.

The Sun doesn't seem to want to hit the bottle. It is dull. Unwarranted. Vermouth has wandered off to unhook himself from the bollard.

SWEETIE: Well, look. Let's get sloshed in September or summat.

KEY: Christ.

SWEETIE: What?

KEY: Well show some optimism. "September"?

SWEETIE: Summer then.

KEY: Spring. Spring, it'll be.

The champagne is back in Key's Puma rucksack now. Pie smiles. Key doesn't.

SWEETIE: Will you walk with Vermouth and I? We're going to take a look at the church, then back down to Joan, you know.

KEY: Pie. I walk. That's what I do. Of course I'll walk with you and your silly little dog.

Pie says something very strong in defence of Vermouth. Key defends himself and Pie says something stronger and Key apologises and they walk.

HERE WE GO ROUND THE MULBERRY BUSH.

DO YOUR WOGAN.

IT was time for the next batch of people to get vaccinated.

If you were over seventy-five, had eczema or could do impressions you were up.

I stood in the queue, kissing my bicep and practising my Wogan.

The lad at the front was doing a medley of Alan Carr, Borat and Professor Brian Cox.

They waved him through and also blasted a couple of old biddies, who didn't even have to do an impression, though one did look like an elderly Su Pollard.

Now I was up.

Blank faces at my Wogan so I boxed clever, switched to Brucie.

The needle was sliding past my humerus before I'd got to "to see you, nice!"

The twerp behind kept chiming in with some "higher higher, lower lower" stuff as the serum spurted out and spread around my networks.

I waddled back to my Volvo, applying pressure with my cotton-wool ball and muttering "good game, good game" into my snood.

CONTROL-P.

Key is walking along the canal. On his side of the waterway: the bars – closed, the weird cafés – closed, the stinking galleries – closed. On the other side: the industry. Warehouses, micro factories, breweries: struggling on. Chimneys: furloughed. Some lathes at a standstill, others still sawing wood, or chipping metal, or whatever it is lathes are supposed to stop doing when a pandemic sweeps in. Early February and some sunshine at last. But the rays are cold by the time they kiss the towpath. You gotta walk. Key's walking to Hackney; spinning his stick like an old-school majorette. Emily Juniper detonates Key's iPhone in his pocket and he answers it in a flash.

JUNIPER: I've ordered the books.

KEY: Emily Juniper!

JUNIPER: I feel sick.

KEY: How many books?

JUNIPER: I didn't know how many to print. I feel sick. Oh, gawd.

KEY: How many d'ya print? Same again?

JUNIPER: Well... I mean I went for more. I need a stiff drink. I've sent you an email.

KEY: Ordered more than the first run, huh?

JUNIPER: Rolled the dice. Gives me the heebie-jeebies, this. I need a gin and peppermint.

KEY: Well... what's the worst that can happen?

JUNIPER: I dunno, Tim! Me with four hundred boxes of books in my lounge? Everyone furious with me?

KEY: Ha!

JUNIPER: Me crawling over the boxes like a weird creature, falling between the gaps, being forgotten about, dying in the shadow of three tons of paperbacks. My antennae –

KEY: Antennae?

JUNIPER: Stretching up to the top of the boxes, to a world beyond the books. Check your email!

Key checks his email. It's a larger figure than he expected. His eyes bulge and pop, and mild panic runs down his cheeks.

KEY: I need a stiffy, too, Em.

JUNIPER: You seen the figure, huh?

KEY: I mean... the key is for bookshops to step up to the plate, that's all.

JUNIPER: They're about to start printing.

KEY: Control-P.

JUNIPER: Oh, gawd, my peppermint's going everywhere. They start printing at ten. Look, can you get someone to say something nice about the book, slap it in the press release.

KEY: "Quotes."

JUNIPER: Frank Skinner? You know Frank Skinner, don't you?

KEY: Um. Let me think. Did I stay in touch with the guy who handed me my Perrier Award? Mm. Guessing so.

JUNIPER: Oh, don't joke, Tim. I'm dying here. What if I've overcooked it, Tim?

KEY: If Waterstones and WHSmith both ask for a couple of thousand, we're rosy. Cool heads, Em. Cool heads.

Key's knees buckle. He spies a bench, drops his fat arse down on it; it buckles. Across the canal: a building. Derelict? Or a going concern? Key screws his nose up, shoves his forearm into his sack. He pulls out his Penelope Pitstop flask, cracks it open, pours 250 ml of Goose IPA from the flask into the lid.

JUNIPER: How are you, Tim?

KEY: Nailing lockdown, Em. Giving it what for.

JUNIPER: My mum was a bit worried about you, that's all.

KEY: Lynne Juniper?

JUNIPER: She's reading the book.

KEY: Oh. Well, tell her I'm doing okay. Lynne Juniper doesn't need to lose sleep over me, Em, I swear.

JUNIPER: She wants me to check you're going out. Taking the air.

KEY: Big-time. Lungs full of that shit.

JUNIPER: It wasn't easy for anyone, that first lockdown.

KEY: Ha. Could have fooled me.

JUNIPER: People present different versions of themselves on Instagram, Tim.

KEY: I had Yorkshire puddings and fish fingers one morning.

JUNIPER: Interesting combination.

KEY: My noggin had shut down –

JUNIPER: Hang on – "morning"?

KEY: I'm out and about this time. Walking. Walk. Ing. I'm not gonna sit in my flat and tie my plonker in knots, tell her. Not this time.

JUNIPER: I'll report back.

KEY: Been there, done that.

JUNIPER: You wrote the book on it.

KEY: Let me tell you this, Em. Some lockdowns, you write a book. Other lockdowns, you unleash it onto the world.

JUNIPER: And then pulp what's left.

KEY: I'll talk to journalists, Em. I'll get the word out.

Key unwraps some foil. A scotch egg. He squeezes it lightly. His fingers are his eyes. His actual eyes continue to look at the building opposite. Its bricks are old. Like some kind of terracotta vibes. Orange, like. What even is it?

JUNIPER: How's your bubble? Making a good account of yourself?

KEY: Going there tonight. Requested fish and chips.

JUNIPER: Requested?

KEY: I'm not in the business of demanding it, Em. Just politely requested it. Cod, chips and mushy peas.

JUNIPER: Fish-and-chip-night!

KEY: Dunno about that. "Fish-and-chip-night". Makes it sound like we're all having it.

JUNIPER: Well, anyway. Take 'em a bottle, eh.

KEY: They have stuff in. That's the beauty of 'em, Em. It's very much *mi casa, su casa*, to be honest. Just phone ahead, get 'em to put it in the fridge. How's Quint?

JUNIPER: Oh, well. Quint's a bloody revelation is what he is. He likes to look after us. Brings round this weird cheese he makes.

KEY: Sounds gross, but carry on.

JUNIPER: We'd be bored to tears without Quint, I must say.

KEY: Everyone has their bubbles.

JUNIPER: 9.58 AM. I'm jelly.

A goose shoots through, honking. Key refills the lid. The orange building appears to be trembling.

KEY: You're obsessed with time, Em.

JUNIPER: Ha.

KEY: What?

JUNIPER: So funny you say that.

KEY: Yeah?

JUNIPER: I'm drawing clocks.

KEY: Quite right, too.

JUNIPER: Well, I'm all locked down and you aren't writing –

KEY: I can't, Em. I won't.

JUNIPER: So, now I have tons of time on my hands. May as well draw the stuff.

KEY: Time?

JUNIPER: Exactly.

KEY: Depictions of time.

JUNIPER: That's the idea.

KEY: Reflections on time.

JUNIPER: In charcoal.

KEY: Is there any other kind?

JUNIPER: 9.59! I can't bear it. Printers'll be firing up. I'll call you later.

Key's eyes widen. The orange building opposite is beginning to judder.

KEY: Go to your clocks, Em. Lots of love.

The walls of the orange building momentarily illuminate. He can hear presses firing up inside. The printing house? Key places his lid down, takes a couple of steps out onto the water and cups his ear. The second edition begins to print. Thunk thunk thunk. The stink of ink spews out of the chimneys.

†**JUNIPER:** But how do you *expect* them to do it?
KEY: It's just a poem, Em. I'm not saying I've got the answers.
JUNIPER: Pour all the vaccine into the sea and everyone has to go swimming and swallow what they can?
KEY: Pardon me?
JUNIPER: Because it's easy to sit on the sidelines and make snidey comments and write poems about it.
KEY: You think writing these is *easy*?
JUNIPER: Well, I mean...
KEY: This ain't easy, what I'm doing. I'd happily swap jobs with these guys.
JUNIPER: You wouldn't last a week.
KEY: We don't know that.
JUNIPER: You'd get swamped by the emails. End up with vax sitting in vats and everyone with empty biceps.
KEY: Right, and meanwhile The Maestro's biting his biro and pulling his plonker and trying to think of a decent poem.
JUNIPER: I definitely don't think you should swap jobs.
KEY: It'd be carnage, Em. Utter carnage.

SHORT.[†]

THE drugs guys basically said yes to everyone so now they didn't have enough serum to go round and there were loads of continental Europeans banging on the door.

The CEO called a meeting.

It was a mess.

Five chairs between twelve drugs guys and two four-packs of *all-butter croissants* to go round.

Italians and Danes slapped the windows with their palms as the drugs guys looked for a solution.

There wasn't enough proper coffee for everyone so some people were having to inject themselves with instant.

Bohnson was on the screen, in all his glory.

He was saying they needed to dilute the vaccine.

He was saying they should cut it with water and he was laughing, but also crying.

"Cut it with grapefruit juice, who cares!"

Drugs guys leant on fax machines and nibbled buttery crumbs.

"Cut it with piss! What's the difference?!"

The drugs guys fiddled with their ties, bared their teeth nervously.

"Hell, I'll cut the stuff myself!" Bohnson went on.

CAN I QUOTE YOU ON THAT?

It is extremely brisk. Sub-zero. Mother Nature's turned it right down and Key's jiggling around on a Highgate doorstep, his bollocks clinking together, his fingertips deep purple in his Thinsulate gloves, his eyebrows heavy with frost. He shoves his mask on, whacks the old-school bell with his stick and retreats to a safe distance. He fondles one of the three stone lions that stand like sentries, guarding the modest mansion. Key is humming by the time the heavy front door swings slowly open. And now the great Frank Skinner stands in the doorway. He is wearing a thick blue track-suit and his hood is up. His eyes twinkle above his West Bromwich Albion FC mask.

FRANK: Tim!

KEY: Hello, Frank!

CATH: *(From off)* Who is it, Frank?

FRANK: It's Tim Key. How are ya, friend?

CATH: *(Off)* There's a pandemic, Frank!

FRANK: I'm vaccinated, babe!

CATH: *(Off)* Why's Tim Key round?

KEY: I've just popped by, Cath! I'm masked up to the nines!

CATH: *(Off)* Fuck's sake. Coffee?!

KEY: Mocha, please!

CATH: *(Off)* How the fuck am I making a mocha?!

The two men stand. The Perrier Winner 1991, and the recipient eighteen years later, in 2009. Now masked up in a city overrun by bugs. They are shivering.

FRANK: When you asked for my address I thought you meant you were going to post me something.

KEY: Nah.

FRANK: Doorstep in the pandemic. One way of doing things.

KEY: I'm on my stiffy, Frank.

FRANK: Huh?

KEY: Stiff walk, this is nay bother, promise. You got the jab, huh?

FRANK: Yeah, I'm a dinosaur me. Blasted me with that shit early doors.

KEY: Any side effects?

FRANK: I wrote a book about Prayer.

KEY: Okay.

Key pulls his own book from his Puma rucksack. It absorbs the light from the Sun and the street goes dark for a split second. Frank blinks and the scene is lit once more.

KEY: Well, anyway, thought I'd pop over, Frank. Give you a copy of my one.

FRANK: We're all at it.

CATH: *(Appearing)* I'll disinfect it.

The book disappears. Key lolls against a lion once more. Bobby belting the ball. Nobby dancing.

FRANK: Cath disinfects stuff.

KEY: Fair play.

FRANK: Runs apples through the dish-washer.

KEY: You can't be too careful.

FRANK: They taste like Persil.

KEY: In a good way?

FRANK: So what d'ya want? A quote is it?

KEY: Gotta shift some units over here, Frank.

FRANK: I give quotes in my sleep, believe me.

KEY: We've printed too many, so some kind words from you wouldn't go amiss. Might mean we have to pulp less, if you catch my drift.

FRANK: Well, what about "Key takes you on an unexpected journey, he –"

KEY: Well, you can obviously read it first, Frank.

FRANK: "At its heart, Key's is a tale of loss."

KEY: I mean, as in, give it a read and then see what you think. Then you can give a quote sort of like from the heart, you know.

FRANK: I'll be honest, Timbo. I ain't reading it.

KEY: You're not?

Cath re-emerges. The book is dripping wet. She hands it to Frank and puts a West Bromwich Albion FC mug on the wall bit for Key.

KEY: Mocha?

CATH: Crumbled a couple of Pro Plusses into a hot chocolate.

KEY: Fair play.

CATH: Why don't you two go for a walk?

FRANK: Cath.

CATH: Go on, Tim. Not now but, yer know. Give the old fossil something to look forward to, eh.

KEY: Yeah, I'll walk the guy.

CATH: He'd never ask you himself, that's all.

KEY: Ha. Couple of Perrier winners, strolling around on the heath.

FRANK: Ha! The old Perrier Award! Don't even know where mine is these days! Lost in the mists of time.

KEY: Ha ha, yeah.

FRANK: Bet yours is pride of place in your lounge, is it?

KEY: Nah.

FRANK: Cobblers, on a plinth by your telly I bet!

KEY: Nah, not currently on display, eh.

FRANK: Good man.

KEY: Meaningless twaddle, eh.

Key's pack is heavy on his back. He leans forward slightly so he doesn't fall backwards.

CATH: Well, look, let us know when's good for you.

KEY: Happy to go for a stroll, Frank. Couple of entertainers taking the air, why not?

CATH: This is great. Any unwanted attention, he'll look after you, Frank. He gets so much hassle on that bloody heath, Tim –

FRANK: I like it.

CATH: He likes it, but you know. Man of the people and all that. Gives everyone the time of day, always has. But, you know, bit much sometimes.

KEY: Welcome to my world –

CATH: If you're with him, you can keep a lid on it.

KEY: Oh.

CATH: What "oh"?

KEY: Well, it's just... I think we might be double trouble if it's the two of us, that's all.

CATH: What double trouble?!

KEY: We'd be like Ant and Dec up there, Cath.

CATH: Ha ha. *(And now serious)* I mean as in, Frank's famous.

KEY: I was in One Day with Anne Hathaway, I played "customer".

FRANK: Do you get hassled, then?

KEY: I get my fair share, Frank, believe me.

Key looks at the four questioning eyes, imagines the mouths twisted into squiggles of disbelief beneath the masks. Sips his approximated mocha.

CATH: A nice little walk for you, Frank. Sounds okay, doesn't it?

FRANK: I wouldn't mind a trundle, no.

KEY: Well, I'll be off then, try out a few routes.

FRANK: Do you want the book back?

CATH: He wants you to read it, Frank.

FRANK: I ain't gonna read it, honestly I'm not.

The book is handed back. Key clamps a sad Thinsulate glove around it. Its cover is frosting up.

KEY: You're in it, you know.

FRANK: Huh?

KEY: Namecheck.

FRANK: Gimme that.

Frank grabs the book back, starts forcing his thumbs between its pages. His tongue is out now, he is mouthing "Skinner".

CATH: Leave it with us, Tim.

Key chugs down his turbochoc and moves away, clapping his hands together to try to get his fingers back from black to something more purply.

CATH: Toodle-oo then!

Cath is waving. Key waves back. Frank's nose is buried deep, deep in the solemn pages of the first lockdown.

NOW YOU SEE ME.

THEY started going door-to-door.

A rozzer unfolded a photo of *the variant*.

"Seen this?"

Steve Grunt peered at the photo, bleary-eyed; his pyjama bottoms riding low on his arse.

"Naw."

"Who is it, Ste?!" Lynne made eggs with Tabasco in the kitchen.

"The fuzz, honey!"

The rozzer frowned.

He looked past Steve, squinted down the hall.

"Eggs, is it?"

"Yeah," Steve's breathing was shallow.

The rozzer folded the photo up; rain trickled off his helmet, sploshed onto his epaulettes.

The rozzer nodded; Steve shut the door.

And now the variant emerged from the shadows.

"Nice," he said, his smile sick, poisonous.

Steve flinched, tried to push the variant away with his walking stick.

The variant slithered towards the kitchen.

"How my eggs getting on, Mrs G?"

The variant was leaving a thin, green trail in his wake and Steve muttered something about this under his breath.

WE'RE GONNA HAVE TO LET YOU GO. †

I RETIRED my bag.
We had gone beyond the point where
you would "need a bag".
I sat him down and told him this.
Of course he didn't understand.
Try explaining a pandemic to a bag.
Impossible.

♥

†**JUNIPER:** Ha ha, I got rid of my wallet!
KEY: Shoved it in a drawer, wait for the tills to whirr back to life, type of thing?
JUNIPER: Threw it in the sea more like.
KEY: With all your cards in?
JUNIPER: Ha ha.
KEY: That's a shame.
JUNIPER: Photos, too. Whoops!
KEY: That is "whoops", Em.
JUNIPER: That's why I'm saying "whoops".
KEY: Why'd ya have to go and do that, yer daft apeth?
JUNIPER: Drove my van home, got my wetsuit.
KEY: Went in after it?
JUNIPER: It was nighttime, Tim.
KEY: You really are a beauty, Em.
JUNIPER: In the end I had to get rescued, ha ha!
KEY: This is bananas, Em. You're putting them in danger, too, yer know.
JUNIPER: These big old frogmen, hauling me onto their rubber speedboat thing
like a seal, ha ha!
KEY: Ha ha. It's not a bad anecdote, to be fair. Ha ha.

PRESS.

Key has come off the heath and has bought his sausages, and now he descends the hill, swinging them by his hip. In his ears, a journalist, eager to find out about the book so he can tell his readers what's what. His voice is a miserable, caustic affair. It goes right through Key. All his theories about lockdown, his probing questions about the bar supervisor, his tangents about the pandemic's impact on live comedy: they all grab at Key's nerves and squeeze them tight.

PRESS: And you work with "Emily Juniper". She's your designer, right?

KEY: Someone's read the press release.

PRESS: And how was your experience of collaborating with a designer?

KEY: Jesus wept.

The voice, spearing into his brain, making his eyes water.

PRESS: Would you work with her again?

KEY: Have you got the book in front of you?

PRESS: Erm...

KEY: Have you got the book in front of you?

PRESS: Yes, yes I do.

KEY: Then what do you think, mate?

Key squeezes his sausages together and uses them to prod the button on the traffic lights. The traffic is quelled and Key crosses, pausing to punch a car bonnet as he walks.

PRESS: And so, from what I can gather, you printed a few thou to test the water?

KEY: What the fuck kind of phrase is that? "A few thou"?

PRESS: And sold them to your Instagram followers.

KEY: Jeez Louise. Yes. And now we're printing a few thou more.

PRESS: That's good going.

KEY: You think I don't know that?

PRESS: And have you been pleased with the reaction?

KEY: What do you think, Einstein?

Key walks down past a stone camel. He can hear the breathing of the journo. Short. Stressed. And he can hear paper. His notes? The book itself? No, not the book. The sound isn't luxurious enough.

KEY: Got your notes?

PRESS: I wonder, would you mind if I spoke to Emily?

KEY: Why would I mind?

PRESS: Don't know, worried I might find out she's the brains of the operation!

There's a bollard. And an empty Cherry Coke can on it. Key winds up his sausages and swings them at it. The can goes flying into the road, it strikes the windscreen of an Ocado van and flies into orbit.

KEY: She doesn't like being interviewed.

PRESS: Well, I can perhaps drop her an email, see what she reckons.

KEY: She exists in the shadows.

PRESS: The power behind the throne.

KEY: She doesn't like a fanfare, that's all. She likes to be left alone.

PRESS: I get it: you're protective. Keep her to yourself.

KEY: Let's talk about Partridge, can't we. Happy to say something controversial.

PRESS: Do you get lonely in the lockdowns?

KEY: Nope. Next question.

Key is across the road from his flat now. He looks up at his window. Where he must go next. Reincarcerate himself. The door locked behind him.

PRESS: How much of the book is true?

KEY: The million-dollar question.

Key leans back on the wall. His fat arse perched on the edge. The questions continue to scrape into his earholes like wire wool.

PRESS: Those conversations, I mean. How many were real?

KEY: You haven't actually said you like the book yet.

PRESS: As in, I mean you obviously weren't talking to a mouse, ha ha.

Key doesn't laugh.

PRESS: But, I mean do you have rules? For what goes in, what doesn't.

KEY: Yeah. Yeah, there's rules.

PRESS: There's rules.

KEY: Put it this way, this'd go right in.

PRESS: Ha ha.

Key stares up at his flat. Remembers the conversations. He screws up his eyes into two foul squints. In the amber glow of the lounge he thinks he can see his own silhouette. Its ear to his iPhone.

PRESS: And are you doing another book?

KEY: You never know. You never know what these lockdowns will do to a man.

PRESS: "You never know", he says.

KEY: If I was, this'd walk in, this stuff's gold.

PRESS: Fair enough.

KEY: I encounter a gel, such as your good self, this goes straight in.

PRESS: Gel! Ha ha. But I mean, would it?

Key pulls out a sausage; starts to "write" with it on the wall.

PRESS: Come on, buster, *are* you writing another book?

KEY: I just said, you never know.

PRESS: And when you say "gel". That's negative, isn't it? Hope it's not a hatchet job!

KEY: I'm not writing another book.

PRESS: But if you did you'd portray me as a gel.

KEY: You're getting bogged down in whether or not this will be a piece in my new book.

PRESS: Shitting myself now.

KEY: I might not write one.

PRESS: You "might not"?

Key stops "writing". There's soft meat on the brick.

PRESS: I liked the book, I mean that.

KEY: Thank you.

PRESS: So if I'm in the next one... well...

KEY: I'll go easy.

PRESS: Right.

KEY: Some stuff about your voice at the top, then selected highlights, you know.

PRESS: About my voice, huh?

KEY: Yes, and then selected highlights.

PRESS: Are you recording this?

Key holds his hand up to a truck, crosses the road in front of it.

PRESS: I enjoyed you in Peep Show.

KEY: "Where can people buy the book?"

PRESS: Sorry?

KEY: You need to tell people where they can buy the book.

PRESS: Oh, yes, of course. Where can people buy the book?

KEY: Waterstones is the dream.

PRESS: It's in Waterstones?

KEY: Emily Juniper's website's your best bet at the mo.

Key's at his front door now. Spiritually at least, his sausages are already in his mouth.

KEY: Well, thanks for that, anyway.

PRESS: I should be thanking you.

KEY: I think we're both winners, aren't we?

PRESS: And what now? Back into your flat? Reacquaint yourself with your bear?

KEY: Ha ha. Don't believe everything you read.

PRESS: Ha ha, yeah. I don't know what's true and what isn't any more.

KEY: Nor me, pal. Nor me.

The journalist hangs up. There's a beat, Key's iPhone steadies itself, then a faint click and music pours into Key's ears. It is Laura Marling, and she washes away the gristly residue the journalist's voice has left in Key's skull. He inserts his key into the lock and as he does so the loneliness from within seizes it and makes it unbearably cold in his hands.

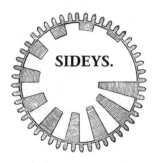

SIDEYS.

T HE serum gushed out of the needle and away into the deepest recesses of my bod.

The side effects were more or less immediate.

Massive boner and yelling some kind of weird language that certainly felt Scandinavian.

Also, coughing up some thick bluish stuff and my ceiling trembling and eventually collapsing.

I lay in the rubble, clutching the nurse's hand.

She also had side effects.

Her dress was on fire, her eyes were the wrong size and she couldn't remember what plans she had for that evening.

BIG TOP.

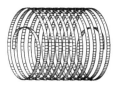

HOLEPUNCH HUGHES finished his home cinema and grabbed himself a beer at his home pub.

He stared at a clearing in his yard, pulled his pad out.

He started doing some very early sketches for a home circus.

In his mind's eye he could already see the thick ropes pegged taut.

He could already hear a ringmaster's whip cracking ferociously.

DOWNING STREET.

Late evening. Baltic London. Key sweeping in bigger circles. Trudging along The Mall, Bucky P soft and golden in the background. Key's Gazelles iced-up and clinking on the tarmac. Skating right, cutting through St James's, unvaccinated geese honking on moonlit ponds. Key's AirPods jammed so far into his ears they touch one another.

KEY: 'Course I heard the bloody briefing, Em.

JUNIPER: A hundred thousand.

KEY: Yeah. Yeah I seen the tolls, Em.

JUNIPER: A hundred thousand, though.

KEY: It's grim stuff alright.

JUNIPER: Poor sods.

KEY: I know they're poor sods, Em. I know that much.

Key breaks left onto Birdcage Walk. He whacks a pillar-box on the head with his stick. Then left again: Whitehall. His shins brittle with the cold; he clips on past The Red Lion: closed. Nothing. Dead as dial-up. Key puts his hands together, prays for the boozer.

JUNIPER: That's the equivalent of The Nou Camp.

KEY: What do you know about The Nou Camp?

JUNIPER: I did a stadium tour there once.

KEY: What the – ?

JUNIPER: What?

KEY: What do you mean "what"? This is madness.

JUNIPER: I was in Barcelona teaching English as a foreign language.

KEY: You see Messi?

JUNIPER: Not on the stadium tour.

KEY: Of course not on the bleeding stadium tour! You see him play?

JUNIPER: He's a magician.

KEY: I know he's a magician, Em! Did you see the little master play?

JUNIPER: A few times, yeah.

Silence from Key. The Gazelles stop. Everything stops.

JUNIPER: Tim?

Key is stock-still. Awestruck. The vast black, wrought-iron gates. The weird hut. The police presence. The weight of history seep-

ing through the railings. Key is outside Downing Street. His knees buckle. He fixes them. Stands up straight. Salutes the police presence.

JUNIPER: If you must know, I saw him score four against Real Betis, and put one on a plate for Xavi.

KEY: Hold on, Babe.

JUNIPER: "Babe"?

Key puts his designer on hold. The AirPods go flat, the sound of the world seeps in. Not much of it. A distant ambulance. A gull above, taking in the historic sights, squawking sporadically at the relics of power beneath it. Key stands in front of the police presence. Without moving, he nods to them. They motionlessly nod back. A citizen and his guardians.

KEY: So.

PC: So.

Key smiles. Looks at his feet. Looks back at the police presence. Looks beyond them.

KEY: So, is the big man in?

PC: Huh?

KEY: The Maestro.

PC: Can't say.

KEY: Well, you ain't standing there with a machine gun and those thick trousers on if The Maestro ain't in.

The rozzer has a puffy face, covered up with a despicable beard. His submachine gun is the blackest thing Key has ever seen. So black it is shapeless.

PC: You can't stand there.

KEY: Free country.

PC: Step away from the gates.

KEY: Yeah, you'd love that, eh.

PC: Sir.

KEY: Yes, constable?

The rozzer lifts his submachine gun at Key. Key frowns. The rozzer smiles. A gold tooth flashes in the moonlight. Key raises his jaw, addresses the WPC.

KEY: Come on then. He in?

WPC: We're not allowed to say.

PC: Don't go asking her, I already told you.

KEY: See the tolls today?

Key mimes a graph. His palm soaring upwards at forty-five, fifty, sixty degrees.

KEY: Woosh.

WPC: We ain't meant to talk about the tolls.

KEY: The equivalent of The Nou Camp.

WPC: Not allowed to say.

KEY: Well, it is.

PC: Barcelona.

KEY: Yeah, I think I know where The Nou Camp is, cheers.

PC: Saw Messi tear Valencia a bunch of new ones there.

KEY: For fuck's sake.

PC: They couldn't get near him.

WPC: Be on your way.

KEY: Nowhere to go. Dopy old sod shut the boozers, didn't he?

Key gestures behind him. Swings an arm back towards The Red Lion.

KEY: His nibs should be opening that up. It's what, three hundred yards away. He should stroll down, snip the chains himself. That's what he should do. Bung some dough behind the bar, get the place bouncing.

PC: Step away, I swear.

KEY: 'Stead of sitting in there, tugging his boy, boasting about the tolls to anyone who'll listen.

WPC: He's not boasting.

KEY: Yeah, well.

WPC: Sir, we must insist you leave.

PC: We're warning you, in fact.

KEY: Oh, right, you're warning me. Well done. How does that work then?

From nowhere the clack of the bolt carrier being shoved rearward and then the deafening volley of machine-gun fire as the rozzer peels off ten-dozen shots into the sky. Key throws himself to the floor, clamps his ears, wails into the concrete. Then silence. Presently the gull – torn to ribbons by the government-sanctioned brass bullets – plummets from the heavens, falls into our scene. Stunned, its body disgraced by gunfire, it looks blankly at Key.

KEY: Wow. That's...

Key stands. The WPC adjusts her specs on her nose, moves towards the stricken bird. She stands over it. Key watches. The silence oppressive. The WPC pulls a pistol from her utility belt, finishes the gull off with a clean shot to the neck.

PC: See?

Key nods. It's cold, his chest is trembling.

KEY: Okay.

To his right, Key hears a buzz and an unlocking mechanism. He looks across. A plump man in a long black coat, his hood pulled over his head. One or two yellow fronds peaking from under. In one fist: a Pret paper bag; in the other: a 500 ml can of Heineken. Key frowns.

PC: *(To the plump man)* Sir.

MAN: *(Some yards away)* Constable.

KEY: Huh?

The vast figure squeezes through the gate and moves down the road. His hips swing lavishly. Key peers at his gait, squints at his Pret bag. His nose twitches. Swedish Meatball Wrap. Key's lips quiver. He knows that man.

WPC: Come on then.

The machine gun, waving vaguely at Key's throat. The end of his time here. Key nods at the police presence. He looks past them. The figure has disappeared into the darkness, towards the houses, replaced by a thin fog, illuminated by the Moon. Key pulls his iPhone, slides to unhold, moves towards Traf. Square. Emily Juniper's voice. To calm him. To steady the ship.

JUNIPER: I saw them all.

KEY: Hey, Em.

JUNIPER: My boyfriend knew a government official, he had tickets coming out of his arse.

KEY: Oh, right. Well, you landed on your feet, Em.

JUNIPER: I liked Iniesta the best.

KEY: Well, now you're talking.

The road bends and Key glimpses Nelson. His shoulder's thrown back. Proud. Strong. His right hand stuffed up his jumper.

HERE WE GO ROUND THE MULBERRY BUSH.

PHARMACEUTICALS.

A PILL was developed to ward off the loneliness.
I took it down with a quart of sherry.
A feeling of warmth rushed through me.
My phone started pinging like nobody's
business.
Long lost pals,
Colleagues and clingers-on from before the
locks turned,
Employees and shareholders of the
pharmaceutical company who developed the pill.
Everyone getting in touch.

Week VI.

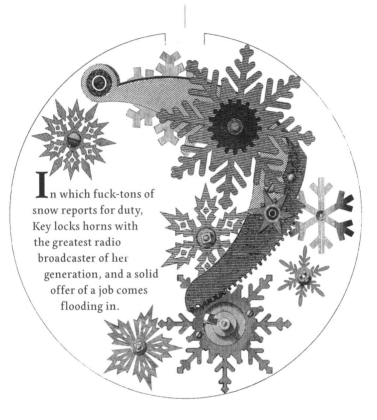

In which fuck-tons of snow reports for duty, Key locks horns with the greatest radio broadcaster of her generation, and a solid offer of a job comes flooding in.

HERE WE GO ROUND THE MULBERRY BUSH.

FROSTY.

E VERYONE'S worst nightmare:
Snowmen could get it!

The government stepped in quickly and decisively as per.

Children were still allowed to build them but they had to put a mask on them once they were done.

You weren't allowed to build two *right next to each other,* you couldn't bring them into your house, and no one was allowed to sleep with the snowmen.

At night the army came round in trucks and vaccinated the snowmen.

If they resisted or were lippy they were melted down with government-sponsored flamethrowers or smashed apart with bricks.

MOCHA IN THE SNOW.

Snow. Everything white. Like A4 paper, before The Poets have emptied their guts onto it. A winter wonderland. And in its depths, yeti-like, stooped and dusted white, a figure. His familiar red Norway bobble hat winking at us through the flakes. Hunched and alone, he moves through the conditions. An old-school Sasquatch, mocha in hand. The beast knocks some white clods from its eyelashes. Everything obscured by the whiteness. An iPhone is raised? Its ear is blue?

KEY: Emily Juniper. Book angel.

JUNIPER: Foyles have put in an order.

KEY: Huh?

The snow dissipates, The Poet is revealed.

JUNIPER: Foyles, Tim.

KEY: What?

JUNIPER: Foyles. The bookshop.

KEY: I know what Foyles sell, Em. I spent half my thirties in that bloody shop.

JUNIPER: Me, too! I used to go there when I lived in London!

KEY: Foyles have put in a bloody order!

JUNIPER: I was rudderless, Tim. Lost. I'd always end up in Foyles.

KEY: Me too, Em. Me too! And The Wheatsheaf, I'd go to.

JUNIPER: I was like a young Scandinavian girl, flouncing round a bluebell forest!

KEY: The Montagu Pyke. That was another classic.

JUNIPER: Foyles! Actual Foyles!

KEY: They put in an order, huh?

JUNIPER: One hundred books.

Key lies down on the pure white carpet. His smile stretches off his face, falls into the snow, creates two pleasing pools.

KEY: So that's made a dent in the stock, huh?

JUNIPER: Could do with Waterstones.

KEY: But it's a start, huh?

JUNIPER: It's two boxes.

KEY: How many boxes we getting?

Silence. The longer the silence goes on, the more boxes Key imagines. By the time Emily Juniper speaks, there is a tower of boxes as high as The Gherkin itself.

JUNIPER: Our book's going to be in shops! Shops, Tim!

Key moves his arms up and down in the snow. Up and down, like a stricken marionette; shovelling the snow this way and that.

JUNIPER: Now did you speak to the journalist? Butter him up?

KEY: Putty in my hands, Em. And tomorrow...

JUNIPER: Yes? Yes?! Tomorrow?!

KEY: Tomorrow I shall be speaking to a certain Laur–

JUNIPER: Lauren Laverne!!!

KEY: I'm going on, Em. Talk about the book.

JUNIPER: With Lauren Laverne!!! Tim!!! Lauren actual Laverne!

Key raises his mocha to his lips. He's prone, though, so this doesn't work at all. 90% bad outcome.

KEY: Bleughhhh.

JUNIPER: What Bleughhhh?

KEY: Just... hang on.

Key hauls himself on to his haunches, scrambles to a snow-topped log, leans back against it, his lips burning, in distress.

JUNIPER: What bleughhhh, Tim? Our book's gonna be on shelves! Oh, I could cry! I could cry!!! And you rabbiting on to Lauren about it! I love her, Tim! What's wrong, are you choking?

KEY: No I just...

There is mocha in Key's snood. There is mocha sloshing against Key's throat.

KEY: Nah, nah. Spilt my drink, that's all.

JUNIPER: Ha ha, it was all going so well.

KEY: It's filled my snood up, that's all. Mocha everywhere, that's all.

JUNIPER: Another day, another mocha!

KEY: What's that supposed to mean?

JUNIPER: You know... it's Valentine's Day on Sunday.

KEY: Huh?

JUNIPER: I know where you got that mocha.

KEY: You don't know the first thing about anything, Em, I swear.

JUNIPER: You've been back to your fancy lady, you've been batting your eyelashes.

KEY: This is a scandal. It's slander, Em. Plain and simple.

JUNIPER: She's been shovelling marshmallows in like there's no tomorrow. Blowing kisses into her mask.

Mocha is seeping through the zip of Key's Mountain Warehouse anorak. Mocha is streaming down his tracksuit top. Mocha is seeping through that zip, too. Mocha trickling down his tummy. Marshmallows in his naval. Marshmallows from his fancy lady.

JUNIPER: You have to ask her out, Tim.

KEY: It's embarrassing. What if she says no? No, I can't!

JUNIPER: Why's she saying no?

KEY: Aagh! She'll say it so nicely.

JUNIPER: You've not even asked her yet, you big bowl of custard.

KEY: I'll ask her out, she'll say no, I'll put it in a poem, and so it goes on.

JUNIPER: Why write it up?

KEY: Hammer it out on Valentine's Day, I can see it now.

JUNIPER: You'll be with her on Valentine's Day.

KEY: Let's talk about Foyles, Em. Let's talk about the financial deal you've made with Foyles.

Mocha seeping down his knickers, mocha in the very wrinkles of his nutsack, mocha down his thighs.

JUNIPER: Take her out, Tim!

KEY: And the regs?

Key pulls the purple notebook out of his anorak. It's grown and is now as thick as fuck. A two pound lump of dos and don'ts. Not that there's many dos to write home about.

KEY: What am I gonna do, Em?

JUNIPER: What do you mean?

KEY: Well, it's alright for you. You've got a great big boyfriend. You can have a cosy –

JUNIPER: Stu's stuffing a bird inside another bird, the dopy sod. He's bought special wood, which smells like maple syrup when it burns. Light that, watch The Apartment.

KEY: You see.

JUNIPER: Quint's the only fly in the ointment.

KEY: Quint wants in?

JUNIPER: Saying the bubble don't stop for Valentine's Day.

KEY: Quint's a handful.

JUNIPER: Quint sits in Stu's chair.

KEY: Honeymoon's over.

Key waves a fist at an imaginary Quint.

JUNIPER: It stops snowing on Friday. Go for a walk with the coffee girl. I'm serious. Wind up on some nice bench somewhere. A pocket of hope in the madness.

Pages of the notebook tear away from the spine, lime-green Post-its break into the air, flap amongst the snowflakes.

JUNIPER: A bench, Tim. Away from it all.

KEY: There's one that overlooks the city.

JUNIPER: So ask her out. Take up some treats.

KEY: She's not a dog, Em.

JUNIPER: Well, in the end it's up to you.

KEY: And the regs? They're not for The Maestro's own health yer know.

JUNIPER: The whole thing's madness, you know. You think The Maestro would mind you canoodling with the coffee girl? He'd be cheering you on, Tim.

Key's heart races to his fingertips, forces the notebook back into his pocket.

JUNIPER: Well. I need to make space for these boxes in the lounge. No use Foyles riding in on a white horse if all the books have been left out in the elements.

KEY: He'd be cheering me on, wouldn't he, Em?

JUNIPER: Ha ha. He would!

Mocha dripping from Key's walking trousers, mocha streaming off his Gazelles. Mocha in the snow.

LET IT SNOW.

"YEEEEE!!!!"

Bohnson was sledging now.

"Yeeeee-haaaaa!"

His cowboy hat was sailing behind him, the strap cutting into his chins.

"Yes, Bohns! That's what I'm talking about!!!"

Moggeth ran down the hill in his weird clogs.

He retrieved Bohnson and walked him back up to the top of the hill.

Matt Boytwitch was up there and the education twerp, too.

"Well sledged, Sir!"

There was a scramble to elbow-bump Bohnson, who was giggling and whacking his damn fists together excitedly.

"A proper snow day!"

His face was red, radishy, and he was shoving snow down his tennis shorts to quell his stiffy.

DICK TRACY.

I GOT pinged!

I'd clipped someone in Tesco's and now I had to lock myself in my bedroom for ten days.

I stared at the message.

The language was very disrespectful.

It called me "irresponsible", "reckless", "sloppy", and "a complacent shit-for-brains, who's clearly brushed past someone".

It told me I wasn't allowed to watch telly or have any baths or browse any dating sites or have any cakes or wine, and I wasn't allowed to daydream or text.

It concluded by saying, "Anyway, well done thicko, cheers for fucking it up for everyone."

I said goodbye to the lads and plodded morosely back to my flat.

Another ping.

"Bit quicker, cunt."

I broke into a half-run.

JUNIPER: Stu's not doing any of that stuff.
KEY: No? Not getting involved?
JUNIPER: Pretends to photograph the code thing, never actually unlocks his screen.
KEY: Knows his own mind, that one.
JUNIPER: His thing is he's never been ill.
KEY: Yet.
JUNIPER: Ha ha! That's what I say! "Yet!"
KEY: What does he say?
JUNIPER: When?
KEY: When you say yet.
JUNIPER: Oh right. Just says he doesn't plan on getting ill, and the government needs to relax.
KEY: Famous last words.
JUNIPER: Ha ha. Well, he's dodged it so far, anyway.

HOLLYWOODISH.

Snow. Falling in thick clods. Key gazes through it. His eyes are trained on the cinema: closed. Time stood still. "Tenet" plastered on its front. Vast posters advertise screenings six weeks in the past, all adding to the confusion. Key gazes up at The Protagonist, who seems to be shrugging: he doesn't have a fucking clue what's going on. Key pulls his Penelope Pitstop flask from his Puma rucksack. He puts the whole damn thing to his lips; drenches himself in English bitter. He reflects on his own film career. His scenes, his paychecks, his costume fittings. His iPhone trills. The agent. Another 200 ml down the throat. Click. Connection.

KEY: Chiggy!

CHIGGY: Darling boy! I bring good tidings! Are you nice and cosy in your flat?

KEY: Exposed to the elements, I'm afraid, Chig. Out on a walk. What good tidings?

CHIGGY: Walking in this! You'll turn into a snowman, my lad!

KEY: Ha ha. Not if I keep it over four mph I won't, Chig. What good tidings? Work?

CHIGGY: Always walking! Richard Ayoade saw you walking. Noel saw you walking.

KEY: Sightings.

CHIGGY: How much are you walking?

KEY: Quite a lot. Is there a job, Chig? What are the tidings?

CHIGGY: Blummy. More than an hour a day?

KEY: Yes, Chig.

CHIGGY: Most you've done in a day?

KEY: Fourteen hours, Chig.

CHIGGY: You walking through the night?

Key sips. He leans back against the front of Mountain Warehouse. His arse adheres to the icy glass. He stares at "Tenet".

KEY: What good tidings, Chig?

CHIGGY: A rather lovely little acting job –

KEY: You know what I wanna do, Chig?

CHIGGY: Can I tell you about this job, though?

KEY: I wanna do what the lads from A League of Their Own do. That's my dream, Chig.

CHIGGY: Okay. What do they do?

KEY: Road trip, that's what! Whitehall, Redknapp, Cordon, Freddie Flintoff: into the Land Rover and off round the country! Just having fun! Roll camera! Pissing themselves!

CHIGGY: Who would you do that with though?

KEY: I don't know, Chig! Get my gang together –

CHIGGY: What gang?

KEY: Let's say it's me, Rob Brydon, Sophie Ellis-Bextor, Ken Dodd –

CHIGGY: Dodd's dead, love.

KEY: Ken Hom then.

CHIGGY: I think those things are all about the chemistry.

KEY: I know that, Chig!

CHIGGY: So they're friends – that's why it's fun. They know each other.

KEY: We'd get to know each other.

CHIGGY: Let's focus on the here and now. This acting job:

KEY: You don't think me and Ken Hom could have a laugh together on camera?

CHIGGY: It's a straight offer.

KEY: Keep talking.

CHIGGY: Are you sitting down?

Key's Puma backpack slides down the Mountain Warehouse window and now Key is on his fat arse, sat in the snow, feet outstretched. Sipping from his flask.

CHIGGY: Well, it's a lovely little movie, starring a certain Saoirse Ronan?

KEY: *(Choking on his Boddingtons)* The new Saoirse Ronan picture?!

CHIGGY: Straight offer. Your scenes will be with Saoirse and –

KEY: Saoirse Ronan! Fuck me, Chig! A Saoirse Ronan picture!

CHIGGY: And Sam Rockwell.

KEY: Fuck off! Rockwell?

CHIGGY: Ronan and Rockwell.

KEY: Together at last. Fuck me, Chig! The new Sam Rockwell picture! What is going on here, Chig?!

Key throws his head back, puts it through the Mountain Warehouse window, some sleeping bags and flasks fall on his head; he shakes off the glass, pulls himself back into the elements.

KEY: Saoirse Ronan!

CHIGGY: I know! Although it's pronounced Saoirse, of course.

KEY: Saoirse, yes! I adore Saoirse Ronan.

CHIGGY: But you keep saying "Saoirse". It's "Saoirse". Very important.

KEY: What's the picture called, Chig?

As Chiggy tells him, so the vast posters on the cinema morph and twist. Now they are advertising this new film. A twenty-five-foot Saoirse Ronan cackling as a stacked Key fires a machine gun at a Nazi.

CHIGGY: Now, it's a small part.

KEY: There are no small parts, Chig.

CHIGGY: It's four lines.

KEY: It's what you do with 'em, Chig, I swear. I'll get huge, no question about it.

CHIGGY: Don't be a scene-stealer.

KEY: How am I stealing a scene from Saoirse Ronan, Chig?

CHIGGY: "Saoirse". She's been nominated for four Oscars.

KEY: Four, Chig! Count 'em!

CHIGGY: Rockwell's won one.

KEY: They won't know what's hit 'em, Chig.

CHIGGY: I'll send you the script –

KEY: No need, I work on instinct, Chig, I fucking promise you.

CHIGGY: You happy?

KEY: Happy?! This is the dream, Chigworth! I am lovin' this lockdown! Lovin' it!!!

Key brushes some glass off his head, reaches inside Mountain Warehouse, treats himself to a Kendal Mint Cake and some salopettes.

CHIGGY: Now, you'll need to get tested.

KEY: Huh?

CHIGGY: Someone will come around and do a test on you.

KEY: Huh? Test? What test? Screen test?

CHIGGY: Covid test, of course.

KEY: No. No, no, no.

CHIGGY: You'll have to, love.

KEY: No, I'm not having some thug reaching down my throat thanks, Chig. Not my style.

CHIGGY: Well, it's fairly quick and easy, I think.

KEY: Not happening, Chig.

CHIGGY: But I mean, you can't do your scenes without a negative test.

Key whines silently amongst the snowflakes.

CHIGGY: Saoirse will be tested. Sam will be tested.

KEY: Ronan and Rockwell.

CHIGGY: Look, do you want the job or not?

KEY: 'Course I want the job, Chig! I want the job!

Key slams his head back once more and what's left of the windowpane comes down like a guillotine. Portable stoves fly into the air, a tent pings up, head torches ignite, waterproof trousers march about the shop floor. He rocks forward, back into the street; staggers to his feet.

CHIGGY: Then you'll need testing, I'm sorry.

Key nods, walks zombielike through the flakes. Crosses the empty street. Plods through virgin snow. Trudges towards the cinema.

CHIGGY: It won't be so bad once we've all had the jab.

KEY: Yeah. The jab. The jab. You up for one, Chig?

CHIGGY: Cheeky sod! How old do you think I am?

KEY: Ha ha! Right, sure.

CHIGGY: The sooner I get me a shot of that bloody virus the better.

KEY: Vaccine, Chig. You mean vaccine.

CHIGGY: Well, at this point, either'd do. It's the waiting around I can't stand.

Key smiles. Writes down "vaccine/virus" on his hand.

CHIGGY: Okay, I'll send the script through, and you'll get a date for the test in the next couple of weeks.

KEY: Yes, Ma'am.

CHIGGY: Exciting though! Little part in a film!

KEY: Time will tell what size the part ends up being, Chig. Ta-ra!

Key hangs up. He rattles the heavy chains that shackle the cinema's magical doors. He moves away. Northwest. His figure is gradually wiped out in the snow. The scene is engulfed in whiteness.

JAMMED AND RAMMED.

Now you had to have two swabs jammed up your nostrils at all times.

I blanched at the diagram in my government-issued pamphlet.

You also had to have one rammed down your throat, except for when you were eating or talking about how mad everything was.

I turned back to the cover.

Bloody Bohnson, pointing at me with his divvy beret on.

I flicked forward to the diagram again.

Great, you had to have a needle jammed in your backside the whole time, too.

You were obliged to constantly pump vax into your arnuzzi.

I flicked back again, to the cover.

Bohnson was nodding now, great swabs hanging out of his hooter.

I threw the pamphlet down onto the kitchen table, smashed my Homer Simpson mug down on Bohnson's face.

I waddled into the bathroom to probe and pierce myself for my country.

HOGGING.

A GENTLEMEN'S agreement!

All the best countries got all the vax and began a programme of injecting all their people absolutely shit-tons.

Eventually English people had twelve jabs in their arms and they were a little swollen and merry from all the juice.

The naff countries watched on.

They had fuck all and waddled around all ill or anxious.

More vax became available.

Again: into the English biceps.

More and more gunk flowing into this famous nation's magnificent arms.

People were purple from it now.

Hoping to avoid contact with people from nonsense countries.

English folk going into clinics every 3–4 days to get boosters.

Most people 80% vax by volume now.

Safe as houses.

Looked after.

Their government banging its fists, getting more vax, to top up those who had started to leak.

SNOW DAY.

Snow. The heath smothered in the stuff. Fist-sized flakes of it spinning in the air, a fairy tale, no more, no less. And at its heart, a sledge. Whizzing through the flakes. The Colonel, ears pinned back, his face bright red and taut with excitement. And Key, hanging on for dear life behind him. Wearing his new salopettes, gripping The Colonel's ears, wailing like a banshee. And we are riding with them as they fly down the hill, iced with sweet, sugary snow; on they go, accelerating, bouncing over the moguls, speeding towards the athletics track.

COLONEL: Yeeeee-haaaaa!!!!!

KEY: This is what I'm taaaaaaalking about!!!!!!!

Faster and faster, across the white carpet. The sledge – heavy, wooden – carving straight lines into the snow; tracks, which reach back up to the summit itself. And all around, other tracks, being carved, other sledges shooting like darts from the top of Parliament Hill. And our lads laughing, screaming; the gradient of the hill becoming shallower, and flattening out, and the sledge curving to the left and the sledge throwing our men out into the snow and the sledge travelling another twenty feet and then stillness. The sledge and our men lying in the snow, all three of them laughing.

COLONEL: Yes! Fucking snow day! Get in!

KEY: Again! Again!

COLONEL: High-five!

Key cannot high-five this man. Key is not in this man's bubble. Key runs to the sledge.

KEY: Let's go! Let's go!

And now Key has the thick rope wrapped tightly round his Thinsulate glove and the two men begin trudging back up the hill.

KEY: I'm loving this, Colonel.

COLONEL: And I'm not?

KEY: Thanks for making the trip, eh.

COLONEL: Never knowingly missed a snow day, I'll say that.

KEY: I can rely on you, Colonel.

COLONEL: And the sledge? You likey?

KEY: I likey. How am I not likeying it?

COLONEL: Fixed her up last night, replaced a slat, added the handle, eh.

KEY: You sure did.

COLONEL: Get a bit of grunt up at the top, with the handle.

KEY: It's a beauty, John. I have to hand it to you.

They move up the hill, dragging the rope, the noble feat of engineering purring behind them. On they go, towards the bench.

COLONEL: Started building a bar, you know.

KEY: Pardon me?

COLONEL: You 'eard.

KEY: What bar?

COLONEL: I ain't waiting till 2025 to have a proper pint, I swear. I'm building one. Right in my garden. That's my project.

KEY: A real-life pub!

COLONEL: Fix it up real nice. Big old kegs in there. Barrels, yer know. Old-school pumps, big old bell. What you havin'?

KEY: Ha! Very kind of you, I'll have a Camden Pale, please, good sir.

COLONEL: Ha! See! We are weeks away. I'm measuring up, getting the wood.

KEY: I'm getting the wood thinking about it, believe me.

COLONEL: You'll be getting the wood when you see the sign. Neon. "Cheers".

KEY: You ordered the sign, huh?

COLONEL: Bright red.

KEY: A pub in your garden, man!

COLONEL: Regretting your choice of bubble, wha?

KEY: 'Course. Bleeding boozer in your back garden! Ha!

They laugh. They trudge. They sweat. The Sun kisses the snow. As they near the summit, the jet-black lines of the bench become crisper on the horizon.

COLONEL: Valentine's Day tomorrow.

KEY: Yeah, well.

COLONEL: Well, what ya doing?

KEY: What do you think I'm doing?

COLONEL: I think you're watching Rick and Buddy canoodling on the sofa, that's what. I think you didn't think it through.

KEY: You can still meet people, yer know, one-on-one. So long as there's an element of PE involved.

COLONEL: What's all this? You telling me you got a date?

The Sun flogs the hill and floods Key's eyes. He winces.

KEY: You romancing your good lady, I hope.

COLONEL: Gab's cooking a stew where she's using a skull.

KEY: What the fuck?

COLONEL: There's a skull in the recipe.

KEY: What skull? Animal?

COLONEL: 'Course animal.

KEY: What animal?

COLONEL: *(Grinning)* Who you meeting one-on-one then?

KEY: Who says I'm meeting someone one-on-one?

They march in silence. They're short of breath. The sledge is heavy, the materials are quality. The slats all come from the same white oak tree. The nails are copper.

COLONEL: So?

KEY: What? What "so"?

COLONEL: Where you gonna take her?

They keep plodding, towards the bench. The bench at the top of the hill. Key's bench.

COLONEL: Switch bubs, you can bring her to my pub.

KEY: Finished building it have you?

COLONEL: I will if I've got customers. If there's a booking I'll pull my finger out.

KEY: We're leaning against the bar are we, you all ears, cramping my style.

COLONEL: So there is a date!

KEY: I haven't said there's a date!

COLONEL: I'll keep your tankards topped up, put it that way. If that's what you mean by "cramping your style".

Key smiles at his friend. He gazes up at the bench once more. It appears to glow. Carpet seems to emerge around it, a standard lamp seems to shoot from the earth; cushions, candles, Key's record player spinning next to it. They plod towards it.

COLONEL: It's all go, eh. Pancake Day on Tuesday.

The Colonel's miming tossing 'em. Tossing and catching, jiggling them above the heat; tossing them once more.

COLONEL: Got forty-eight lemons in, me and Gab. We're gearing up. Man, I wish you were coming.

KEY: Don't do this, John. You know I ain't coming.

COLONEL: Bought a new pan, we have. Just the £34.99. Knob of butter in that, nice and hot. Remember last year?

KEY: I long for it. Everything before this I long for.

COLONEL: I guess you're bubbling up on Tuesday, too, huh? Watching on as Rick makes a disgrace of himself at the Zanussi. Scrapes what's left of his cruddy old mixture off the pan, splats it onto your plate, tries to salvage it with Jif Lemon and granulated sugar.

KEY: What's wrong with granulated?

COLONEL: Nah, I wish you well. You had to pick a team.

KEY: It wasn't like that.

COLONEL: That's why I came down here. To say, I wish you well over here. And I'm right by your side this lockdown. I ain't going anywhere.

KEY: You can't.

COLONEL: No one can.

They are at the bench now. They are knackered. But they do not sit. They just catch their breath because they want to go down. They want their ears pinned back. The Colonel slaps the bench with his ski glove. He winks at Key.

COLONEL: Right here. This'll be you. Tomorrow evening. I can imagine it, you know.

KEY: Me too, John. Me too.

The two men smile at one another. The Colonel climbs onto the sledge. Key crouches down, grabs the handle. He rocks back on his heels. Rocks forward, then rocks right back. Then goes. Runs, hard, fast through the snow, ten metres, fifteen, the sledge getting away from him as he leaps in at the final second, and they tuck down and they accelerate down the hill. Away from the bench. Hurtling from heaven.

HERE WE GO ROUND THE MULBERRY BUSH.

9 AM.

THE covids had a meeting.

The lot of them, all crammed into this weird boardroom.

Croissants, lukewarm coffee, some of the covids not wearing ties, some of them guffing, spitting on the floor.

The main covid was working the OHP, showing graphs, sweating hard.

"Well, we're getting there, chaps."

The other covids murmured and scribbled notes.

"But this is not a time for complacency, that I will say."

The main covid turned to the variants now.

"Stellar work, lads."

The variants nodded and blinked and farted.

Some of the other covids turned to the variants and did the "we are not worthy" gesture.

♥

LIVE AT THE BBC.

Snow is falling. More snow. Snow on snow. Six inches of the stuff on the summit of Key's red Norway bobble hat. Below that a thick, crisp snood. Then his salopettes. They're an interesting number, these salopettes. The design is very much "come one, come all" with streaks of electric pink and mad blotches of green and orange. He has a couple of scarves, too. A Zenit St. Petersburg one and kind of a black knitted one. Key's head is cold. But his mind is warm. He is talking to Lauren Laverne. He is on 6 Music. They're chatting away.

LAVERNE: *(The Sunderland accent, like warm honey)* In normal times you'd be in here with me.

KEY: Yeah. Drinking black coffee.

LAVERNE: You brought me a doughnut in one time!

KEY: These ain't normal times, Lauren.

LAVERNE: Certainly aren't, Tim.

KEY: There's the lockdown for a start-off.

LAVERNE: Ha ha! There is! There is. You in your flat then?

He's not.

KEY: Good guess, Lauren!

LAVERNE: Ha!

KEY: Ha ha. *(Sarcastic; euphoric)* Nooooo – I'm out and about, evading lockdown!

LAVERNE: Ha ha!

He is, really.

KEY: Breaking into restaurants –

LAVERNE: Ha ha, Nando's for breakfast, is it?

KEY: Ha ha. Then off to the theatre, actually! Cheeky matinée.

LAVERNE: Ha ha! Les Mis?

KEY: Ha ha! Yeah, then The Mousetrap! Make a day of it!

Lauren Laverne is laughing. Laughing at something Key has said. Key has made Lauren Laverne laugh. His toes heat up.

LAVERNE: Well, I hope you're nice and warm, wherever you are.

KEY: Mm-hm.

Key is outside. He is on Portland Place. He is leaning against a wall opposite The BBC. It's 8.45 AM. Key's lips are blue, dancing to Lauren Laverne's tune.

LAVERNE: I'm toasty in my studio, and I'm in conversation with the brilliant Tim Key about his new book "He Used Thought as a Wife".

"The brilliant Tim Key". Key's lips crack and curl.

KEY: It's nice to talk to you, Lauren.

LAVERNE: Well, I've got to say it's an amazing book.

KEY: *(Choking up)* Huh?

The brilliant Tim Key's head falls forward on hearing Lauren's optimistic vibes sprinkled onto his publication. He smiles up at the windows. She's behind one. Lauren Laverne.

LAVERNE: You okay?

KEY: Just means a lot. No I'm fine, of course. I...

LAVERNE: It's a beaut, I have to say.

KEY: I listen to your show, Lauren.

LAVERNE: Aww.

KEY: Keeps me going. My lockdown soundtrack. Never touch the dial. Glued it down. Bust the radio in the end. It's too quiet now. I have to put my ear right next to it. Sorry. I've interrupted your flow, Lauren! you were saying about the book!

LAVERNE: I'm sure people will read your book, Tim.

KEY: Yeah.

LAVERNE: People read anything these days, just to help each other out, yer know. It's a team effort.

KEY: Yes. Yes it is! We just need to keep going, don't we, Lauren?

LAVERNE: We do. We do. Now, I've got it right here in front of me, your book. It's easy on the eye, I must say. It's like a kind of *objet d'art*.

Nothing back from Key. His voice box beginning to freeze up. Dead air. He rubs his snood, get his cords moving.

LAVERNE: Tim?

KEY: Sorry was that to me or to your flock?

LAVERNE: Flock! Ha! Well, sort of both really.

KEY: It's escapism, Lauren.

LAVERNE: Yuh! Not sure exactly about that.

KEY: For people who want to escape from Lockdown Three back to Lockdown One.

LAVERNE: Ha ha, yeah! Out of the frying pan.

KEY: A change is as good as a rest.

LAVERNE: It's the closest you're going to get to a holiday!

KEY: Without being vaccinated!

Lauren Laverne laughs. The brilliant Tim Key gazes at the building. Good old Auntie. At the heart of everything. Emitting warmth and information to the masses. Never mind the Sun, this is what's keeping lifeforms going. This and food. The brilliant Tim Key raises a mitten, salutes the building. He tries to clench his fist. Tries to get his blood moving round his body. But his hand is locked solid in its salute. Like a seal's hand. Only Lauren Laverne can keep him from freezing solid and snapping in two.

LAVERNE: The design's lush I must say.

KEY: Emily Juniper.

LAVERNE: Oh, yeah?

KEY: She designed it.

LAVERNE: "Emily Juniper".

KEY: She's an avid listener.

LAVERNE: Aw.

KEY: Can you say "hi" to her?

LAVERNE: I certainly can.

KEY: She'd love that, I know she would.

LAVERNE: Hi Emily Juniper –

KEY: I call her Em.

LAVERNE: But also, Emily Juniper, what you've done here is extraordinary. It really is. It wouldn't really matter if the actual content was utter tripe –

KEY: It's not, I don't think.

LAVERNE: Your design's so good, Emily Juniper, this'd still walk into my top ten books, no matter what the words were.

KEY: Top ten. Wow.

LAVERNE: Irrespective of what's going on with the content.

KEY: Content's fine though, no?

LAVERNE: Content's a winner, Tim.

Key smiles and his mouth snaps in half. His teeth begin to chatter. He wants to hug the building. He moves towards it.

KEY: Emily'll b-b-be thrilled you like her d-d-design.

LAVERNE: You sound cold. You should put the heating on!

KEY: I'm a c-c-cold boy.

Key tightens his scarves round his neck. Winds them round and round. His chin is pale blue, his cheeks mauve, his brain now crushed ice. He stamps his feet, stands at the base of the building now. Looking directly up. The building stretching towards the unavailing Sun.

LAVERNE: Will you come back in and see us when all this is over?

Key nods. His teeth are so cold they are sticky.

LAVERNE: Now you've chosen a song for us.

KEY: D-D-Donna S-S-Summer.

LAVERNE: Donna Summer. In the depths of winter. Run yourself a bath then, Tim, I would.

KEY: Thanks, Lauren. Thanks for l-l-letting me t-t-talk about the b-b-book.

LAVERNE: "Love to Love You Baby".

Donna Summer kicks in, moving like a tide over Lauren Laverne's butterscotch burr, sweeping it out to sea. The brilliant Tim Key stretches his arms around the building. Encompasses the whole lot. Moves his cheek onto its bricks. They are warm. Key defrosts instantly. He glows like amber.

BUBBLING UP NICELY.

FRIDAY night!

Big Oliver got his bubbles together for some Heineken and chilli.

They hadn't all met one another and some registered surprise at the extent of Big Oliver's network.

"Some network," Jim Slab said, the pungent mince melting away between his teeth.

"Cheers Jim," Big Oliver said, squeezing his can and swaying his hips to his always enjoyable Hot Chip CD.

"What the fuck is happening here? You're in nigh on twenty bubbles!" Sinead and Eloise looked vexed.

"Cheers," Big Oliver doinked them on their heads with his ladle, his hips still going.

He filled the ladle with meat and wandered round the flat, touching his loyal, twinkling bubs with his elbow.

It was weird seeing them all together like this.

JUNIPER: How many bubbles were you allowed?
KEY: I think one was the idea.
JUNIPER: Oh yeah, that sounds about right. Quint certainly didn't have other bubbles.
KEY: No one else would have taken him.
JUNIPER: Don't even joke about it.
KEY: Do you still hear from him?
JUNIPER: I said don't joke about it, Tim.
KEY: It's hardly a joke, Em.
JUNIPER: It's no laughing matter.
KEY: No, quite right. No more Quint talk.
JUNIPER: Please.

LOVE POTION.

I STOLE 250 ml of vaccine and gave it to my sweetheart.

"Happy Valentine's, dearest."

She chugged it back and we kissed.

I could feel the protective qualities of the sweet, chemical fluids as they surged around our tongues.

Our lips detached.

Her eyes were alive, her body: protected.

"I got you this," she said.

Yes! A Moby CD!

She'd picked up on my hints.

THE OVERLOOK.

Key and the coffee girl are sitting on the bench. The black, cast iron bench. At the very top of Parliament Hill. Night has fallen and the Moon skims off what snow remains. They are silhouettes. Before them: everything. A city on hold. Lit up. London. Its intermittent glow occasionally picks out details on their faces. It is cold, they are warm. Same old story.

KEY: Yoghurt?

COFFEE GIRL: Oh my. You really know how to show a girl a good time.

Key pulls two yoghurts out of his Puma rucksack. He pulls two teaspoons out, too. He goes to doink her on the nose with his teaspoon and she laughs. She really does laugh.

KEY: Bop!

COFFEE GIRL: Ha ha.

He places her yoghurt on the bench. There is a gap between them but it certainly isn't two metres. It's maybe ninety centimetres and, once you take into account the romance and the electricity within this gulf, you could say they are sitting right next to each other. Key gestures at the city with his teaspoon.

KEY: That'd be crawling with lovers most years.

COFFEE GIRL: Such a shame, eh.

KEY: What has become of us?

COFFEE GIRL: Valentine's Day on a bench.

KEY: With the coffee girl.

They stare across the cityscape. No music. No honking limos. No fantastical orchestras. London on ice.

COFFEE GIRL: The whole city, look.

KEY: At our mercy.

COFFEE GIRL: But off limits.

KEY: Not forever.

COFFEE GIRL: No.

KEY: I'll show you a date, when this is all over.

COFFEE GIRL: Is that a threat or a promise?

KEY: Either way, we'll be in that lot. Me and you.

COFFEE GIRL: I'd settle for the pub at this stage.

KEY: Yeah well, you won't have to.

COFFEE GIRL: A pint of knockout juice and a decent jukebox.

KEY: We can do better than that, I'm saying.

Key smiles, tears the foil off his yoghurt. They gaze out across the city. Key holds up his spoon like an artist sizing up his muse with his paintbrush. He closes one eye, lines up the teaspoon with The Shard.

KEY: Ever heard the phrase "rosé champagne in The Shard"?

COFFEE GIRL: Is it?

Key lifts the spoon, gets everything in perfect alignment, and doinks it down on the top of The Shard.

KEY: Bop.

COFFEE GIRL: Bopping The Shard.

KEY: We'll bop the lot, I really do mean that.

COFFEE GIRL: Show me a good time, is it?

KEY: Rosé champagne and olives. Then into Theatreland.

COFFEE GIRL: Now you're talking.

Key moves his hand in the night air, starts tapping his spoon on the distant theatres.

COFFEE GIRL: What are we watching?

KEY: Well, what do you fancy?

COFFEE GIRL: It's up to you!

KEY: This isn't about me.

COFFEE GIRL: Matilda then.

KEY: Has to be.

COFFEE GIRL: I'll get us halftime ice creams.

KEY: Naughty!

COFFEE GIRL: Sometimes you have to be!

KEY: Huh?

The coffee girl's eyes burn with mischief.

KEY: I'll go to the bar, get us craft IPAs.

COFFEE GIRL: What about the queue?

KEY: I've got elbows. Bash my way to the front.

COFFEE GIRL: Matilda!

KEY: Where next?

The coffee girl is laughing, pointing at London. Pointing at the future. Key stretches an arm behind her. Grips the bench, loosely. Five centimetres. But gloved.

KEY: You hungry?

COFFEE GIRL: Chinese, please!

Key bops his teaspoon on the lanterns of Chinatown. Two figures running beneath them. Hand in hand, her spinning round in an emerald frock; him, jubilant, in a dark-pink shirt and navy-blue tank top. Pause. Back on the bench. Key looks to his right.

KEY: Who here fancies a boat ride?

The coffee girl's hand shoots into the sky, almost clipping a star.

COFFEE GIRL: This is a wild night!

KEY: Why wouldn't we go on a boat? I thought I said I was treating you?

COFFEE GIRL: Of course we go on a boat. We're not idiots.

KEY: The date of the century!

COFFEE GIRL: Megadate!

KEY: If you like.

COFFEE GIRL: I do like. Who's bank-rolling all this?

Key taps his breast pocket.

COFFEE GIRL: I'll pick up some more bubbly for the boat then!

KEY: A date without a stop-off at a Sainsbury's Local isn't, in my opinion, a date at all.

COFFEE GIRL: I'm getting fags, 'n' all.

KEY: Well, we're hardly gonna speed down the Thames without a couple of cigs dangling out of our mouths, now are we?

Key's reaching his spoon into the river now. He dips it in and the surging tides of the Thames slosh past it in a fury. The river water flows down the handle and wets Key's Thinsulate glove.

COFFEE GIRL: I've never been on a boat trip. What next?

KEY: Another boozer.

COFFEE GIRL: And what if I'm done with boozers?

KEY: Oh yeah?

Key looks at the coffee girl and then back out into the city. It is a dreamscape. A future.

COFFEE GIRL: Come on, it's getting cold.

Key moves his teaspoon across the city. Bends his elbow, draws it back to NW5. The trees and the buildings evaporate. Everything falls away. Just his flat is visible. He clinks his teaspoon on his living room window.

COFFEE GIRL: Oh, I see.

The coffee girl smiles.

COFFEE GIRL: A nightcap.

KEY: I've got champagne. In the fridge. Won it on Richard Osman's House of Games.

COFFEE GIRL: As long as it's wet and fizzy I don't much care whose show you won it on.

KEY: I have a record player.

COFFEE GIRL: Oh, you do?

They lean forward on their bench. They can hear music. The record spins, The Rolling Stones reach out of the flat and onto the heath. "She's a Rainbow" sweeps up the hill. The two of them gaze out onto the city.

KEY: *(Into the void)* When all this is over.

We are behind them now. In the background: the city; amber, shimmering. And in the foreground: the bench. But on it, there are not two silhouetted figures. There's just one silhouetted figure. And it is Key. His arm is stretched across the back of the bench. We can hear him muttering into the night. He reaches down to his second yoghurt. He momentarily looks for his teaspoon. Then he realises he is holding it. He has been using it to mark through his imaginary date. To his imaginary date.

HERE WE GO ROUND THE MULBERRY BUSH.

A REAL SNOW.

THE snow settled and wiped out the virooze.
They unlocked the boozers.
Chains on the pavements.
Snow on the chains.
The citizens in the pubs.
Lashed off our tits.
Reminiscing about the lockdowns.
Sharing bag upon bag of Quavers.
Zero distance between *anyone*.

Week VII.

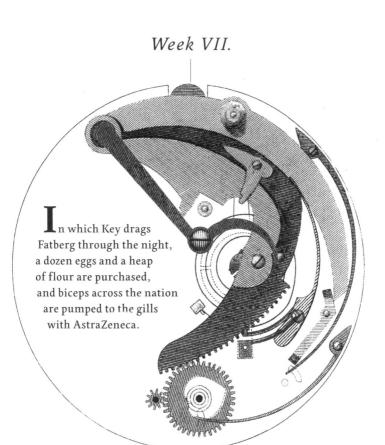

In which Key drags
Fatberg through the night,
a dozen eggs and a heap
of flour are purchased,
and biceps across the nation
are pumped to the gills
with AstraZeneca.

.

A ROYAL BICEP.[†]

"GET your jabs, yer selfish cunts."

No one had really seen The Queen like this before.

She was chewing gum, too.

A few people muttered as they watched.

Fill your own arm up with nonk, Ma'am – don't tell the rest of us we gotta do it!

Others nodded along, though.

They were like: fair play, best place for it, good on the old hen for leading the way.

Most people just couldn't believe she was wearing jeans and shades.

She looked really with it!

---

†**JUNIPER:** Why do you always bring her into it?
KEY: "Always"? I don't, Em. I just think it's nice to give her a run out. Some people like to see her on the page.
JUNIPER: Poor Queenie. I bet she loathes the pandemic.
KEY: I'm sure she's dead against it. She'd never say it but I bet she's privately very anti.
JUNIPER: That's what I mean, she's an advanced version of us, that lady.
KEY: I can't exactly argue with that, Em.
JUNIPER: I wonder what she'll do once she stops being Queen.
KEY: Oh I think she'll die in the job, Em, think that's the idea.
JUNIPER: It's all so sad, isn't it?

MOONWALKING.

Darkness. A Moon. In front of it, a poet in silhouette, bent forward like a beggar man. And behind him, being dragged along by The Poet's fist: a bear. Five foot tall, his paws being pulled through the dew. They move slowly across the skyline. Sometimes they rest, then they move on once more. Key turns, says something to the bear. Then he uses his spare hand to pull his iPhone from his dark-blue Mountain Warehouse anorak. He thumbs a number. A poet, calling into the abyss. Emily Juniper, elsewhere in the abyss, picks up immediately.

JUNIPER: You obviously know it's half past four in the morning.

KEY: You're obviously up.

JUNIPER: I'm obviously trying to organise two hundred and fifty boxes of books.

KEY: Obviously the second edition has arrived.

JUNIPER: We've obviously ordered too many books.

KEY: Oh.

Key shares a look with his bear. They come to a bench by a streetbin, flop onto it. Key sits up straight, stiff as a guardsman, stares across the heath. The bear is momentarily upright. Then he falls forward, bends in half. His ears between his ankles. His snout in the turf.

KEY: You shouldn't be organising boxes at half past four in the morning, Em.

JUNIPER: I've been up since three. I'm like a baker.

KEY: Ha. A baker who's accidentally ordered ten thousand doughnuts.

JUNIPER: At least if I was a baker I could occasionally take a bite out of one of the doughnuts.

KEY: Don't eat the books, Em.

JUNIPER: I'm not going to, Tim. Honestly I'm not.

KEY: Just because we may have printed too many, doesn't mean we should be eating them.

JUNIPER: I'm not going to eat the books.

KEY: We'll shift 'em, Em.

JUNIPER: What were we thinking?

KEY: Waterstones'll come in. They just will. They're obsessed with books down there.

JUNIPER: Hang on, gonna take you the other side of the boxes.

KEY: What?

JUNIPER: *(Whispering)* Quint.

KEY: Quint's there? Quint's with you?

JUNIPER: He's curled up on the rug in front of the fire.

KEY: Make him sound like a dog.

JUNIPER: He's forty-eight, how's he a dog?

KEY: Behaves like a dog, that's all. Bloody Quint.

JUNIPER: A dog who makes cheese.

KEY: Curled up in front of your fire at half past four in the morning.

JUNIPER: *(Even quieter)* He's doing my head in.

KEY: Quint is?

JUNIPER: Why are *you* up?

Key reflects upon this. His tap is broken so he has to turn it on and off with a mole grip. But is that why he is walking a bear at half past four in the morning? He doesn't think so.

KEY: I'm still going from the day before, Em.

JUNIPER: Walking.

KEY: My Fitbit's saying I've done too many steps.

JUNIPER: It's half past four in the morning, Tim.

KEY: Need to walk backwards. Get rid of some.

JUNIPER: This is madness, Tim. Why are we both up?

KEY: Well, you because of the boxes thing and me... general... you know. I don't know, Em.

JUNIPER: I'm having a bad bit of lock-down, Tim.

KEY: Em, I've just walked in circles for seventeen hours with a bear.

JUNIPER: I want to go to Greenwich.

Key nods, he lifts his bear up, gives him a look. Sit up straight, Fatberg.

KEY: Greenwich?

JUNIPER: I don't wanna be surrounded by boxes any more, not in lockdown.

KEY: They'll be out of your hair soon, Em. Just need WHSmith to –

JUNIPER: I wanna see the clocks.

KEY: You don't half like a clock, these days, Em.

JUNIPER: I'd love it there, I know I would.

KEY: You'd have the time of your life in Greenwich.

JUNIPER: Ha. I would actually. I've got all these sketches. All these bits of time. You know. Just... nowhere to put them.

She sighs. Key can picture her perfectly. Emily Juniper, stood there in her glasses. Her dungarees streaked in charcoal. Surrounded by boxes. Thinking about time.

JUNIPER: Oh, it doesn't matter. Who cares? I just wish...

KEY: What?

JUNIPER: *(Hopeful)* You writing?

KEY: I'm surviving.

JUNIPER: Staying afloat.

KEY: Just want it done, Em. I wanna escape.

JUNIPER: I know.

KEY: Like Andy Dufresne.

JUNIPER: What's Andy Dufresne?

KEY: You know, when he's walking across the beach, walking towards Red.

JUNIPER: Oh, Shawshank Redemption.

KEY: I wanna be free, Em. Walking towards my pal.

JUNIPER: I cry when I watch that.

KEY: Two old pals, through the worst of it. Hug it out, Andy Dufresne creaming himself about Red's boat.

JUNIPER: They say The Maestro's going to do a roadmap next week.

"Roadmap". What even is a "roadmap"? Key and Fatberg shake their heads.

JUNIPER: He never goes home, Quint. Trying to freeze him out of Pancake Day.

KEY: You can't do that, Em. You must at least give him Shrove.

JUNIPER: He's given me a whole list of toppings he wants.

KEY: That's the thing with me, Em: I add value. I helped shave Rick's hair off the other night.

JUNIPER: What's he shaving his bonce for?

KEY: Oh, I dunno. But I was shearing up the sides like a madman.

JUNIPER: How'd we end up with Quint?

KEY: Ha! Should be me!

JUNIPER: Can you imagine! You in our bubble?

KEY: *(Firmly)* Yes.

JUNIPER: Try telling me we wouldn't have made another book if we'd been in a bubble together.

KEY: I'd never try and tell you that, Em.

JUNIPER: You pounding it out with the orange pen, me plonking it on Fabriano –

KEY: Fabri...?

JUNIPER: That's the paper we use, Tim. Wake up.

KEY: Well. I'm in the capital. Bubbled up with Rick and Buddy.

JUNIPER: And we've got Quint.

KEY: And his cheese.

JUNIPER: Next lockdown. Me and you. I swear. Cooped up, making literature.

Key mimes taking the lid off an orange pen. Mimes writing in the sky. "Week One".

JUNIPER: Well. I'd better see if Quint wants some water.

KEY: Quint's a leech.

JUNIPER: They may be saying that about you.

KEY: Ha. I hope not.

JUNIPER: Bye, Tim.

KEY: Bye, Em. We'll shift 'em, Em. The books.

JUNIPER: I know. There's a lot, Tim. Bye, then.

Key hangs up. He remains upright for a moment. Then his head becomes heavy and takes him forward. And he folds in half. And now his ears are between his ankles. And his snout is in the turf. Next to Key's skull, in the frigid mud: the orange pen. Barely covered, its lid glistening. Fatberg looks down and folds his arms.

HERE WE GO ROUND THE MULBERRY BUSH.

TWO LARGE EGGS.

BOHNSON was wearing a divvy old chef's hat that covered about two thirds of his grubby old fringe.

He whacked his frying pan with his egg slice and spoke slowly into the camera.

"Listen up, folks. No one is cancelling Pancake Day. Neh-uh. Not happening. Not on my watch!"

Half a dozen Jif Lemons leapt about on his lectern as Bohnson became more animated.

"I for one am having some lads from work over, and I suggest you do the same."

Matt Boytwitch grabbed The Moneyman's knee and smiled.

"You want me to put a figure on it?" Bohnson let his question hang in the air.

He lifted his crop top up by a couple of inches and slapped his belly with his egg slice.

"Thirty," he winked and licked his lips and chin.

He was drooling hard now.

"Thirty pancakes for I!"

He mimed tossing and the journalists blushed.

PANCAKE DAY.

The bubble floats down the street, the Sun shining off it. Three bodies inside it. Anoraks and snoods, shades and bobble hats. As it moves past William Hill's – closed, and Gail's café – open for takeaway, it elicits jealous glances from those walking in ones and twos along the pavement. Rick is swinging a Tesco bag and Buddy is dancing. Key, in a daze, is swept along by it, the inner film of the sphere occasionally tapping his arse and pushing him forward.

RICK: We start savoury.

BUDDY: Just a bit –

RICK: Savoury, savoury, savoury; crank open some Hofmeisters, live like kings. Then – when we can't do any more – we tap the coffee, turn up the heat and we go sweet.

KEY: And do I have a say in all this?

RICK: You can have as much say as you like, but that's how things gonna be.

BUDDY: Well, there you go! The master has spoken!

KEY: Tosser-in-chief!

BUDDY: Ha! Yeah, head tosser!

RICK: I'm wearing a chef's hat, believe me. That's going on. Get my Ramsay on, yell at the pair of you!

BUDDY: We're your *sous chefs*, now? Charming!

RICK: Get me my fucking eggs!

KEY: Well, I'm taking a pass on the savouries, cheers.

RICK: Then you're mad.

KEY: Wait for them to go sweet, then I'm in.

BUDDY: What's the sense in buying proper ham –

RICK: Not to mention the brie –

BUDDY: And brie! Exactly! And you're sitting out the savouries???

KEY: Wake me up when the Jif Lemon starts squirting, that's all.

RICK: Suit yourself, I'm tossing ten before we switch to sweet, I swear.

BUDDY: He will 'n' all.

KEY: I'll nurse my Hoff, cheers. Wait for the good times.

RICK: Whoop whoop whoop!!!

Rick bounces up and the top of the bubble bulges.

RICK: *Ich liebe* Pancake Day!

BUDDY: We all do, Rick.

KEY: Exactly, mad if you don't. Pancake Day in the bub! Did anyone order a perfect evening???

They link arms, and the jealous glances intensify. Key's iPhone goes. His niece. He drops back, the bubble freeing him, closing behind him. A perfect orb, shimmering once more.

KEY: Niece!

MAGGIE: Uncle Timmy!

KEY: I want a word with you!

MAGGIE: Well, I want a word with you!

KEY: What the hell do you want for your birthday, sweet niece?

MAGGIE: Ha ha!

KEY: Forty-pound budget, but as we both know that's just a guideline.

MAGGIE: It's a starting point!

KEY: What do you get an eleven-year-old trapped in the clutches of a pandemic that doesn't know when to say "enough is enough".

MAGGIE: A dress from Next, thank you. My sister'll be in touch with the link.

KEY: Leaving nothing to chance.

MAGGIE: Smashes the budget.

KEY: What are budgets for?

MAGGIE: Ha ha.

Key tickles a cashpoint with his stick. The note dispenser curls into a smile.

MAGGIE: And, and... Uncle Timmy?

KEY: Yars, Maggeth?

MAGGIE: Well, the thing is can you come to our house on my birthday?

KEY: I'm there, Mag, believe me. Set your watch by me.

MAGGIE: No, I know, I know, I know. But the thing is, I mean can you actually come inside? As in not just your gate stuff, you know.

KEY: Huh?

Key looks ahead. The bubble, shimmering. His friends inside. Buddy dancing. Rick juggling Jif Lemons.

MAGGIE: Uncle Timmy?

KEY: You see, sweet Maggins, this ain't... I mean –

MAGGIE: Because if you come inside we can have cake and play Names In The Hat like before.

KEY: Mag –

MAGGIE: We can make videos!

KEY: I work with Steve Coogan, babe. Doubt I need to make vids with my niece.

MAGGIE: But... I mean... Daddy'll get some weird beer in specially!

KEY: Magpie, I'm in my bubble –

MAGGIE: No, no, I know. The thing is –

KEY: I can't get out of the bubble, can I?

MAGGIE: Bubbles are easy to break out from. Uncle Timmy!

The light's too good. A burnt orange, sprayed across the street, bouncing off of windscreens, splattering the flats above the health food shops – open, and the charity shops – closed. Caressing the tree trunks and streetbins.

MAGGIE: Daddy said if you have a gap you can switch bubbles, that's all.

KEY: Oh, he did, huh?

MAGGIE: So if there's a gap you can make the switch! That's my thinking. The government says it's okay.

KEY: Yeah. Think that's maybe right.

MAGGIE: See!

KEY: But once I'm in a bubble... I... that is...

MAGGIE: So when did you last go inside their house? And then we can work it out.

KEY: Erm... Friday night.

MAGGIE: Okay, okay. So last time with them: Friday night –

KEY: We got lashed and watched Dead Man's Shoes –

MAGGIE: Okay, so that makes Saturday day one. So we need ten days. So Saturday, Sunday, Monday, Tuesday. So that's already four days. That's today.

KEY: So I can't come today.

MAGGIE: I know, annoying, we're having pancakes, could have been

good. But anyway, it's the 25th that's the main thing.

KEY: Always.

MAGGIE: So Wednesday, Thursday, Friday, Saturday, Sunday, Monday, Tuesday, Wednesday, Thursday. So hang on. That's Saturday to Saturday, so that's seven and then Sunday – eight – Monday – nine –

KEY: Any joy with getting into those schools in the end?

MAGGIE: Tuesday – ten. So my birthday's on Wednesday! So it works! It works, Uncle Timmy! *(Off)* Dad, it works! It works!

Key moves in a trance behind the bubble. Behind Pancake Day. Behind the flour and the milk, the eggs and the music, the lard and the laughs, the warmth, the citric drizzle, the ring pulls, the sofas, the songs, the joy.

MAGGIE: All you need to do is not go in their house again and it works!

KEY: You know I can lean on the gatepost, Maggeral.

MAGGIE: But that's the whole point, which you don't seem to be getting. You don't need to lean on the post! You can walk right on in!

Key nods.

MAGGIE: Your new bubble! The best bubble! Starring your favourite niece: Maggie Key!!! I'm going to tell Dad!

KEY: I'll bring your dress, either way.

MAGGIE: Bye, Uncle Timmy. Stop saying "either way"! Byeee.

The iPhone is dead, gone, in his pocket. Key's feet are heavy, slow. He needs to catch up to the bubble, in the bubble he can float. The bubble can propel him.

BUDDY: *(Shouting)* Hey! Bublé! Are you part of this bubble or nay?!

Buddy has her hand pushed through the gossamer-thin sheen of the bubble; gunk dripping off her wrists. The bubble shimmers more as Key approaches. He can see his reflection in its curve. Because the curve is not in his favour he looks portly, concerned.

†**JUNIPER:** He didn't cancel Pancake Day, did he?
KEY: I guess the point I'm making here is it would have been bloody typical.
JUNIPER: Quint came over –
KEY: Oh he did, huh?
JUNIPER: Had his own ideas.
KEY: I thought we weren't talking about Quint.
JUNIPER: Kept on insisting on thick mixture.
KEY: Thick mixture?
JUNIPER: Sneaking more and more flour in when we weren't looking.
KEY: Christ.
JUNIPER: It wouldn't pour, Tim.
KEY: Your mixture wouldn't pour?
JUNIPER: And Quint laughing. Squeezing lemons directly into the sugar bowl, making a weird paste thing.
KEY: Deary, deary me.

TOSSPOT.[†]

"**P**ANCAKE Day's off, folks."

Bohnson looked fucking miserable.

His crop top was damp with tears; it was obvious the big man had just taken a bollocking.

"It's because... well, it's because... Slappo –"

The slaphead bunged a slide up with the tolls.

Bohnson was reading from his teleprompter, his voice breaking, flour on his cheek.

"If you've got way too much batter in, I can only apologise."

He had a Jif Lemon in one of his fists and occasionally he'd move it towards his mouth.

"I was daft thinking Pancake Day would be any good, should have known that'd end up being gash, too."

He squeezed the lemon and the citric jet fell short of his rubbery old lips, splashing onto his mic and making it sizzle.

IT'S IN THE BLOOD.

A brighter day. The sky is Barclays Bank blue, and Key gushes onto the heath once more. On Key's head, a new hat. The Norwegian bobble has departed; now a mustard-yellow cap is stuffed on his bonce. Across the front, five black letters: Y-O-U-N-G. The grass is a deeper green now, replenished by the rain, honoured by the Sun. And Key moves with pace, deeper, deeper into the verdant expanse. Other people mill about. It is more... populous than before. Microscopic families. A young lad with a wooden sword and no one to fight. Key's walking trousers begin to rattle. He pulls out an iPhone. Mother.

KEY: Mother!

CAROL: Well, we're done!

KEY: You are?

CAROL: All jabbed up.

KEY: They rammed it in, huh?

CAROL: Gallons of it. Jabbed up to the nines!

KEY: Quite right, too.

BILL: *(From off)* I'm invincible, Son!

CAROL: He keeps saying that.

KEY: Grain of truth in it, probably. All went off okay, did it?

CAROL: Oh, you should see it up there, Tim. It's so well organised. Everyone with their arms, and these lovely little nurses squirting gunk into them.

KEY: Where d'ya go for it, Ma?

CAROL: Up at the sports centre.

KEY: Ha!

BILL: *(Off)* Oooooh yaaaa!

CAROL: Basketball hoop at each end. Everyone lined up. Lambs to the slaughter!

KEY: World's gone mad. Jabs down the gym now.

CAROL: We were saying they should bung a ball in there, let people shoot some hoops while they wait.

KEY: I suppose they're focusing on the needle. Getting it into the arms.

CAROL: Your father was talking to all sorts of doctors, trying to get a game going.

KEY: The important thing is you've got your "I've been jabbed" badges –

CAROL: I mean people were already in

singlets, Tim. Bung 'em a ball! Sport does wonders for people's morale.

Key is staring at the football goals. They are shackled to one another on the halfway line. A depressing embrace in the centre circle. Key wills the goals to crack apart. For a game to form in the space between them. Tuesday football! Comedians charging about in their little shorts. But the goals stay in their bonds. The young lad is whacking the posts with his toy sword. Key waves his stick vaguely in the air.

CAROL: Now you must get yours. Have they been in touch?

KEY: I mean... not... no, they haven't.

CAROL: They've done fifteen million, now. They're whipping through it. You're vulnerable, they'd love to pop a shot into you, I bet.

BILL: *(Off)* Ooooooh yaaaaa! Yer bugger!!!

KEY: What's up with him?

CAROL: Side effects, little pain in the upper arm, that's all.

BILL: *(Off; slapping his bicep)* Ooh yaaaa! Down boy!

CAROL: It's no use walloping it, Bill. You'll only thicken it up. Just keep it still.

BILL: *(Off; whacking his arm against a grandfather clock)* I wanna get back on the horse, man!

KEY: Still riding his horse, huh?

CAROL: Thinks he's Vladimir bloody Putin, Tim.

KEY: He's going tops off, is he?

CAROL: Seventy-five and he's riding a bloody horse round the village.

KEY: What's it called?

CAROL: I don't bloody know. Daft old thing, stupid long head, massive eyes.

KEY: Well, that's just its face, Ma. It's a horse.

CAROL: He's bought this ruddy great saddle off of eBay.

KEY: Oh.

CAROL: Pink saddle, it is. Pink as your bottom.

The child with the sword has spotted Key. He holds his weapon up like Mel Gibson himself. Key holds his up, too. Chal-

lenge accepted. The lad smashes his sword against the post again. Clonk.

CAROL: Honestly, Tim. Why can't he just quietly lock down and wait for it to, you know, fizzle out?

KEY: Is he happy?

CAROL: Can't wipe the smile off his face.

KEY: Well, that's something, I suppose.

CAROL: Oh! We got your email! Saoirse Ronan!

KEY: Yes!

CAROL: You're gonna be a star! Finally!

KEY: *(Stamping his feet)* Didn't I tell ya, Ma?! Didn't I always say? "Hollywood'll come calling!" Didn't I always tell ya that?!

CAROL: Atonement! Brooklyn! Little Women!

KEY: Yes! That Saoirse Ronan.

CAROL: "Saoirse", isn't it?

KEY: Huh?

CAROL: You said "Saoirse". I hope you iron that out before you meet her.

KEY: I'm sure they'll send someone round. These productions are swimming with money. They'll have a dialect coach for that type of thing.

CAROL: To help you say the name of the lead?

KEY: Great news though, Ma, ain't it! Covid test next week.

CAROL: Yuk.

KEY: I need to be safe for Saoirse.

CAROL: "Saoirse".

In Key's peripheral vision: a sword. The boy, from nowhere: charging. Key gets his stick up just in time. And now he is in combat with the young lad; parrying haymakers, wooden chips flying off his stick; Key coming back now, feinting to strike the lad's right flank and then driving his stick down, obliterating the lad's puny sword, splitting his own. The kid runs off, back to his parents, tears flooding down his spaceman costume. Key slings what's left of his stick onto the ground. His nose crinkles in dismay.

KEY: My stick!

CAROL: Tut, Bill! Leave your bloody bicep alone, I swear!

BILL: *(Off, pained)* Disperse! Disperse, dammit!

CAROL: Stop whacking it! Let it do its thing. We want it to be right for Saturday.

KEY: What's Saturday?

CAROL: Pardon me? What's Saturday? It's the funeral, Tim. Keep up.

BILL: *(Off, pained)* Captain Tom, you moron.

KEY: Quite right.

CAROL: They're ringing church bells across the country. Out of sheer respect for the man. A hundred dongs.

KEY: I'd say that's the minimum.

BILL: *(Off, in agony)* A hundred seconds, for us all to reflect upon the great man's life.

CAROL: A communal pause, to contemplate.

KEY: I'm on it, Ma. No bigger fan of the good Captain than I.

CAROL: You stop what you're doing. Put your beer cans down. It's not much to ask. Thirty-two point eight million, the guy raised.

KEY: The man was a saint, Ma.

CAROL: What have you ever done?

KEY: Huh?

CAROL: The least we can do is pull the handbrake on for a couple of minutes.

KEY: If they did *a thousand* dongs for the guy I'm not batting an eyelid.

CAROL: You're a good boy.

KEY: Puff my chest out, shut my eyes, think of the money.

More garbage in Key's peripheral. Some parents are moving towards him. Behind them, the Spaceman, a mess of tears, his sword in bits. Key moves down the hill. As they speed up, so he speeds up, too. He heads vaguely towards the ponds.

KEY: Love you, Ma. Speak soon.

CAROL: Bye-bye, then, Son. Lots of love.

Key is now running. Running hard towards the ponds. The adults trample his buggered stick as they pursue him.

HERE'S LOOKING AT YOU, KID.[†]

A NEW variant.

This one spread through eye contact.

This was all the beleaguered United Kingdom needed.

Grubby little covids swimming through gazes, diving into irises.

The government compulsorised eye masks with immediate effect.

You were allowed to take them off to sleep, drive and flirt.

But otherwise you were stuffed up the arnuzzi.

Some companies printed designs with horses' eyes or Union Jacks or parrots.

Other companies opted for plain eye masks in bold, single colours.

[†]**JUNIPER:** Quint came back one time –
KEY: Quint again.
JUNIPER: I know, I know. But he came back one time with a full facemask made out of cling film.
KEY: For someone who doesn't want to talk about Quint –
JUNIPER: I know, I know.
KEY: Let's order two more Bulmers and have a break from the poems, eh.
JUNIPER: Okay, I might hit the pear one.
KEY: Cling film though?
JUNIPER: With holes pierced through with a biro for his mouth and nostrils.
KEY: Quint.
JUNIPER: Sitting there in Stu's chair, this cling film rustling. You could hear it from the kitchen, Tim.
KEY: "It".
JUNIPER: Yeah. "It". Quint. "It".

EN SUITE WITH COMPLIMENTARY TOILETRIES.

Now you had to quarantine for one night before you went up the shops.

I packed my duffel bag and got an Über to the Jurys Inn, Euston.

I got a good night's sleep and in the morning I breakfasted heartily, then walked up to Tesco's to pick up the parsnips.

Another Über and home.

I boiled and minced the 'snips.

Fuck! No butter!

I made another reservation at the Jurys Inn and scooped the dry, beige mash into a Tupperware container; popped it in the fridge.

I packed my duffel bag again and sat on it.

I watched my animated Über as it clunked towards my apartment.

WALKING FRANK.

Key is walking Frank Skinner. Two men: two different generations. Key, still stuffed in his dark-blue Mountain Warehouse anorak, his mustard-yellow cap on his bonce; his stick absent, his legs unsteady. Frank is bedecked in a Japanese longcoat that's skimming his shins. He's wearing a thick cap, too. In his early sixties, he wants to retain all the heat he can. They move through the heath. There's definitely more life on it now. It's... nice.

FRANK: I'm just not sure you can tell someone they're name-checked in your book when they're not.

KEY: And I'm saying you are, Frank. You're name-checked.

FRANK: I've gone through it, I'm not in.

A jogger, pounds through, salutes Frank as he goes past. Frank smiles.

KEY: And I'm saying you're in. You're in, Frank.

FRANK: Well, I didn't see it.

Key's eyes are suddenly drawn beyond his mentor. He sees the policeman, right across in the distance there, his badge flashing like a diamond. Key waves. The policeman raises his coffee cup. He's what, two hundred metres away this guy, but the acrid stink of mocha hits Key's nostrils like a sledgehammer.

KEY: I don't know what to say, Frank, you're name-checked.

FRANK: Well, what am I doing in it?

KEY: Have you read it?

FRANK: I'll read it once I find myself in it, that's what I'm saying.

They split either side of the footpath, let a lady with a pram go through. The lady smiles and mouths "huge fan" at Frank. The baby gawps and gurgles "Skinner".

KEY: Look, Frank, if you just read the thing you'll find the ref as you go.

FRANK: Just tell me the page number.

KEY: It's your own name, Frank, you'll spot it. Read the book.

A couple spot Frank and wave, he waves back. One of them shouts "Hey Frank". Key waves back and shouts his own name over to them. They say "Hey Frank" some more and "where's David?" and "Fantasy Foot-

ball League". Frank nods and waves like the Queen Mum.

KEY: That ever piss you off?

FRANK: That? No, they're my people.

KEY: In your grill the whole time.

FRANK: I'd be worried if they stopped, put it that way.

Key processes this. He continues to process it for about three hundred metres. More people greet Frank. He is much loved and sometimes bows when they coo at him.

KEY: Well, anyway, thanks for mentioning it on your radio show. The book, I mean.

FRANK: Oh, I'll mention anything on that thing.

KEY: Even so.

FRANK: Any old crap, I've gotta fill three hours.

KEY: Well, it meant a lot.

FRANK: I once talked for half an hour about some weird exhibition about prisms.

KEY: What prisms?

FRANK: Hadn't seen the exhibition, me. Why do I wanna waste my time walking amongst prisms?

KEY: I mean, it seemed like you were more interested in the design than the words, but anyway. Right, what are we doing here?

They are at the foot of Parliament Hill. Key stares up towards its summit. His facial expression implies it's one of the great peaks. A Blencathra. A Mont Blanc. Frank begins the ascent. His size sevens tapping evenly on the path.

FRANK: Come on, ya pussy. Let's just get it done.

KEY: You can cope?

FRANK: The fuck is that supposed to mean?

KEY: Well, I dunno, do I? I've never done this with anyone much older than... yer know.

FRANK: My girlfriend makes me drink a weird green drink in the mornings.

KEY: Oh.

FRANK: I'm effectively mid-forties.

KEY: Ah. Welcome to my world.

Key's iPhone rings. It's Emily Juniper. Key pulls off a Thinsulate glove, looks across at Frank.

FRANK: Busy boy.

KEY: I gotta get it.

FRANK: The world hasn't stopped. Take the call.

KEY: It's Emily Juniper.

FRANK: That girl's a genius.

KEY: You kept saying on your show.

FRANK: And quite right, too. Where'd'ya find her? That girl knows how to place text, I'll say that. Say hi from me, will ya?

Key slides the ball across. Connects with his designer.

JUNIPER: Boxes hacked open, up to my tits in books, perched on the top on my laptop. Are the orders coming in?

A distant ping.

JUNIPER: Yes.

Key closes his eyes. Imagines postmen the world over, pushing books through letter boxes, the thud of the paperback on the mat, the adults tearing through the cardboard, diving onto sofas, chowing down custard creams, sating themselves on Key's words. Key opens his eyes. Frank's looking across at him, his features sharp, interested.

JUNIPER: Are they coming in frequently enough?

Silence. No ping.

KEY: I'm just walking Frank Skinner, Em.

JUNIPER: I love Frank Skinner.

FRANK: Tell her she's a genius, Tim.

KEY: I'll call you back, Em.

JUNIPER: Tell Frank I love him, Tim.

Ping.

KEY: Another sale?

JUNIPER: Quint. Putting his dinner order in.

KEY: Speak later, Em.

Key puts his iPhone back in his pocket, peels

his Thinsulate glove back over his knuckles. The two men walk at Frank's pace.

FRANK: What do you mean "walking" me. You're walking with me, surely.

KEY: She's got an open fire, that girl.

FRANK: "Walking Frank Skinner". Makes me sound like I'm a dog.

KEY: No, I know. I know that, Frank.

The men are almost at the summit. Frank is a bit ahead now. Key can hear his calves as they stretch and grab, propelling the great man to the peak. He stops at the cairn and is overwhelmed by well-wishers. Delighted to have run into him, baying at a respectful distance. Key watches. Fire runs through his hamstrings. He harnesses the flames, completes the ascent.

FRANK: What kept ya?

The crowd roars. Key gets his breath. Then he addresses Frank's people.

KEY: I'm Tim Key!

FRANK: You got any bananas in that bag of yours?

Key ignores Frank, piles into the throng.

KEY: I'm off the fucking telly! Let's be having you. I've appeared along-side Alan Partridge! I used to be a live act! I've met Anne Hathaway! Who wants some?!

Frank bows his head. Key marauds into the people, catches a member of the public, wrenches their scooter from them, starts trying to sign it with a Sharpie he has on him. The member of the public escapes and the crowd disperses, tending one another with Dettol and distance. Silence. Key and Frank at the cairn.

FRANK: You gotta keep it together, lad.

KEY: You're so graceful with them, Frank.

FRANK: You gotta keep it together though.

Key nods. He opens his bag, hauls out the 'nanas. They sit and peel and load up with potassium; consider the urban stasis beneath them.

HERE WE GO ROUND THE MULBERRY BUSH.

DEEPER.[†]

EGGY asked his wife three thousand questions.

He wanted to find out more about her.

He loved her too much.

With each answer he loved her more.

As he scored lines through his questions, he could feel his heart swell.

He could barely hold his clipboard.

Every one of her answers made his body convulse with affection for this beautiful, beautiful woman.

[†]**JUNIPER:** Why's this one in?
KEY: Dunno.
JUNIPER: Padding?
KEY: Guess so.
JUNIPER: It's got nothing to do with anything.
KEY: Well, I mean it's got something to do with this chap, Eggy, I suppose.
JUNIPER: I guess.
KEY: And his missus.
JUNIPER: Oh yeah, I can see that.

†**JUNIPER:** Ha ha. Is that Daniel?
KEY: Yuh.
JUNIPER: Ha ha. From the conversations.
KEY: The same.
JUNIPER: And The Colonel.
KEY: 'Tis indeed.
JUNIPER: Funny seeing 'em in a poem.
KEY: They're good men, Em, them two.
JUNIPER: And Gracie! Who's Gracie then?
KEY: Made up.

GOING ABOUT MY DAY.[†]

[barcode]

I MET Isy and Daniel for brunch and then me and Daniel went and played five-a-side down at Elmers End.

The Colonel was there, too, and he and I grabbed a beer in a BrewDog on our way home.

I had a shower and then went and met Gracie Winch for dinner.

We decided on a whim to go to the cinema and it's then, while I'm watching this James McAvoy thing, I remember the pandemic!

"Fuck."

Gracie looks at me and I whisper the oversight into her ear.

"Oh bollocks." She'd clean forgotten, too.

We downed our popcorn and shuffled out sheepishly.

As we left I mouthed to the projectionist that the bloody pando's still raging and he needs to press stop and get the fuck home.

Once on the street I took a deep breath and I swear didn't exhale until I was sat in front of Newsnight.

Listening to the soothing interrogations of Maitlis, I began going through my diary, scoring thick red lines through the glorious plans I'd inked in for the week, while my guard was down.

"Come on, man," I muttered, crossing out Zumba.

"Discipline, bro."

ON POND SQUARE.

Key is sat on Pond Square, in the cool, thin air of Highgate Village. There are people on the square. Too many people. Loose. Key squints through them and past them, squints at the pub. Squints at the Prince of Wales. He smiles, remembers the good times he's had in its innards. His eyes narrow. The Sun bounces off the white-washed walls and Key squints through them, too. He watches shots racing down throats, pints being poured into hand-bags, fags chain-smoked in the gardens, staff having quiet words. Key continues to squint, imagines the silken pong of the Thai food, snaking out of the locks. He watches himself being flung out of the door, stum-bling across the square, splatting into an Über, speeding down the hill.

POLICEMAN: One of your old haunts, eh?

KEY: Ha! PC Gourd, as I live and breathe.

The rozzer's arrived. His nose is redder than ever. His chinstrap can barely contain his face; the features look sore.

KEY: *(Gesturing to the boozer)* Must be a way round this.

POLICEMAN: *(Cross-eyed, tongue out, salivating in its direction)* Mm. I wish.

KEY: Bet you lot have got one you all go to. The fuzz, like.

POLICEMAN: Secret boozer, typa thing?

KEY: Ah ha! So now it comes out.

POLICEMAN: Naw, we don't have a secret boozer. I wish we did. Not a bad idea that.

KEY: Mm.

POLICEMAN: They're as much closed for us as they are for you, I'm afraid.

KEY: *(Winking heavily)* Except... are they?

POLICEMAN: What?

KEY: Well, what if a policeman were to "go rogue"? What if he were to accidentally on purpose find himself inside one of these places? What if he were to breach the doors on a certain premise, trouble the pumps?

POLICEMAN: "Trouble the pumps".

They stare across at the boozer. The Sun beats down. The shackles glint. PC Gourd's face glistens in the midday Sun.

KEY: Well? Are you thinking what I'm thinking?

POLICEMAN: I'm thinking I'd be slung on the scrapheap without any pension if I forced the locks on that tavern.

KEY: Exactly! Force the locks! That's what I'm talking about. Let's do it!

The copper is drooling onto his brass buttons. He, too, knew of a life before this. He, too, remembers belting out the Welsh national anthem; slamming down tankards; quiz machines; dancing; dust-ups. He scoops a tear from his eye, flicks it onto the slabs. Licks his thick old lips, blinks at the boozer.

KEY: I could keep watch, yer know. You could jimmy it with your wrench.

POLICEMAN: What wrench?

The two men stand, their tongues resting in the dust at their feet. Key notices the police-man has a drink in his fist. Steam emanat-ing. A hot one.

KEY: Got yourself a little coffee, is it?

POLICEMAN: Aye, Sir. A mocha.

KEY: *(Nodding. Looking away)* It's a mocha, huh.

POLICEMAN: From the heath.

KEY: The heath?

POLICEMAN: Yeah, the – I don't know what you'd call it – the coffee...

KEY: Wagon?

POLICEMAN: Was gonna say cart, but yeah. Thanks for the recommen-dation. Can't get enough of it.

KEY: *(Muttering)* Down on the heath there.

Key's head rocks back and he looks up at the sky. It is full of marshmallows in soft, luxuriant shades. He turns to PC Gourd. His moustache is damp and glistening. His eyes bright.

POLICEMAN: The girl at the wagon, by the way. Coo-eeeee! She –

KEY: What we gonna do about this little lot, anyway?

Key wafts his arms across the square. There's a big group of maybe eight by the vast oak next to the bogs. They have a disposable barbecue and one twerp in particular is getting huge with a diabolo.

KEY: I mean, shouldn't you be dispersing that sort of thing, I thought.

POLICEMAN: Oh, right. Well, I mean, I'm policing by consent.

KEY: What the fuck does that mean?

POLICEMAN: Means I asked them if they fancy moving along and they've said they're happy to stay, for now.

KEY: Policing by jizz more like.

The group of eight are marking out hopscotch. Some drink wine, others wear bandanas or smoke rollies. Their leader wears a technicolour dream anorak. He is wetting himself as he marks out the squares in the dust with his stupid little clogs. A topless fella stretches his hamstrings, ready to hop.

KEY: You gotta move this shit on. Clamp down, man.

POLICEMAN: Well, hang on one second, a minute ago you're asking me to break us into the pub, drain their barrels.

KEY: That's what I'm saying. Make your mind up, that's all. Which side of the law you on?

POLICEMAN: I'm on the side where I drink my mocha then maybe try and move those two old biddies on over there.

KEY: Nah, you gotta swing your bat at the big groups. Hurl a couple of these guys into next week. Tops off, look! I'm trying to flatten the curve over here. These guys are pulling my plonker.

POLICEMAN: I don't like it, that's all. Having to go up and confront the cool crowd in my divvy helmet.

KEY: Group of eight, that. Barely a cigarette paper between them. Diabolo!

POLICEMAN: Diabolo's no good?

KEY: I'm pretty sure the nerds would go mad if they knew the hippies had dug out their diabolos.

POLICEMAN: I gotta say, I've lost track to a certain extent.

KEY: You need to be on top of this shit, Gourd!

POLICEMAN: *(Staring down at his bollocks)* I'm a briefing behind.

The cool cats are playing a new game now. They are stretching the technicolour dream anorak to breaking point, about ten of them; pulling it taut. And the jacket's owner is bouncing at its very centre, flying high into the air, somersaulting and landing back down in the pliant heart of their makeshift trampoline.

POLICEMAN: *(Frowning at the chaos)* I'd rather stop here for a mo, sip my mocha.

He lowers himself onto a bench. Key stares at the mocha. Stares at PC Gourd's ruddy fingers, his thick thumbs.

KEY: You talk to the coffee girl, huh?

POLICEMAN: Florence?

Key nods. "Florence". He starts to walk away.

POLICEMAN: Hey, what's happening here. Let's have a little drinkie on the bench, can't we? I'll confront these guys in a sec, I swear. Just wouldn't mind enjoying my mocha first, that's all. Hey!

But Key has gone. Key is stung. His shadow is jet black and small under the midday Sun, he must leave Highgate Village now. He looks up once more into the marshmallow sky. A bright red diabolo plummets past his nose and lands in the dust. Key boots it as hard as he can, sends it crashing against the roof of the Prince of Wales. It clatters against the tiles and bounces back down, resting by his Gazelles once more. He can hear hippies screaming at him as he takes aim again. This time he clears the roof. He cups an ear, hears it bouncing in the direction of Jacksons Lane.

HERE WE GO ROUND THE MULBERRY BUSH.

ROUND AND ROUND.

ANOTHER walk.
The same loop.
Eyes closed.
No longer necessary.
Sometimes opening one a tiny
bit to see where I'm going.

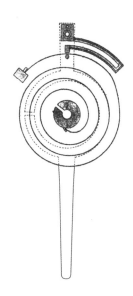

Week VIII.

In which a giant pugil probes a poet's tonsils, a niece clambers into a birthday frock, and a roadmap is unveiled.

HERE WE GO ROUND THE MULBERRY BUSH.

STUCK.

THEY tried to lift the lockdown, but it wouldn't budge.

They'd had it on for so long it was stuck fast.

People were drafted in from other sectors to help the engineers, but no, it wasn't shifting.

The government started changing their messaging.

Huge posters appeared with the phrase "this is us now" alongside images of the great leader shrugging.

People accepted it.

They made placards saying "Okey-dokey".

They marched about philosophically in their lounges.

THE COVID TEST.

Drizzle. 11.55 AM. A car park. Usually used by the gym – closed, the pizza place – takeaway only, and the office complex – God knows. The occasional zephyr whizzes through, troubling a puddle, rattling a streetbin. It is dark, the sky is filled out with thick, grey clouds. Key is moistening next to a Daihatsu. He's wearing his House of Games bathrobe, grey tracksuit bottoms and carpet slippers, which draw the rainwater up into his feet, soaking his metatarsals. The driver's door opens, a lady steps out.

TRISH: Tim?

KEY: Hulloo, hulloo!

TRISH: Tim Key?

KEY: The same.

TRISH: I'm Trish. Covid test?

Her cheeks are red, her glasses vast. A spear of sunlight catches them and a rainbow fills the car park, then it disappears, overtaken by the gloom.

TRISH: Daft all this, eh?

KEY: Fucking bleak.

TRISH: Sweary!

KEY: No, I mean. Mad. Doing it in a car park.

TRISH: I couldn't park right outside your flat, that was the only thing. Ha! Slippers!

KEY: It was a two-minute walk, no worries. I'm always nipping out in 'em.

TRISH: Well, it's mercifully quick this. I'm a dab hand now.

KEY: Swabber to the stars!

TRISH: Indeed I am.

She gloves up and pulls a six-inch long sachet from her coolbag.

TRISH: Indeed I am.

She rips the top off the sachet, reveals the end of a swab. Key squints. She begins to pull the swab from the sachet. It comes and it comes. Like a magic trick. It's a foot long minimum and keeps coming.

TRISH: So who do you play for?

KEY: Huh?

TRISH: As in I do Chelsea and Totten-ham, but I don't follow football, not really. Don't know whose throat I'm going down half the time.

KEY: Oh... well...

TRISH: Oh, and I do some actors, too. Are you an actor?

KEY: Erm... well...

The swab's out now. Eighteen inches and glistening as it collects water from the late-February air. Trish is holding it in a fist, like it's a rounders bat or a sickle. Key nods proudly.

KEY: Chelsea.

TRISH: Oh, you're a Chelsea player. Lovely.

KEY: Yes. Yes I play for Chelsea.

TRISH: Oh, I did Harry Kane! He's one I did know. Obviously I knew Harry Kane.

KEY: England captain. Spurs, Kane is.

TRISH: Fantastic lad. Very brave. Let me go right in with the swab, did Kane.

KEY: Oh, he did, huh?

TRISH: I was scraping the top of his lung by the end of it. Ever so brave. And the Korean fella.

KEY: Son, I bet.

TRISH: He was lovely. Biting the swab out of my hand, was Son. Now then. Bop bop bop.

She taps Key on the head with the swab and his mouth flips open. She stands on her tiptoes and Key relaxes his knees, bobs down a foot or so. The rain is getting a little heavier.

TRISH: So... ha ha.

She scratches her nose with the swab, laughing.

KEY: What?

TRISH: Well, I dunno if this makes sense as a question. What position are you?

KEY: Oh, that makes sense, for sure!

TRISH: I know nothing! I remember in some World Cup or other I cheered when what's he called, looks like Shrek – well, anyway, everyone was smash-faced, this is twenty years ago, and he had to go in the bin or something and I'm cheering. Anyway, the point being I did it wrong and my kids hated it!

KEY: Maybe that's Rooney getting sent off.

TRISH: God, I wish I'd had you there – I could have shouted that out!

KEY: Ha!

TRISH: So, yeah, what position are you for Chelsea?

KEY: Um I play... well, I'm a midfielder.

TRISH: Nice. Bit of everything.

Key nods. The shaft of the swab clicks against his teeth.

TRISH: Helping out whoever's struggling type of thing. How old are you?

KEY: Forty-four.

TRISH: Is it? Right, just need to skim some crap off your tonsils and we're golden.

She forces the swab further into the depths. It touches the tonsil. A bell tolls.

TRISH: Oh.

Another bell. And another. Seven, eight, nine.

TRISH: Oh. Oh I see. It's for Captain Tom. We'll hold on.

KEY: Ng.

She pauses her work. The swab deep inside Key's airways. The bells continue to toll. Key tries to speak once or twice. Forty-five, forty-six... For The Captain. The fallen hero.

TRISH: It'd take most people a hundred lifetimes to achieve what that man did in the last year of his life. I swear to God. Sorry, shut up, Trish. Respect the bells.

Seventy-eight, seventy-nine. The swab pushing into the tonsil like a wren's beak trying to get inside a plum.

TRISH: Think we're almost there.

There is a peace around the nation. Key's eyes are watering. He glances past the

nurse, to a patch of grass by a parked moped. A daffodil has emerged and gleams in a ray of sunlight. Ninety-nine, a hundred.

KEY: D'ya get it?

Trish pulls out the swab, examines it.

TRISH: Oh yeah, more than enough. Now I just need to go up your nose and I think we've cracked this.

She goes hard at Key's hooter, then snaps the swab. Shoves it in a small plastic canister from the cool-bag.

TRISH: There. Not so bad, huh?

Key wipes his nose like a bear who's just had a run-in with some bees and isn't sure if he's been stung yet. Trish zips up her cool-bag, wanders back to the Daihatsu.

TRISH: Off to do Sam Rockwell now, if you can believe that. The Hollywood actor, woo-hoo.

KEY: Glamorous old life, huh.

It continues to piss down.

TRISH: Who have you got this weekend?

KEY: Huh?

TRISH: Who are you playing?

KEY: Oh right. Um... Crystal Palace.

TRISH: Ooch.

KEY: Ha, yeah. Should be alright.

TRISH: Zaha playing?

KEY: Huh?

TRISH: Is Zaha playing?

KEY: Dunno. Um... I think.

TRISH: Makes a difference if Zaha plays. Might be helping out your right-back if Zaha's on the wing.

Key nods. Trish is in the car now. The window winding down. The engine starting.

TRISH: You'll get a text, letting you know if you're clear. Keep your shin pads on ice till Wednesday, I would. Adios!

Key navigates the puddles as he walks after the Daihatsu. The indicator is warped by the rain. A flashing blob of orange. Key is blinking, too. His eyes are watering.

SCUTTLING.

I WHIPPED away my Shreddies box and sure enough: there he was.

A bloody covid.

Loathsome, skinny.

Fucking gross, to be fair.

"Finally," I said, laying down my magnifying glass.

"Who the hell are you?" he hissed.

I picked him up by the neck.

He had about fifty legs.

"Who the hell am I? I'm a fucking human, that's what."

He smiled.

"Big wow."

I squeezed him and his smile seemed to widen.

SHIMMERING.

I WENT round to my bubble, banged on their door.

"We're having a night in, I'm afraid."

I picked up a dustbin lid, smashed it against their car.

"I'm in your fucking bubble!"

They looked tired, she was wearing two towels.

"It can't be every night, that's all."

I pulled the paperwork from my briefcase.

"Oh can't it???" I said, waving the small print in their faces.

"Next Saturday, we'll have you in. We'll have another film night."

I whacked the dustbin lid against their car some more.

"I demand to be invited into this fucking bubble!"

The car alarm was wailing, the rain was piling down, the bubble was looking thick, impenetrable.

WATER RATS.

Blue skies: cloudless. Key's in his mustard-yellow "Young" cap, walking along the canal. Towards Warwick Avenue this time. Where it all began. The towpath is more populous than before. Thickening up with Londoners. Braving the plague, jostling for position, elbows sharp, eyes small. "Meet up with someone from another household providing it is exercise". Pah. Sometimes Key is knocked towards the canal. Sometimes Key's Gazelles clip the fat metal mooring rings. Occasionally Key yells. The iPhone. A clarion call. His erstwhile designer inside it. Click.

KEY: Emily Juniper!

JUNIPER: Why have people stopped buying the book?

Key changes lane, hugs the wall. His right hip scraping along the ancient brickwork, his left hip buffeted by surge upon surge of his compatriots. Locked-down humans flowing east and west in the sunshine.

KEY: How many boxes we got?

JUNIPER: I'm staring at my website. No ping! No ping!

KEY: This is madness. It's a lockdown, Em! Why aren't they reading? *(To the gushing hoards)* Hey! Why aren't you reading?! Go back to your houses and read!!!

Key reaches back into his Puma rucksack, pulls out books, hurls them into the torrents of people.

KEY: Read, Goddamn you!

JUNIPER: Maybe it's all done, huh? Ordered too many, take it on the chin. Phone round some pulpers.

KEY: Nothing from Waterstones?

JUNIPER: Maybe people don't want to read about a lockdown when they're in a lockdown?

KEY: Maybe I don't give much of a flying fuck what they want to read, Em?

JUNIPER: Maybe we need new ideas, we gotta shift units!

KEY: Maybe this is what I've written and they'll just have to read what they're given.

JUNIPER: These people don't wanna look back, that's the problem.

KEY: Well, maybe they should. That was a proper lockdown, Lockdown

One. Everyone towing the party line. These people don't know they're born.

JUNIPER: Maybe they're reading other stuff.

KEY: Well, good luck to 'em, that's all I can say. How many boxes we got?

JUNIPER: I'm not with them. I had to get out. They were depressing the hell out of me. I can't see the carpet for the boxes.

KEY: The wood for the trees.

JUNIPER: I've come to draw.

KEY: Oh yeah.

JUNIPER: Set up with my charcoals here, in the square.

KEY: Depicting a clock, is it?

JUNIPER: There's a lot of people here. They're eating ice creams.

KEY: It's loose, Em. They know something we don't.

Emily Juniper's clock starts striking twelve. Key is boshed towards the bank. He bares his teeth at a teenager.

JUNIPER: Quint's reading it.

KEY: I beg your pudding.

JUNIPER: Quint's reading your book.

KEY: Quint?

JUNIPER: Takes it into the garden, smokes and reads, yer know.

KEY: Quint?

JUNIPER: Can't move for him this end.

KEY: Fag on the go, flicking through it, huh? Guess we take what we're given. A reader's a reader.

JUNIPER: I wish you'd write another one.

KEY: For Quint?

JUNIPER: For me. I loved designing your book, last lockdown.

KEY: You've got your clocks now, Em.

JUNIPER: Feels like a waste of a lockdown, that's all.

Key's eyes are wet to the core. He blinks.

KEY: I loved writing that book, Em.

JUNIPER: It was an anchor. Kept me from floating away, that's what.

KEY: Scribbling in the evenings. Fuck off, man!

Key gets a push in the side, bends over at the hip like a rubber man; his ear nicks the surface of the canal. He springs back up, swings his fists.

JUNIPER: Hello? Tim.

KEY: It was a source of great comfort.

JUNIPER: I love imagining you scribbling away in your divvy little pad. Pint of beer in attendance.

KEY: And a fig roll.

JUNIPER: Oh, please let's do it again.

KEY: I'm not writing poetry without fig rolls, Em, I swear.

JUNIPER: I'll get a consignment delivered. On my honour, I will.

KEY: There's not a poet on the globe who's getting shit done without fig rolls, Em.

JUNIPER: Seamus Heaney?

KEY: That a poet?

JUNIPER: Yeah. He's lush.

KEY: Then yeah, I think he's chowing back fig rolls, I really do.

JUNIPER: Washing 'em down his throat with beer.

KEY: I wouldn't blame him, Em. Ink and drink.

JUNIPER: Lockdown One. You can't stay angry with it.

KEY: It's done now, Em. These days I just read it.

JUNIPER: Oh, so do I. In the evenings.

KEY: Lock my door, unlock my drinks cabinet. One movement.

JUNIPER: I touched up the gin and peppermints last night, I must say.

KEY: You see.

JUNIPER: Lit the fire, popped my readers on.

KEY: Good Lord, Em. If we're finding time to read it why can't these jizzhounds?

Key is walking now on a thin sliver at the edge of the canal. One foot in front of the other, like Nadia Comăneci herself, fiddling about on her beam.

KEY: And Quint?

JUNIPER: Quint what?

KEY: He enjoying the book?

JUNIPER: He says he is. Keeps saying

the guy who wrote it's mad.

KEY: *(Spitting into his iPhone)* Charming.

JUNIPER: Purrs over the design.

Key leaps away from the hordes; leaps onto a buoy out on the water. He steadies himself, his Gazelles slipping about on the thick orange plastic.

KEY: *(Yelling at the hordes)* Hey guys! Guys!

JUNIPER: Tim?

KEY: Guys! I'm la la, apparently. Don't take my word for it though. Man called Quint says so! Extra extra!

JUNIPER: You did go cuckoo in that lockdown, Tim, by your own admission.

KEY: *(Bawling now)* Read all about it!

JUNIPER: Who are you shouting that to?

KEY: *(His voice splintering)* Poet goes la la in first lockdown! Extra! Extra! Keeping it together in this one though! Aaggh!!!

Blackness. Time passes. Key is now dressed in his red tracksuit. He is walking on the heath again. The Sun is low in the sky. Key's hair is still wet. He picks up.

JUNIPER: Finally! Where the hell did you go? You were screaming!

KEY: Nowhere, it's all good.

JUNIPER: Did you fall in the canal?

KEY: No I didn't "fall in the canal".

JUNIPER: Were you pushed in?

KEY: I'm dry now, Em.

JUNIPER: Oh, Tim! You need to look after yourself.

KEY: No one fell in any canal, Em. Believe me.

JUNIPER: I'll let you know about Waterstones. You look after yourself.

KEY: This is no kind of lockdown, Em.

JUNIPER: Not if you're falling in canals, it isn't, Tim.

KEY: "Canals"? One canal, Em. Week eight. One canal.

The Sun dips. As it gets closer, Key can feel his hair crisping up very nicely indeed, thank you. His Gazelles continue to leave wet footprints on the footpath.

†**JUNIPER:** June seemed such a long way away then.
KEY: Wrote this in Feb. So... four months.
JUNIPER: Feels like a lifetime.
KEY: I remember thinking, we ain't getting out of this.
JUNIPER: Oh, don't.
KEY: Stood with my hands on my hips in the middle of the street.
JUNIPER: I know.
KEY: Spinning slowly round.
JUNIPER: Yup.
KEY: Just quietly going, "This feels permanently fuckerooed."
JUNIPER: There's always hope.
KEY: Easy to say that when you've got down the mountain.
JUNIPER: Yeah.
KEY: When you're lost at the top of Helvellyn and Pete Moore's brother's holding the map upside down and the weather's come in, it's hard to envisage the warm pint of bitter in the youth hostel.
JUNIPER: Oh, okay.
KEY: You get my point?
JUNIPER: I don't know who those people are but yeah, I think so.

THE FUTURE.[†]

"**S**LIDE me up, Scotty!" Bohnson stood behind his lectern.

His humour: unshakable; the last bit of his lunch: still in his fist.

A spod threw up a slide; Bohnson waggled his lips at it.

"We'll be getting out of this mess in..." Bohnson heaved some air into his lungs.

His tennis shorts were glistening with sweat.

"... June!!!"

Bob Piston ITV was like a rat up a drainpipe, pointing at the slide.

"It says 2025!"

"Yeah but," Bohnson grinned so wide his ears began to bruise, "June though."

He poked at the word "June" – which was very big – with his chicken drumstick.

2025 was written very small underneath.

"June 2025's four years away, Captain."

Bob Piston ITV was like a dog with a bone.

Bohnson dabbed at "June" again.

"Bulmers in a pub garden anyone? A day at the cricket? Don't mind if I do!"

Rivulets of sweat poured down Bohnson's shins, collecting on his tennis shoes.

"Dear old June," he went on.

He was almost inaudible now and he was cuddling his lectern like it was a loyal Great Dane.

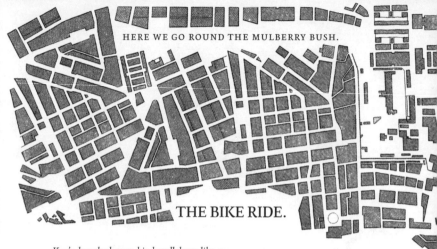

HERE WE GO ROUND THE MULBERRY BUSH.

THE BIKE RIDE.

Key's hunched over his handlebars like a young Laurent Fignon, cycling into the wind and the rain. His iPhone gaffered to his wrist, his route barely visible amongst the blobs of water, which build and build and then are whisked into the air by the miserable gusts of wind, and away. Through the tides on his screen he can barely discern the blue dot edging deeper and deeper into town. In his ear: The PM. He who must be obeyed. Outlining his roadmap. Presenting his route out. Swinging his arms towards an exit. An exit from all of it. The PM in the dry, strapped to his lectern. Key in the elements. Rain pouring off his chin, his eyes floating in a cm of UK rainwater, his buttocks glistening. His head down. Hunched. Like a young Laurent Fignon.

...THANKS TO THE VACCINATIONS THERE IS LIGHT AHEAD...

Key's thighs, slender, nimble. Thumping up and down like pistons. The blue dot quivering in the wash. Key peering through his eyelashes. Squinting at the signs. Lost in Soho, looking for Waterloo.

...WE CANNOT PERSIST INDEFINITELY WITH RESTRICTIONS THAT HAVE SEPARATED FAMILIES AND LOVED ONES FOR TOO LONG...

Water sloshing across Key's helmet, Key's eyes gawping through the cascade. Berwick Street. D'Arblay. Wardour, Brewer, back onto Berwick. The chain, squeaking, moaning as Key turns the cogs. Like a young Laurent Fignon. The PM in his ears. The roadmap being outlined.

...THREATENED THE LIVELIHOODS OF MILLIONS, KEPT PUPILS OUT OF SCHOOL...

The rear wheel sliding on the asphalt. Water flinging itself at his ankles. Water from every direction. His front wheel blowing into shop facades, his nose blowing into signposts, flying down side streets. Key ringing his bell, like Laurent Fignon himself. The PM in his ears. Key spills

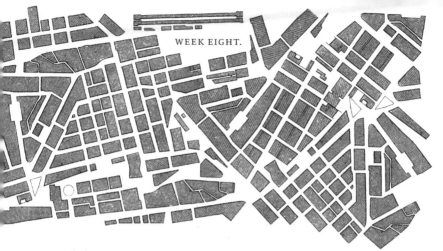

out onto Shaftesbury Avenue. The Curzon cinema – closed. Chinatown – a ghost town. Fopp Records – closed, chained, a relic. Right at the lights. Wrong turn. Onto the pavement. Water gushing through his veins. South, South.

...LEADING US TO A SPRING AND A SUMMER...

Key, head right down, teeth gripping the handlebars, feet stomping the pedals down again and again and again. Trafalgar Square inching towards him, Nelson clicking his fingers to the incessant tune of The PM's speech. The rain easing. The rain easing.

...LOOKING AND FEELING INCOMPARABLY BETTER FOR US AND FROM WHICH WE WILL NOT GO BACK...

Now on the Strand. The theatres. Closed. Chained. The actors motionless on the stage; frozen; set in aspic, preserved for later use. And now, the rain easing. The

locks loosening. Key opening his eyes, Key knocking half a pint of rain off his lashes, Key shaking his torso like a post-pond Alsatian. He moves into top gear. Ten mph. Approaching the lights. The Lion King on his left. A stiff arm out to his right. Onto Waterloo Bridge.

...THE END REALLY IS IN SIGHT...

And, as Key moves over the river, the clouds break above the city. And the Sun smashes into it. And The Shard throws its rejuvenating qualities down the river. And it is no longer raining and Key's wheels are beginning to dry, and the clouds part and Key's snood dries to a crisp and he pulls it down below his throat, and he lifts his hands from his handlebars and he stretches his frame in the warmth. And he is cycling no-hands now, like a young Laurent Fignon, celebrating a famous victory on La Plagne. And Key's lips curl with hope. And the blue dot is big and distinct. And he puts the hammer down. And he pedals to his niece's.

COVERT OPS.

THE variant got a little cute.

Mutated itself, did a pretty good impersonation of the vaccine itself!

It was laughing into its sleeve as it snuck its way into syringes.

Every time the doctor said, "Okay, here comes the vaccine then," the variant shut the fuck up, hid behind doc's wrist, held its despicable breath.

This lowlife imposter bubbled and gurgled, waited to be pumped straight into these poor old blighters' veins.

Once inside, no particular plan, just typical variant mayhem.

GEOFF.

ONCE you were vaccinated you got a cape.
Folk with these capes could do anything.
Go down the boozer, pile into the ballet,
hug other cape-wearers on the street.

If you didn't have a cape you were
basically a no-mark; a jizzhound.

Some people knitted their own capes.

But the authorities spotted these folks
easy enough.

Their capes were woollen and rough
rather than the sheer, red, government-issued
capes of the brave folks who'd had the elixir
plunged deep into their quivering wings.

A CAGED BIRD.

Key is leaning on the gate of a serious house on a pleasant street. In front of him: an ice-cold bottle of continental lager, resting on the top of the gatepost. The Sun shines onto the green glass. Condensation runs down its flank. Key's bicycle helmet is clipped onto the lock of the gate. On the other side of the gate, in the front garden, a niece. Strutting about in her new dress, the front door open behind her. She is beaming from ear to ear.

KEY: I've said it before, and I'll say it again. That is one helluva frock.

MAGGIE: Thanks, Uncle Tim.

KEY: Too easy, your big sis set the whole thing up. Just click on the link, jam my card details into Next's website and here we all are.

MAGGIE: My first frock.

KEY: Well, there you go.

MAGGIE: It's really annoying I can't wear it anywhere.

This dress is a beaut alright. Yellow and green, with great slices of watermelon all over it. She's glugging apple juice from a carton. Eleven years old already.

KEY: Eleven years old, huh!

MAGGIE: Oh oh, and I got Playmobil and I got a weird book about acting and I got earrings with teddy bears on them.

KEY: Ha! Not a bad yield, as they say.

She twirls again, spinning and spinning until she's dizzy. Key pretends to be the assembled fashion photographers, snapping away with his imaginary camera. Through the door we hear laughter. Maggie moves closer to the gatepost. Key takes a step back. As if he's being approached by a cow.

MAGGIE: What are my family doing, do we think?

KEY: They'll be getting your cake ready.

MAGGIE: Oh!

She puts her hand over her mouth and her eyes light up like Catherine wheels.

MAGGIE: Is that why they went quiet and were all winking?

KEY: When a family starts whispering like that: it's cake time.

MAGGIE: They said I didn't have a cake, because of lockdown.

KEY: Yeah, that's a cover-up. They're jamming the candles in as we speak.

MAGGIE: I hope it's red velvet, do you know that one?

KEY: Do I know red velvet?

MAGGIE: Yeah.

KEY: Yeah. I know all the cakes, believe me.

MAGGIE: Tut.

Maggie's suddenly deflated. The melons suddenly appear dull, lifeless. The eyes, brown, regulation.

KEY: What's up?

MAGGIE: Why can't you come in, Uncle Tim?

KEY: Do you want me to read out the regs, Niece?

MAGGIE: But –

KEY: You know the drill, I'm in a bub, gotta stay on the gatepost.

MAGGIE: Tut. What's the difference? If you come in we can all play Names In The Hat again! Like a proper birthday.

KEY: I know. But that shit don't fly, not in Lockdown Three.

Maggie is deflated. Some watermelons drop from her frock, splat on the floor.

MAGGIE: Well, what did you do on your eleventh birthday?

KEY: Ah, now you're talking.

It is Key's eyes that have ignition now. He slurps from his Peroni, stretches his arms in the heat.

KEY: We went up the woods, Niece. All piled into Volvos, drove out to Harlton Woods. My old man –

MAGGIE: Big Grandpa!

KEY: – built a roaring fire and we toasted dampers on it –

MAGGIE: What are –

KEY: Then into a clearing and Big Grandpa hammering cricket stumps into the turf for a couple of hours of rounders. He'd got a policeman's truncheon, God knows where from, and that was the bat.

MAGGIE: Two hours of rounders!

KEY: The Sun kissing the bases! Then into the Volvos and back into town. Parking up and wandering arm-in-arm down to the cinema. Police Academy Four, Citizens on Patrol. Faces stuffed with pick 'n' mix, pissing ourselves at these bloody recruits! Ha!

Continental lager gushes down Key's throat. He's in the cinema now. Stuffed between Hammers and Bacon, cigarette smoke diffusing in the beam of the movie being thrown from the projector to the screen.

MAGGIE: Have you been vaccinated, Uncle Tim?

Key looks at his niece. She shrugs.

KEY: Soon. It's coming. I can sense it.

MAGGIE: They should have special cinemas for everyone who's vaccinated. Then at least some people would see some movies.

KEY: You're not an idiot, Maglight.

MAGGIE: Then tell everyone all about them.

KEY: I'll be your eyes and ears, Niece. If I get some gunk in my arms.

MAGGIE: I can't even go round to Abi's.

KEY: Never heard of her.

MAGGIE: You're allowed to walk around on your own at least.

KEY: Like a madman, yeah. Never stops. The loops.

MAGGIE: Why can't you come through!

KEY: Soon, Niece, soon.

MAGGIE: We've got a badminton net up!

KEY: You have?

Key squints through the front door, past the silhouettes, plunging candles into sponge, through the kitchen window. The bright white tape of a badminton net flashes in the sunshine. Key frowns. Oh, to "go through". It's too much.

KEY: I'd destroy you, darling. It'd be a humiliation.

MAGGIE: Dad lets me win.

KEY: Am I Dad?

MAGGIE: No, I'll get good by the time you can come through.

KEY: Your best won't be good enough. I'll run rings around you, hun.

MAGGIE: We'll see.

KEY: You'll wish I'd never come through.

Maggie smiles. She's good at sport. It'd be tight.

MAGGIE: I mean, look at us. It's like you're at the zoo, visiting a camel.

KEY: Ha. Yeah, that's nice.

MAGGIE: It's not funny!

They are laughing. The situation, ludicrous. A badminton net fifteen metres away, and they can't play. An eleven-year-old niece muddling through a birthday and you can't even hug the poor sod.

KEY: It's not long now, Maggo.

MAGGIE: The problem is, when you think about it, it's ten percent of my life.

KEY: Yeah, so far. That'll go down.

MAGGIE: Oh, yeah.

They nod at one another. It won't last forever. There is a roadmap. There will be a future.

MAGGIE: Maybe we should go and see Matilda, when it's over?

KEY: Yes. We should. That's what we'll do.

MAGGIE: And I can wear my new dress!

KEY: If you haven't grown out of it.

MAGGIE: Huh?

And now the rambunctious strains of Happy Birthday rise up from inside.

KEY: Yes, Niece, you wear the dress. I'll bang on a suit. A night at the theatre!

MAGGIE: Yes!

They cheers. Peroni and apple juice. Together at last. And a red velvet cake emerges into the sunshine. Eleven candles burn as the Sun continues its descent, and behind the cake: a family. Full of love, singing tunelessly but together. And it is nice to hear the song in its full glory. Not just as a muttered accompaniment to bloody hand washing.

†**JUNIPER:** Oh, right, gotcha. You're saying it was arbitrary, what they loosened and when.

KEY: I am, Em. And I'm saying it with poetry.

JUNIPER: As per. So you're saying they picked stuff at random, like it's all out of a giant hat?

KEY: I don't know about a hat.

JUNIPER: I'd have chosen specific things, I think, if I'd been in the old war rooms.

KEY: What would your priorities have been then?

JUNIPER: Me?

KEY: Sure. You're leaning on the bar with The Maestro –

JUNIPER: Gawd help me –

KEY: What would you have brought back first?

JUNIPER: Well I like a flutter, me.

KEY: Get the bookies open?

JUNIPER: Fiver on some nag, cheer her on, you know.

KEY: So bookies before schools, for you?

JUNIPER: Oh yeah, schools. Forgot about schools.

KEY: Schools have to be a part of the conversation.

JUNIPER: Bugger me, tricky innit? When you stop to think about it.

A ROADMAP FOR A BETTER FUTURE.[†]

BOHNSON pulled a shitty little deck of playing cards out of his tennis shorts.

"How's your luck, chaps?"

He shuffled the cards, fanned them out.

The broadcast journalists watched on from their screens.

"Roight, may I have a volunteer?"

Matt Boytwitch leapt up from his little stool.

He prodded three cards and scampered back to his seat giggling and bowing.

Bohnson read from the first card, a three of hearts augmented with a Sharpie.

"Schools."

A spod whacked up a slide, with a graphic of some stuff going a bit wrong in a physics lesson.

"Ha! Old-school!" Bohnson pointed at the next card, "Haircuts!"

He ruffled his notorious mop and mimed cutting it and shooting himself in the head.

He took the final card.

"Saunas," he shrugged at the gallery, some grunts of approval, a slide of some old fat guys sweating their nads off.

Bohnson licked his lips, slotted the cards back into their pack and waddled away, his hips rocking as they receded into the darkness.

A NEW CURRICULUM.

North London. A park. A table tennis table. On one side, the side nearest us, Key. Stuffed inside his red tracksuit, he pushes the ball over the wooden net with his Stiga Royal 5-Star. Again and again he chips it over. And again and again it comes back, more firmly, crisper. Across the table: Younguzi. Lean, athletic, 38. His hair is short, his wrists thick. The more Key dabs the ball over the net, the more it comes back. They talk as they play.

KEY: You gotta help me out, bro.

YOUNGUZI: Yeah, you know I would if I could.

Key's shots are sullen, flat. They sit up, present themselves to Younguzi as a gift. Younguzi plays within himself. He can open his shoulders any time he likes, destroy The Poet. But for now: doink. Suit jacket buttoned up. Patting and talking.

KEY: Come on, bro, you're killing me here.

YOUNGUZI: We haven't got the budget.

KEY: Yeah, I get it. Schools have budgets.

YOUNGUZI: They do.

KEY: Gotta stick to the budget.

YOUNGUZI: Hands are tied.

KEY: You're the head, man.

YOUNGUZI: I'm sorry, bro.

KEY: School's gotta have books, Len.

In the middle of the table, on Younguzi's side, lying by the wooden net, is Key's book: "He Used Thought as a Wife". Its cover, a perfect blue, reflecting the light. Winking in the afternoon. It's Younguzi's copy. Well-thumbed.

KEY: You're killing these kids, bro. What they reading?

YOUNGUZI: Ah, you know –

KEY: Just take three hundred, man. What's it matter? You give me three grand we say no more about it. What they reading?

YOUNGUZI: Ah, you know. Steinbeck.

KEY: Okay.

YOUNGUZI: Shakespeare.

KEY: Lucky them.

YOUNGUZI: We can't just –

KEY: I know your school, bro. I've been there. That's what you forget.

YOUNGUZI: We can't just buy books, there are –

KEY: Don't tell me: "protocols". I know your school. You ain't proto-colly. No, Sir.

YOUNGUZI: We've carved our own path.

KEY: You've got a farm, man!

YOUNGUZI: Yeah. Yeah, we do.

KEY: Farm ain't standard issue. There's no school like yours, I'll admit it. What other school brings the goats in?

YOUNGUZI: We're proud of what we do.

Younguzi curves his back, his joints harmonise, his tendons secure them in place, his arm cracks like a whip, the ball speeds off the bat, kisses the table and disappears into the distance. Key collects it, jogs back, leans on the table. Beads of sweat glimmer on his knuckles.

KEY: So buck the trend, bro. Burn the bard, there's a new poet in town.

YOUNGUZI: We're not burning Shakespeare.

KEY: Nor should you. I don't wanna barge him out the way. Not my style, never has been. Just try my book on 'em, that's all.

YOUNGUZI: Yeah... yeah.

KEY: A minute ago you're texting me saying you love the book.

YOUNGUZI: It's a great book.

KEY: Yeah, but not "great" enough to put it on your syllabus, apparently.

YOUNGUZI: It's a brilliant account of a man falling –

KEY: Of Lockdown One, yes.

YOUNGUZI: You did do a great job. Really.

KEY: So let's get their snouts in it, man!

Key's holding the table tennis ball. He is perspiring heavily and his sweat is soaking into the paper-thin sphere. A pond is forming inside; sweat falling into it in steady drips from its ceiling.

KEY: Well, how is it up there?

YOUNGUZI: School?

KEY: You hanging on in there?

YOUNGUZI: Toughest year of my life, next question.

KEY: When d'ya get your kids back?

YOUNGUZI: I'm hearing March.

KEY: You're a leader, Lenny, that's the truth of it.

YOUNGUZI: Went for a long walk last week.

KEY: Big wow, I'm always walking.

YOUNGUZI: Needed to clear my head, eh.

KEY: Oh, aye.

YOUNGUZI: Found a bin, up near the fire station. Needed a moment. Sat on this bin, you know.

KEY: That's a new one.

YOUNGUZI: Ate six cherry Bakewells.

KEY: Right, on the bin, there.

YOUNGUZI: It's a lot of responsibility, being the head, you know.

KEY: You wear it well.

Younguzi is impressive. His face is serious, but he's unbowed. The book on the table. The Sun in the sky. He's enjoying his downtime is the truth of it.

YOUNGUZI: Rick said you've been drinking a lotta mochas, trying to get in with the —

KEY: Maybe you take one-fifty.

YOUNGUZI: Ha.

KEY: We see how you go with those, they work out, we do a couple of dozen more.

YOUNGUZI: Look, are we playing table tennis or not?

KEY: We're talking. That's what. Table tennis is a smoke screen, you know that as well as anyone.

Younguzi leans over, picks the book up, opens it. He smiles as he lands on different pages, different moments in the book. He looks up at Key. Then down at the book. Two men. Two different places in the lockdown. Leaning on the same concrete table tennis table. Key bites his top lip. Tastes a sale. Younguzi reads out loud.

YOUNGUZI: "Moggeth continues to tease the cat's penis absent-mindedly".

Key nods. It sounds good, having a big-hitter in the education sector read his lyrics.

KEY: You have to remember it's a political text, also.

YOUNGUZI: We have modules on New Labour.

KEY: I bet you do.

YOUNGUZI: Just this is...

KEY: What?

YOUNGUZI: "Yolk ran in rivulets amongst the deep wrinkles of his nutsack".

KEY: You're deliberately picking bits that –

YOUNGUZI: Difficult to ask a teacher to guide teenagers through a text like this.

KEY: Do we do things because they're easy?

Younguzi shakes his head. He smiles as he folds a corner of the book, slides it up to the wooden net. Key bounces the ball a couple of times and sweat sprays out of it onto the table.

KEY: Play to serve?

Key removes his headband, reassigns it as a flannel, deletes the puddle.

YOUNGUZI: We're playing a game?

KEY: While you think about what you wanna do.

Serve. Return. Both players starting slow. Cagy. The table tennis ball is weightless. Seemingly it floats on thermals. Their bats wave as it moves to and fro. The clouds race across the sky.

YOUNGUZI: Ha. Yeah. Yeah, I'll have a think, bro.

With his left hand, Younguzi is unbuttoning his suit jacket. His eyes narrow. He'll take the win here.

†**JUNIPER:** Crab says he'll never have a vaccine passport.
KEY: Now, who's Crab?
JUNIPER: He's a creel roper.
KEY: Pardon me?
JUNIPER: Wears a leather hat, sometimes rides his trike up to us.
KEY: What the fuck are you talking about?
JUNIPER: Just that Crab isn't into vaccine passports.
KEY: Well, with respect to Crab, he sounds like he's all over the bloody show.

FOR ALL YOUR NEEDS.[†]

Vaccine passport photo booths shot up across the UK.

You sat in 'em, pulled the curtain, spun the seat to the right height, bunged your four nugs into the slot and posed.

A flash.

And the needle flying into the bicep.

Another flash.

The gloop pumped deep into your veins.

A third flash.

The needle hoicked out and back in its cradle.

A final flash.

The cotton-wool ball on the scratch.

And now, groggy, leaning on the side of the booth.

Nonk churning round your channels.

A whirr and a clonk.

The passport and lollipop dumped in the bucket.

Barely able to focus now:

Lolly popped in the gob, passport stuffed in the back pocket.

Staggering towards a Wetherspoons or a zoo or an airport or a boating lake.

Access all areas.

PING!

A North London running track. Key and The Colonel troubling the cinders. Key in his red tracksuit; The Colonel wearing his green job. Orange streaks down the sleeves, and a couple down the legs, too, for good measure. Both men wear Adidas headbands and both are shuffling along at a certain pace. Is it "exercise"? You could certainly have a good go at claiming it was exercise. Ah leave 'em be, they look sporty enough. Both are drinking cans of Goose IPA. No one else is on the track. No one else has thought to vault the fence. No one else has any ambition any more.

KEY: He's saying June 21st, Colonel.

COLONEL: I'll believe it when I see it.

KEY: Saloon doors flying open, the drinkers charging in. The crush.

COLONEL: "No earlier than".

KEY: Yeah, I heard the briefing, cheers.

COLONEL: No. Earlier. Than.

KEY: *(Brightly)* 21st though.

COLONEL: At. The. Earliest.

Their hips swing as they come into the back straight.

KEY: Won't have to piss around with this nonsense anymore. We'll be sat in the damn corner. Seeing away packet upon packet of Quavers. IPA gushing down our throats.

COLONEL: I'm not getting a hard-on about the 21st, believe me.

KEY: Well, I am. I've whacked the dates in my diary.

COLONEL: Pencil, I hope.

KEY: Ink, brother. And if I had anything stronger I'd have used it. June 21st. Pubs. March 17th: groups of six.

COLONEL: No hard-on.

KEY: Five weeks away from being able to sit down within earshot of your best pal and get lashed without some policeman touching your collar.

COLONEL: I ain't getting a hard-on about any of this stuff.

KEY: Well, I am. I've got a monster in my pants over here, and I don't care who knows it.

COLONEL: I'm old enough to remember Christmas.

KEY: Bugger me, Colonel. He *wanted* us to have a nice Christmas, man!

Let it go!

COLONEL: Been stung before by this clown.

KEY: So, no hard-on?

COLONEL: When some poor lass takes my payment remotely and some weird robot plonks my beer in front of me, then and only then will I get a hard-on.

KEY: Doiiiiiing.

They carry on walking. Walking in circles. Every day another loop, every week another ring. When will it end? Even when an end comes, is that the end? Or is it just the start of another circle? Another lap chalked off. Round and round. Spiralling into insanity. Nooses and haloes. Eternity.

KEY: Driving much?

COLONEL: When I can, aye.

KEY: Must be nice. The open road.

COLONEL: Still trying to work out what an essential journey is.

KEY: After all this time.

COLONEL: Is driving to a football stadium and sitting outside imagining it's full essential?

KEY: They can't steal our dreams.

Hips swaying. Three mph. Swigging Goose. Headbands filling with sweat.

COLONEL: Like, if I'm getting charcoal or something, is that essential? You could maybe argue I could cook just on the hobs or in the microwave.

KEY: You ain't flame-grilling a rump steak in a microwave.

COLONEL: Right. And once I've bought the stuff all bets are off. I've gotta come back, haven't I?

KEY: Oh, I see.

COLONEL: I can't exactly stay at Sainsbury's.

KEY: No.

COLONEL: So once I've got the stuff, the next bit's essential.

KEY: Yeah.

COLONEL: Any court in the land –

KEY: Oh, they'd be tripping over each other to acquit you.

COLONEL: Yeah. Ha ha. "Get this twerp out of my court!"

Key's iPhone chirrups. It's in his hand immediately. His beak clacking on the screen as he reads the text.

COLONEL: Who is it?

Key looks up to the heavens. His lips go dry, his eyes go wet. He slows to two mph. The Colonel turns.

COLONEL: Who is it?

KEY: The text.

COLONEL: What text?

Key stops, looks at The Colonel.

KEY: It's *the text*, John.

Dear Mr Key, you have been invited to book your COVID-19 vaccinations. You must wear a face covering and clothing with easy access to your upper arm...

KEY: Simples. I'll wear my Kraftwerk singlet.

COLONEL: The jab?

KEY: Huh?

COLONEL: You getting the jab?

Please attend alone unless you need a carer. Please click the link to book your vaccination times.

KEY: Fringe benefits, Colonel.

COLONEL: Fringe benefits of vulnerability.

KEY: Happy to be vulnerable me, if it gets me shunted up the old jab queue. A hundred percent.

COLONEL: You're getting the vax.

They move off again. Elbows like pistons.

COLONEL: Well, we need to celebrate. No doubt about that.

KEY: Invincibility party.

COLONEL: Ha. Yeah, this is good stuff. Arm full of gunk for Mr Key.

KEY: Fill 'er up, Sir.

COLONEL: Pisses me off.

KEY: Huh? What does, sorry?

COLONEL: Nah, nothing. Just –

KEY: Thought we were gonna stop going on about the bubble.

COLONEL: This is inhumane.

Key slows for a second. Thinks he sees a stick, beyond the sand, by the railings. But it is too short.

COLONEL: My old pal getting jabbed and I can't even ladle some chilli onto his plate.

KEY: Ha. That'd be something.

COLONEL: I've started putting chocolate in it.

KEY: Finally.

COLONEL: Bunged a whole Kit Kat in last time.

KEY: Kit Kat. Huh?

COLONEL: You gotta come over man. Bust out ya bubble. This is madness. He's getting jabbed and he won't come over; won't split a damn keg.

KEY: Sorry.

COLONEL: I build a bar in my garden. Kegs coming out of my arnuzzi. And he won't come.

Key looks at his friend. Imagines clambering onto a barstool, angling his tankard.

KEY: D'ya get the bell?

COLONEL: Yes! I love the bell, bro. "Time at the bar!"

KEY: Can't have you building a bar without a bell.

COLONEL: *(Sighing; gravely)* Had to pour half a keg away the other day, need your help over there.

KEY: My half, huh?

COLONEL: Down the sink.

KEY: Yeah.

COLONEL: Should be going in there!

The Colonel points at Key's throat. Key opens wide. Imagines four pints of Siren sloshing down it like a dam's been breached.

KEY: Nature's sink.

They walk in silence. The Colonel's hurting. His green and orange tracksuit stretches with the pain of it all.

KEY: Believe in the roadmap, Colonel.

COLONEL: I know.

KEY: Five weeks, bro, and we're meeting up without these.

Key pings The Colonel's headband. The Colonel pings Key's. They retreat to two metres and walk in silence. They pass the finish line, and as they cross the white paint, they start their loop again.

†**JUNIPER:** 2028.
KEY: Ha ha.
JUNIPER: Well, it's 2021 now.
KEY: Yuh.
JUNIPER: And it's over.
KEY: Looks like it.
JUNIPER: Well, it is.
KEY: Does feel like it.
JUNIPER: It is, Tim. It is. It's over.
KEY: Yuh.
JUNIPER: Tim, it is.

STOP STRUGGLING.[†]

EVERYONE was chill now.

2028 and it was all "smoothed out" if that's the phrase I'm after.

We were used to it now anyway.

Some rules were still kicking about.

When you weren't protesting or stuffing your face you did have to wear a mask and have a couple of swabs hanging out of your hooter, and pubs were sealed over.

And you couldn't mix much, but that was about it.

You were totally allowed to jump on a Zoom though, or talk about going on holiday.

And things like chowing back rice and dancing with your wife in a secure tent were 100% okay.

If you liked, you could also dream of a better future, the government let you do what you wanted in your brain, that was your area.

"Dream away," was their vibe: "Fill yer boots."

You were free to imagine yourself on some sun-licked European beach or text pint emojis to your pals, and you were allowed to draw pictures of yourself in groups of ten, wrestling, getting sloshed, dancing in the Sun.

Week IX.

In which Key dares to dream, the acting boots are laced up, and a grim force appears in NW3.

HERE WE GO ROUND THE MULBERRY BUSH.

FIRE WITH FIRE.

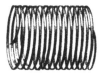

SPRING came.

They started training up wasps to go after covids.

Covid-scented hankies were dangled in front of wasps' hooters.

And then away they went.

These furious insects.

Hunting down covids.

Plunging their stingers into their flanks.

Like grubby little spitfires in a bleak new war.

Focused, angry, some of them high on ket, the wasps laughed as they worked.

WATERSTONES.

The Sun is shining and Key has a new stick. It is heavy and long and brilliant and it has a duck's head on the end. Key marches through Regent's Park, in his other hand: a cold mocha. His Puma rucksack dances on his back, a smile plays on his lips. He flows down Regent Street; washes up in Piccadilly Circus. There's an energy down there. Everyone examining their road-maps, buzzing about the future. Some drink juice, others wear low-tog puffer jackets. In the shadow of Lillywhites – closed – they stand. Key moves to the statue that glints in the Sun. It is of Eros, the sexual Greek. The lucky so-and-so has wings and a bow and his nappy is loose. Tourists clamber up his thighs and rub his winkle for good luck. Key's phone is ringing. Emily Juniper. Click.

JUNIPER: Tim, we did it. We actually did it.

KEY: Emily Juniper!

JUNIPER: Are you sitting down?

KEY: Never!

JUNIPER: Waterstones have ordered –

KEY: Fuck me, no! They've put in an order?! Waterstones! No! Em?! No!

Key tries to sit down. On a streetbin, on a fire hydrant, on his stick. Anything, anywhere. His legs are buckling, his knees flicking the cobbles like spaghetti.

JUNIPER: They've pulled the iron out of the fire, Tim!

KEY: Blown the cobwebs off of their filthy old chequebook! Waterstones!

JUNIPER: Do you even want to know what they've ordered?

KEY: Well, books, I'm guessing.

JUNIPER: But how many?

KEY: You're hardly phoning to say Waterstones have ordered new tills.

JUNIPER: What they do with their tills is nobody's business but their own.

KEY: So it's books? They've ordered books!

JUNIPER: I've emailed you the figure.

Key spins round and round like a cork-screw, drives himself deep into the ground as he checks his phone. He yelps like a puppy; punches himself hard in the jaw. Unscrews himself, puts Emily Juniper back to his ear.

KEY: So what does this mean, Em?

JUNIPER: It means I've cracked open the gin and I'm hacking up the peppermint as we speak. Where are you?

Key doesn't know. Key is disorientated. Unanchored. Key is sur the plage in Saving Private Ryan. Flailing, walking without direction, like a duck. Past Barbour International – closed; past Grom Gelato – closed. Swallowing hard. Quacking.

JUNIPER: It means boxes start moving. It means I get my lounge back.

KEY: Lose the boxes!

JUNIPER: Exactly.

KEY: Pack 'em off to Waterstones.

JUNIPER: Well, this is it, Tim.

KEY: Not our problem any more. Fuck the boxes!

JUNIPER: I'm sitting on one now. Legs dangling.

KEY: In your little red shoes.

JUNIPER: It means I can get some order in here. It means I can set my easel up.

KEY: I'm getting my vax, Em.

JUNIPER: *(Surprised)* Oh you are?

Key nods. His vast webbed feet slap the paving slabs of Old Piccadilly. His mocha now warm again. Heated by the Sun, nuked by the vast order of books. Past NatWest Bank – dead.

KEY: Lord's Cricket Ground, Em. Bicep full of nonk. Yes please, Louise. Bang it in, baby.

JUNIPER: Well... I mean, how old are you?

KEY: Huh?

JUNIPER: Just 'cos, I mean –

KEY: Well, I'm not sixty-to-seventy, Em, am I?

JUNIPER: I'm just trying to work out why...

KEY: Lucky break.

JUNIPER: Am I being thick?

KEY: No, no. No. Well, anyway, I'm going up Lord's –

JUNIPER: Home of cricket. I wonder if

they'll have the players doing the jabbing.

KEY: Ha ha, yeah Jos Buttler himself, slamming in the lamb.

JUNIPER: Buttler's in India, isn't he? Twenty20's.

KEY: Ha!

Key stops in his tracks. Outside the next shop. He is mesmerised.

JUNIPER: Quint's taken a turn for the worst; he's stopped wearing trousers. Takes them off like they're a coat, hangs them up as he comes in...

But Key isn't listening. He is outside Waterstones – closed. The bookshop – closed. 203–206 Piccadilly – closed. Key stares through the glass. The books, gathering dust. The Osmans and the Highsmiths, the Childs and the Mantels. In all their glory. Uplit by Habitat floor lights. And beyond them more shelves. The Carvers and the Chandlers, the Faulkses and the Franzens, the Wodehouses and the Woolfs. And nobody in there. Midday and empty. Just the books. The words. Millions of them. Billions. Behind windows. Emily Juniper is still talking; Key tunes back in.

JUNIPER: ... only thing that shuts him up. It's like a pacifier.

KEY: Huh?

JUNIPER: Just sits there spooning soup into his trap, hoovering up the book.

KEY: Quint?

JUNIPER: Yes, Quint. Who'd'ya think?

KEY: The man has taste, that's what.

JUNIPER: Can't get it off him.

KEY: His Cold Dead Hands.

JUNIPER: Obsessed with it, he is.

KEY: Good old Quint.

JUNIPER: What? No! Bad old Quint!

KEY: But he's reading the book, Em. People have gotta read the book. He's reading it. Quint! Ha! Difficult to stay angry with him.

JUNIPER: He dribbled onto it last night.

KEY: Oh. Dribbled on the book, huh?

JUNIPER: Quint's a bloody nightmare, is what Quint is.

KEY: Fuck Quint.

JUNIPER: Yes! Why's he coming round? That's what I wanna know.

KEY: You chose him. For your bubble?

JUNIPER: Biggest mistake of my life. He's stolen our rug.

KEY: Quint has?

JUNIPER: Blank space on the floor.

KEY: *(Distracted)* Definitely Quint?

JUNIPER: He loved that rug. It's Quint alright. Quint...

Key's gone again. Staring through the glass. The books are now transformed. Now, every last one of them is his. A sea of blue in the window. Every book, his book. His words. Emily Juniper's design. And now the whole place populated by people. The great and the good traipsing, pulling the blue book from the shelves, dunking their snouts in, waving the books above their heads, scuttling to the tills, bagging them up, making way for others. Hugging their purchases to their chests. Key blinks. The shop is empty once more. The display reforms. The O'Briens and the Baddiels. The syrup bubbling in Key's ear reforms itself once more into Emily Juniper.

JUNIPER: I've dismantled a clock.

KEY: Okay.

JUNIPER: I've laid the parts out.

KEY: Okay. And what? Draw the parts?

JUNIPER: I wish I didn't have to.

KEY: Are you okay, Em?

JUNIPER: I wish you'd write. I wish we were doing it again.

KEY: We're in the shops, Em.

JUNIPER: It feels like the end.

KEY: Em?

JUNIPER: No it's good. We're in the shops. It's a good thing.

KEY: You betcha, Em!

Key plunges his phone into his pocket. He barely hears her voice breaking into pieces. His chest is far too puffed out for that. His fist clasps his duckhead walking stick, he strikes out towards Hyde Park Corner. His mocha is burning his other hand. He pulls his sleeve down to protect himself against its heat. Past The Ritz – closed, shackled, dark.

VEES.

BENNY ST. EDMONDS got muddled and said vaccine instead of virus.

Poor sod, just lost it for a second, said he'd got his text asking him to come and get the virus next week.

But he'd meant to say vaccine.

Lol.

He went bright red!

"Sorry, I meant vaccine, I'm getting the vaccine."

Oh, well.

The other people on the Zoom call smashed through their screens, chased him into his kitchen, tore him apart limb from limb, and ate him.

◀

NEW AND IMPROVED.

THERE was a new variant.

It made your boy double in size, plus it gave you loads of energy, and if you were a slaphead your hair grew back.

Bohnson called a briefing.

"Realistically, this is a good variant, folks."

He shrugged and glanced down at his tennis shorts.

The spods were flanking him.

One of them's hair was growing back – he'd got it alright.

The other spods were trying to touch this first spod's skin and were brazenly wafting his breath towards them.

Bohnson dabbed at his tennis shorts with his fists.

He was licking his lips and purring deeply.

†**JUNIPER:** He's got a nice job.
KEY: Em, he's got a bloody tricky job.
JUNIPER: Trundling round with a wheelbarrow full of coins, scooping out a bunch for anyone who fills out the right forms.
KEY: There's more to it than that, I expect.
JUNIPER: Just think it's bloody generous of him, that's all.
KEY: It's not his money, Em, you do know that?
JUNIPER: In his little tie, cheering people up with his coins.
KEY: Em, it's not his money.
JUNIPER: Uh-huh.
KEY: Do you know that, Em?
JUNIPER: Well, how comes he's got it then?

WOODEN NICKELS.[†]

RISHI PERFECT was stood with his divvy little briefcase, Bohnson just behind, fists down his tennis shorts, bouncing up and down excitedly.

"You think I've run out of money?"

Bohnson could barely contain himself.

"'Course he bloody hasn't!"

Rishi Perfect half turned to him, "Let me do it, eh."

Bohnson pointed at his charge, did a double thumbs-up, gestured zipping his mouth shut, mimed counting a large stack of banknotes.

The capitalist addressed the mic once more.

He cleared his throat and coins fell from his lips, lodging in his cummerbund.

"Ever heard the phrase 'furloughs are on me for the foreseeable'?"

Bohnson could contain himself no longer, he put a vast arm round the millionaire's shoulders.

"I fucking love this cunt!"

Rishi Perfect blushed.

His divvy briefcase clicked open and loose Coke sloshed down the steps of the Bank of England.

He regained his composure; poured what was left into his cakehole, wiped the budget on his trousers, peeled it open and began to read.

PITCH PERFECT.

Key marches up through the heath. He climbs through the daffodils, his duck-head walking stick clipping their ears. He reaches a tree and sits his fat arse down at its base; he leans back, sighs. Key can feel the tree's craggy bark through his Puma rucksack. He leans back and stares down at the football pitch below; its goals shackled together in the centre circle. Key unfolds his roadmap on his lap and pours himself 100 ml of Pale Fire from his Penelope Pitstop flask. He squints at the pitch. Beer in his moustaches. His iPhone begins to chir-rup: Daniel. Key frowns.

KEY: There's a roadmap, Daniel. Don't you get it? A roadmap! So I don't need you phoning and telling me not to get carried away or not to celebrate or not to feel happy or any of that stuff. There is a roadmap. Do you understand me? A roadmap. This thing is done.

DANIEL: Good morning, Tim.

KEY: Yes, Daniel! It is a good morning. I'm on the lash! I'm getting the vax! The Sun's shining! You haven't got a leg to stand on, bro. This is happening.

DANIEL: You're getting the vax? What?

Key smiles, peels back his sleeve. Some early bees buzz around his bicep.

KEY: Ha! Yeah! Right in there. Glomp! Arm full of the stuff. Then the old heart pumping it round the bod. I feel it in my fingers –

DANIEL: How the hell are you getting the vax?

KEY: I feel it in my toes –

DANIEL: You're younger than me!

KEY: We're done! Vaxxed-up poet, marching into the sunset, I'm tell-ing you, Daniel.

DANIEL: You vulnerable?

KEY: I'm vulnerable.

DANIEL: Vulnerable how?

KEY: I think when someone says they're vulnerable you just have to accept it, not try and make them confess to having fucked-up lungs or whatever it is you're doing.

Key is on his feet and dancing now, the Sun

kissing his yellow cap, licking his peak. A vulnerable poet, gambolling amongst the daisies. He falls back against the tree, stares at the football pitch.

DANIEL: Just keep it together, that's all.

KEY: No way, not happening.

DANIEL: You live in your head.

KEY: Respectfully disagree.

DANIEL: I'm rereading your book –

KEY: Can't get enough of it, huh?

DANIEL: It's fantastic, it really is. But be careful. Don't get complacent. You're a fantasist.

KEY: No one knows what you mean.

DANIEL: D'ya get the stick?

Key glances down at his stick. The duck winks back at him.

KEY: Hello, Ducky.

DANIEL: To replace the one you smashed up –

KEY: I'm looking at the footy pitch, Daniel, that's what.

DANIEL: *(Wistful)* Comedians' Football.

KEY: Aha. Now he perks up.

Key's iPhone begins to shake and clatter. Key just knows Daniel's booting his Mitre Delta Cosmic about in his little courtyard bit.

DANIEL: You can't get ahead of your-self, that's all. I want to play football as much as the next man –

KEY: Dare to dream, Daniel.

DANIEL: Dare to wait. Don't spin stories in your mind. Tick the dates off, that's all.

Key looks at his roadmap. "Team sports: March 17th". Not long now. He blows a kiss at the pitch. The goals seem to be struggling to get away from one another. He can hear the sad clink of the chains even from here.

KEY: I need to be playing, Daniel.

DANIEL: Even if everything goes according to plan with the roadmap –

KEY: I'm some player, Dan.

DANIEL: I know. I know you are.

KEY: When I think of all the games I could be bossing –

Suddenly, a thunder crack from the centre circle. The locks burst open and the goals begin to step away from one another. Key sips his Pale Fire.

DANIEL: Roadmap's saying no football till spring.

KEY: Which is upon us. I'm not sitting here twiddling my plonker. I'm dreaming. Then I'm playing.

DANIEL: Live for the day.

KEY: Pah! You still bunging stuff, huh? Filling skips with trophies and plasterboard?

DANIEL: Trying to buy my bed back.

KEY: Oh?

DANIEL: Been reading up on the benefits of beds.

KEY: Of course there's benefits, man.

DANIEL: That's what this article was saying, yah. I've offered the guy twice what he paid for it.

KEY: You've thrown out too much stuff, man. You've been too ruthless.

DANIEL: I'm not saying I'm on top of things this lockdown. I'm not saying I'm the blueprint.

The goals have reached their rightful stations. They stand proud in their six-yard boxes. They throw nets over themselves like widows organising their cloaks.

DANIEL: Here's my view, for what it's worth –

KEY: Jack Shit.

DANIEL: You need to write.

KEY: Naw. Been there, done that, met Lauren Laverne.

DANIEL: You need to. Otherwise it just stays in your brain.

KEY: Interesting theory.

DANIEL: Becomes gunk.

KEY: Gunk now?

DANIEL: Dig out the orange pen.

KEY: Slung the pen.

DANIEL: Well, unsling it.

KEY: Or sit tight. Wait for the whistle.

A referee appears and blows a whistle. Comedians jog out onto the pitch. They are in poor condition.

KEY: Listen, pal. I'm not delidding my pen on your say-so. Who are you to tell me to write?

DANIEL: So who you listening to then?

KEY: I'll take advice from my old man. Or if God pokes his beak in I'm listening. Not from you, I swear. I'm happy imagining booting a ball, frankly.

DANIEL: You think I don't need to be playing, too? You think I can't play?

KEY: Oh, I know you can.

DANIEL: I turn up in my little pink shorts.

KEY: You organise it, Dan. Of course you deserve a run-out.

DANIEL: Scored my fair share of goals. Nutmegged Lee Mack once. I can play a bit, no?

KEY: Daniel, you send the emails out. No one minds you joining in. We'd be a cold-hearted old bunch to let you organise it –

DANIEL: And pay for it –

KEY: And not let you join in.

Key leans forward, watches the game. Watches himself. Resplendent in a Spartak Moscow shirt and white tracksuit bottoms. Collecting the ball on the halfway line, ghosting past three portly comedians, passing the ball expansively with the outside of his right boot. Andy Zaltzman, controlling on his chest, Key making a lung-busting run into the box, Zaltz skipping past some other satirist and swinging the ball in, Key defying physics, leaping, contorting, his boot coming past his ear, his laces smearing into the ball; the props comic in nets: helpless. Key slathering his fingers across Daniel's face, Key yelling, "Too Easy", other comedians pulling Key back from Daniel, restraining Key, getting him off the pitch, putting him on the tube.

DANIEL: How's the pitch looking?

KEY: Goals are shackled.

DANIEL: You see. Not worth thinking about. Not yet.

Key can hear Daniel's Mitre Delta Cosmic ricocheting off his barbecue. He can hear Daniel's pain as the wait for football continues. Key sips his Pale Fire. He is wearing football boots. His studs twitch as he watches the ghosts.

†**JUNIPER:** First one about Cumdawg, eh.
KEY: He had a quiet lockdown.
JUNIPER: Loud first one, mind.
KEY: The star that burnt too bright.
JUNIPER: Licking his wounds, most probably.
KEY: Licking his plonker, most probably.
JUNIPER: Plotting, I expect. Polishing his grenades.
KEY: Ha! I like that! Polishing his grenades indeed!

THE BRAIN WITH THE VEIN.[†]

CUMDAWG wandered into a booth, hoiĉked the sleeve of his cardy up.

"Vax me up, Buttercup."

The doĉtor filled his syringe from the nonk-buĉket.

"Hang on, aren't you –"

Cumdawg pulled down his mask, pushed up his shades in one movement.

The doĉtor nodded.

Cumdawg's cords were halfway down his thighs, he was working on a Pret Swedish Meatball Wrap.

"We don't usually eat when we're being injeĉted, that's all."

Cumdawg took a big mouthful, pulled a Punk IPA out of his record bag.

"That's really intereŝting, great ŝtory."

Cumdawg's upper arm rippled as the nonk flowed in.

"This is the Pfizer, it –"

"I know what it is, pal, I organised this lot, ĉheers."

Cumdawg grabbed the syringe, suĉked his beer into it.

"I'm sorry, I didn't know you were responsible for... before you..."

Cumdawg wasn't liŝtening though.

He'd punĉhed the needle into his heart and was pushing 330 ml of IPA into his epicentre.

Then he swayed out into the ŝtreet, clambered into his car, turned the ignition, teŝted the vax.

JUMBO.

Key and The Colonel are out for a walk. Taking their form from the track into the streets. Their headbands are on and their arms are exposed in their little singlets. They look like old-school twerps as their trainers peck at the wet paving slabs and their little bottoms wiggle down The Broadway.

KEY: Month more max. Dig deep, huh.

COLONEL: You think I ain't digging deep?

They pause at the butchers – open. They gaze through the window, eyeing up the flesh. Licking their lips. The meat-whacker brings his cutlass down on some dozy pig. They move off, hips dancing like magic beans. Two men. Straining to smile. Battling through a lockdown.

KEY: Fuck me, I ate a lot of biscuits this morning.

COLONEL: Oh, you did, huh. How many's a lot?

KEY: You know how many a lot is.

COLONEL: Five?

KEY: What the hell is five?

COLONEL: Well, I don't know, do I?

KEY: You think I'm bringing it up if I'm eating five biscuits in a sitting?

COLONEL: "Sitting"?

KEY: These lockdowns. They drive me to it. Urge me towards the fig rolls, do these lockdowns.

COLONEL: Pain in the balls is what they are.

KEY: You think I don't know lock-downs are a pain in the balls, John?

COLONEL: There's Jumbo, look.

KEY: Who's Jumbo?

COLONEL: Over there, look.

KEY: Who the fuck is Jumbo?

COLONEL: Gotta say hi.

KEY: In a pando? Yeah and let's have a group hug while we're at it. Have you finally lost it?

COLONEL: Come on, it's just a quick stop-and-chat.

KEY: Perfect! Shall I pick us up some hotdogs and then maybe the three of us can break into a hotel and fuck?

COLONEL: Huh?

KEY: Let's swerve him, man. He's a big brute, I don't want him gassing me if he's got it.

COLONEL: Huh? Let's say hi.

They cross the road. This man Jumbo's had a couple of good lockdowns, it looks like. His hair is wild. Red and tons of it. His vast tummy reaches up to his tits. John salutes as they cross.

COLONEL: *(Shouting)* Good day to you, squire!

KEY: What the fuck?

COLONEL: *(Sotto)* It's how we talk to one another.

KEY: Bugger me.

They land. Jumbo's eyeing Key and licking his lips.

JUMBO: Good morrow, fine sir!

COLONEL: This is my mate, Tim.

JUMBO: Of course! Verily. I have been enjoying your turn in "Pls Like" on the much-maligned BBC. Sterling work, old boy.

KEY: Jesus wept.

JUMBO: Good morrow, Squire. I go by Jumbo.

KEY: So I hear. Tim.

COLONEL: So how goes your lockdown then, Jumbo?

JUMBO: How goes anyone's lockdown, Sir?

Jumbo's the worst. Key has no option but to look up at the sky. The clouds are getting on with it. No difference up there from 2019. None whatsoever, clouds just filling up with water, spilling onto the city when they're full. Key mouths, "Good old clouds". Jumbo's jabbering away.

JUMBO: ... then Carlie gets the dreaded lurgy. So I light the old lamp and do my best impression of Florence Nightingale, tending to this poor sparrow.

KEY: Hang on, your girlfriend got the bug, huh?

JUMBO: Verily, temperature: volcanic –

KEY: Never mind all that. Have you got it?

JUMBO: I hope not!

Jumbo, lurches towards Key like a zombie,

Key pushes him back with his stick. The duckhead right in his throat.

JUMBO: Negative test. She's on the mend now, we...

As Jumbo drones on, so Key starts spinning gently around. His coat is hanging off him and arms are outstretched. Like the poster of the film Shine, with Geoffrey Rush, who watched Key's stage show in Melbourne in 2010. Round Key goes. His eyes are open, the damp air moistening them further. He glimpses a toyshop – closed, a child's face pinned to it, a mother chivvying him along. Key spinning. What has this world become. Everywhere locks. Everywhere masks. Everywhere nothing. Key gropes his roadmap in his pocket. Squints at a framing shop – closed.

JUMBO: ... but the new normal keeps changing, of course. I think the powers that be might have to just nuke the word "normal" and start from scratch!

COLONEL: Lol.

JUMBO: This could be another five years, methinks.

COLONEL: Don't say that, Jumbo!

Key covers his ears. He imagines not going into the framing shop. He imagines not talking to a kind man. Not handing over a poster for a show that Key never performed. Not picking out a frame. Black, matte, heavy. Key not paying the deposit. Key not shaking the man's hand. Key not stuffing his ticket in his pocket. Key not immediately losing the slip.

JUMBO: ... and her sister's in our bubble so we have her round with the gossip.

COLONEL: *(Waving a thumb at Key)* Yeah this guy should be in mine.

JUMBO: Oh, right, you bubbling with Partridge then, are you, Sir?

KEY: Probably could.

JUMBO: Ha ha.

KEY: "Ha ha".

But Key's now revolving again. The deserted buildings are vaporising and penetrating him like gas. Everything gone. Where has it gone? Where have we come to? And Jumbo. Jumbo. This lad Jumbo.

COLONEL: Well, I think I need to walk

this one back to his sanctuary, Jumbo.

JUMBO: Good man and true! Well, 'twas well met, Jonathan.

KEY: "Jonathan?"

JUMBO: Nice to meet you, Good Timothy.

KEY: 'Twas an honour, fine sir.

JUMBO: Ha! Splendid.

They move off. Key looks over his shoulder. Jumbo seems to be wearing – not that it matters – a kind of harness thing, like you'd wear if you were being instructed in the art of abseiling. The Colonel clicks his fingers in Key's face.

COLONEL: What happened there? We lost you.

KEY: Don't know. I just don't know. Oh, John.

Key is heaving. Something is trapped in his chest. A lungful of lockdown. Key needs to keep it together. He angles himself away from The Colonel. Come on Keyzee! Keep it together, man!

COLONEL: It's called a wobble, that's all. Perfectly normal.

KEY: Yes. That's what it was.

Key turns to The Colonel, nods.

KEY: You and Jumbo going at it, me having a wobble.

COLONEL: I didn't get out of bed yesterday.

KEY: What the fuck? Why not?

COLONEL: Point is, we're almost there. That's what.

KEY: Yeah, but... not getting up? What's happened there?

COLONEL: I dunno.

They walk down the hill.

KEY: No I don't know either. You gotta get out of bed, Colonel. That's the basics.

They walk on past a pub. It is a quarter to six now. The air is filled with a fine, fine rain. Like a mist, almost. The light is all but gone. Their hands are pink. They look at the pub. They don't even look at one another. Just one foot in front of the other. Move out of the pub's emotional glow. Move to where it's just dark trees and occasional cars speeding by on the wet tarmac.

LOFTUS.

I MET a covid online and started dating her.
She was tiny and I called her Mini
and always came to the pub armed with a
magnifying glass along with my phrase book.

I wondered if she'd ever heard of Chris
Whitty or any of the other state heroes.

When I asked such questions she'd simply
blush and switch the subject to either wild
swimming or her beloved QPR.

POP!

"**W**E'RE going to have to let you go."

I was sat in my bubble, across the table from my sponsors.

The bigger one read out a list of issues they had with me.

The little one could barely look at me.

The thrust was I was "too much" or "always there", or however they phrased it.

I glanced across at the window.

A face pressed up against the glass.

They'd got someone lined up, clearly.

I signed the paperwork and slipped out the back.

I could feel the bubble shimmering behind me as the Sun dipped over the hill and I waddled up the lane.

ACTION.

Movie cameras! Boom operators! Vast lights, huge drapes, cables everywhere. A film set! On location, in London's famous West End. A sliver of Hollywood, jammed into a side street just off the Charing Cross Road. The Sun beating down. Pin-drop silence, apart from the skilful warblings of the actors, carving words into the open-air. A director watching on, his megaphone held tightly in his fist, his mask clamped round his face. The crew all masked-up 'n' all, eyes narrowed. The camera eating up the action, swallowing the drama into its guts.

DIRECTOR: Aaaaand cut! And turning round. Nice work, Saoirse! Lovely stuff, Sam. Onto your single next, Sam. Relax for a second!

Sam Rockwell and Saoirse Ronan. Together at last. They turn, move towards the chap who does the coffees. His machine's already making a helluva noise. Sam fist-pumps Saoirse.

SAM: Good job!

SAOIRSE: Give me coffee!!!

Key is there, too. Scuttling along behind them in his little costume. All miked up, theatrical make-up trowelled onto his skull, a custodian's helmet stuffed on his bonce; he's playing a policeman! In the 1950s!

KEY: *(Shouting after them)* You can see why they pay you the big bucks, Miss Ronan!

The three amigos collapse onto special chairs and coffee is plunged into their fists. Sam jabs an earphone into his lughole; flicks his eyes closed.

KEY: Antisocial bugger, ain't he?

SAOIRSE: Oh, he's learning his lines. The guy's a pro.

KEY: And I'm not?

SAOIRSE: Well, have you learnt your lines?

KEY: I'm on nodding terms with them, let's say.

SAOIRSE: You're reaching for them a bit.

KEY: I just sort of open my trap, see what comes out.

SAOIRSE: You like an ad-lib, huh?

KEY: Might have some fun when the camera's on me, put it that way, once I've found my confidence.

SAOIRSE: Try any of that shit in my scenes and I'll have you marched off set before they've yelled "cut".

KEY: Huh?

SAOIRSE: *(Smiling)* Jokes jokes jokes. We all have our own approach.

KEY: Oh, ha ha! I see.

SAOIRSE: *(No longer smiling)* But seriously. It helps the editor if you do it the same each time.

KEY: I'm a pro, don't worry about me.

SAOIRSE: You were mouthing "Hi, Mum" down the camera this morning.

KEY: It's Mother's Day next Sunday.

SAOIRSE: The film won't be out till next year.

KEY: I'm all over the place, if I'm honest, Miss Ronan.

SAOIRSE: Saoirse.

Key takes his custodian's helmet off, pulls his shitty sheets of A5 out from underneath, starts scanning his lines.

SAOIRSE: You're doing great. Your mum okay, is she?

KEY: I watched Brooklyn with her. She can't believe this is happening.

SAOIRSE: Aw.

KEY: I'm the first person in my family to work with you.

Wiry men climb ladders and angle lamps behind them. Sam Rockwell mouths his lines. Saoirse Ronan blows on her coffee. The film industry roaring back. A Covid officer waddles by. He looks fucking pissed off and has loads of sprays and covid-swats on a trolley.

SAOIRSE: *(Sipping coffee)* Acting's not your main thing, is it?

KEY: Huh?

SAOIRSE: It's not your main thing. Is it?

KEY: Oh, I see. Yeah, I write. Probably that's my main thing. You knew that, huh?

SAOIRSE: No. Just the state of your acting.

KEY: Oh.

SAOIRSE: *(Cracking up)* Jokes jokes jokes! Nah, Sam said you gave him your book in the make-up truck.

KEY: Oh, yeah. Yeah, sure, I write. But I mean, acting's the thing, really. Well, you know how it is. You gotta do your acting, don't ya.

Key does a few facial expressions and waves his arms about before chowing down on a blueberry muffin, most of which explodes down his police cloak. Saoirse watching on. Sam learning his lines. A film set. Key's body tingling.

KEY: Hey, we should compare awards at lunchtime.

SAOIRSE: Ha ha!

KEY: I know! But we should. I'd love to see an Oscar, that's for certain. Hey, Sam! Oy!

Key jabs his truncheon into Sam Rockwell's flank. He pulls his earphone out, smiles.

KEY: Just saying to Miss Ronan –

SAOIRSE: Saoirse. It's Saoirse.

KEY: Yuh, saying we should compare awards at lunch. Finally see how the old Oscar measures up to the Perrier, you know. See what all the fuss is about.

SAM: Ha ha!

KEY: I'm serious, bro.

Key boots his Puma rucksack, winks at the assembled.

SAM: Ha ha! This guy is the bomb! Ha ha! Imagine, bringing your Oscar onto set! Ha ha, that's fantastic!

KEY: Ha ha!

Key does his best to keep laughing. He sees the humour in the situation. To bring an award to work would be ridiculous. Sam Rockwell plunges his earphone back where the Sun don't shine. Key detonates another muffin. Saoirse brushes some debris off his PC's uniform with a kind knuckle.

KEY: Crumbs.

SAOIRSE: Bless. You must have a fair bit of imposter syndrome, huh?

KEY: Dripping with it, if I'm honest. All your acting trophies and whatnot.

SAOIRSE: Ha! I know it sounds really naffo but I don't really do it for the awards and whatnot.

KEY: Whatnot! Ha!

SAOIRSE: I don't! I'm just more, you know, in it for the acting. Really.

KEY: Yup, totally get that! Who cares about the accolades? The great thing about my 2009 Edinburgh show was that the audiences wet themselves watching it. Every. Single. Night. And if my suitcase was 2.8 kg heavier on the train home, so be it.

SAOIRSE: Well, I'd love to be able to write, that's for sure.

KEY: How much does an Oscar weigh?

SAM: *(Opening an eye)* Eight and a half pounds.

KEY: There you go.

DIRECTOR: Okay, let's get you lovely people back on set, please.

And up they get. And Key's crumbs jump like fleas and a lady with a weird hoover comes charging back in and gives Key's chest a good going over.

KEY: It's fine.

SAOIRSE: Your character wouldn't be covered in crap, that's the thing.

KEY: Believe me, ain't no one gonna be looking at the crumbs when I'm acting. They'll be focussed on my expressive eyes and throbbing jugular. They start counting the crumbs, something's gone bloody wrong.

SAOIRSE: Counting the crumbs, ha ha.

And now they're moving back into their positions, outside a red door, next to a billboard that the masked art department have knocked together. And the make-up girls are swarming in. And they have plastic visors on and they look like cheerful little welders.

DIRECTOR: Okay, we're on you this time, Sam. Saoirse, you're being a delight as always. And... turning over...

And the cameras whirr back into life and the little fella with the boom lifts it up and Sam Rockwell smacks himself in the mouth a couple of times to get himself going and Key wiggles his truncheon and smiles.

DIRECTOR: And... action!

†**JUNIPER:** I seem to remember the vax stuff going okay though.
KEY: Yeah, they rolled it out.
JUNIPER: You make out like people were trying to scoop it out of folk.
KEY: Yeah for the poems, Em. Just for the poems.
JUNIPER: Write whatever works best for the poems, type of thing? Or is that an oversimplification?
KEY: I'd say that's quite a big undersimplification.
JUNIPER: I'd say I want another Bulmers.
KEY: I'd say I'm what I'd like to call "nicely lashed".
JUNIPER: I'd say we have nowhere to be.
KEY: I'd say it's a slight case of another Bulmers for Miss Juniper.
JUNIPER: Yay. Cider and poems.
KEY: Together at last.

GIFT RECEIPT.[†]

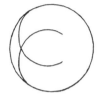

GLUNCH marched back into the vax hall.

He was mad as hell.

He grabbed the first person he saw with a stethoscope round their neck.

"You've injected me with the wrong gear, pal!"

Glunch slapped his bicep and snarled.

The physician fella gave him a dopy look.

"Both vaccines have great efficacy, which one did you have?"

"The lamo one, you spoon!"

Glunch waved the article he'd printed out from www.bbc.co.uk/news/uk in his face.

"Kindly extract this nonk and bung in the good stuff!"

Glunch's upper arm glinted under the strip lights above.

The cavernous hall was teeming with biceps and needles.

What was this place in normal times?

An ice rink?

Could be, certainly would explain the cold, unforgiving floor.

A bigger doctor had hold of Glunch's arms now and was sliding him towards the changing rooms.

Great, finally, someone taking him seriously.

HERE WE GO ROUND THE MULBERRY BUSH.

Today 07:22

Sorry not answering phone.
Drawing clocks in weird places.
Dreamt last night you wrote second
book and I designed it? Em. xoxoxo

ORCHID.

Moonlight. Key picks his way through the heath. Leaning hard on his duckhead walking stick. There is a ringing in his ears. But no one is picking up. He cancels and redials. His Gazelles kiss the thin veil of water that spreads across the bridleway, like a glistening sheet stretched across a mattress. His Gazelles have come this way before. His Gazelles are tired. They cast looks at the streetbin and at one another. The ringing in his ears. She will not pick up. Key drapes himself over the streetbin like pastry being draped over stewed apples. Moonlight.

BILL: *(From nowhere)* Don't go in the bin, Son.

Key turns round. A horse. Its coat like silk, muscles twitching in the moonlight, teeth wretched, eyes thick, dead.

BILL: You're almost there, Son.

And on the horse: Key's father. His chest bare. A bicycle helmet strapped to his skull, reflective armbands laced round his biceps. Other than that everything as per the horse's description above.

KEY: My own father. On a horse in London.

BILL: They always end, Son. Lockdowns.

KEY: I know, Pa. I'm keeping it together. I have the roadmap.

BILL: You'll feel better once you've got a pint of vax in your arm.

KEY: They pour it in next week, Pa. The Pfizer.

BILL: Me too. Pfizer till I die.

KEY: If you die.

BILL: Doesn't feel likely. Best I've felt in years. Carried the fridge to the duck pond this morning.

KEY: Oh, you did, huh?

BILL: Wasn't doing that pre-vax.

KEY: Why d'ya carry the fridge to the duck pond?

BILL: Tossed it in like a caber.

Bill Key raises himself up to his full height on his bright pink saddle. He starts doing muscle man poses. He grins and a gold crown flashes in the depths of his mouth.

KEY: So you rode your horse to London, did ya? Ya mad sod.

BILL: M11.

KEY: Old-school.

BILL: Busier than I'd hoped.

KEY: I bet. People are allowed to travel now, Dad.

BILL: They were winding their windows down, making that exact point. Being mean to the horse.

KEY: Beeping their horns, too, I bet.

BILL: Stressing Barnard out, yuh. Swerving into his flanks.

The horse blinks. He bows his head, drinks from a puddle next to the streetbin.

BILL: Things are loosening. You can break city limits.

KEY: Why'd ya come, Pa?

BILL: You're lost.

KEY: Huh? How'd ya know that? Lost? What lost?

BILL: You gotta write, Son.

The horse is going mad in the puddle, his vast tomb-like teeth, churning up the water.

KEY: Naw. Not this time.

BILL: That was a proper book, that last one.

KEY: I'm good, Pa. I'm good, I promise.

A tring on the phone. A text coming in. It ain't Emily Juniper though.

BILL: Half the village have read it. Calling you the new Pepys.

KEY: I ditched the pen, Pa. I'm in the acting game these days.

BILL: So your mother said. Running rings around Hollywood's finest.

The horse neighs, lifts its head back up, shakes out its mane. He looks puzzled. Key leans against the streetbin. Considers flomping onto the bench.

KEY: I dunno, Pa. I dunno what I'm doing, if I'm honest. I was on fire this time last year, then bam! The bugs fly in. I'm stuffed up the arnuzzi.

BILL: You had stuff lined up, huh?

KEY: D'ya think this was the plan?! D'ya think I had 2021 earmarked for waddling around the heath, lapping up mocha, befriending policemen?

BILL: I've become a horseman.

The old nag smiles. There's a bloody pen in its mouth. Key's orange pen! Right there! In its damn gnashers! The horse's eyeballs glisten like lychees. Bill Key reaches down, pulls the pen from Barnard's teeth. Lobs it to his son. Key grips the pen in both fists. The horse nods at the pen; he is trying to do a wolf whistle.

KEY: What the...

BILL: Get it down, Son. Tell the world.

KEY: Mm.

BILL: Alert Emily Whats'ername. Choose a font. Disgrace the paper with your words.

KEY: Emily Whats'ername's gone AWOL, Pa.

BILL: She'll be back, Son. No one's gone far. Just seems like it. Lockdowns take a bit of getting out of, that's all.

The horse guffs. The Moon blinks. Key rubs his heart with his pen.

BILL: You know what you'll write about?

KEY: Yuh.

BILL: You do, huh?

KEY: Yuh.

Key smiles. Saxophone begins to ring lightly around the heath. Bill Key grimaces at the treacly tones. Key shoves his pen down his drawers.

BILL: Now. Two weeks' time. You can come and see me and your mother. She's chomping at the bit as you can imagine.

KEY: I can and I will.

BILL: The roadmap's terrific.

KEY: I know.

BILL: We're getting lashed with Ron and Shirley on April Fool's Day. All above board.

KEY: Homebrew?

BILL: Ron'll be sloshed, Son. Can't cope with my homebrew. He'll be going to his shed, getting his trombone.

KEY: I'll be along, Pa. A matter of weeks. Mum won't know what's hit her.

BILL: Did ya drink the champagne?

The House of Games stuff?

KEY: Kept it back, Pa. We'll get sloshed on it, believe me. You, me and the mothership.

BILL: And you'll call her on Sunday, too. Mother's Day.

KEY: Don't I always?

BILL: To be fair you're not bad on that front.

The two men stand in the moonlight. One deep into his seventies, the other pissing about in the foothills of his mid-forties. The horse – eleven.

BILL: Well. That's me, Son. Better head. Your mother doesn't exactly love it when I'm out on the horse.

KEY: Will you stop on the way?

BILL: We'll go straight through, I think.

KEY: Sixty miles though.

BILL: He let the side down in the services on the way here. We'll go straight through, I think.

Bill Key reaches down to his panniers. Places a couple of Schweppes lemonade bottles full of homebrew on Key's bench. He adjusts his stirrups whilst he's down there. Swats a horsefly from his mount's penis.

KEY: Ride safely, won't you.

BILL: Put this bit in the book, eh. Our little chat.

KEY: Yeah.

BILL: Say I've got my top off and I rode down on a horse.

KEY: You *have* got your top off and you *did* ride down on a horse.

BILL: *(A smile; a wink)* Love it.

The thick splat of the hooves slapping the mud becomes quieter leaving the sax as the only sound issuing around the heath. Key becomes woozy and falls backwards onto the bench. He hoicks his pad from his Puma rucksack, pulls his pen from his drawers. An old-school desk appears before him and he hunches over it. The nib connects with the paper and ink comes out like a cobra emitting a thick black stream of potent venom. "Tim Key Tim Key Tim Key 4 coffee girl I heart coffee girl book 2 I love you coffee girl".

HERE WE GO ROUND THE MULBERRY BUSH.

MORE.†

I locked myself deeper and deeper.

The more I locked, the more hooked I got on locking.

I bought locks for the kitchen, the bedroom.

I commissioned a vast lock for my bed.

You wanna lock me up, huh?

Let's do the job properly.

I locked my ears to my pillow.

Locked my eyelids to my cheeks.

Shoved my thumb in my gob.

Clamped my gnashers into my knuckle.

---

†**JUNIPER:** I get this.
KEY: Mm.
JUNIPER: It was stressful. Everything unlocking like that.
KEY: It's the not knowing that kills you.
JUNIPER: And the virus, obviously.
KEY: And the virus, yes, Em.

Week X.

In which a bubble's walls evaporate, shimmering ales emerge on the horizon, and Key is reacquainted with a pink-snouted ghost from a bygone lockdown.

HERE WE GO ROUND THE MULBERRY BUSH.

AND ON AND ON AND ON.

I PHONED up the helpline.

Just wanted to double-check this thing was still going on, really.

They said it was and I said oh okay.

I put the phone down and sat back on the sofa.

I was surprised it was still going on.

It felt like it had been going on quite a while now.

I watched four episodes of Masterchef and did a press-up.

I phoned up my pal Ian and the two of us chatted about how it was going on quite a while and how one of the guys on Masterchef had knocked up some purple shit and undercooked his pears.

ENDGAME.

Key is frowning in Holland Park. Standing on a vast outdoor chessboard, he scratches his head like a latter-day Stan Laurel. The board's black-and-white squares are weather-beaten, its pieces: heavy, plastic, classical. The Sun beats down, picking out turrets and crowns, orbs and manes. Key stands on D4, fingering a rook. He is white and a piece up. He shields his eyes from the Sun, speaks quietly across the board.

KEY: How do you mean "switch bubble"?

Buddy leans on a pawn on H3. She is wearing thick shades and bows her head.

KEY: How do you mean "switch bubble" though?

Rick is pissing about on a horse on F8. Slapping its flanks with his palm. Pretending to hold onto its painted-on reins.

KEY: Bud? How do you mean "switch bubble"?

BUDDY: The fact is... *(Her voice is faltering)* It's my sister's birthday next Wednesday.

KEY: *(Almost inaudibly)* "You're fired."

BUDDY: You're not fired.

RICK: More of a hiatus, bro.

BUDDY: I just need to have some clear water if I want to see her, that's all. Need the gap.

KEY: She on her own?

BUDDY: Lives on her own, yuh. She can jump across. It's all legit. Switch her in, switch you out. Then switch her out, switch you back in.

RICK: Simples.

KEY: I see. I see, obviously, I see.

BUDDY: We've never spent a birthday apart, that's all.

KEY: Yet.

BUDDY: Well, I mean that's what I'm saying, we're trying to keep the streak going.

KEY: The streak. Of course.

Key looks into the middle distance and beyond. He drapes himself around his castle; peers into an arrow loop, hides his face.

RICK: Your move, buster.

Key looks up; tries to compose himself. He fetches up his castle, shuffles along, deposits it onto D8. He reaches over his shoulder into his Puma rucksack, stuffs a pair of shades on his snout.

KEY: And does this mean... I mean this is as of when?

BUDDY: The point being, we get the birthday done, cocktails, dancing, hoovering up romcoms, *et cetera* –

KEY: Okay, okay, I get the idea –

BUDDY: And then another ten days and you're back in.

KEY: Back in. Exactly.

RICK: Like a bad penny!

BUDDY: Rick!

KEY: Like I never went away.

BUDDY: Exactly.

KEY: Slot right back in. Just need to... I mean it's only, what, two weeks.

BUDDY: Three weeks all told. Ten days either side. I mean...

Key heaves a gigantic cloud of air into his lungs and his ribs creak.

RICK: Twenty-one days! Use it to write.

KEY: Huh?

Key's hand is in his pocket, his fingers curled around his orange pen, the blood in his veins is moving quickly.

RICK: Yeeeee-haaaaa!!!

Rick makes his horse ride up, jabs his filthy spurs into its flanks and takes two steps forward, one to the right. Tethers him on D7. Grins.

RICK: Check!

BUDDY: Oh, don't put him in check, you mean sod. That's all he needs.

KEY: *(Staring at his castle)* No it's okay, Bud. I'll be fine.

BUDDY: *(Brightly now)* Oh, Tim! You can shack up with the coffee girl.

RICK: Ha ha! In his dreams.

BUDDY: But why must it be in his dreams? Why not in real life? You'll be a free agent, Kiddo. Invite her round for an M&S Dine In. She lives alone, right?

RICK: Ha ha!

BUDDY: You could heat up some moussaka okay, couldn't you? Have it on your terrace!

But Key is dreaming of more. More than moussaka and lemon meringue pie. More than Malbec in the drizzle. He leans on his turrets, imagines the coffee girl tethering her horse outside, imagines her lifting up her skirts, plodding up the spiral staircases, her hems barely kissing the joyless steps. Imagines her joining him at the battlements; pouring her mead, drinking from chalices. Imagines them both descending to the keep, retiring to a stone bench, banging on Jeeves and Wooster, twirling her medieval locks in his gnarled fingers, smoking menthols. He blinks; steps back from the castle, surveys the board.

KEY: And there's no probs with me coming back in?

BUDDY: None.

KEY: I love our bubble, that's all.

BUDDY: You're back in, I swear.

KEY: I can do better, you know. Bring me back in, I'll do better. I'll work twice as hard. I'll bring round cheese, I'll... yer know...

BUDDY: You don't have to do more.

KEY: I'll paint your lounge.

RICK: You're not painting our lounge.

BUDDY: Rick.

RICK: Well, he's not. He'll fuck the whole thing up.

BUDDY: We can have a painting party, for sure. Could be fun.

RICK: Fun getting flecks of yellow paint out of the sofa for the next six months, sure.

BUDDY: You're coming straight back in, we promise.

Key wanders over to his king. He turns from his friends, wipes the inside of his shades with the top of his snood. Focuses on his breathing. In for five; out for five. He edges his king out of danger, sits cross-legged on E7.

KEY: And tonight?

Buddy lowers her head. She is upset.

KEY: I'm still up for watching Harry and Meghan.

RICK: Spilling their guts. Ha!

KEY: Watch Oprah poking away, chow down on some pizza, Bananagrams. If we can sneak it in.

BUDDY: It's Sunday today, that's the only thing.

Buddy's pulled a hankie from the very depths of her bag and is stuffing it between her eyes and her shades.

KEY: Am I out the bubble already?

BUDDY: Just because... it's Sunday, so the clock's sort of started ticking. Sort of as of today.

RICK: We can order the same pizza at the same time in our own homes, watch along on Zoom. Do it that way.

BUDDY: Could be nice?

Key nods. He stands up on E7 and pushes past an errant pawn. Then he walks diagonally across the board like a bishop. Arrives at H2.

KEY: I'll be there. Three weeks today. I'll bring the bubbly. We'll talk about our adventures.

BUDDY: We will.

RICK: We can have Lord and Megan round by then, pretty much.

KEY: *(Welling up again)* The roadmap.

BUDDY: Another month and you can go in whoever's house you like.

KEY: I can?

RICK: People you know!

BUDDY: Yes, it has to be people you know.

Key smiles, throws his arms round Rick and Buddy. Sets the clock back to zero again. Pulls his friends towards him.

KEY: I fucking love our bubble.

Rick uses one of his size twelves to quietly push the black queen onto H5. And now the clock starts once more. Tick tock.

BUDDY: Best bubble in town.

Key wanders, disorientated, over to his king. He brushes his neck with his knuckles as he surveys the board. His friends are smiling; Buddy through tears. Flashes of light fly off Rick's teeth like lasers. Key glimpses the black queen and nods. Checkmate.

†**JUNIPER:** You don't really imagine *him* getting jabbed, do you?
KEY: Leading by example, I s'pose.
JUNIPER: I guess most celebs will have got done.
KEY: Oh, God yeah.
JUNIPER: Bill Bryson.
KEY: Yup, I expect Bill will have got the jab, Em.
JUNIPER: Gail Emms.
KEY: The badminton player?
JUNIPER: Suggs.
KEY: Yeah, a lot of people in the public eye will have been vaccinated, Em.
JUNIPER: It's actually quite reassuring.
KEY: Yeah.
JUNIPER: Titchmarsh.
KEY: The great and the good.

ONE UP THE BUM.[†]

BOHNSON reversed into the jabbing cubicle.

"Fill 'er up!"

The doctors dunked their needles into buckets and sucked up the nonk.

Other doctors from other cubicles smelled the stardust and waddled in with full syringes, too.

"Sterling work, chaps!"

Bohnson had on his West Cornwall Pasty Co. singlet, fresh tennis shorts and leadership clogs.

"The more the merrier! On three?"

Other doctors and some of the goons from the front desk squeezed into the cubicle – there must have been eighty of them now, their thick serums glistening on their needles.

Sir Matthew Boytwitch was dancing about excitedly as the dripping tips hovered around Bohnson's biceps, bollocks and bottom.

"Like an old-school pin cushion!" he bayed. "One, two, three! Let him have it!"

Plungers depressed.

Flashbulbs detonated.

Party poppers discharged.

Geronimooooo!

Bohnson's lips appeared to inflate slightly as pints and pints of nonk slipped through his hide and gushed around his vitals.

PENNY.

I SHOVED my swab stick thing so far up my hooter it came out with thoughts on it.

I examined the glistening pugil.

Tiny, smudged, broken thoughts.

Fears about incoming restrictions.

Mad hopes for the summer.

Squished daydreams of barbecues and ice-cold ciders.

♥

OUR CHILDREN ARE OUR FUTURE.

THE kids went back to school.

They all had to wear gas masks and shin pads and wicket-keeping helmets and jab themselves the whole time.

Their books had to be glued closed and painted with a "Dettol gel".

Teachers faced away from class and bounced their lessons in off vast teaching mirrors.

At lunchtime the government abandoned the experiment and the kids were placed upside down in buses which took them to hotels near airports for ten days and then home, where they had to type up their notes and scratch their heads and hope for the best.

FOE.

Key is lost. He's gone too deep into a spinney and now he's struggling to get back out. Brambles cling to his flanks. He is snagged, right enough. He stamps his Gazelles. The ground shakes, sending vibrations up the trees, rippling through the trunks and spewing out of the uppermost branches, making the clouds judder.

KEY: Dammit Janet!!!

He squirms and thrusts and ultimately, through sheer force of will, unhooks himself from the cloying knives of the scrambling furze and pitches forward, splatting into a glade.

MOUSE: Ha!

Key looks across the glade. A mouse. Stood, stock-still, in the middle, by some bone-dry leaves. Its pink nose glistens, its whiskers appear brittle from the cold.

KEY: Who are you?

MOUSE: Mouse.

KEY: I can see you're a mouse, pal. Your rancid whiskers were the giveaway.

MOUSE: Hello, Mister.

An impasse. Key squinting at this pale being. He must not weigh more than two ounces, and yet here he is, standing his ground. Cool as you like. A mouse.

MOUSE: Well?

KEY: Well, what's going on? What's your name?

MOUSE: How's your lockdown?

KEY: Do I know you?

MOUSE: "Does he know me," he asks.

Key squints. A flashback. A lightning strike. Trauma.

MOUSE: Lockdown One?

Key's eyebrows knit hard. They knit so hard the top of his face is dragged together and becomes bunched, inflating the lower portion as a consequence.

MOUSE: I spent ten weeks in your flat?

Key's eyebrows unravel and separate and his jaws deflate and swing.

KEY: You have got to be fucking kidding me.

Key looks around flabbergasted. The mouse takes a step back, leans lavishly on a discarded 660 ml bottle of Asahi.

KEY: The mouse from before, huh?

MOUSE: You slung me out.

KEY: You had no right to be there.

The mouse nods, straightens a whisker. He's put on weight since before. Key nods, too. Bites his lip.

KEY: Fix yourself up with somewhere okay, did ya?

MOUSE: Yeah, I mean... yeah...

KEY: As in?

MOUSE: We had a few days where we were trying to work it out.

KEY: The fuck does that mean?

MOUSE: Well, the missus didn't want just any old place, yer know. None of us did.

KEY: Well, beggars can't be choosers, surely.

MOUSE: She likes a bath, basically.

KEY: Oh, sure, welcome to my world. That's my refuge, the bath.

MOUSE: That and the booze.

KEY: Huh?

MOUSE: Nah, fair play, you know. Fiddly things to negotiate, lockdowns.

KEY: Watching me getting sozzled, was it?

MOUSE: Ha ha. Yeah. I guess.

KEY: So what? So I open the odd can in lockdown.

The mouse doesn't say anything. Key bows his head.

KEY: And what do you drink? Lemme guess.

MOUSE: Water.

KEY: Yeah, knew it. Water. Soooo adventurous.

MOUSE: Well, what do you want me to do? Go buy myself a can of Diet Coke? Spend the best part of a week trying to get the cunt open?

KEY: Come on. Let's sit.

Key gestures to a tree trunk, fallen in olden times. They take a seat. The mouse's legs swing. Détente. Key pulls out his Penelope Pitstop flask.

MOUSE: I don't drink hot drinks, cheers.

KEY: What hot drink?

Key opens his flask. Pssscht. The flask breathes an amber mist into the glade. The mouse's nose quivers.

KEY: Wait a second, wait a second.

MOUSE: What?

KEY: Your missus. Was she taking baths in my bath?

MOUSE: What are you talking about? I already told ya – she likes a bath.

KEY: Jesus wept.

Key pours out two vessels. The two life-forms clasp them. The mouse takes a sip of Jaipur IPA. Nanoscopic bubbles go up his snout. He likes it.

KEY: I'm saying... how does she draw it?

MOUSE: Nah. Nah, she'd wait till you were asleep in the tub, then she'd hop in.

KEY: What?

MOUSE: While you were wallowing.

The mouse takes a bigger sip. It's going down okay, this ale.

MOUSE: She appreciated the candles, I know that. You vaccinated?

KEY: Where the fuck's that come from?

MOUSE: You're vulnerable, huh?

KEY: *(Thrown)* Reading my mail, too?

MOUSE: The missus heard you on a call to the hospital.

KEY: *(Flat)* Oh, she did, huh?

Key tops up the mouse. The mouse necks it and jumps down off the log. He's unsteady on his feet. His eyes gleam.

MOUSE: Well, listen – nice to catch up, mate.

KEY: I had a mouse in my bath for three months. Jesus.

MOUSE: Ha, yeah. Live and let live.

KEY: It's fucking gross.

MOUSE: Don't say it's fucking gross. That's my wife.

Key nods. He refills his cup and screws the lids back on the flask. He slings the flask in his Puma pack. Sighs.

MOUSE: I gotta get back. He opens the door at six, we all pile back in.

KEY: Where'd'ya end up this time then? Who opens the door?

MOUSE: You know Stephen Merchant?

Key almost chokes on his Jaipur.

KEY: You're in with Merchant now?

MOUSE: He's fantastic.

KEY: Yeah I think I know Stephen Merchant's fantastic, cheers.

MOUSE: Yuh. Guy's got a big house. Doesn't know we're there.

KEY: Another lockdown, another comedian, is it?

MOUSE: We all love his stuff.

KEY: Watching The Office is he? You all stealing a look over his shoulder?

MOUSE: He's funny in real life. He's an enjoyable presence. You know.

KEY: And I wasn't?

MOUSE: You're both very different.

KEY: I'm not at my best in lockdowns, that's all! I'm best when stuff's unlocked. Don't judge me on lockdowns. Come see the shows!

MOUSE: I seen the shows, I told ya. I love the shows.

Key nods, shuts the hell up, shoves his thumb in his mouth.

MOUSE: I saw you down Dalston once. Snuck in at the back.

KEY: Yeah, yeah The Arcola.

MOUSE: I love what you do. I mean I don't reckon I get it, not all of it.

He does an "it goes over my head" gesture. Points at Key.

MOUSE: You're looking good.

KEY: Thirteen thousand steps a day.

MOUSE: That'd do it.

The mouse picks up his bindle and is away. Key sits back on the tree trunk. Delves into his bag. Hunts for the flask once more.

HERE WE GO ROUND THE MULBERRY BUSH.

JUPITER.[†]

ELEANOR Jupiter, flying through the air.

Typewriters, spinning to earth around her.

A rain of ink, coming down in jet-black spears.

Above her, in a despondent descent, a poet.

Wrapped in a fleece, his sallow hand reaches for her as he tumbles past.

Grasping into the chaos.

Trying to spring Eleanor Jupiter from her wondrous vortex.

He offers her scraps to type on her plummeting machines.

He offers her company as their fall accelerates.

[†]**JUNIPER:** *(Eyes glistening)* Is that me then?
KEY: It's Eleanor Jupiter.
JUNIPER: It reminds me of my name a bit.
KEY: Yuh-huh.
JUNIPER: I'm usually in the dialogues. Don't usually crop up in the poems.
KEY: I was worried about you, that's all.
JUNIPER: You put me in a poem.
KEY: I was glad you turned up, let's put it that way.
JUNIPER: Like a bad penny.
KEY: Nothing good ever happened without a designer in tow.

BUCHUNG UND STORNIERUNG.[†]

Shane Width phoned the travel agency.

"I'd like to book and cancel a holiday to the Black Forest, please."

The lady on the phone was marvellous with him.

She found a hotel just outside Furtwangen and booked and cancelled a double room for ten nights.

Then she booked flights to Baden-Baden and a train, which would take Shane and his fiancée from Baden-Baden to Furtwangen, and a taxi to the hotel.

She then cancelled all of that lot, too.

Shane placed his phone back in its holster and waited for his emails to come, confirming his bookings and cancellations, so he could then delete those, too.

While he waited for them to drop he grabbed his diary, his Parker fountain pen and a tub of Tipp-Ex and texted Marlie, boasting about how *ruthlessly* efficient he was being.

[†]**JUNIPER:** Booking and cancelling.
KEY: Yup. Rick and Buddy had one cancelled. Booked the hell out of it. All the flights, everything. Then whoomph.
JUNIPER: Whole thing cancelled.
KEY: Ended up having to cobble something together in Wales.
JUNIPER: The old staycation, huh. Oh, your vein on your temple's popped out a bit.
KEY: Well, yeah, anyway they went on holiday to Wales. West Wales, it was.
JUNIPER: 2021. The year of the staycation. Your vein's throbbing a bit.
KEY: It's certainly a year for holidaying in the UK. Can't rely on the flights.
JUNIPER: Yup. Make do with a staycation this year. Then maybe next year... your vein on the other side's gone a bit now. It's purple, like an aubergine.
KEY: I'm going to get some air.
JUNIPER: We're outside.
KEY: Well, either way, I'm going to walk down to that tree and back.
JUNIPER: Okay, I'll man the fort.

CLOVER.[†]

ST. Paddy's Day down the jab centre!

Green dye in the vaccines and Guinness hats all round. My doctor had gone the extra mile.

He was wearing what he explained to me was a Piggyback Paddy's leprechaun costume.

And he was giving the accent a good old go, too!

There was certainly some Irish in there, along with a soupçon of Geordie.

He slapped a sticker on my chest and shoved me into the waiting pen.

I chiselled open a can of "da black stuff" and slung that down my throat, too.

"Nature's vaccine," I mouthed to the rosy-cheeked fiddler.

He smiled back.

He'd been injected with something or other, too, I reckon.

His knee was going like the absolute clappers.

---

†**JUNIPER:** You wrote this on St. Patrick's Day.
KEY: Yuh.
JUNIPER: Quint made Guinness soup.
KEY: I really think... I mean Quint's gone now and it does you no good wasting your time thinking about him.
JUNIPER: Heated up a four pack with some butter, dropped in some clams and winkles, handful of whole black peppercorns.
KEY: Jesus wept.
JUNIPER: I stormed out, right there. Hated seeing that lot coming together on my hob.
KEY: Aye.
JUNIPER: Sat down on the marina. Tried to forget about him.
KEY: Guy's a maggot, right enough.
JUNIPER: Mm.
KEY: A Maggot. No more or less.

MOTHER'S DAY.

Key is sat on the foothills of Parliament Hill. A sunny day. Daffodils everywhere, strong, ambitious daffodils, surging up towards the blue skies. A patchwork of green and yellow with paths stitching through it like seams. And beside the paths: benches, Victorian. And on one such bench: The Poet. Sat with a mocha in one hand, his iPhone in the other. Across the daffs, on another bench: an old lady. Well, not old, but... Mid-seventies. She has a bunch of flowers on her lap. Key blinks. Blinks hard. Pushes it all back. Sweeps life into his iPhone, sweeps to favourites, sweeps to Ma, sweeps to give the old hen a ring.

CAROL: What do we think? He unlocking us? Always looks like it. Then he holds another briefing, fesses up, says he's welding us back in.

KEY: Hi, Mum.

CAROL: Hi, Son.

KEY: Happy Mother's Day.

CAROL: I got the flowers. They're beautiful.

Opposite, the old lady's phone is going. She places her bouquet down on the bench next to her, goes into her handbag, re-emerges with her phone. Some weird Nokia, uphanded to her from her progeny. She answers it and her face is animate now. Smiling.

KEY: The kicker is, it's not just that one bunch, Ma. You get another one in April and another one in May. It's a subscription.

CAROL: I know, you put all that in the note.

KEY: You could choose twelve months, six months or three months.

CAROL: And you went for three.

KEY: There's method in my madness, Ma! It takes us up to the end of lockdown. Everything's sorted by May. Everything's back up and running.

CAROL: So you say.

KEY: The roadmap, Ma. Believe in the roadmap!

CAROL: Well, it's a lovely gesture,

Tim. That's what it is. I've put them in that filthy great vase you got us from Kiev.

KEY: Filthy?

CAROL: They look beautiful. I love them. They've brightened up my Sunday, that's what.

Key smiles. The old lady across the daffodils appears to smile back. She is nodding, listening, smiling. Occasionally she strokes the flowers, as if they are sentient. As if their fronds connect in some way to her son's limbs. She opens her mouth to speak again. Not that Key can hear her. He is out of earshot.

CAROL: We've got daffs in the garden. I'm sat in there now, on the bench.

KEY: I like that bench.

CAROL: Surprised you remember it.

KEY: It's only been a year, Ma.

CAROL: You were lashed last time you were on that bench.

KEY: Ha.

CAROL: The good old days.

KEY: You got that right.

CAROL: Disgraceful, really.

KEY: Dad's homebrew, eh.

CAROL: He put sixty gallons of the stuff into bottles last night.

KEY: Oh he did, huh?

CAROL: He was singing about getting unlocked.

KEY: You have to remain optimistic.

CAROL: I dug out your brother's trumpet. I was playing that. Your father singing. Beer flowing into bottles.

KEY: Schweppes bottles, huh?

CAROL: Yeah. Yeah it was flowing into Schweppes bottles, Son. And him singing about that, too.

KEY: Where is he now?

CAROL: Where do you think?

KEY: Riding Barnard Castle?

CAROL: Riding Barnard Castle. Guy's a lunatic.

KEY: You've gotta have a project, Ma.

Key wipes his eyes. The old lady across the way wipes hers. But she is also laughing. Which brings us back to Key, because he is also laughing.

CAROL: Ah, Son.

KEY: Mother.

CAROL: It's our fiftieth wedding anniversary in April.

KEY: I know, Mum.

CAROL: I guess he'll find a way of bollocksing that up, too.

KEY: He usually does.

CAROL: Weird little man, locking our doors for the best part of a year.

KEY: We'll be able to do something, trust me –

CAROL: I think you should be able to apply for - what's the word? - say "it's our bloody golden wedding anniversary, throw us a bone!"

KEY: "Dispensation."

CAROL: Never mind that, I want to see everyone! Take the grandchildren to Center Parcs.

KEY: That ain't on the roadmap, Ma. Not for April.

CAROL: I wanna see my grandchildren hurtling down the rapids.

KEY: That's what we all wanna see.

CAROL: Their hands grabbing onto your father's ankles.

Key nods. Heaves in a vast breath, heavy with the fresh, rehabilitating perfume being honked out by the daffs.

KEY: I'm getting my jab tomorrow, Mum.

CAROL: It's the anniversary of the first lockdown.

KEY: And I'm getting a needle up my bum.

CAROL: Well, you must do something nice after. Doughnuts or something.

KEY: Getting smash-faced with John.

CAROL: Good. Because you must. You'll have earned it.

KEY: You feeling healthy?

CAROL: It's taken years off me. The stuff's a miracle.

KEY: It's what's getting us out of this mess, Ma.

CAROL: Your father thinks it's made his beard thicker.

KEY: The guy's lost it, Ma.

CAROL: He stuck a fork in it and it didn't fall out.

KEY: Stuffing forks in his beard now.

CAROL: He's had it in for a fortnight now. Thinks it's a sign of strength. Will we see you on the Zoom at five thirty?

KEY: Don't you always?

CAROL: You're always there, yes.

KEY: There or thereabouts.

CAROL: Sometimes you miss it.

KEY: I do indeed.

CAROL: But not often.

KEY: I like to put in an appearance.

CAROL: Well, it's Mother's Day today.

KEY: I know, Ma. I'll be there.

CAROL: I'll put the lovely flowers in shot when we Zoom.

KEY: It'll be nice to see them.

CAROL: "In shot". Sound like Spielberg over here. No but I'll put some thought into the shot.

KEY: If you could, ha ha.

CAROL: I bet you've drunk your House of Games champagne have you?

KEY: No, Ma. We'll drink that together, in the sunshine.

CAROL: Lovely, nice little family lash.

KEY: Love you, Ma.

CAROL: Ha ha, get on with ya.

Key hangs up. Chews on his mocha thoughtfully. The mother across the way has finished her call, too. She sits in the Sun, like a terrapin. The Sun's rays warming her, a salve to her heart's bruises, bashed about by the separation. She smiles at Key and he smiles back. She waves. Key blinks tears into his eyelashes. He waves back.

†**JUNIPER:** Ha ha. Like tartan paint!

KEY: Well, no. I mean not really. This one's about linking good vax to patriotism.

JUNIPER: I'm sure the jocks are proud of their tartan paint.

KEY: Huh? No, this is the one where politicians have a ton of flags behind them when they're being interviewed. And then they're saying we're number one in the world and sucking each other off 'cos our nerds made the best vax.

JUNIPER: How do they keep all the different colours separate when it's in the pot?

KEY: Em, there's no such thing as tartan paint.

JUNIPER: You'd think it'd all mix in there and it'd be purple or something by the time you painted it on.

KEY: (*Sipping, frowning, sipping, nodding*) Yeah. Yeah you would.

JUNIPER: It's a bit of a mystery, eh.

KEY: Yup. Yup, that is mad how they've worked out how to do that.

JUNIPER: This is why I think they should be proud.

FOR KING AND COUNTRY.[†]

THEY pulled the vaccine.
"Sorry, it wasn't ready, wait a second, wait a second."
They squirted it all back into the vats.
Then they added Union Jack dye.
Buckets of the stuff.
The MPs dunked their fingers into it, it was perfect.
Red, White and Blue.
Brought a tear to the eye.
So much more flaggy.
They ladled it back into syringes, scattered it back into the gyms and hospital hubs, restarted the rollout.
For Britain now.
And as it flowed into biceps, so chests pumped out and chins stiffened and pride was restored.

THE IMPOSTER.

Key is in a new park. He is sitting amongst The Sunday Times, pulled apart like pork, its sections surrounding him, rippling as the breeze moves through it. Various details show themselves as the pages flutter and separate. The Anti-Protest Bill waved through, Jos Buttler smiting eighty-three not out in Ahmedabad, Magufuli: dead. Key's orange pen is out. Its lid is off, and Key is circling something. Tears roll down his cheeks. Again and again he circles it. Underlines it, highlights it. Boxes it in. His iPhone is clamped to his ear. It rings and it rings. And then. Click.

KEY: Emily Juniper! You're back! Hi! Amazing news! I'm reading the papers in the park and you'll never guess what? Em?

Key stops chewing his cinnamon bun. Silence. He squints at a distant slide. A chain of children sliding down, running round, spiralling up the steps, then sliding down again.

KEY: Em?

QUINT: Emily ain't in.

Key's tongue is still. Cinnamon bun coagulates around Key's gnashers, slides slowly down into his gum, is absorbed into his blood. Key frowns.

KEY: *(A murmer)* Quint.

QUINT: The same.

Key closes his eyes. He wants Emily Juniper. He doesn't want Quint. Not now. Not ever. Cinnamon blows into the air as he talks.

KEY: Where is she, Quint?

QUINT: She's out of town.

KEY: Out of town how? Out of town where?

QUINT: Drawing clocks, man! Don't you get it! You've driven her to it. She draws clocks now, bro!

KEY: Wait a second, how have I driven her to it?

QUINT: 'Cos you ain't gave her nothing to design, bro! Don't you see? A whole lockdown and nothing to put on the page. She's skipped town, taken her coals. She's sketching

time, man. Sketching time.

Quint's voice is like glue. Sticking to the receiver as it comes out, words gripping onto one another, the whole thing a blob. Key having to stretch it apart to discern what this charlatan is saying to him.

KEY: Well, did she get my letter?

QUINT: What letter?

KEY: Don't play dumb with me, Quint. The letter. I sent her a letter.

QUINT: I haven't seen no letter.

KEY: If you've nicked that bloody letter, Quint –

QUINT: Why am I nicking a letter?

KEY: Because you're a scandal, Quint.

QUINT: How d'ya make that out?

KEY: You have a certain responsibility, if you are invited into a bubble –

QUINT: I offer value, don't worry about that –

KEY: Bad bubbler!

QUINT: No!

KEY: I say you are a bad bubbler!

QUINT: And I say I earn my keep. I make cheese, you've never seen so much cheese.

KEY: Stinking the place out, Quint! That's what!

QUINT: *(With bite)* I know who you are! You're the writer! Tim Key! The writer who ain't writing!

KEY: I could have been down there, Quint.

QUINT: She threw a protective wing around me, pal.

KEY: Should have been nowhere near you, Quint. Should have been round me. I could have caused mayhem in Cornwall, man. I'd have written down there! Believe me. Hammered Emily Juniper's typewriter! Don't worry about that. I'd've fucking battered it!

QUINT: I read your book.

KEY: Huh?

Key falls forward onto his supplements. His elbows digging down into a vast photo of

Sophie Ellis-Bextor in her kitchen.

KEY: Pardon me?

QUINT: Diary of a madman.

KEY: It's an account of the first lockdown, Quint, that's what it is.

QUINT: I can't handle it, that's what it is. It's spinning me out. I pour myself a glass of port –

KEY: Emily Juniper's port –

QUINT: Read it with my mouth open.

KEY: She mentioned you dribbled on it, Quint.

QUINT: I'm not apologising for that.

KEY: It's printed on Italian paper, Quint, but hey-ho, who gives a fuck about that, huh?

QUINT: Spit the port out at times. I'm like, "What the hell is going on with this guy?"

Key nods. His pen on the paper again. Circling.

QUINT: What's in the letter?

KEY: It's chapter one, Quint. I'm writing!

QUINT: Oh, you are?

KEY: I don't know. I... why am I telling you this, Quint? I need to talk to Em.

QUINT: And I'm saying she's out.

KEY: Yeah, and you're in.

QUINT: Yeah, and you're jealous.

KEY: Not of you, Quint.

QUINT: Jealous you didn't get the nod.

KEY: Yeah, how about I come down there, Quint? Have a proper dust-up.

QUINT: Yeah, let's do it. Let's go. How does Monday sound?

KEY: Nah.

QUINT: Yeah, you see.

KEY: Having my vax on Monday, you ignoramus.

QUINT: You're the ignoramus if you're having the vax.

Key rams another vast clod of bun into his trap. Pulverises it, swallows it.

KEY: You're anti-vax, huh?

QUINT: Not having that muck in my arms, cheers.

KEY: *Quelle surprise.*

QUINT: Would you pump gorillas' spunk into your veins if the government told you to?

KEY: I'm not even going to dignify that with a response, Quint.

QUINT: The slapheads okay it, you bang it in, huh?

KEY: If the WHO's on board with it, then yeah.

QUINT: Yeah?

KEY: Yeah, bang it in.

QUINT: Shove it in now, ask questions later.

KEY: Tell her to call when she's home, eh.

QUINT: Oh, not up for the debate, huh?

KEY: You do you, Quint. Tatty bye.

QUINT: You got a message?

KEY: What message?

QUINT: Well, you said you had amazing news.

KEY: Yeah, which I'll tell her when we catch up, cheers, Quint.

QUINT: Sounded urgent, that's all.

KEY: Yeah. Urgent for her ears. Not urgent for your rancid lugholes, Quint.

QUINT: Come on, bro, why not tell Old Quint?

KEY: Because it's news I want to share with Emily Juniper, that's why. Special news.

QUINT: Try me.

KEY: *(Snapping. Proud)* We're in The Times Bestsellers List.

QUINT: Oh, you're hard.

Key hangs up. Quint moves across the kitchen. He is wearing baggy y-fronts and a Phil Collins t-shirt. On the back: tour dates. From '89. On the front, the bald tax-exile himself. Quint grabs the instant Kenco, pours it directly into a mug that still has some tea in it. He bungs some lukewarm water in it from the kettle, stirs it with his thumb and waddles through to the fire. Another Day In Paradise.

†**JUNIPER:** If I got to have a go in a time machine –
KEY: "Have a go in". It's not a dodgem, Em.
JUNIPER: I'd go to Wuhan.
KEY: What the fuck?
JUNIPER: Sneak into –
KEY: Em, you'd stick out like a sore thumb!
JUNIPER: I can be sneaky when I want to be.
KEY: You're an artist, Em. They'd see your scarves and your dungarees a mile off.
JUNIPER: See if I could seal down the lab.
KEY: What do you even mean by "seal down".
JUNIPER: I don't know, do I? New doors. Paint over the cracks.
KEY: Thought it was a wet market, anyway. Bats, no?
JUNIPER: Go there, too, then. Pretend to be a minister, have 'em get their act together.
KEY: Parading round Wuhan, can't speak a word of Chinese –
JUNIPER: Well, where would you go, then?
KEY: 2007 probably. Have another crack at my thirties.

TIME MACHINE.[†]

GREAT Scott!
They invented a time machine!
Finally.
Any date you liked.
I voted for March 2002.
Yes please, Louise!
Back to the The Pickerel please, another evening with Hettie, iron things out, charm her senseless, put a ring on it.
I could barely contain my excitement!
I slapped my digits in.
But, in my excitement, I bollocksed up my numbers!
Accidentally typed in March 2020.
My heart sank.
"You've gotta be fucking kidding me!"
The lights began to flash and the seat was jiggling.
I hated where I was off to.
Pubs open but not meant to go in them.
Keys turning in locks.
Definite year of bollocks sprawling before me.

HERE WE GO ROUND THE MULBERRY BUSH.

TALKS.

"IT'S not a question of compromise, it really isn't, old boy."

Bohnson was on a Zoom call with the head of the covids.

He had on a Pink Panther tie and he'd borrowed the gardener's glasses for the meeting.

"I haven't even said our demands yet," the head of the covids sneered.

His nose was sharp and he had so much gel in his hair it was obscene.

"Ha! Bit late for demands, old boy. We're blasting your mob with vax these days!"

To be fair to Bohnson, he was nailing this meeting.

He grabbed a syringe he'd placed by his Dell and pumped it at the screen.

"En garde!"

The rancid covid flinched.

He'd set up the Zoom summit maybe four months too late.

He had nothing to work with!

He had about a thousand eyes and they flickered and squinted.

He consulted his shitty little notes and picked at an angry boil on his neck.

AND IF IT RAINS?

It is late. Late enough. Key is a dark figure once more, silhouetted on Parliament Hill by an anxious Moon. He is stood on his bench. Surveying his city. A crooked arm presses an iPhone against an ear. A mouth, vexed in the moonlight. A troubled poet with thin, contorted lips. Words spilling into the night.

KEY: ... and that's all really, Em. Just to say "call me". I'm not worried, of course. You're somewhere sketching a clock, I'm sure. Time on your hands, and charcoal down your blouse. And that's your prerogative and... and I think you're calling me! Ha!

A flash of white as the Moon zaps a cheekbone. Key's thumb sweeps his iPhone and he leaps from the bench. And now Key bleats into his phone.

KEY: Emily Juniper!

COLONEL: Nup! *Il Colonnello!*

KEY: *(Faint)* Colonel.

COLONEL: Why'd Emily Juniper be phoning you at midnight?

KEY: Why are you phoning me at midnight?

COLONEL: Because I'm looking at my diary and I've got a social engagement with a certain poet tomorrow.

KEY: Ha!

COLONEL: I'm thinking: last of the lockdown, maybe. As we know it.

KEY: Yes, Colonel. Things are opening up. Pages of diaries are being prised apart. Nibs are being stuffed between pages. Arrangements are being forced in.

COLONEL: I am pouring shit into my diary this end.

KEY: I don't know what I'm doing over here, Colonel.

Key looks down the hill. Shadows, zephyrs, earthshine. A silver badge is bobbing up and down in the distance. It gleams in the moonlight as it moves closer. Then it bobs behind some trees. Disappears.

COLONEL: Let's put some proper plans in. Once we've opened up.

KEY: We have tomorrow night, Colonel. We are where we are.

COLONEL: Proper plans, I'm saying!

Not glugging bottles of liquid faeces in the elements.

KEY: "Liquid faeces"! Eh? "Elements"? We'll be sound, bro.

COLONEL: And if it rains?

KEY: Why's it raining in March?

COLONEL: So you're guaranteeing no rain?

KEY: I'm guaranteeing I'll be stood on your doorstep at 7 PM. I'm guaranteeing I'll have an arm full of vax. I'm guaranteeing we're walking up to Pond Square.

COLONEL: Guarantee me no rain!

KEY: I'm guaranteeing I'll have a Sainsbury's bag full of beers and I'm not ruling out Twiglets.

COLONEL: And if it rains?

KEY: Then we'll find a...

COLONEL: What? Pub?

KEY: I was going to say "bit of corrugated iron".

COLONEL: What?

KEY: We'll find a way, Colonel, that's what. We always do, don't we?

COLONEL: I wanna celebrate your vax, bro. That's all.

KEY: I know.

COLONEL: Can't do that with ten gallons of rain flowing off my nose.

KEY: Okay. Okay, I guarantee no rain, John. You have my word.

COLONEL: Thank you. *(A sigh; contented)* Well, night, broseph.

KEY: We can't break it, Colonel. We can't break the lockdown. Not when we're so close. Night, then.

Key takes a breath. His phone becomes heavy. His arm becomes long. His knees bend. His head lolls on his chest.

POLICEMAN: Almost there, Son.

KEY: Huh?

Key spins round. The policeman's badge, riddled with moonlight, gleams from the bench that Key vacated. Beneath the badge, the face. Redder than ever. Squishy. Kind. And on his lap, a weird case.

POLICEMAN: That your sweetheart?

KEY: Huh? Oh. No. The Colonel.

POLICEMAN: Oh. Thought you might

be hatching a plan to... yer know, get off with some lass as soon as the bells ring out.

Key's eyes sparkle. He stares down the hill. Stares down at the blank space where the coffee wagon once was. Where it will be again. He peers across the city. Where is the wagon tonight?

POLICEMAN: I'm going on a date I think. After this is over.

KEY: Oh, you are?

And now both men are staring at the blank space where the coffee wagon once was. Where it will be again. And Key's eyes disappear down his throat.

KEY: *(Coughing)* Who with?

POLICEMAN: Wouldn't you like to know?

KEY: I would. I'd like to know.

POLICEMAN: Gotta make plans. Going Euros, me. That's happening, yer know. Me and a couple of constables gonna bag ourselves tickets –

KEY: I'd like to go to the snooker.

POLICEMAN: In Sheffield?

KEY: Nooooo. The snooker in Timbuktu! Yes in Sheffield.

POLICEMAN: Exciting, innit? The unlock.

KEY: Um... yeah... I mean... Yeah... Just... Dunno. Sometimes feel like I want to... I dunno...

POLICEMAN: Stay locked? Is that what you mean? Stay locked?

Key becomes aware he is clutching his pen in his pocket. Clutching it hard, making its shaft bulge either side of his fist. He holds it out to the policeman. As if the pen is the answer to everything.

POLICEMAN: Oh, I see. Well...

And now the policeman taps his case.

KEY: What's that then?

POLICEMAN: Got me through, this did.

KEY: What is it, I'm saying.

Key squints. What's in the case? A gun? Has the policeman brought a musket to the top of Parliament Hill? Is this how the policeman unwinds? By firing shots across the city?

KEY: On the one hand I want it all back. All of it. I want my diary flooded, you know. On the other hand I want to weld the cunt shut. Am I making any sense? Everywhere I look I'm accidentally making plans.

POLICEMAN: Now then... .

KEY: What?

POLICEMAN: Just... Well, what do you reckon? Early summer, you and I dunk our beaks into a couple of draught beers. I know you're saying –

KEY: Aaaaaagggggghhhh!!!!

POLICEMAN: I'm gonna pop us in for June 2nd. We can always change it.

PC Gourd scribbles in his little notebook.

KEY: *(Quiet; dismantled)* Is that why you came up here? Huh? Collar me for a post-lockdown knees-up?

POLICEMAN: Oh, God no.

The policeman taps his case. Key admires its bronze lock-clasp. He gazes into his kindly, port-coloured face. He has nothing left.

KEY: Please tell me who your date's with, mate.

POLICEMAN: Ha. *(Wistful)* 'Tis with my music teacher.

KEY: With your music teacher?

POLICEMAN: With my music teacher.

The policeman's eyes are becoming moist and he pulls his helmet down another inch. But his voice is warm with optimism.

POLICEMAN: So we shall see how that goes.

Key nods. He elbow bashes the PC.

KEY: It's important to have hope.

POLICEMAN: We can break it down in the pub.

KEY: Yes, let's *definitely* do that.

POLICEMAN: On the second.

Key nods and begins to walk. And as he walks he hears a click behind him. The brass clasps of the case, no doubt. And he continues to walk. And now the whole of the heath is full of thick, syrupy music. And Key smiles. And he doesn't need to turn round. He knows what is behind him. Silhouetted by the Moon is the policeman, his foot up on the black, cast iron bench, his saxophone gleaming, notes flying out into the dying embers of the lockdown.

†**JUNIPER:** You don't look so fat.
KEY: Yeah, well.
JUNIPER: People had worse lockdowns.
KEY: I lost weight after. I'm talking late spring here.
JUNIPER: How big d'ya get?
KEY: I was buying new jumpers, put it that way.
JUNIPER: New jumpers! Ha ha!
KEY: And had to update my anorak.
JUNIPER: Wowee.
KEY: What wowee? I've slimmed back down now, I said.
JUNIPER: A new anorak though.
KEY: Was staring down the barrel of having to buy a new duvet.
JUNIPER: Gah!
KEY: You've spat your drink out.
JUNIPER: How fat d'ya have to be to buy a bigger duvet?
KEY: "Staring down the barrel," I said. I never bought one, Em.

REMEMBER ME.[†]

I WAS eighteen stone now, I had long thick sideburns and I smoked a pipe.

And now, finally, they unlocked.

Ker-chonk.

I sloshed out into the street, squinting in the sunlight, igniting my tobacco.

The butcher didn't recognise me, of course.

The more I explained who I was, the more he said he didn't have a fucking clue and told me to choose my meat.

"I'm the man who buys pâté!" I squealed, smoke going everywhere.

"So you want pâté?"

He started putting fistfuls of the stuff into a weird sack; he wanted me out.

"I was in here every day!"

I covered my sideburns with my palms and sucked my cheeks in.

He wafted smoke out of his eyes and squinted at me.

"Ah! Yes! Six hundred grammes, wasn't it?"

The guy was killing me.

"Fifty grammes," I said sadly, "I'd generally get fifty."

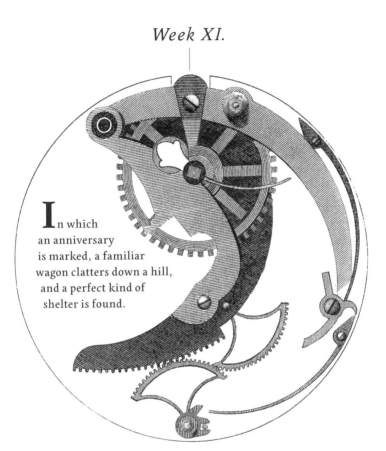

Week XI.

In which an anniversary is marked, a familiar wagon clatters down a hill, and a perfect kind of shelter is found.

HERE WE GO ROUND THE MULBERRY BUSH.

SIGNS OF LIFE.

STUFF started appearing in my diary.

First in a trickle, then a slew.

"Tina and Rod: Sunday roast."

"Barbara W and Fasteyes: Scrabble and soup morning."

"Rounders with the Prague lot."

"Tango lessons with Mr Hill."

Too much.

I slammed it shut.

Plans continued to seep out the side.

"Quiet drink with Beaverboy and the Chaos Brothers."

I threw my diary into the bath and poured kettles of hot water onto it, fighting the plans, boiling them off the pages.

MARITIME.

Key is stood at the top of Parliament Hill. The very top. The crest. His duckhead stick leaning on a cairn. The Sun is beating down. His dark-blue Mountain Warehouse anorak is undone to his belly. He is staring across the city. His Gazelles are baked onto the summit. If he stamped the whole thing would crack apart. There are no clouds, these will come. For now, everything is clear. He can see the lot. Streets heave with bowler hats. Playgrounds sing with children. Traffic snarls. Cyclists fart. Doors open and shut like castanets. Key squints at a window cleaner licking out a Creme Egg on the curve of The Gherkin, his rancid tongue dipping into the fondant, his arse-crack glistening in the breeze. Key folds his arms, gazes over his domain. The city's lifeblood is starting to pump. Key fights back tears. His iPhone springs to life. Emily Juniper. Finally. Key picks up.

KEY: Emily Juniper!

JUNIPER: Howdy stranger!

KEY: It's been six days.

JUNIPER: I fell off the map.

KEY: Where d'ya go.

JUNIPER: Pilgrimage!

KEY: I talked to Quint.

JUNIPER: Ugh – Quint!

KEY: Said you'd skipped town.

JUNIPER: Quint's gotta go!

KEY: Guy's a gel.

JUNIPER: Guess where I am!

KEY: I sent you a letter.

JUNIPER: I have the letter!

KEY: You picked it up?

JUNIPER: Slung it in my case!

KEY: You have it with you?!

JUNIPER: Guess where I am, Tim!

KEY: Have you opened it?

JUNIPER: It says "do not open!"

KEY: I thought Quint had nabbed it!

JUNIPER: I have it right here!

KEY: Are you outside?

JUNIPER: Yes! I'm drawing, Tim!

KEY: But you have the letter?

JUNIPER: I have the letter!

KEY: Open it! Open it, Em!

JUNIPER: Guess where I am!

KEY: Open the letter!

JUNIPER: It says "do not open!"

KEY: You can now, Em! Open it, Em!

JUNIPER: Okay, I'm going in!

KEY: Emily Juniper!

Key falls back onto his bench; black, cast iron. He closes his eyes. Pictures Emily Juniper forcing a fingernail under the seal. Swishing the thing open. Hacking at it, ripping, tearing like a madwoman. Pictures her. Pictures Emily. In the sunshine.

JUNIPER: Ha!

KEY: Well?

JUNIPER: Well, I've opened it!

KEY: You have?

JUNIPER: "Week One". It says "Week One", Tim.

KEY: Then it arrived in one piece.

JUNIPER: What have you done, Tim? "Week One".

KEY: It's just the first chapter, Em. Some possible conversations, yer know. Poems to follow.

JUNIPER: "In which a book spills into the world..."

Key, staring across the city. Listening to Emily Juniper. His designer. His pages offered up to her. His words in her custody. She is welcome to his words.

JUNIPER: The orange pen...

KEY: Delidded. In the evenings.

JUNIPER: Getting your Pepys on.

KEY: I think the way it'll play out is that the first book is about writing a book, and then this second book is about the first book going into the world.

JUNIPER: With me being daft the other end of the line?

KEY: That'll be the spine, certainly.

JUNIPER: Emily Juniper clattering about in Cornwall.

KEY: Set your watch by her.

JUNIPER: The "Key" figure skulking around his flat, is it?

KEY: No, he'll be out and about.

JUNIPER: Oh, I see.

KEY: Stomping about the place. Getting up to God knows what mischief, you know.

JUNIPER: Poems and conversations from outside.

KEY: Ha! Yeah, I'll have that.

JUNIPER: It's certainly not an "unattractive project", Tim.

KEY: Then you'll sign up?

JUNIPER: Guess where I am, Tim!

KEY: Will you sign up?!

JUNIPER: Guess!

KEY: Not Cornwall?

JUNIPER: Nee uh.

KEY: Then... a clock! The fiend Quint said you'd gone to paint a clock.

JUNIPER: Not just any clock, Tim!

Key sits back. Gazes across London. A London on the verge. On the brink. Ready to rock and roll. And then it falls away. Block by block, piece by piece, London evaporates. The Shard, St Paul's, The Gherkin, swallowed by the earth. The London Eye. Tussauds. Disappear. Eros, John Lewis, the lot. Key watching. Buckingham Palace, Big Ben: dust. Until all there is is Greenwich. Greenwich: there. Parliament Hill: here. And on the crest of Greenwich, in the vast shadow of the observatory, her lime-green raincoat glinting in the Sun. Emily Juniper. The size of an ant. As clear as day.

KEY: You went to Greenwich!

JUNIPER: To finish my project.

KEY: Essential journey.

JUNIPER: Not gonna depict itself.

KEY: Painting the time.

JUNIPER: Whilst it's stood still. You have to paint it.

Key squints. Emily Juniper's got her glasses on and black dust down her raincoat. She peers past her canvas. Holds her charcoal in front of her. Key smiles, his teeth gleam. Emily nods, pulls her charcoal back and waves.

JUNIPER: Hello.

KEY: Hello, Emily Juniper.

JUNIPER: It's nice to see you.

KEY: Emily Juniper. At large.

JUNIPER: We'll be in a pub garden before you know it.

KEY: Yes.

JUNIPER: In the sunshine.

KEY: A first draft sat between us.

JUNIPER: A Bulmers on top of it.

KEY: Stop it blowing away.

JUNIPER: I'm ready for the question, Noel.

KEY: Would you do me the honour of designing the book, Em?

JUNIPER: Are you mad?!

KEY: If you've time.

JUNIPER: Does this answer your question?

KEY: *(Laughing)* You're doing star jumps.

JUNIPER: I'll design it.

KEY: I was hoping you'd say that.

JUNIPER: Oh, Tim.

The two vantage points seem to tremble. Then they charge towards one another. And now Key and Emily Juniper are together. Her, holding her charcoal. Key, clutching his orange pen.

JUNIPER: So what now?

KEY: Finish the book.

JUNIPER: You've written the poems.

KEY: And scribbled down chats.

JUNIPER: The jackdaw.

KEY: I'll go somewhere to write, Em.

JUNIPER: But the story's over.

KEY: The tale is told.

JUNIPER: No coffee girl.

KEY: I'll write about the coffee girl.

JUNIPER: But not a love story?

KEY: The story ends today, Em.

JUNIPER: Didn't happen, so it don't go in.

KEY: Not this time.

JUNIPER: Bitter sweet.

KEY: Like Arabica.

JUNIPER: I can't wait to get going.

KEY: The old team.

JUNIPER: Back together.

They smile. And Emily Juniper pirouettes and she recedes and Greenwich goes with her. And now she is 9.4 miles away. And the city sprouts back up between them. And they have a contract now. And they will make another book. And Key falls forward and his face smashes against the hard clay and Parliament Hill splits like a walnut.

HERE WE GO ROUND THE MULBERRY BUSH.

ONE FOR THE ROAD.[†]

STANLEY decided he'd go again – have another lockdown.

He pulled his curtains closed and took his jeans off.

He emailed work and put his phone on airplane mode.

He sat on his sofa and twiddled his nuts.

He smiled.

A cheeky little six-week locky D.

Self-imposed.

With a definite ending.

He cracked open a can of whiskey, slung some Twiglets down his throat.

Nice.

†**JUNIPER:** Why's he wanna do another one?
KEY: I know.
JUNIPER: Bonkers.
KEY: I know he is, Em.

HERE WE GO ROUND THE MULBERRY BUSH.

HUNTED.[†]

A TIP-OFF and now we were scrambling down scree.

Dianne got behind me and I peered into the mouth of the cave.

There was a campfire in there and around it: eight covids, plus another twenty or so leaning against the cave walls.

I backed off and turned to Dianne.

"Go to the car, radio for back-up, we've found 'em, Di. This is their stronghold."

A biggish, thick looking covid appeared at the entrance, clutching a machine gun.

"Hey."

I picked up a length of wood.

"Run, Dianne! Run!"

†**JUNIPER:** Hey! Only seven poems left, look!
KEY: Ha. We got through 'em, huh?
JUNIPER: Buy me enough cider and I'll read anything, I honestly will.
KEY: Another Bulmers for the final push?
JUNIPER: You read my mind.
KEY: Funky berry one, or...?
JUNIPER: Nah, I'll go apple, please.
KEY: Back onto apple for the last big effort.
JUNIPER: I'm having a lovely afternoon.
KEY: And I'm not, Em?
JUNIPER: I know you are. Can't wipe the smile off your chops!

HOP IT, YOU HORRIBLE LOT.

BOHNSON looked agitated at the back.

He was trying to open a Milky Way, listening to the scientists' dull drone.

"Now, more than ever, we need to be vigilant, the variants..."

Bohnson was huffing, trying to tear the thin plastic, getting frustrated with himself, with everything.

Nerdoss continued: "...a final push, we mustn't let our guard down, all our hard work –"

Bohnson snapped.

"No, no no."

He slung his treat down, pulled up his tennis shorts, pushed past the cameras.

He shoved the spod off the side of the stage and staggered towards the lectern.

"You know what?" He patted his hair down, swatted the Autocue away with a fist.

His eyes were big, bovine, as he leered into the nation's screens.

"We're done. I'm calling it."

A couple of nerds blanched.

"We've as near as dammit cracked it, folks. Now piss off down the boozer, before I change my mind."

The nerds were grabbing at his ankles, imploring him to stop.

Bohnson pulled a Bulmers out of his knickers.

"Good work, folks! We got there, give or take! Up your bums!"

He took a long swig of cider.

It was the pear version and this caught him off-guard and some went down his crop top.

DOWN TO BUSINESS.

Key is a bicep now. Floating across the heath. Daisies elbow one another out of the way as they stretch out of the earth, try and drink some rays in themselves. Key's Gazelles crush them as he walks. No paths for Key; the open fields for Key. The heath is becoming a meadow and the bicep ripples in the heat as it moves across it. A bicep. A Kraftwerk singlet. Swimming shorts. Homer Simpson socks. And then the Gazelles. Crushing the daisies. Booting their heads off. Pinning their faces to the turf. The bicep engorges as Key puts his iPhone to his ear.

NHS: Hello, NHS vaccination helpline, how can I help you?

KEY: Yes, exactly. I'm due in this afternoon.

NHS: Okay, can I take your NHS number, please?

KEY: I'm getting done at Lord's, strange to say.

NHS: Yes, I'm based at Lord's.

KEY: Home of cricket and, to be fair, vax.

NHS: What's your NHS number, please?

Other biceps, drifting this way and that. The meadow populated. Spring ushering people from their sanctuaries. In ones and twos they take the air. Sometimes threes. Fours and fives. Wasps getting involved. Sixes and sevens. Boots on the ground. Crushing the daisies.

KEY: Yes, I wonder who the best person would be to talk to about having my vaccination photographed?

NHS: Excuse me?

Key spits on his bicep. He's ready for the gunk alright. He wants it right in there. A hit of the gunk. His veins taking it on a tour.

NHS: Can I have your NHS number, please?

KEY: It's Tim Key.

NHS: Do you have your NHS number?

KEY: With respect –

NHS: Or if I can take your postcode? Tim King, was it?

KEY: No, it wasn't. No one's said Tim King. Who the hell's Tim King?

Key frowns. Listens hard. He can hear the nice lady whacking keys. He can hear her colleagues on other calls, solving other problems. He can hear gunk being plunged into arms, the occasional yelp. The warm hubbub of gratefulness gurgles up into the phone.

NHS: What's your date of birth, please?

KEY: Yeah, well. I look about thirty-six, thirty-seven, put it that way.

NHS: Pardon me?

KEY: September second, seventy-six. Still play five-aside by the way, not listening to the Archers just yet.

NHS: Okay. 02-09-1976.

KEY: Got ID'd two years ago, that I will say.

NHS: Ah, I have you here –

KEY: In a bookies.

NHS: Timothy David Key.

KEY: Huh?

NHS: I have you here, Timothy.

Key looks to the heavens. The odd cloud has come to the party. Blips amongst the blue. Above Key, only optimism. He looks back into the phone. Squints down the mouthpiece. A vague silhouette of a lady at a desk on the outfield, surrounded by lists and syringes and Quality Streets.

NHS: So, I see you'll be joining us at twenty-to-four.

KEY: And I'm asking: who is the best person to talk to about getting the thing photographed?

NHS: Photographed, as in –

KEY: Come on, love, you know what I'm talking about. We've both seen the images.

NHS: Images?

KEY: Famous folk. The great and the good, arm full of gunk, doctor out of focus over their shoulder, big thumbs up, droplets of vax flying through the air.

NHS: Oh.

KEY: Have I got your attention now?

NHS: The thing is, erm... Timothy –

KEY: This is the trouble, you keep

saying Timothy. I mean, even a cursory look at my credits will tell you I go by Tim. Tim Key.

NHS: I'm so sorry, I don't think I'm familiar with –

KEY: Well, I'll start you off with Alan Partridge. That little known character. Then of course there's Peep Show, series nine, just the four scenes. Inside Number 9, anyone? I mean I could go on!

Key realises he's shouting. Other biceps turn to him. He squats down, picks at some daisy heads. Collects his thoughts.

KEY: Listen. We need to get this gunk in folks' arms, ma'am. The sooner we get a photo of me with the plunger halfway down, the sooner we get your numbers up.

NHS: I see.

KEY: If you whack my name into Google, you can find my showreel. Might give you some idea as to how I might be of use to the campaign.

NHS: We don't really watch showreels, that's the only thing.

KEY: Because what's the point of me and you getting jabbed up if there's some twerp who won't take it 'cos they haven't seen enough people off the telly stepping up?

Key is gesturing to the disparate biceps. The folk in the meadow. These people will need jabs, too, if we are to be free again. These people will need luring to clinics. These people will need to roll their sleeves up. Make the effort.

NHS: Erm.

KEY: I mean I shouldn't have to go through my resumé, really I shouldn't.

NHS: Oh.

KEY: What?

NHS: It says "deliberately bad poetry" on your Wikipedia page.

KEY: It's not deliberate.

NHS: We don't have photographers.

Key throws his iPhone down again and again, then chases after it; lifts it back up to his ear.

NHS: You will be allowed to take a selfie, or if you have a carer, they can –

KEY: Why have I got a carer suddenly?

NHS: Do you want the vaccine or not, Timothy?

KEY: Tim Key! PBJ Management!

NHS: Will we see you at twenty-to-four?

KEY: *Avec* bells on! It's not about the photo op, is it? When you really think about it. There's more at stake, eh.

Key continues to walk. The Sun has gone behind a cloud and his bicep is cold now. He tries to pull his singlet strap a bit, make it into more of a sleeve.

NHS: Bye, then.

KEY: What do you get after you've got jabbed?

NHS: I have to take another call, I'm afraid.

KEY: As in, at the dentist you'd get like, a Chewit, or something. Is there any kind of, I dunno, I mean what do you get?

NHS: Just a sense of knowing that –

KEY: I'm talking about food, not the "sense of knowing" something. Is there a Krispy Kreme doughnut in the offing, or... ?

NHS: I'll look out for you.

KEY: You will? The apple one, it'd have to be.

NHS: I'll try and get you a doughnut. Tim Key. I've written it down now. Please don't worry about a thing.

KEY: I'm not.

Where has the Sun gone? Why is it cloudy now? Why's the place stopped heating up?

KEY: Thank you.

Key's slowed right down now. He's covering his bicep with his palm. He can hear his showreel starting before the phone call ends. Click.

† **JUNIPER:** Poor sods.
KEY: Kids have had a rough run, Em.
JUNIPER: If the scientists had anything about them they'd have injected them with some kind of... oh Gawd knows, ignore me.
KEY: What?
JUNIPER: Nah, just feel for the kids, that's all.
KEY: Injected them with what though?
JUNIPER: Well, you know, some drug with all the stuff they've missed out on, all the knowledge. Inject that.
KEY: Catch-up drug?
JUNIPER: Yeah, I mean maybe they got too bogged down in the vaccine stuff to think of other useful drugs. Well, not bogged down.
KEY: No, "bogged down" doesn't sound like the right phrase.

THE LONG GAME. [†]

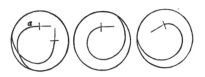

THEY decided to throw it out to the kids.

They now got to choose.

They could either catch up on all the stuff they'd missed because of the jizzhouse virus *now*,

Or they could defer;

Not worry so much about it for the time being, do the extra stuff in their fifties.

The forms came back.

By and large they'd all ticked "fuck this, I'll do that stuff when I'm old, it wasn't my fault, I'll take my chances, cheers."

Schools resumed and were chill.

There were *some* issues with a generation of children, sure, and adults agonised over this.

But in the 2060s it all sorted itself out.

They filled in the gaps and they enjoyed it.

It made a welcome break from the never-ending bullshit you had to endure as a grown-up.

HERE WE GO ROUND THE MULBERRY BUSH.

FREEDOM THROUGH THE WINDOW.

Key tumbles down the hill, smashes into a bus stop. He rises up, sits his fat arnuzzi on the narrow moulded orange bench. And now he waits. Waits for the 46. The 46 to take him to Lord's. Home of cricket. Home of jabs. Home of hope. He looks up at the sky. One cloud. Two. And a nip in the air. Goosebumps on his bicep. He closes his eyes, momentarily. Then. Smack! A slap on the polycarbonate glass and Key spins round. Rick and Buddy! Hand-in-hand, their spare ones spanking the glass. Three friends partially reunited, but it is verboten. They are no longer in a bubble, these three. But there is this polycarbonate glass between them. So they are safe. So all is fine. Slap! Slap!

KEY: Here they are!

But Rick and Buddy cannot hear Key. And now they are laughing and shouting, but they are in another realm, because of this bloody polycarbonate glass.

KEY: Huh?

And Rick and Buddy are excited and Rick breathes against the glass and it steams up a treat and Buddy peels off a mitten and writes on this canvas with her finger and Key squints and goes cross-eyed because the writing is in mirror, and he presses his temple and now the letters twirl around and click into place.

WE MISS YOU!

And Key blinks away tears and smiles through the condensation. And he pulls himself together. And he talks.

KEY: How was your sis's birthday?

Blank faces and Key blows a cloud onto his side of the window. Licks his finger.

HOW WAS YOUR SISTER'S
BIRTHDAY?

STELLAR!
MEGALASH!

And Key furrows his brow. Because, really, they are not in a bubble. And they are at close quarters. And he mouths, "Is this safe?" and Rick mimes something and Key

can't work out exactly what he's saying, but it's certainly along the lines of "If a covid gets through this glass I'll give him the money myself." And Buddy's back at the canvas.

HOW ARE YOU
COPING?

I'M GETTING VAXXED!

YAY!

And Key does a couple of muscleman poses. And the 46 can be heard approaching, and Rick licks his whole fist – punches it against the pane. And he begins to paint his proposal.

SNOOKER WORLD
- CHAMPS -

And Key's eyes widen, and he scratches at the polycarbonate glass.

GO ON

THEY'RE GONNA HAVE AN
AUDIENCE

KEEP TALKING

AM I GETTING TICKETS?

And Rick fiddles with his iPhone and he slaps it against the pane. And the deep purr of the 46 is getting louder, and Key squints through the condensation, and he reads Rick's screen through the glass.

SNOOKER WORLD

CHAMPIONSHIP EXPECTED

TO HAVE A FULL HOUSE

FOR MAY 2 FINAL

And Rick is doing some snooker stuff. Miming taking a pink into the middle pocket, screwing back for a black against the rail. And Buddy's pulling imaginary high-value colours out of imaginary pockets and polishing them with imaginary white gloves. And now Rick's pointing to Key, and he's raising his eyebrow, and Key is thumping his chest and nodding, and now he falls backwards into the 46 and the doors slide closed and Key is away. And things are moving in the right direction. And things are coming back. And now, finally, there is a horizon. And the 46 swings onto Adelaide Road, and surges forward towards the needle.

HERE WE GO ROUND THE MULBERRY BUSH.

EURO-BUFFET.

B<small>IIIIG</small> meeting in Europe.

Tons of croissants and pink wafers and piping-hot coffee and fat politicians and weird flags and PowerPoint and bald translators and doodles on headed notepaper and the tips of the flags going in the coffee and people going for a wee.

Eventually, they agreed to disagree.

They resolved to split the vaccine back up and each country would have one ingredient and that would be "their special ingredient".

Now citizens who wanted vaccinating had to go on a European tour to get 'emselves done.

It was a pain in the neck is what it was.

They'd go to eight major European cities and get a jab of each until they'd got all the stuff they needed into their veins.

They each had a card, similar to a Costa card, that they had to get stamped.

They'd get pumped full of monobasic potassium phosphate in Seville, mark their card, hop in the minibus, then off to Berlin to get some bloody nucleoside-modified messenger RNA into their bicep.

Then onto Geneva, Copenhagen, Lisbon.

Madness.

HEADQUARTERS.

Lord's! The world-famous cricket ground. Key: sat on his fat arnuzzi, leaning back against a sightscreen, his legs stretched before him. He chows down on his Krispy Kreme apple doughnut and surveys the outfield. Thousands of old citizens sitting on thousands of stools, biceps out and ready for lancing. Nurses plunging vax into bloodstreams. The Jabbed saluting, staggering, knock-kneed, off down to fine leg; other silvertops clambering out of the pavilion, shuffling to the stools that the vaccinated have vacated. The whole thing perfectly choreographed. A medical ballet. A triumph. A ringing phone. Chiggy.

KEY: Chig! Guess what?

CHIGGY: Darling boy!

KEY: I'm wearing a sticker, Chig.

CHIGGY: What sticker?

KEY: Wanna know what it says?

CHIGGY: Can we have an ever-so-quick chat about work, darling boy?

Key hauls himself to his feet, starts walking round the boundary rope. Loping like a chimp. It's a gloomy day. Ground staff hover by the covers, ready to tear on should the heavens open.

CHIGGY: What does your sticker say?

KEY: Says "I've had my vaccination", baby.

CHIGGY: Oh! Vaxxed, huh? Where did you get that from?

KEY: They're jabbing at Lord's, Chig. I'm fully gunked-up!

CHIGGY: Oh, you are?

KEY: My arm stings!

CHIGGY: Then it's doing you good!

KEY: Arm full of nonk. I'm emotional, Chig.

CHIGGY: Your voice is trembling, Tim.

KEY: Yuh... yeah.

CHIGGY: How much did they put in?

KEY: Normal amount, I reckon. Walking it in right now.

CHIGGY: Get it circulating, huh?

KEY: I can feel it going in, Chig. I feel strong.

Inside Key's body a trillion soldiers charge through veins, deploying themselves in defensive positions, ensuring there will be no breach. Chiggy's voice echoing around the tubes.

CHIGGY: There's a play with Katherine Parkinson in it, they're checking your availability.

KEY: *(Weak)* Parky, uh-huh –

CHIGGY: She's world class, Tim. Buzzcocks is coming back, too. Revamp. Noel's a team captain. They –

KEY: Dusted down Buzzcocks, uh-huh –

CHIGGY: I've got a list as long as my arm here, it's all go.

KEY: *(Weak)* I don't fear hard work, Chig, believe me. I once did three-and-a-half days in a row on Peep Show. I'm not a shirker.

CHIGGY: There's a film set in Venice, looks like, maybe –

KEY: *(So weak)* Oh, Chig.

CHIGGY: I know. I know. I had one of my other clients say they were petrified about everything coming back to normal.

KEY: I'm not petrified though, Chig. Put anxious.

CHIGGY: How do you mean "put"?

KEY: I'm feeling the squeeze here. I wanna be back in my bubble, Chig.

CHIGGY: You're not in your bubble?

KEY: Bubble went pop.

CHIGGY: Oh, darling.

KEY: No worries, they're gonna reblow it. Just it's a lot, Chig. Shackles all falling away at once.

Key looks up at the famous scoreboard. No runs and wickets, no batters and bowlers. The whole lot replaced with tolls and jabs. Huge garish numbers shining out into the gloom. An animation underneath: The PM, pumping a syringe, splurting vax into the air. Key looks at the heavens.

CHIGGY: It's the anniversary, you know. Today.

KEY: It's mad, Chig.

CHIGGY: Of the keys turning in their locks.

KEY: I know, Chig.

CHIGGY: Remember how we felt?

KEY: Yuh.

CHIGGY: All that work, stolen away by the bloody virus.

KEY: Mm-hm.

CHIGGY: Our lives wrenched from their moorings.

KEY: I know, Chig. I know.

CHIGGY: Latitude looks like it's happening, they've asked –

KEY: I'm writing a book.

CHIGGY: *(Phone thrown across room, Chig's voice now distant)* For fuck's sake.

Key's phone trings. A text message. A smile plasters itself onto Key's face. Rick and Buddy. "Tickets secured, Crucible. All three sessions! Miss ya!" Yes. The snooker. Key shuts his eyes. When he opens them, the cricket pitch is transformed. Snooker players dominate the square. Jack Lisowski stood in full cricket whites, wielding the willow; Mark Selby steaming in; Lisowski nicking off, Shaun Murphy leaping to his left, pouching the catch. Key blinks. Gone. Back to the jabs. Docile relics being pumped with formula. Key smiles.

CHIGGY: How do you celebrate your jab? If you're not in a bubble, I mean.

KEY: I'm seeing The Colonel, Chig. We're walking to Pond Square.

CHIGGY: It's supposed to rain tonight, no?

Key looks across to the square in the middle. The umpires are in discussions. They look to the clouds. They peer at their light meters.

CHIGGY: Get your diary out. Let's bung some stuff in. Come on.

KEY: It's in my veins, Chig.

CHIGGY: AstraZeneca?

KEY: Book two, Chig. Book two.

CHIGGY: *(Hesitant)* The character of Chiggy in there again, is she?

Key glances down. His pen is in his hand now. Its barrel throbs like a hornet's abdomen.

KEY: Lockdown Three, Chig. All what's gone on. Flow it through the hand, into the barrel, splosh it on the paper.

CHIGGY: Emily Juniper designing it?

KEY: Nooooo, you don't say. Thought I might just do this one myself. Slap it in Dom Casual, splatter a bunch of WordArt on the cover, see who salutes.

CHIGGY: But it will be Emily designing it, right?

KEY: The offer's out. She seems interested. If she can squeeze it in, in between her clocks.

CHIGGY: I mean. If you want to write a book...

KEY: No.

CHIGGY: No what?

KEY: I don't want to write a book. There is a book, Chigmond. And it wants me to write it.

CHIGGY: I think you'd be a good game show host, personally –

KEY: When the genie's on your shoulder...

CHIGGY: Huh?

KEY: It won't wait, Chig. I swear.

CHIGGY: I know, darling boy. I know.

Key spins his arms round like a helicopter. He's at the opposite end of the ground now. He sits down. Leans back against the sightscreen. Stares up at the media centre. Smiles.

KEY: I'll type the book, Chig. Once my arm's stopped stinging. I'll type the shit out of it. I know what I'm doing.

CHIGGY: You can look after yourself.

KEY: I can, Chig.

CHIGGY: You're fortified now.

KEY: I know I am, Chig.

CHIGGY: You must do what you must do.

KEY: And I will.

Key squeezes his pen. Slaps his bicep. Yelps.

KEY: I'd actually love it if that stupid virus tried it on now. Veins full of the good stuff. All I can say is good luck to it. Good bloody luck.

Key squints up at the commentary box. Aggers is purring into his microphone. Describing the glistening needles sinking into the nation's beleaguered limbs, tarnishing the skin, fortifying us against the wicked bug. Occasionally Tuffers peers up at the sky. He's worried.

†**JUNIPER:** That's horrible.
KEY: I mean, I knew it must have been going on.
JUNIPER: Merlin and Ken used to drive to Penzance. It's maddening.
KEY: Who? What?
JUNIPER: I towed the party line.
KEY: Me, too. Yawnfest!
JUNIPER: I think there was about eight of 'em. Used to have Europarties.
KEY: What's a Europarty?
JUNIPER: I know. Doesn't really appeal.
KEY: I don't think I'd do very well at a Europarty.
JUNIPER: No, it annoys me they were doing it. That's all.

MUGGINS HERE.†

"**L**ASHED off our tits! Ha ha! Anyway, we left at dawn, the eight of us, so as not to arouse suspicion!"

I was enjoying hearing these people's tales of lockdown.

Chris was talking now –

"Yeah me and Beryl used to go over to CJ and Diane's most Fridays, too."

I nodded; so Chris and Beryl were having dinner parties at The Wilsons', were they?

"That you did, Chris," Diane was laughing hard, "not forgetting Rob Pilchard and the Dutch girls piling in with their bloody cigs!"

Everyone seemed to have had a great lockdown, very sociable.

They were looking at me now.

"What about you, Nige? Get up to no good? Or tow the old party line?"

"I stayed in my flat, I –"

Beryl was bent double, laughing; Chris was drawing a square in the air with his fingers.

And now they were all laughing.

As if the whole thing had never happened.

As if this wasn't a reunion at all.

As if this was a continuation of what they'd been up to since last effing spring.

HERE WE GO ROUND THE MULBERRY BUSH.

BON ANNIVERSAIRE.

THE anniversary
Of the doors slamming shut, the keys clinking in the locks.

The dear old govt. brought out a coin with all the gang on it.

Bohnson, nice and stiff in his tennis shorts, a big iron key stuffed in his trap.

Sir Matt Boytwitch laughing his head off, spurting his syringe in the air like a madman.

Rishi Perfect, squeaky clean, pressed tie, glugging Coke, strumming an abacus.

Other stalwarts and slapheads, arms crossed, chests puffed out like robins, on this beautiful, precious coin.

And behind them all, chiselled in soft focus by the engraver: Cumdawg.

His cardigan falling off his shoulders, his steering wheel in his hands, and above his insipid hooter: the castle, reflected in his commemorative spectacles.

A LIFT.

Key's road. Where it all began. And Key walking up it. With a Sainsbury's bag in his fist, he plods. Past the Thai Café – closed; past Costcutter – open, absolutely rammoed; past the pub – its locks trembling. There are no needles on the pavement now, no snow. Key looks up, rocks his head right back, flicks his sunglasses onto his top lip. He examines the clouds. There are many, their guts bright white as the Sun tries to find a way through; their edges silver. Key bares his teeth at these clouds. Warns them with his eyes. Warns them not to empty their load. Warns them not to drench The Colonel. He waggles a Sports-Direct umbrella to the heavens.

KEY: No. Don't.

And now a clatter, from behind him. Key turns; stands open-mouthed. A tricycle. Hurtling down the hill. And behind it – munching on the towbar – a wagon, painted pink, its shutters bolted closed. The spokes glint and bend as the vehicle skims across the asphalt. And on the seat, being jolted and juddered and jiggled and jounced:

KEY: *(Whispered, besotted)* The coffee girl.

Key's arm swings from his body. And his middle finger kisses the traffic light button. And he wills the lamps to turn to red, to clothesline the coffee girl...

KEY: *(Under his breath, guttural)* Stop. Please.

And the coffee girl clatters along, and Key wafts his SportsDirect umbrella at the lamp. But it won't go red. And he starts to beat the lamp, but it will not change. But the girl stops. In spite of the green light she stops.

KEY: Um.

And the coffee girl sits on her tricycle, and her wagon pulsates behind her and a bus sounds its horn and swerves past and a fist is shaken and it roars off down the hill, and now it is just Key and the coffee girl, on the street.

COFFEE GIRL: Need a ride?

KEY: Huh?

And the coffee girl slides her bum across and she pats the leather seat and her eyes glint. And it is like a fifteenth-century horse and cart, but with pedals now, where once there was a rancid nag.

COFFEE GIRL: Where you headed?

KEY: No, I'm...

And Key is headed to The Colonel. But is he really? Because now his SportsDirect umbrella is between his knees, and his fat arse is sat next to this coffee girl and she's pedalling and the coffee-equipment is rattling behind them and they're picking up speed down the hill.

COFFEE GIRL: Where am I taking you?

KEY: But...

COFFEE GIRL: Ha ha! This is hilarious!

And it is. And the breeze is gushing through the coffee girl's hair and she is laughing and her blackcurrant fingernails are squeezing the handlebars bit. And the chain is whizzing round and there is optimism but also the first spots of rain.

KEY: I'm off to see The Colonel. I was –

COFFEE GIRL: What's The Colonel?

KEY: He's my friend, The Colonel. We're celebrating.

COFFEE GIRL: We can cycle down to Regent's Park, you know. We can get an ice cream. We can look at the penguins.

And the coffee girl has a dress on, and the dress is the colour of pear drops and it is flowing across the seat and Key is sitting on its hem and the coffee girl's legs are awash with goose bumps and Key is tingling, too. And their faces are both pointing forward and they are both smiling.

KEY: Penguins?

COFFEE GIRL: I know a bit of a gap, where you can peer through.

KEY: Peer at the penguins?

COFFEE GIRL: Dopy sods!

KEY: Peer through the fence.

COFFEE GIRL: They walk funny!

KEY: Ha ha! I know!

COFFEE GIRL: But... if you have to go to The Colonel...

KEY: I've purchased the Beck's Viers.

COFFEE GIRL: Celebrating with Viers! Not much of a celebration then.

And Key's eyes wander, and they rest in front of the coffee girl's face, and it is the second time his eyes have borne witness to her unmasked mouth. And they revel in her glistening teeth, and her playful lips, and her flickering tongue, and then they wander back into Key's sockets and they look out onto the road.

COFFEE GIRL: Where's The Colonel then?

And now they are at a fork in the road. And the coffee girl's blackcurrant fingernails are on the brake lever, and there is a sign saying Highgate, Crouch End, all that stuff.

KEY: Highgate.

And there is another sign saying Camden, Regent's Park, West End, all that stuff. And they are at a fork in the road. And the coffee girl is smiling at The Poet.

COFFEE GIRL: We can cower under my awning. Does The Colonel have an awning?

KEY: We're going to sit on a bench, up on Pond Square.

COFFEE GIRL: You'll get drenched.

And Key's eyes begin to revolve and flash as three months of lockdown pulsate in his skull.

KEY: Can we feed the penguins? Can we get right up close? Can we stop and buy sprats? Can we feed 'em?

And the coffee girl looks to the skies. And the skies frown down and the coffee girl's smile becomes a frown, too.

COFFEE GIRL: You stopped coming.

KEY: Huh?

COFFEE GIRL: To the wagon.

KEY: Naw.

COFFEE GIRL: Yah! I've made maybe five mochas in the whole of March.

KEY: I was walking.

And Key is staring at the signs and some dots of rain are troubling his shoulders.

COFFEE GIRL: So, what's it to be?

KEY: It's just... The Colonel.

COFFEE GIRL: He's starting to hack me off, this "colonel".

KEY: I must go to him.

COFFEE GIRL: And what? We meet next week?

KEY: Yes! What? Meet how?

COFFEE GIRL: Meet however. I know

a place. A hatch. They serve take-away beers through the hatch. We can sit outside their pub.

KEY: Eating olives.

COFFEE GIRL: We can eat olives, yes.

KEY: Chow down on our olives –

COFFEE GIRL: Put the world to rights.

KEY: With our faces stuffed full of olives.

COFFEE GIRL: Maybe ice cream, too.

KEY: Naughty.

COFFEE GIRL: Sometimes you have to be.

KEY: Ha!

COFFEE GIRL: Next week... If you're putting things in your diary that is.

And Key has his diary in his hand already and he opens her up, and he blows all the appointments off the pages, and they flutter into the sky and mix with the spicks and specks of rain and Key's orange pen is in his fist.

KEY: Name your day.

And the blackcurrant fingernails pour into the diary and find a virgin page and now the orange pen is in her fist and it sinks into the page like a magic wand into snow. "Olives and wine with Flo." And then numbers fall from the pen, one after another until there are ten. And then the diary is closed. And distant thunder can be heard. And the clouds are so heavy, so low, their udders almost clip the top of the wagon.

KEY: Plans.

And the cabin fizzes. And the street is electrified. And the city is coming back to life.

COFFEE GIRL: Now what about these penguins then? Could be good!

And a single drop of rain blots the coffee girl's hem. And Key looks to the heavens.

COFFEE GIRL: Be a bit spontaneous?

But spontaneity was shot to pieces a year ago today.

COFFEE GIRL: Or am I dropping you at this bloody colonel's?

And the lights go amber. And the lights go green. And the Sun peeps between the clouds. And Key reaches across the coffee girl to her bell. And he rings it. And Lockdown Three is over.

HERE WE GO ROUND THE MULBERRY BUSH.

THOSE WERE THE DAYS. †

I cut my diary from its Cellophane.
I flicked through.
January.
February.
White as snow.
March.
I pulled out these futile pages, fed them
to my hog.
I wanted them out of my sight.
Let's make April a fresh start.
Let's give May a fighting chance.
Why risk June catching what March had?

†**KEY:** I did this, Em. Ripped it asunder.
JUNIPER: You did?
KEY: On the anniversary of the first lockdown.
JUNIPER: Uh-huh. The day you got your jab.
KEY: I've had 'em both now.
JUNIPER: I talked to you that day.
KEY: You did, Em.
JUNIPER: You were in good spirits.
KEY: *I* was in good spirits? *You* were doing star jumps!
JUNIPER: That was a good day.
KEY: The beginning of the end.
JUNIPER: The beginning of the start.
KEY: I'll drink to that.

CHEERS.

Key's main finger reaches out, depresses The Colonel's doorbell; returns itself into Key's pocket. And now he waits. His other hand grips his SportsDirect umbrella, which prevents the heavens from emptying themselves completely onto his bonce and shoulders. And there we have it. Key. Waiting for The Colonel. In the rain. The rain that The Colonel feared.

KEY: Bugger me.

Movement behind the glass, and The Colonel ambling to the door, a sketchy silhouette becoming a colourful blob. Then the door opening. And The Colonel stood there in his little tracksuit. In his house. Holding a Phillips screwdriver.

KEY: Nice weather for ducks.

COLONEL: I'll be honest, I don't even wanna hear it.

KEY: I know. Our worst fear, eh. Monsoon season, in all its glory.

COLONEL: In all its jizz, I think you mean.

KEY: Well, you say that, Colonel...

Key gestures to the Sainsbury's bag between his legs. The first bottle of a six-pack of Beck's Viers peeps out past the handles. Key stares at the bottle top. Closes his eyes. Imagines it being flicked off in the sunshine. Imagines two of these bottles clinking together, The Colonel roaring with laughter. The bottle top landing on a buttercup. He opens his eyes. The Colonel's face, a dough of disappointment. Trying to remain positive. In the rain.

COLONEL: So, where we headed?

KEY: Pond Square, eh.

COLONEL: I don't have an umbrella.

KEY: The trees have grown leaves, John.

COLONEL: And when they're full of rain, what then?

KEY: It'll ease up.

COLONEL: Leaves not gonna do shit against this. Fill 'emselves up with rain, then tip the lot on our heads, that's what.

The Colonel reaches a hand under the weather, to check the moistness of the drops. His palm is quickly filled like a queen scallop shell. He turns it over, pours it away. He is in pain. He looks at Key.

COLONEL: Aw, man. It just had to go and rain, didn't it?

KEY: Yuh. 'Course it did. 2021, eh.

COLONEL: In a nutshell.

Lightning. And thunder in the post. Key looks up past his SportsDirect umbrella. The sky is dark. The heavens have more rain up their sleeves. And The Colonel in pain.

KEY: Hey.

COLONEL: What "hey"?

Key shrugs his Puma rucksack into his arms. Unzips it. Dunks his hand in. Winks at the Colonel.

COLONEL: *(Whispered)* Champagne.

Key nods. He is holding his House of Games champagne aloft. Jules Rimet still gleaming.

COLONEL: Champagne's for your mum, I thought.

KEY: Felt like we should do something special, that's all. To mark the...

Key mimes piercing his arm, plunging the syringe, cavorting like Popeye. The Colonel's head bulges at the insanity of it all.

COLONEL: Quaffing champagne on Pond Square though! It's impossible! It's not who we are!

KEY: We'll be fine once we get into it!

COLONEL: I've got a pub in my garden! A pub! A pub, man!

Key nods.

COLONEL: And you can just come through. And there's an awning –

KEY: I know there's an awning, John.

COLONEL: I mean that'd be special. Save the champers for Carol, you know.

Key stares at his foil-clad cork.

COLONEL: *(Waggling his Phillips)* I've just screwed your bell on. It's a beauty! Last orders at the bar! Not rung it yet, mind. The devil's own job fixing it up 'cos it's a proper bell, you know. Weighs a ton, but it's up now. It's seen some action that bell, I bet.

KEY: Got it off eBay. Pub had closed down.

And now the thunder. Quelle suprise.

COLONEL: It's okay, let's wait. I know you can't come through. It's madness! I'm sorry. Jeesh. Okay, let's wait. What's another two weeks? What's the difference?

The rain is pouring off Key's SportsDirect umbrella. They're a metre apart, no more. Key in the elements, The Colonel in his slippers. Key peers past his friend. Past his coats and his shoes and his banisters. He can see the kitchen, and beyond, he can see the garden. Rain coming down in spears, Key squints. There's the pub. Some job The Colonel's done. Rain pours off the awning. And, through the cascade, two dry bar stools. On top of the lot: a large, red neon sign. It flickers on and off as it takes a pounding from the rain. But when it's on it says "Cheers". It is heart-breakingly beautiful. Key blinks back the tears. There's enough water about without his soppy ducts adding to it. Then he smiles.

COLONEL: What?

KEY: What?

COLONEL: Why you smiling?

KEY: I'm not in a bubble, John.

And the rain coming down. And the neon light flashing. And the blankness of The Colonel's face.

KEY: They let me go. They had to bring another into their fold.

COLONEL: They let you go?

KEY: Buddy's sister. I had to make way.

COLONEL: Then...

KEY: What have you got on tap?

And The Colonel stepping forward. And The Colonel's face, finally emerging into the light. His eyes ignited. His irises disappearing momentarily, replaced with flagons, then a blink, and back to eyes. Lit up. Excited.

COLONEL: I've got Tropical Deluxe.

KEY: 3.8% abv.

COLONEL: Last time I checked, yes!

Key is beginning to drool. He licks his lips lavishly.

KEY: "Something special."

COLONEL: Leave the cork in the bubbly.

KEY: And that's on tap, the Tropical Deluxe?

COLONEL: It's a keg. It's on its side. It's hooked up to the tap, yes. I don't have snacks. Are you coming in? I mean... Are you coming through????????

Key nods. The Colonel grabs the handle of Key's SportsDirect umbrella, forces it through the door. Grapples with it like an alligator, tumbles onto the floor with it, eventually gets it down. Pulls himself up to his full height.

KEY: I'll come through.

COLONEL: So we're in a bubble? Me and thee?

KEY: Yes.

COLONEL: For the final throes.

KEY: The last vestiges.

COLONEL: See it in together.

KEY: I'm in your bub, bro!

Two men. Stood either side of a doorframe. Rain filling Key's hair, pouring down Key's face, running down his dark-blue Mountain Warehouse anorak, flowing down his thighs, spattering on his Gazelles. And now his best foot moves forward. Towards the threshold. Towards the warmth. The hospitality. And now his toe, his sole, his heel sweeps through and Key's foot is inside. And his ankle creaks and his body leans forward and now the rest of him follows suit and he is inside. Key. Inside The Colonel's house.

COLONEL: He's in.

KEY: He is!

COLONEL: Come through. Come through!

And the door shuts behind them. And the two figures move away, and occasionally a flash of red neon emerges behind them in a blur. And there is laughter. Joy. And now they are gone. Away to the garden. To the pub. To ease open the faucet, to fill their cups. To drink under the awning. To discuss the roadmap and the future beyond. And then to ease the faucet open again. Cheers.

"CHEERS!"

EPILOGUE.

IN THE SUMMERTIME.

A pub garden. Alive. Thriving. Thrilling. Stuffed to the gills with smiling goons, young and old, fat and thin. Squeezed onto tables, squidged onto benches. Glasses being clinked, tankards being smashed together, flutes exploding in the sunshine. Hips next to hips, lips sucking on shoulders. No distance, none. And The Poet slaloming in between the joy, bouncing through the laughter, down towards the river. At the last table he slams on the brakes, plonks down his tray. Two pints of cider – rammed with ice – leap an inch in the air! Emily Juniper jumps, too.

KEY: Bulmers o'clock!

JUNIPER: You genius!!!

Key transfers the cider onto the table, hurls the tray into the river, and plonks his fat arse down on the bench. Opposite his designer. His muse. His friend. Opposite Emily Juniper. In the summertime.

JUNIPER: *(Smiling)* So this is it?

Emily Juniper is waggling the manuscript. Seventy thousand words, driven out of Key by Lockdown Three, sploshed onto pages, printed out by Connie, the girl with the spectacles at Ryman's. "Here We Go Round The Mulberry Bush."

JUNIPER: I think I'm going to pop!

KEY: Something to dig those horrible little talons of yours into anyway.

Emily Juniper stretches her fingers out, starts clawing at the title page.

KEY: I'm still tweaking; still polishing; still licking it into shape.

JUNIPER: May I turn the page? Head on in?

KEY: You'd be ever so welcome, Em.

JUNIPER: Ooh la la!!!

KEY: Usual rules apply. A poem here, a dialogue there.

JUNIPER: I just want to eat it up, Tim.

KEY: Try not to eat it, Em.

Emily Juniper sinks through the title page, comes to rest on a poem. She reads; she smiles.

JUNIPER: "The Best Laid Plans".

Key nods; drinks his Bulmers; licks his lips. Emily Juniper's sunglasses are on her head, Key peers into them, spies his reflection, a poet in the sunshine, the river behind him, and beyond it: cows. Key clonks his pint against the specs and Emily Juniper looks up.

JUNIPER: I want to read them all.

KEY: What's stopping you?

JUNIPER: Gah!

KEY: We have nowhere to be!

JUNIPER: Fuck! A book!

She takes the whole lot in her hands, waves it above her head.

JUNIPER: You could really clobber someone with this.

KEY: Huh?

JUNIPER: *(Suddenly serious)* And I have something for you.

KEY: You do?

Emily Juniper smiles her most mischievous smile yet. She reaches into her beach bag, pulls out an A4 piece of card; pushes it across the table. Its corners are folded up slightly and have some satsuma on them. Key stares at his designer's offering, mouth open, tongue in his pint. Splashed across the middle, Emily Juniper's ink.

KEY: *(Into his cider)* The cover.

JUNIPER: Early stages.

KEY: Lush stages.

JUNIPER: Well.

A bumblebee buzzes into the scene. He hovers above the cover, taking in the design. The sharp teeth of a key, moving through fruit; juice flung over the words, dripping off the edges. The bumblebee's buzzing becomes higher and higher-pitched as he appreciates the simplicity of the idea, the clean lines of the design. The whole thing a bust-up between artistry and economy. Key's buzzing too.

KEY: Dragged yourself away from your clocks, huh?

JUNIPER: I'm going all out on this. I'll have it on your desk September second. Designed.

KEY: A sprint to the finish.

JUNIPER: Fire it off to the printers.

KEY: Spit it out into the world.

JUNIPER: See who salutes.

KEY: Shit, I like that cover.

JUNIPER: It'll change.

KEY: I know.

JUNIPER: Oh, Tim!

Emily Juniper seizes the manuscript once more. Cleaves her palm into its depths, finds another poem, licks her gnashers.

JUNIPER: "Love Potion".

KEY: Let's go from the start, Em.

JUNIPER: I know, I know!

Emily Juniper throws the manuscript high into the air, like a pizza chef trying to attract a mate. It crashes down and she pulls it open onto the second poem. She looks up, smiles at The Poet. Bites the lid off a pink felt tip.

JUNIPER: I might draw a little heart next to the ones I like.

KEY: Oh.

JUNIPER: Whole manuscript peppered with hearts, ha ha.

KEY: You didn't draw a heart by that first one.

JUNIPER: I hadn't started the system yet.

KEY: Well, less is more, Em. Obviously don't pepper the thing with hearts.

JUNIPER: Can I have seven?

KEY: I couldn't give a fuck, Em.

Emily Juniper laughs and licks her pen. Key smiles. Vast clods of cigarette smoke drift above the tables and Key breathes in deeply. Everywhere, nimble fingers lace into tobacco pouches, construct dainty little cigs. There are butterflies, too. Key's phone judders. A text.

KEY: My mother.

JUNIPER: Aw sweet.

KEY: Seeing her tomorrow. The whole lot of us. Fuck me. Hug the old hen.

Emily Juniper smiles.

KEY: Cracking open the House of Games bubbly. Ha.

JUNIPER: The prodigal son.

KEY: The hungover son, to be fair.

JUNIPER: Ha ha. Yes, let's get trolleyed!

KEY: We made it through, Em.

JUNIPER: I'm seeing my lot at the weekend.

KEY: I've got people coming over Saturday night.

JUNIPER: "Over".

KEY: I know, right. Ten of 'em. Rick and Buddy, Lord's mob, The Colonel –

JUNIPER: The characters from the book.

KEY: The characters from my life, strictly speaking.

JUNIPER: Chilli & Heineken all round.

KEY: Something like that. This cover!

JUNIPER: This book though! Gah, I want to eat it!

She pulls a dialogue out from the middle. Something with Key and The Colonel, shoves it down her throat, washes it down with Bulmers.

KEY: Let's eat it with our eyes, Em.

JUNIPER: You read it out. Read out the poems.

KEY: Okay.

JUNIPER: We're almost out of Bulmers.

KEY: I'm so happy to see you, Em.

JUNIPER: Finally.

KEY: It all seemed so far away.

JUNIPER: Look at your bloody smile, you daft sod.

KEY: Look at everyone's smile, Em. It ain't just me.

They gawp at the other tables. Faces taut with happiness.

KEY: Okay, this one's called "Locking".

JUNIPER: Takes me back.

KEY: Deep breaths. It's from January.

JUNIPER: Yuk.

Emily Juniper grabs both of Key's hands and pulls him towards her, across the table. What's left of the Bulmers goes everywhere. Key is now slopped across the table like a stricken seal. The collaborators unlink their hands and hug. Then they rock back. And then they smile. And the bumblebee drinks the spillage greedily.

KEY: "A key. Cold, heavy, shoved in a lock."

JUNIPER: Very poetical.

KEY: That's the general idea, Em.

The bumblebee is woozy. He staggers from the sweet puddle; shakes his furry legs. Then he runs. Faster and faster until he runs out of table and leaps; soaring into the air, high above the pub garden, and the river, and the town, and beneath him the world is moving once more, and he licks cider from his beak and he smiles. And he accelerates in the direction of a meadow he enjoys.

ACKNOWLEDGEMENTS.

Key is wearing Levi 501 jeans. They're new. Pristine. Hell, they were dangling in a boutique in Carnaby Street not six hours ago. He slaps his ass, leaps up, clicks his heels together. He's got on a dark-pink shirt and a navy-blue tank-top, too. His toffee-coloured fashion-boots kiss the cobbles as he picks his way through SE1. His duck-head walking stick is smiling, winking at the crowds. A single red rose peeks out of Key's battered Puma rucksack. Emily Juniper is in his ears, talking admin. She's walking, too. She's on a beach. The Sun is beginning to dip over her right shoulder. She sounds happy.

JUNIPER: Okay, so I've got Sam and Cherry, and basically everyone at Calverts.

KEY: Yup. Sure. Gotta thank the printers.

JUNIPER: And then Pongo, just because I'd have gone mad if I didn't have her to walk, and –

KEY: Are you joking?

JUNIPER: Huh?

KEY: Are we thanking dogs now?

JUNIPER: Just Pongo. We were like a team.

KEY: And what, am I thanking my cheese plant?

Key winks at an old man in a tracksuit.

JUNIPER: You can do!

KEY: Yes, thank you cheese, for all your support in this challenging era.

JUNIPER: I think that sounds perfectly normal. If it helped you while you were writing the book –

KEY: No, Em. No plants, no dogs. Let's get some humans down. My cheese plant's never gonna read this bit.

JUNIPER: But you don't put people in the acknowledgments so that they see themselves there –

KEY: What are you talking about, Em? That's the entire point of this shit. It's what these folk get off on.

JUNIPER: You think people are searching themselves in The Acknowledgments?

KEY: I always have a peek.

JUNIPER: What peek?

KEY: See if they've recognised my contribution.

JUNIPER: In which books?

KEY: Any. You never know.

JUNIPER: Surely you know if you've helped with someone's book.

KEY: You can help without realising it though. That's my point. I checked my Franzen this morning.

JUNIPER: And?

KEY: Well, he hasn't acknowledged me.

JUNIPER: Right. I mean... Right.

A bark, Emily Juniper's end. A projectile being bunged. A tongue flailing. Excitable feet running off.

KEY: Come on then, Em. More names, more names.

JUNIPER: Well... Just Sam and Cherry, I think.

KEY: For my part I'd like to thank Sweetie Pie and Breeno and, for that matter, Marina.

JUNIPER: Okay.

KEY: Do you want to know why?

JUNIPER: I expect they... did they read early drafts?

KEY: They ploughed through a load of gash, yes. Poor sods.

JUNIPER: Oh oh, what about proof-readers?

KEY: Yup, yup. Always thank the proof-readers.

JUNIPER: Beady-eyed buggers.

KEY: Pete, LK, Phoebe.

JUNIPER: Feels like we're not thanking enough people.

KEY: I'm sure if people feel like they should have been thanked, they'll get in touch.

JUNIPER: Angry agents, asking where their bloody names are ha ha.

KEY: Good point, shout out to my agents.

JUNIPER: Oh, by the way, I was thinking. We can maybe print individual pages out, you know, on lush, lush paper stock, and maybe people can buy them. You know, sort of frame a double page spread, that type of thing. For people who really love the book.

KEY: Focus, Em.

JUNIPER: Oh, right.

KEY: Focus on The Acknowledgments.

JUNIPER: Yeah, good point.

KEY: Focus on who "chipped in".

JUNIPER: Can I thank my Mum?

KEY: Is this The Oscars?

JUNIPER: No, but –

KEY: You're not Winslet, Em. Always remember that.

JUNIPER: Well, Lynne Juniper deserves a mention, I think.

KEY: And Carol Key doesn't, all of a sudden?

JUNIPER: Well, she's mentioned in the book, isn't she? Carol is.

KEY: So I'll slot a mention of Lynne in.

JUNIPER: Oh, okay.

KEY: As a treat. In the main book bit.

JUNIPER: She'll love that.

KEY: Oh, and let's thank, you know, everyone who read the first book and was nice about it.

JUNIPER: Tut.

KEY: What?

JUNIPER: Well, if I'd said that you'd be saying something snarky about me being a lamo or something.

Key rounds a corner and stops, in awe. He gazes up. Up to the top of The Shard. And it is impossibly tall, and has no ending. And Key stops, staggers backwards, leans on a bollard.

KEY: No, I wouldn't.

JUNIPER: You would!

KEY: I'd have welled up if you'd have said it.

JUNIPER: I dunno.

KEY: I'd have said, "Oh, lovely touch, Em" or words to that effect.

JUNIPER: Mm.

KEY: Do you think it's lamo?

JUNIPER: No. I don't think we could have done it without 'em. They're the best. We'd be nothing without them, really.

KEY: Mm.

JUNIPER: What?

KEY: Well, that's getting a little closer to lamo, in my opinion.

JUNIPER: See! One rule for one, one rule for another.

KEY: I know. I know it is, Em. It's awful, really.

JUNIPER: Well, look; I'm where I need to be now.

KEY: And I'm not?

Key pushes off from his bollard. His toffee-coloured fashion-boots twitch; awed by the selection of revolving doors before him; revolving doors that spin you into the bowels of The Shard.

KEY: Well, look. Lemme know if you think of any other goon who helped us out particularly.

JUNIPER: I will. Have a lovely evening, Tim.

KEY: I will, Em. You too.

JUNIPER: Let's catch up tomorrow about things like press and distribution, all that jazz.

KEY: Yawn.

JUNIPER: I know, Tim. But it's important.

KEY: Bye, then, Em.

And Key reaches back and gropes for his rose. And his hand finds it and he pulls it out, sniffs the business end. And he lets out a lungful of breath. And he marches forth, into the glass spire.